STORIES FROM
IRAN

A Chicago Anthology
1921-1991

Edited by
Heshmat Moayyad

MAGE PUBLISHERS
WASHINGTON, D.C.

Biographical sketches written by Michael C. Hillmann
and updated by Sunil Sharma and Tony Ross

Author portraits by Maryam Zandi

Bazaar Photographs by Mehdi Khonsari

Cover Photograph by Laurence Lockhart courtesy of The Lockhart
Collection at the Faculty of Oriental Studies, Cambridge University

LIBRARY OF CONGRESS CATALOGING-IN-PUBLICATION DATA

Stories from Iran: 1921-1991: a Chicago anthology 1921-1991 /
edited by Heshmat Moayyad. p. cm.
1. Short Stories, Persian—Translations into English.
I. Moayyad, Heshmat.
PK6449.E7S86 1992
891'.553010803–dc20

PAPER ISBN: 0-934211-33-7
CLOTH ISBN: 0-934211-28-0

THIRD EDITION

MANUFACTURED IN THE UNITED STATES OF AMERICA

Mage books are available through better
bookstores, or directly from the publisher.
Call toll-free 1-800-962-0922 or 202-342-1642
Or visit Mage's home page at http://www.mage.com

For Ruth, Leyli and Shirin

C O N T

E N T S

Preface

Persian prose and Persian women have one bitter experience in common: they have both been suppressed for many centuries, women by men, prose by poetry. The Persian literary tradition has been dominated by poetry for at least twelve hundred years. Prose was not perceived as being capable of artistic expression. It served the purpose of expressing thought and communication in philosophy, theology, some secular sciences, and history. Only occasionally did a work of prose hit the target and become a literary masterpiece. The best examples are Abu'l-Fazl Bayhaqi's History (451 A.H./1059 C.E.), the *Monājātnāmeh* (Prayerbook) of Abdallah Ansari (d. 481 A.H./1088 C.E.), the Persian Epistles of Shehab al-din Sohravardi (d. 587 A.H./1191 C.E.), some of the writings of Sufi mystics and a few of the ethical-didactic treatises of the "mirrors for princes" genre and, most of all, Sa'di's *Golestan* (Rose Garden, written in 656 A.H./1258 C.E.).

In the course of Iran's struggle during the last ninety years of modernization and change, Persian prose has scored the greatest success. It has gone through a process of healthy development and has attained unprecedented beauty and power of expression. Two groups of the Iranian intelligentsia may take credit for this achievement: scholars in humanistic disciplines and writers of fiction. It is the work of the latter group with which the present volume attempts to acquaint the English reader.

This is not the first, but is probably the largest collection of Persian short stories in translation ever to appear in a Western language. Several other writers might deservedly have been included in this book had it not already grown beyond its intended capacity. The selections focus on no single, specific topic. Such an approach would have narrowed the scope of the volume and unduly restricted the pool of suitable writers and stories. The variety of situations illustrated in these stories has the advantage of offering a wider spectrum of the concerns of the Iranian people in this century.

A number of Persian writers make their first entry in English through this volume. Stories which had previously been translated and published elsewhere, even some that admittedly are more sophisticated, were deliberately excluded from this volume. A concession, however, had to be made with regard to three stories: Jamalzadeh's "What's Sauce for the Goose...," Golestan's "Esmat's Journey," and Amir-Shahi's "Brother's Future Family." These have been included by gracious permission respectively of their original editors Ehsan Yarshater and Michael Hillmann, and the translator Michael Beard. The brief overview with notes and a short bibliography, and also the biographical information, are intended to serve the academic community, particularly students who may wish to pursue the subject further.

The available biographical information on a number of the authors was incomplete. Professor Michael Hillmann of the University of Texas at Austin offered to provide the needed data and, in the process, helped in finalizing all of the biographical sketches. Without his generous and expert assistance, many details would have remained missing.

The preparation and execution of this work was made possible by the enthusiastic cooperation of the University of Chicago Persianists who did the actual work of translating the stories. While the responsibility for the choice of stories, as well as any possible oversight in the translated text, rests entirely with the editor, they deserve sincere gratitude for any merits attached to this anthology. Professor John Perry saw the entire text through press, polishing its style and preparing the glossary of terms. His contributions are gratefully acknowledged.

No words can adequately express my warm feelings for Najmieh and Mohammad Batmanglij, who embraced the project even in its raw form, most generously supported it at every stage, and spared no trouble and expense to facilitate its completion. Without Najmieh and Mohammad, whose friendship I dearly cherish, the publication of an anthology of this kind would perhaps have remained a dream.

— HESHMAT MOAYYAD

The Persian Short Story: An Overview

Heshmat Moayyad

Modern western fictional genres, particularly the short story, are relatively new in Persian literature. The writing of Persian short stories began in 1921 with the publication in Berlin of *Yeki bud yeki nabud* (Once upon a time),[1] a collection of six stories written by M. A. Jamalzadeh during the previous four to five years and printed in *Kaveh*, a Persian monthly magazine published by a group of distinguished Iranian scholars in Berlin. In these stories Jamalzadeh had criticized the social and political conditions of his homeland in a charming style replete with colloquial words and idiomatic expressions. However, it was not the stylistic quality of its language, nor even the author's critical views, that made this little volume a real novelty. Both characteristics had already appeared several years earlier in certain journalistic writings of the time, most notably in *Charand-parand*[2] (Balderdash), a series of satirical articles by the encyclopedist A. A. Dehkhoda. The Constitutional Revolution of 1906-11 and the subsequent period of relative political freedom had prepared the ground for the mushrooming of countless newspapers filled with open attacks on the government and the country's estab-

11

lished institutions.[3] It was rather the charming plots of the short stories in the garb of an alien form that captivated readers' minds and marked the birth of the new genre in Persian literature. Jamalzadeh, who by then had spent over ten years in Europe, was well aware of the need for a radical departure from the norms and traditions of classical Persian prose.

The reaction at home to this rather harmless volume was nevertheless tumultuous, particularly in the clerical circles, not unlike the uproar raised against Salman Rushdie's *The Satanic Verses* in recent years.[4] Eventually, however, it won the hearts of its Iranian readers and is recognized as the turning point in the history of Persian prose, with Jamalzadeh himself being hailed as the pioneer of modernistic fiction in Persian.

Although the Constitutional Revolution failed to fulfill its promise to usher in an era of political freedom and social justice, it did break many old barriers and set the history of Iran on a new course of radical changes. It marked the beginning of an unending struggle which even now, after eight decades, is far from having achieved its ultimate goals. And yet, it did provide the right atmosphere for the gradual appearance of a new cultural awareness. It succeeded in making headway for a cultural revolution, even though the political one continued to show few, if any, signs of permanent success.

Jamalzadeh (b. 1892), the son of a politically engaged, liberal nineteenth-century preacher, was too deeply rooted in his background traditions to be able to shake them off completely. His predilection for opulence in vocabulary deprived his later stories of technical sophistication, rendered his characters as lifeless figures, and stopped his plots from developing smoothly and naturally. The role of the true founder of the genre in Persian was reserved for Sadeq Hedayat (1903-51), the son of an aristocratic family who had spent four years studying in France. Upon his return to Iran in 1930, he began a period of hectic literary activity. Within the span of seven years he published three volumes of short stories, one volume of pungent satirical sketches called *Qaziyeh*, a longer piece of fiction of devastatingly critical purport called *Alaviyeh Khanom*, and a short novel, *Bufe kur* (The blind owl). The last, more than anything else, has contributed to his reputation, both in Iran and the West, as the most pessimistic and lonely figure in the history of Persian literature.

This remarkable outburst of creative writing, entirely during the period of Reza Shah's dictatorial rule, slackened, oddly enough, in the years of unprecedented political freedom that followed upon the abdication of the Shah in 1941 and ended, for Hedayat, with his suicide in Paris in 1951. One last volume of short stories, several more sketches (*Qaziyeh*), and one more novelette, titled *Haji Aqa*,[5] were the only pieces of fiction published by Hedayat during those ten years. Social and religious conditions were never favorable for the publication of another major piece of satirical writing, *Tup-e morvari* (The pearl cannon), which has been printed by Iranian scholars only in exile and only since the Islamic Revolution.[6]

Hedayat was intimately familiar with and infatuated by European literature, particularly the decadent trends of the post-World War I period. Hopelessly skeptical, he found no attraction in life and remained chronically despondent and obsessed with death, which is present almost everywhere in his fiction. In *The Blind Owl* Hedayat has presented an enigmatic, multifaceted, psychological type of story which escapes the dimension of time and mingles the pseudo-reality of life and dreams in the frame of an unusual structure that is hard to follow. Passionately attracted to Khayyam, he wrote a lengthy essay on the *Ruba'iyat* which was a real breakthrough in the study of that poet. He also felt an affinity with Kafka, whose *Metamorphosis* he translated into Persian. His nostalgic remembrance of Persia's ancient glory did not minimize the contempt he felt for the corrupt institutions and degenerate masses of his own people, nor was the spark of hope which the leftist ideology may have kindled in his heart any more than a furtive flirting with a rapidly spreading vogue of the time.[7]

The turbulent political conditions of Iran during the forties, in no small part the result of the Allied occupation of the country, was accompanied by a high rate of inflation and economic ruin. These conditions favored the flourishing of the Marxist Tudeh party, which attracted large segments of the intelligentsia, including some prominent poets and writers. Political instability and chaotic economic conditions kept the country in turmoil, with strikes and demonstrations, stimulated by conflicting parties, paralyzing the normal flow of activities in schools and factories. The struggle to deliver the nation from the grip of poverty, attempts at stopping foreign manipulations and interference in the internal affairs of the country, and the desire to establish the rule of law and democracy finally crystallized in the nationalistic movement of the old aristocratic statesman, Dr. Mohammad Mosaddeq, who enjoyed the overwhelming support of the masses, including both the Communists and the traditional classes of merchants and professionals.

The overthrow of Mosaddeq in August 1953 practically ended a period of roughly twelve years during which poets and writers felt free to speak their minds and criticize all and any of the established institutions. During the next quarter of a century, 1953-78, freedom of expression was curtailed and censorship plunged writers and poets into a state of confusion. They were forced either to avoid treating sensitive subjects openly and to resort instead to a veiled style of symbols and allegories, or else to risk the consequences of disregard for the rules and provocations of the state authorities. The resulting conflict led to hostile confrontations between writers and the government, causing years of enforced restrictions, suffering, and bitterness. Admirable acts of courage in resisting state pressure and a determination to win freedom of expression were common. They served the youth as models of commitment and supplied the writers with fresh subjects. The struggle, however, led a group of so-called engagé writers to employ the wrong means for the right ends. In order to undermine the credibility of the state authorities they used the tactics of lying and falsifying the facts, spreading fabricated rumors, denouncing what deserved approval and support, and making common cause with individuals and circles whom the intelligentsia themselves had long since declared reactionary and antiquated. This deplorable state of affairs grew worse in the late fifties and continued for the next two decades as well.

During the period in question, 1941-53, several new talents of superior quality emerged. Oldest among them and belonging to the "first" generation was Bozorg Alavi (b. 1904), who had published his well-received first collection of short stories, *Chamedan* (The suitcase), in 1935 and had spent four years (1937–41) in prison because of his linkage with the nascent Marxist group of Tehran. Upon his release in 1941 Alavi resumed his literary activity with the publication of *Varaq-pareh-ha-ye zendan* (Scrap papers from prison),[8] followed in 1951 by the novel *Chashmhayash* (Her eyes),[9] and a third volume of short stories called *Nameh-ha* (Letters). Between 1953 and 1978, teaching as a professor at Humboldt University in East Berlin, he concentrated more on scholarly activities, authoring several books and translating from Persian into German and vice versa. In 1978, even before the Islamic Republic was established, Alavi reentered the literary scene with the publication of two collections of stories, *Mirza*[*] and

---

*. Asterisk denotes a story included in this anthology.

Div! Div! (Demon! demon!), as well as a small novel called *Salariha*.
His forthcoming novel, *Muryaneh* (Termite), is in essence about the
social and political ailments of Iran under the old regime.

Social concerns and attempts at discrediting the regime are obviously the thrust of Alavi's works, as well as of the fiction of another
like-minded writer, Mahmud E'temadzadeh Beh'azin (b. 1915),
whose novel *Dokhtar-e ra'iyat* (The serf's daughter), published in
1951, describes the plight of one such girl who struggles to liberate
herself and join the working class. But no writer conscious of his art
can afford to subdue the gift of his pen exclusively to mere propaga-
tion of a political ideology, repeating it in so many stories. Alavi's
Her Eyes may owe its success to a degree to a romantic flavor that
makes it enjoyable reading beyond the party line. Another trait of
Alavi's fiction is his predilection for detective plots, evident in both
Her Eyes and *Mirza*. As for Beh'azin, his *Mohreh-ye mar* (The snake
stone),* is a fantastic tale which uses symbolic elements reminiscent
of the Biblical story of Eve, the serpent, and the loss of paradise.

One of the brilliant novelists to emerge during the forties was
Sadeq Chubak (b. 1916), whose first collection of short stories,
called *Khaymeh-shab-bazi* (The puppet show, 1945), proved his
power of naturalistic description combined with penetrating insight
and a compact style. The level of sophistication displayed in this volume was maintained in his second book, *Antari ke lutiyash mordeh
bud* (The baboon whose buffoon was dead,[10] 1949). His characters
represent neglected, downtrodden elements of society, which had
hardly ever caught the attention of writers. A reticent person by
nature, Chubak kept aloof from engagement in fashionable political
activities. For over thirteen years he remained silent, until 1963
when his first famous novel, *Tangsir*, appeared, followed by two story
collections, *Ruz-e avval-e qabr* (The first day in the grave) in 1965,
and *Cheragh-e akher* (The last offering) in 1966. His second novel,
Sang-e sabur (The patient stone)[11] remains his last published work.
Tangsir is the dramatic unfolding of the allegedly true story of a
young man of Tangestan (the mountainous hinterland of Bushire)
who, being cheated and robbed of his savings, takes the law into his
own hands and kills, within a couple of hours, the five "respectable"
swindlers before sailing away with his wife and child.[12] The breath-
taking linear development of this novel is in marked contrast with
the multilevel, complicated, dense thought process and substance of
The Patient Stone which, in its stream-of-consciousness style, illus-

trating the utter despair and misery of several characters, represents a major highlight in the history of Persian fiction.

Another influential writer to start his career in the forties was the more famous, hotly debated, and politically controversial figure of Jalal Al-e Ahmad (1923-69). Being enormously talented, energetic, and passionately interested in the fate of his nation's culture and political future, Al-e Ahmad played a decisive role in shaping the mind and actions of an entire generation of young intellectuals. Restless, impatient, and aggressive by nature, Al-e Ahmad showed the marks of his future career both as writer and social critic even in the stories of his first collection, *Did-o bazdid* (Exchange of visits, 1946). Three more volumes appeared between 1947 and 1952. He also wrote four novels. The shortest and least successful among them, *Sargozasht-e kanduha* (The Tale of Beehives, 1955), was an allegory of the exploitation of Iranian oil by foreign companies. In 1958 came *Modir-e madraseh* (The School Principal), which was enthusiastically received by the public. It decries the deplorable conditions of Iranian education through the example of an elementary school in which children coming from needy families suffer from malnutrition and funds are not sufficient for the purchase of facilities. The principal of the school, who perfectly mirrors the narrator and is identical with Al-e Ahmad himself, reappears ten years later in the novel *Nefrin-e zamin* (The Cursing of the Land) as a school teacher in a village which, in the wake of Iran's land reform, is losing its traditional system of agriculture in exchange for modernization and mechanical tools. The resulting confusion and failure, as depicted by Al-e Ahmad, is meant to lend credence to his basic thesis, forcefully detailed in a most influential sociopolitical essay called *Gharbzadegi* (*Plagued by the West*),[13] according to which imitation of the West and the latter's exploitation of the East are at the root of the ruin and backwardness experienced by Eastern nations.

In 1961 Al-e Ahmad published his third novel, *Nun va'l-qalam* (*By the Pen*),[14] an allegory expressing the interaction between government and society and the role of the intellectual elite in Iran. Told in the form of a historical tale projected back into sixteenth-century Safavid times, it offers a detached statement about religion and government in Iran and the fate of political movements. Al-e Ahmad's typical telegraphic prose, revealing both arrogance and impatience even with grammar and syntax, became the model for some aspiring talents. He impressed his audience as one who knew the diagnosis and had the remedy for the troubles of his country. Some termed him "the wide-awake conscience of the nation." Nobody, even among his opponents, would deny his power of intellect and sharp insight. It is his vital contribution to the establishment of an even less progressive and democratic regime, with all the devastating consequences of political upheaval, that is held against him. He undoubtedly was, and will be remembered as, an outstanding though controversial figure of Iran's intellectual life during the fifties and sixties.[15]

In the hands of these and a number of other writers of fiction, Persian prose, which for over a thousand years had been treated as the illegitimate child of Persian literature, achieved great maturity and, in the appealing form of short stories, assumed a social responsibility greater than poetry had ever displayed. The rapidly politicized mind of the Persian people turned from the other-worldly and religious themes of the past millennium to secular problems. The imported genre of short stories lent itself as the most suitable vehicle for direct exhibition of social concerns as exemplified by countless daily incidents. The group of distinguished writers mentioned so far was joined in the fifties and the following two decades by a host of promising talents. The momentum gained from over thirty years of experience, fueled by fresh ideas offered in translations from numerous languages and cultures as well as ever increasing personal contact with the outside world, produced an intellectual atmosphere that was both inspiring and challenging. Censorship blocked publication of many works and inflicted considerable pain on a number of poets and novelists. But it was not able to break their pen or their will to continue blasting what was wrong and defending human rights and dignity.

Many are the writers of Persian short stories, some associated with only a few stories, others with entire volumes.[16] However, in this introductory essay we must pass over the majority and devote a few words to only four writers who have emerged as leaders in the field.

Ebrahim Golestan (b. 1922), published his first volume of stories, *Azar, mah-e akher-e pa'iz* (Azar, the last month of autumn), in 1948, demonstrating his mastery of technique as well as his unusual gift and taste for linguistic refinement.

Three more collections, published in 1955, 1967 and 1969, were followed by a masterful satirical novel, *Asrar-e ganj-e darreh-ye jenni* (The secrets of the treasures of the enchanted valley)[17] in 1974. Golestan's fiction offers scenes of middle-class daily life, narrative recollections, romantic episodes, and some flashbacks to familiar religious myths daringly satirized. His vocabulary is carefully selected and elegantly arranged. The flow of harmoniously measured sentences causes his prose to glide smoothly into a semi-poetic mode. His story, *Safar-e 'Esmat* (Esmat's journey),* is one of the jewels of modern Persian literature.

Gholam Hosayn Sa'edi (b. 1935, d. 1985 in Paris), was a courageous radical writer and, under the pen name Gowhar-e Morad, Iran's greatest playwright ever. He was a towering figure of creative writing with an inexhaustible wealth of ideas and, unlike Chubak and Golestan, not frugal with the power of his pen and mind. He wrote over thirty volumes of stories, plays, essays, and ethnographic studies. In addition to being a professional psychiatrist, he was the founder and editor of the important periodical *Alefba*. Like Al-e Ahmad, he was at the forefront of the protest movement. His stories are the voice of political dissent, mostly veiled in allegories with grotesque figures of village dwellers or masked foreign intruders. He often treats simple peasants and their fortunes with sympathy and feeling for their own sake and not for the symbolic role they are often assigned to play.[18]

Another superbly gifted writer of fiction, Hushang Golshiri (b. 1938), established his fame as a leading stylist almost overnight with the publication of the short novel *Shazdeh Ehtejab* (Prince Ehtejab)[19] in 1968. It focuses on the decadent figure of a Qajar prince who is vegetating with his memories of the past and his terminal tuberculosis. Following his brilliant debut, Golshiri has published numerous other volumes and remains a central figure among novelists still living in post-Pahlavi Iran. He is known for his sophisticated technique as well as for his meticulously chosen phraseology, which is characterized by many abrupt switches from one person or time or situation to another. (This calculated process is abetted by the lack of gender in Persian nouns and pronouns; thus his stories mostly remain beyond the comprehension of untrained readers.)

Mahmud Dowlatabadi (b. 1940), the youngest among the top novelists of Iran, is the author of a monumental ten-volume saga, called *Klidar*,[20] which in size—and very likely also in significance—has surpassed all novels ever written in Persian. It is remarkable for its fascinating plot, the poetic quality of its prose, tremendous wealth of imagination, an appealing blend of political heroism and penetrating psychological insight, the perfect dramatic development of the story through to its tragic climax, and the variety of its characters and rural scenery. Like so many of the best Iranian writers (Alavi, Al-e Ahmad, Sa'edi, Beh'azin, Baraheni...), Dowlatabadi was—naively perhaps, and out of the sheer goodness of his heart—committed to an ideology that has never provided the country with anything other than unrest and social turmoil. In *Jay-e khali-ye Saluch* (The missing place of the Saluch), another large novel, Dowlatabadi demonstrates the plight of a village that is hard hit by the consequences of poorly planned agricultural reform and is plunged into greater misery than before. The story *Edbar* (Hard luck)* is only a sample of his great literary achievement so far.

The present essay would grow far beyond its limited scope if it yielded to the temptation of saying a few words about the many other writers of rank. One characteristic of Iran's intellectual development during the period covered by this volume is the sudden eruption of creativity in literature and the arts, like the waking of an old genius from over two hundred years of deep slumber. In modern sciences and technology even decades of hard effort and new learning will not enable Iranians to claim to have bridged the gap between themselves and the progressive nations of the world. In the arts and belles-lettres, however, a creative potential has been the hallmark of the Iranian people throughout the ages, dormant at times of severe adversity and cultural decline, but rising with renewed vigor in moments of improved hope and prosperity. In this century Iran has experienced one of those outbreaks of energy in numerous fields of literary and artistic creativity, including even the indigenously "unsavory" fields of music, painting, and theater.

In the field of imaginative literature Persian women, having achieved a certain degree of emancipation, hold an important position and the number of emerging talents among them is growing rapidly.

Simin Daneshvar (b. 1921), is the first outstanding female novelist of Iran; her earliest volume of short stories, *Atash-e khamush* (The quenched fire),[21] appeared in 1948. Her preoccupation with the plight of Persian women was more outspokenly expressed in her second collection, *Shahri chun behesht* (A city like paradise, 1961), and in the rest of her writings through the years. Her real fame rests upon *Savushun*,[22] 1969, an extremely popular political novel that depicts the tense living conditions of a family in Shiraz during World War II when foreign troops were present in Iran.

Mahshid Amir-Shahi (b. 1940), the author so far of four volumes of delightful stories and a novel, *Dar hazar* (At home, 1986), does not dwell only on the dark side of life, as had been the overriding concern of many other writers. Her characters are mostly normal middle-class individuals caught in the hustle and bustle of their daily lives with all their sunny or gloomy moments. Beautiful and often humorous memories of a happy childhood, touching expressions of affection, particularly for a gentle mother, reminiscences of school years, and teenage pleasures, as well as later disappointments in life, are just some of the enjoyable qualities of Amir-Shahi's fiction.

A quite different tone, that of a psychological approach to society and social life, rings through the fiction of Shahrnush Parsipur (b. 1946), the author of a well-known novel *Tuba va ma'na-ye shab* (Tuba and the meaning of night, 1987) which, in spite of—or perhaps because of—its complicated and perplexing plot, has captured the imagination of several critics and inspired different interpretations. In it Parsipur has presented a combination of political, religious, and social factors in the personal fate of a girl who passes through changing times and the ordeals of both old-fashioned and modernized family life.

In an earlier, equally fascinating novel, *Sag va zemestan-e boland* (The dog and the long winter, 1976), she had already treated (though without much symbolic allegory) the similar subject of the oppressive political atmosphere of the time and the agony inflicted by middle-class traditions and religious norms; the former she condemns, the latter she considers moribund.

Parsipur's emancipated, somewhat resigned, mental attitude and approach to love and life is demonstrated in her story *Tajrebeh-ha-ye azad* (Trial offers),* written in 1970.

Generally speaking, it must be admitted that Amir-Shahi, Parsipur, and Golestan are not exceptional in their preference for scenes from middle-class problems and occupations. Numerous other novelists likewise write about the habits, vanities, and moral or immoral behavior of Iranian bourgeois and nouveau riche circles, deriding their emptiness and devotion to fun and base pleasures. One such story is *Malahat-ha-ye panhan va ashkar-e khordeh-borzhua'ha* (The discreet & obvious charms of the petite bourgeoisie)* by Fereydun Tonokaboni (b. 1937), mockingly portraying the hothouse atmosphere of a party where funny men and women enjoy their drinks and vulgar jokes, and yet profess nostalgia for the good old days.

Moniru Ravanipur (b. 1954) is a fast-rising, prolific star who began her career after the Revolution. Her subjects are mostly inspired by living conditions and experiences in the coastal regions of the Persian Gulf. Amin Faqiri (b. 1943) has been a school teacher in rural areas of the south and writes with sensitivity about the natural beauty and also the practical difficulties of village life. *Baradaran-*

e ghamgin (The sad brothers, 1984),* however, seem to offer a political allegory. It shows greater technical maturity with a well-
presented symbolic substance. Ahmad Mahmud (b. 1931) is intimately familiar with the poor neighborhoods around the oil cities of
Khuzistan. In *Pesarak-e bumi* (The little native boy)* he is more concerned about the rising tide of anti-Western sentiment which,
during a political demonstration in Abadan, costs the lives of a small
English girl and a little native boy who has developed an innocent
affection for her. Mahmud's amiable disposition contrasts with the
chauvinistic views of, for example, Mir-Sadeqi as expressed in his *Az
posht-e pardeh-ye meh* (Through the veil of fog),* or of Al-e Ahmad's
unwholesome purpose in *Showhar-e Amrika'i* (The American husband).* Al-e Ahmad's case is no match for Chubak's more realistic
one, the European wife of an Iranian husband in Tehran in *Asb-e
chubi* (The wooden horse).* Perhaps nobody among the Persian
writers, not even Hedayat, brings Kafka more to mind than Nazari
(b. 1933) in his sketchy, hazy, dreamy pieces. He has never published
a volume, and the five "stories" included here, plus a few more,
appeared in the literary magazine *Sokhan* in the mid-seventies.

It is true, as many would say, that Iranian novels and short stories
are usually depressing and leave the reader with the impression that
Iranians are a nation of mourners with no glimmer of joy and hope
and no trace of humor visible in their lives. Without venturing to
explain the historical reasons for this sad reality, one might qualify
this assumption as only partially true. Iranian writers, especially after
1953, may be divided into two distinctive groups, with only a few
being in the middle or completely beyond the borderlines: the committed, anti-establishment writers, led by Al-e Ahmad, who fought
the regime; and those for whom the overthrow of the monarchy did
not constitute the exclusive purpose and motivation for writing. Several novelists belonging to the first camp made politics and political
issues the substance of their stories. With them the meaning of their
craft became identical with their political stance, a trend that can
hardly be rated positively. Among the second group we find some of
the best novelists and poets, who are more flexible in the choice of
their subjects. Even within the limits of this anthology there is no
shortage of stories that dilute this purported seriousness with a dose
of healthy humor (by Jamalzadeh, Amir-Shahi, Tonokaboni, Daneshvar, and even Golestan). Some others may not be uplifting but
neither are they depressing; they are rather descriptive or political or

even suspenseful in type (e.g. Taraqqi, Sadeqi, Parsipur, Alavi, Ashurzadeh, Khaksar).

As a whole, it seems that Iranian writers, and poets as well, have grasped the opportunity to tear the veil aside and publicly expose the reality of life in their country after centuries of oppression, plunder and torture, neglect and abuse of all human rights by authorities of whatever stamp, whether in the name of God or of the State, but in reality to quench their own bestial thirst for money and power. These courageous poets and writers have tried, with more sincerity and honesty than any other leaders and institutions in the past, to open the minds of a nation. To a certain extent, they have succeeded. This intellectual movement started rolling with the Constitutional Revolution. Since then it has been supported and fed by a variety of fundamental changes, and no power has been able to slow its momentum.

During the last twelve years a number of poets and writers, together with artists and scholars, have chosen to live in exile. Several of the most brilliant among them have died either at home or abroad. Many others are enduring the pains consequent upon resistance at home. And a generation of promising new talents is now also rising. They could not, except for three or four, be included in our anthology; they need, and deserve, a separate volume to themselves.

Notes

1. M. A. Jamalzadeh, *Once Upon a Time*. Tr. H. Moayyad and Paul Sprachman, Modern Persian Literature Series, no. 6, Bibliotheca Persica, New York 1989.

2. A. A. Dehkhoda, *Charand-parand*. It appeared first as a column in the weekly *Sur-e Esrafil* in 1908, and has been printed separately many times. See also E. G. Browne, *The Press and Poetry of Modern Persia*, 1914, reprinted Kalimat Press 1983.

3. Browne, ibid., offers a complete listing of them.

4. H. Moayyad, "Jamalzadeh's Life and Work," *Once Upon a Time*, p. 10, no. 24.

5. Sadeq Hedayat, *Haji Agha: Portrait of an Iranian Confidence Man*. Tr. G. M. Wickens, University of Texas at Austin 1979.

6. Sadeq Hedayat, *Tup-e Morvari*, edited with introduction and notes by M. J. Mahjub, Arash Forlag, Sweden 1990.

7. The literature on Hedayat is vast. See H. Kamshad, *Modern Persian Prose Literature*, Cambridge 1966; Michael Beard, *"The Blind Owl" as a*

Western Novel, Princeton 1990; E. Yarshater, "Sadiq Hedayat," in *Persian Literature*, Columbia Lectures on Iranian Studies, no. 3, ed. E. Yarshater, New York 1988, pp. 318-35 and Bibliography, p. 514.

8. Donné Raffat, *The Prison Papers of Bozorg Alavi, A Literary Odyssey*, Syracuse University Press 1985.

9. Bozorg Alavi, *Her Eyes*. Tr. John O'Kane. Modern Persian Literature Series, no. 9, New York 1989.

10. Sadeq Chubak, *The Baboon whose Buffoon Was Dead*. Tr. Peter Avery, *New World Writing* 11 (1957), pp. 14-24.

11. Sadeq Chubak, *The Patient Stone*. Tr. M. R. Ghanoonparvar, Mazda Publishers 1989.

12. "One Man and His Gun" (*Tangsir*). Tr. Marzia Sami'i and F. R. C. Bagley, printed together with translations of five of Chubak's short stories, in: Sadeq Chubak, *An Anthology*, Modern Persian Literature Series, no. 3, New York 1982.

13. Jalal Al-e Ahmad, *Plagued by the West*. Tr. Paul Sprachman, Modern Persian Literature Series, no. 4, New York 1982.

14. Jalal Al-e Ahmad, *By the Pen*. Tr. M. R. Ghanoonparvar, Middle East Monographs, no. 8, Center for Middle Eastern Studies, University of Texas at Austin 1988.

15. For more on Al-e Ahmad see: *Iranian Society: An Anthology of Writings by Jalal Al-e Ahmad*, compiled and edited by Michael Hillmann, Mazda Publishers 1982; M. Hillmann's Introductions to Jalal Al-e Ahmad's *Lost in the Crowd*, tr. John Green, Three Continents Press 1985, and Al-e Ahmad's *By The Pen*, see 14.

16. Hasan Abedini, in his *Farhang-e dastan-nevisan-e Iran* (Bibliography of Iranian writers), Tehran 1990, lists over 600 names. Even if we omit ninety percent of them for a variety of reasons, there still remain more than sixty names, many of whom are indeed better than mediocre writers.

17. For a summary of this novel, see: Paul Sprachman, "Ebrahim Golestan's *The Treasure*: A Parable of Cliché and Consumption," *Iranian Studies* 15 (1982), pp. 155-80.

18. For translations of Sa'edi's stories see: *Persian Literature*, p. 515. For his plays see: *Iranian Drama. An Anthology*, compiled and edited by M. R. Ghanoonparvar and John Green, Mazda Publishers 1989; Gisele Kapuscinski, "Modern Persian Drama," *Persian Literature*, 392-97; *Iranian Studies* 18 (1985), pp. 133-36 and 257-323.

19. "Prince Ehtejab," tr. Minoo R. Southgate, in *Major Voices*, pp. 205-303. For a short autobiography, ibid. pp. 245-50.

20. This novel took almost fifteen years to write and six years to publish. See Hamid Dabashi, "Who is Who in Klidar? Society and Solitude in the Making of a Character," in *Papers in Honor of Professor Ehsan Yarshater*, Brill 1990, pp. 48-59.

21. Simin Daneshvar, *Daneshvar's Playhouse. A Collection of Stories.* Tr. Maryam Mafi, Mage Publishers, Washington 1989. For Daneshvar's biography, see Mafi's "Afterword," pp. 173-83.

22. Simin Daneshvar, *Savushun: A Novel about Modern Iran.* Tr. M. R. Ghanoonparvar, Mage Publishers, Washington 1990.

For further reading, in addition to *Persian Literature*, (Columbia Lectures on Iranian Studies, no. 3, 1988) and other sources and translations mentioned in the endnotes, the following books are recommended:

Major Voices in Contemporary Persian Literature. Edited by Michael C. Hillmann. *Literature East and West* 20, 1976 (published 1980).

Modern Persian Short Stories. Edited and translated by Minoo Southgate. Washington: Three Continents Press, 1980.

Stories by Iranian Women since the Revolution. Tr. Soraya Paknazar Sullivan, Introduction by Farzaneh Milani. Austin: Center for Middle Eastern Studies, University of Texas, 1991.

M. A. Jamalzadeh

1892-1997

Sayyid Mohammad Ali Jamalzadeh was born in Isfahan to a religious family of Shi'i Muslim clerics. Shortly before the execution of his reformist preacher father in 1908, Jamalzadeh went to Beirut and then to France and Switzerland to complete his education. From 1916 to 1930, he worked for the Iranian Embassy in Berlin.

In Berlin in 1921 Jamalzadeh published *Yeki bud yeki nabud* (Once upon a time), the first collection of Persian short stories ever published. The volume featured a preface which served as a manifesto for modernist Persian prose writing, while its six anecdotal stories treat events of the 1910s in Iran with unprecedented realism and local color. A translation of the stories titled *Once Upon a Time* was published in 1985, while the preface appeared in *The Literary Review* 18, 1974–75.

Jamalzadeh published nothing further in the 1920s and 1930s, in part because of strident, negative reaction in Tehran to his satirical portrayal of Shi'ite clerics in *Once Upon A Time*. From 1931 to 1956 he worked for the International Employment Office in Geneva. Following retirement, he has remained there, with an active schedule of writing and corresponding. A flood of books came from his pen from the early 1940s into the 1970s. Among Jamalzadeh's published fiction from this period are: *Dār al-majānin* (Insane asylum, 1943), *Sahrā-ye mahshar* (The plain of judgment, 1947), *Kohneh va now* (Old and new, 1961), *Āsmān va rismān* (From the sublime to the ridiculous, 1964), *Talkh va shirin* (Bitter and sweet, 1964), and *Qesseh'hā-ye kutāh barā-ye bacheh'hā-ye rishdār* (Short tales for bearded boys, 1973). Typical of Jamalzadeh's later writing is the autobiographical *Sar-o tah-e yek karbās* (Cut from the same cloth), published in English as *Isfahan is Half the World: Memories of a Persian Boyhood*, 1983.

In recent years, much of Jamalzadeh's fiction and essays have been reissued in Iran, including: *Khāterāt-e Sayyed Mohammad Ali Jamālzādah* (1999), *Qesseh'nevisi* (1999), *Ashnāye bā Hāfez* (2000), *Dāstān'hā-ye Masnavi: bāng-e nāy* (2000), *Qesseh-e mā beh sar resid* (2000), *Qultashan divan* (2000), *Haft keshvar* (2001), *Kohneh va naw* (2001), *Qesseh'hā-ye kutāh barā-ye bachcheh'hā-ye rish'dār* (2001).

What's Sauce for the Goose…

Translated by Heshmat Moayyad and Paul Sprachman

Habit truly is like a beggar from Samaria or a pet cat or a Jew owed money or an Isfahani jakesraker (or "dustman" as they say in Tehran): no matter how many times you throw it out one door, it'll always return through another. Even after a lifetime of living abroad, it's still amazing what pretexts one will sometimes harbor, to what notions one will succumb, and where one's inclinations will lead. In a strange land, a person merely has to think of something from home once and he becomes the proverbial elephant who dreams of India. Even a completely rational person will act like a pregnant woman, set upon by uncontrollable cravings, unable to tell day from night.

Just recently, while in the very heart of Europe, I was suddenly, for no reason at all, reminded of the warm, snug baths of Iran and the bathmitt rubdowns of our masseur Karbala'i Thursday. Things reached such a state that I was actually ready to give a month's pay to have the prophet Khizr appear and pour a goblet of water over my head, so that when I opened my eyes, I'd find myself back in the privacy of our local *hammam*, stretched out on its scorching marble slabs, a folded bath towel supporting my head and two under my body, and Karbala'i Thursday with his coarse fiber mitt—the tips of two of his hennaed fingers poking out of it—beside me and as gently and mildly as possible, but not leaving out any of the formalities, giving me a massage from head to foot.

From the moment this thought entered my mind, it became a fiendish obsession; peace and quiet turned their backs on me, and my head never touched a pillow. I searched high and low and asked about, until I finally learned of a Turkish bath where the masseur, they say, had been in Iran once and was especially skilled in the art of bathmitt rubdowns. Laying down my life, I thought, would not be too high a price for this piece of good news, so I dropped my work and responsibilities and made for the Mecca of my dreams. All along the way I had visions of the damp, weathered steps of my old *hammam* in Tehran with the famous changing room and its painted vault on which a forked-bearded Rostam was disemboweling the White Demon. I especially recall the plaster on the ceiling just where the Demon's punctured belly had fallen off, and peeking through was a touch of black that got bigger each week I visited the bath.

I found the head bathkeeper with a beard that matched Rostam's, sitting behind his black wooden cashbox, constantly saying "Bless you" and puffing on his wood-bowled waterpipe. But, God! Where were they hiding all the good things in this European version of a bath? Where was the bowl of prune juice, the piping hot sweetwater tea, and the long-stemmed pipe filled with fine tobacco? After they took the posted fee from me in advance, they gave me a ticket and crammed me into a bare and dank room embellished only with a rusty faucet emerging halfway up the wall, a shower head suspended from the ceiling, and a hook like a meat hook that they'd hammered into the back of the door to hang clothes on. That was it. And they had the nerve to call this a bath!

I wasn't in the room long before the door opened, and without so much as a hem or a haw, the attendant turned up. I was about to cover my privates, but realizing that my ancestor, the prophet Adam, wouldn't even have bothered to cover up in this place, I also refrained. As soon as the guy took a look at me and realized from the blackness of my hair and my bandy legs that I was an Easterner, he smiled. But when he learned that I was a native Iranian, he grinned from ear to ear. He immediately doused me with water and left. When he returned, I saw that he had brought back one of those coarse bathmitts that we used back home. God, just the sight of it was worth an entire village! He laid me down and began to give me an Iranian-style rubdown (but without the head support and the long bath towel). Now I won't tell you how good this made me feel—just as merely saying *halva* does not sweeten the mouth. The point is that as soon as I saw that the fellow was really an expert, with all the ins and outs of the trade down pat, I lapsed into total bliss. Just to be friendly, I said, "Master, I've heard that you were in Iran."

He held up the mitt, which he wore like a glove, and said, "Here's the proof."

"What were you doing there?" I asked.

He laughed and said, "Guess."

"Did you perhaps travel back with one of the kings of Iran who visited Europe?"

"No," he answered.

"Were you by any chance some tourist's serving man?"

"No."

"Maybe you stole something and wanted to go to a safe place, beyond the reach of the police?"

"No."

"When you were young, an Iranian nobleman took you to Iran?"

"No."

"I give up," I said. "Now tell me why you went to Iran."

"I was an adviser, my good man…"

My mouth opened as wide as the *hammam* plunge tank in amazement. My eyes were as round as the windows of its skylight domes. "You were an adviser," I said.

"Yes, an adviser," he said. "And why not?"

"Where were you an adviser?" I asked.

"The ministries of the Interior, Foreign Affairs, Finance, Justice, Defense, Education, Religious Endowments, Public Works, Post and Telegraph, Customs, Trade, to name a few."

I was about to laugh, but I saw that the fellow was not one to make jokes and that he seemed to believe that he was not just whistling into the wind. "Granted, whatever you say is possible, but be fair; believing that you were an adviser in Iran is not the easiest thing in the world."

He smiled and said, "It's obvious that you don't know your own Iran. Do you know how they celebrate the carnival in Europe?"

"Of course I know. People get dressed up in weird costumes and masks and lose themselves in carousing and carrying on. But what does this have to do with the matter at hand?"

"Although I didn't spend more than eighteen months in Iran, this much I know: the whole country is like a carnival where anyone can wear whatever costume he pleases and doesn't owe anybody an explanation."

"This is quite true," I said. "But about your being an adviser..."

"Then listen and I'll tell you the whole story, although I've written a day-by-day account in my travel diary, and if you're interested, I can show you that."

"I'd be much obliged, but now that we've got the opportunity, why don't you, for the time being, recite part of your diary to me from memory so that it'll become clear just how the person kneeling beside me and massaging the dead skin off my back became an adviser in eight of Iran's ministries and important bureaus."

With a swipe of his mitt, the fellow removed the furled pieces of skin that had gathered on my chest. He then washed me down with a small bucket of water and said, "My father was a masseur and bathman in this city, and from early childhood I have known nothing but the *hammam*, soap, and massage. Exactly twenty years ago, one of the city's famous people fell ill. They took him to all the reputable doctors in Europe, but nothing worked. By chance, the sick man came to the bathhouse where I worked and, hoping to get a fat tip, I gave him an ample rubdown.

"The next day he returned and said, 'Last night was the first blessed time in six years that I've been able to sleep comfortably. It seems that I owe it to your massage. I've come today just to make sure.' To make a long story short, he came every day thereafter. Evidently my massages produced effects that I hadn't known about before. I was in clover now; the man's faith in me grew stronger day by day. He was not going to let anything spoil our arrangement, so he had a small bath built right in his own home and hired me to be his private masseur. He gave me a place to live in his compound, where eventually I became like one of the family. About this time it just so happened that the government of Iran wanted to import advisers from Europe. The fellow I worked for was chosen and was allowed to select several people to work under him in Iran to 'reform' the government there.

"At first he was peeved about having to let me go. But all at once, I don't know how, he came up with the devilish idea of having me along as an uninvited guest, and just so he wouldn't have to lay out any of his own money, he named me to his advisory team. And I played my part to the hilt.

"Once we got to Iran, though I had to give the Sahib his secret massage every day, as soon as I left the bath I became a 'monsieur,' a 'sahib' in my own right, endowed with grandeur, glory, and standing.

"In the beginning they put me in the Postal Bureau. In Europe everybody knows a little about the post office. Everybody knows, for example, that the postman wears a special uniform and that every neighborhood has a local post office and that there's a postbox on every street. I was more or less able to set up the same things in Tehran, and you wouldn't believe what a hit it was. The shah gave me medals and titles, newspapers carried stories about me, poets wrote poems in praise of me, minstrels made up songs. It wasn't long before I was the talk of everybody in town, both high and low. Parliament even gave me broad discretionary powers, and slowly but surely several other ministries came under my control. At this point the reforms just rained down from me. I kept presenting measure after measure to the Majlis, the government, and the court and started a chorus of groans that no *ta'ziyeh* could match.

"But the problem of the man's massage would not go away. Since he was the only other one in on our game and could have given me away any time he wanted, I was forced to appear every morning, the time when Muslims were at prayer, in the private bath of my former master and, despite the fact that my rank had outstripped his by several grades (most represented on a chest full of Lion and Sun insignias and by all manner of scientific medals) give him a rubdown and a massage. As always, the fellow would nod his head and smile, but would never condescend to mention our secret, and likewise, neither would I.

"It wasn't long before I found myself a man of some means, and I remembered something from *The Adventures of Hajji Baba of Ispahan*, a book that I had read while I was in Iran: Friends, never trust Iranians; they are a faithless lot. Lying and treachery are their weapons of war and their instruments of peace. For next to nothing, they'll put a man on the scaffold, and no matter how much you try to help them, they'll try just as hard to ruin you. The lie is their national disease, their native flaw; nothing bears this out more than the oaths they swear. Just look at how many things they swear by! Why would the plain truth need this much swearing? 'Upon your soul. Upon my soul. By the death of my children. By the spirit of my father and mother. By the shah's head. By the gemstone in the shah's turban. Upon your death. By your beard. By "hello, how-are-you." By the breaking of bread. By the Prophet. By the Prophet's unblemished

ancestors. By the *qebleh*. By the Koran. By Hasan. By Hosayn. By the
Fourteen Innocents. By the Twelve Imams. By the Five sheltered
under the Prophet's mantle.' All of these are part of an oath vocabulary that runs from the spirit and the souls still with us and souls
departed to the heads and the eyes of their dear ones and their own
blessed beards and mustaches, broken teeth and severed arms, to the
hammam furnace, its lanterns, and its wash water—all in the name of
telling the truth!

"This was why I made caution my first concern, thinking that it
was a good idea to collect my riches as quickly as possible and get
back home. Since remaining in Iran presented a thousand risks, and
knowing Iranian ethics, more or less, the way I did, I was afraid the
rascals would try to pull something when I wasn't looking. Briefly
then (why bore you), I converted what I owned to gold coins and,
pretending to be sick and forced to return to Europe for treatment, I
packed my bags. And just to tour a bit more of Iran, I chose the
southern route through Qom, Kashan, Isfahan, Shiraz, and Bushire.
The day of my departure from Tehran will truly live on in history:
the whole city turned out to escort me a few stations outside of town
replete with ties and straps, bundles and baggage, tents, pavilions,
and gear. They put up triumphal arches, showered my path with
flowers, slaughtered cows and sheep, recited long odes, and wept,
but I hadn't even reached Qom when a band of thieves attacked me
and took everything I owned. And there I was without a penny to my
name. But after a thousand adventures and loans and promises to
repay, I somehow managed to get to Europe. High authorities in
Iran have been working day and night for fifteen years now to cap-
ture the thieves and return my property. They've given their word a
thousand times and their promises a hundred thousand, and I still
haven't received one blessed cent. In Europe poverty and hunger
have forced me back to my old profession, and as you see..."

At this point in his adventures, the fellow poured another small
pail of water over me, sighed and lost himself in his own thoughts. I
seemed to remember hearing a similar story when I was a boy and
recalled being amazed by what went on in Iran and by the antics of
my fellow countrymen. I thought to myself that such a people truly
deserve advisers such as my masseur. I smiled a half-smile and said,
"*Bile dig, bile choqondar.*" The fellow understood the word *choqondar*
and asked me why I was talking about beetroots. I told him that it
was a Persian proverb. He asked me to explain it to him. I agreed,
but no matter what I did I wasn't able to express the meaning of the

proverb properly, and since my allotted hour was up, I dressed and left the cubicle. As I was leaving the building, I saw the fellow coming toward me with a notebook in his hand. He said, "When I was in Iran, I wrote down my impressions of some of the things and people there, their morals and the odd ways they did things. You might like to have a look at them and return the notebook the next time you visit the *hammam*." I took the notebook, and in that special state of bliss that comes over one leaving the *hammam* after a good rubdown, I went home. When I got there I began to read the notebook.

The man, I saw, had really written a page or two! I had a fine time with them. As he was only vaguely educated and imagined the whole world to be just like Europe, once in Iran, Mr. Foreign Adviser apparently found the new world quite strange. He wrote naively and simply, never disguising the surprise and shock in his observations. The notebook, nearly a hundred pages long, had numerous parts. As a sample, I will pass on this chapter from his writings:

Chapter III
The People and State of Iran

Iranians are generally of average height and have wheat-colored complexions. They like to talk a lot, but do little. While they are very droll and love to laugh, they also cry a great deal. They have the kind of tongue that can talk a snake out of its hole. The children are bald; the men shave their heads and let their beards grow. But one strange thing about this country is that, apparently, there are absolutely no women in it. You see little girls, four or five years old, in the alleyways, but never any women. No matter how much I thought about this I could never figure it out. I had heard that a "city of women" existed somewhere in the world where there were no men, but I've never heard of a "city of men." Back in Europe people say that each Iranian has a harem full of women; good God, how little my fellow countrymen know about the world! In an Iran where you cannot find one single woman, how could each man have a house full of them? Such stupidity! One day I saw people in the bazaar crowded around a person who had long hair, was clean shaven and wearing a white dress and a silk sash. I thought this certainly had to be a woman and, overjoyed, I ran to see my first Iranian woman, but alas, she turned out to be a dervish. "Dervish," that means "singer." Since they don't have opera or theater in Iran, the singers sing in the streets, and instead of selling admission tickets the way we do, they give each person a green leaf. Though it's still very cheap here, there is no necessity to pay! Pay or not, it makes no difference to them.

I once asked an Iranian with whom I was very friendly, and who had several children, where his wife was. I noticed that he reddened at once, his eyes bulged crazily from their sockets, and his mood changed completely. I saw that I had made a huge faux pas and apologized. Ever since that day, it has been quite clear to me that not only didn't women exist in Iran, but even to mention a woman was impossible there.

Another thing that is very strange about Iran is that a substantial part of the people, about half the population of the country, wrap themselves from head to foot in black sacks, not even leaving a space to breathe. And that's how they go about the alleyways, in that black sack. These people are never allowed to speak and have no right to enter a teahouse or any other place. Their baths are also separate and, at public gatherings like passion plays and Moharram mourning, they have their own viewing sections. As long as they are alone, you never hear a peep from them, but as soon as they get together, they start cackling weirdly. I believe they are a form of Iranian priest, similar to the strange types of priests we have back home in Europe. If they are indeed priests, the people do not seem to hold them in much respect, for they have dubbed them *za'ifeh*, which means "weak" and "insignificant."

Now a few words about the men. The men are distinguished by the hats they wear. There are three basic groups, each having its own special circumstances and qualities; they are the Yellow Hats, the White Hats, and the Black Hats. The first group, mostly called Mashdi or Karbala'i, are generally peasants and servants. I don't know why they have vowed to work as hard as they can all their lives and to present the other two groups, the White Hats and the Black Hats, with the fruits of their labor. They are so insistent upon this that often both they themselves and their families starve to death or die from the cold and are buried without so much as a shroud, while the Black Hats and the White Hats have profited so much from the Yellow Hats' suffering that they have no idea how to spend their money. So they spend money on weddings for Arab bachelors and pitch huge tents in their compounds, where they serve tea and sherbet, sometimes rice and meat, to anyone who comes around making

his face look a bit long and sorrowful, offering their condolences for
the souls of the dead White and Black Hats.

All the White and Black Hats ever think about is how to possess
more Yellow Hats. They're forever involved in buying and selling
them. They cost so little that the whole time I was in Iran I never
saw Yellow Hats bought or sold one by one, but just as we in Europe
market honeybees along with their hives, in Iran they deal in Yellow
Hats along with their homes, households, hamlets and villages, as a
package deal. For example, they say that today so-and-so purchased
the deed for a certain village that has a hundred Yellow Hat families
for such a price!

The nation of Yellow Hats enjoys all the blessings of liberty, frater-
nity, and equality, things that get talked about a great deal in Europe,
but that are nowhere to be found. Their liberty, for example, goes so
far as to enable them to sacrifice their goods and belongings, their
honor and reputation, and even their souls and those of their family,
to the Black and White Hats, and no one tries to stop them. The
same thing goes for their equality: if you were to visit a thousand of
them, you would not find one who possessed something the others
did not. They enjoy complete equality in their poverty and want and
even in their demise; they do not mark their graves with a stone or a
brick or a sign of any kind, just so they will be equal to one another. It
doesn't take long before the wind and the rain wipe out any trace of
their graves, and they all become one with the earth. As far as frater-
nity is concerned, the Yellow Hats practice it to such a degree that
they all call one another *dash*, which means "brother."

Now we come to the White Hats, who are called *shaykh* and
akhund. These the people hold in special esteem and, since they are
distinguished by their turbans, whenever they can get their hands on
some cloth they wrap it about their heads and go about looking like
minarets with storks' nests on top. I once asked an Iranian why they
cover their heads this way. He said, "Haven't you ever noticed that
when you cut your finger, you have it bandaged with an old cloth?
There's probably something wrong with their brains and they don't
want to let the fresh air get at their wounds."

The White Hats are very grave and dignified. In order to maintain
their balance and equilibrium, to keep their weighty turbans from
toppling them over, they grow their beards as bushy as possible.
Their famous turbans at one end of their faces and their woolly
beards at the other make them look like half-white, half-black pestles,
the middles of which have been decorated with eyes and eyebrows.

These White Hats are such dignified and solid figures that when they cross the street, one has no choice but to salute them, but despite this, every year there are a couple of months when they go mad. They mount their horses, donkeys, and mules and gallop all day and night through the streets and the bazaars, yelling and screaming until people finally take pity on them. Gradually the sound of weeping and mourning fills the air and things reach such a state that the Yellow Hats, always ready at a moment's notice to sacrifice life and limb for the other two groups, wind themselves in shrouds and, with a kind of dagger called a *qameh*, lacerate their heads and faces, making blood flow in the streets and the bazaars.

The whole time I was in Iran I desperately tried to find out what these White Hats did for a living, but never could. Whatever they do, it must be a very confidential profession, performed far from public view. I believe that it may be some kind of handicraft, for people generally kiss their hands. One day I said to one of my Iranian acquaintances, "I know that these White Hats work with their hands, but I don't know exactly what they do."

"Yes," he said, "it's an important craft that nourishes our country and without which the wheels of government would grind to a halt and the fabric of enterprise would unravel."

I asked what the name of this distinguished profession was.

"*Reshveh*," he said.

I was ashamed to admit that I didn't know the meaning of this word, but I didn't let on. I still haven't found out what the word means, and it's quite possible that the fellow was pulling my leg, because during the same conversation, when I said, "Yes, I've seen how the hands of most White Hats are red; it must have something to do with the profession you mentioned?" he said, "No, that redness is blood from the hearts of the people." But afterwards I learned that he had made that up; the redness on their hands was really from henna. So my faith in the rest of what he had said was shaken. In any case, the aforementioned craft, whatever it may be, must rely heavily on the use of the thumb and forefinger; the White Hats are continually exercising and doing drills with these two fingers. Day and night they pass a string of round beads through these two fingers over and over again in order to strengthen them.

And now we come to the third group, the Black Hats, called *khans* in Iran itself. All agencies of government, whether in the capital or in the provinces, are in the hands of the Black Hats. They have a large club, similar to a Freemasons' lodge, all to themselves. Anyone who becomes a member of this club has it made for life. The club is called the Divan. The term comes from the word *div*, a demon of Iranian legend famous for its perversity. For example, if you do a *div* a kindness, he'll make you his first morsel; if you speak the truth to one, he'll become your enemy; but, if you lie to one, he'll be your friend. These Black Hats are just like this; they're perverse, and for this reason they call themselves the Divan, which is the plural of *div*.

In order to join the club, people must change their names. Most of the names given to new members are the names of animals or objects of war and battle, like "Dog of State," meaning "jackal," or "Scissors of the Sultanate," meaning "shears." (Confidentially, I must say Monsieur Masseur wasn't too strong in Arabic; he mistranslated *kalb*, "dog" as "jackal." But then again, judging by the old saying "the yellow dog is the jackal's brother," meaning six of one, half-a-dozen of the other, he wasn't too far off the mark.)

One of the articles in their club charter forces the Black Hats never to raise a finger except for their own benefit and never to speak unless for their own personal gain. In Europe I had heard that profit-worship was the invention of an English philosopher, but if the truth be known, long before the philosopher's ancestors ever set foot on earth, his philosophy had reached its zenith in Iran—more proof that all the learning and civilization of the West has come from the East. All of the Black Hats' efforts are directed toward maintaining peace and quiet throughout the land. Aware that money is at the root of all disputes and misfortune, they spend their time and energy seeing to it that money never remains in anyone's hands for long; whenever they learn of some somewhere, they confiscate it. In order to perform this task, they are always sending agents to every part of the country and doing whatever it takes to keep anyone from saving money. This wise policy has prevented all sorts of harmful occurrences and, at the same time, it keeps money from leaving Iranian soil; never straying far, it only travels from Taqi's pocket to Naqi's purse. Surely it's high time our leaders in Europe learned something here and stopped causing the people of their own countries so much suffering!

One group of Black Hats, who shave their beards and curl their mustaches and have shortened their hats several inches, wearing them to one side, are called "Faux-colis." This group backs changes and "reforms" in the charter of the Divan. They claim, for example, that the provisions of the charter concerning the White Hats have not been observed for the most part and that occasionally there have been oversights and lapses in the confiscation of White Hat wealth.

From now on, they feel, everyone should be treated equally; there should be no difference between Yellow Hats and White Hats. In my opinion these Faux-colis are right, and we have our own culture in Europe to thank for it. Because of the effects of our culture, these young Black Hats, calling themselves "Western-oriented" and presenting themselves as experts in Western learning, have found a sense of equality and, moreover, want to spread this fertile seed in their own country.

Another point well worth mentioning is that Esperanto, which I'm told is composed of words from various languages and ought to become the international language and which they try so hard to popularize and spread among us in Europe, is already spoken in Iran. All the Faux-colis speak nothing but Esperanto. Understanding their language, which is composed of words from various European languages and even, on occasion, words from Persian, Arabic, and Turkish, presents absolutely no problem for us. This has been a summary of my observations about the women and men and the nation and the government of Iran.

Thus ended the third chapter of Monsieur Masseur's essay. I had a great time reading it and, after writing the following words at the end in Persian, mailed it back to its author:

Oh, such women, such men!
Bile dig, bile choqondar!
Such a nation, such a government!
Bile dig, bile choqondar!
Such a bureaucracy, such an adviser!
What's sauce for the goose is sauce for the gander!

Sadeq Hedayat

1903–1951

The fiction writer and scholar Sadeq Hedayat came from a prominent and educated Tehran family and attended Tehran's best schools. In 1926 he went to Europe to pursue university studies, but spent his four years there mostly getting familiar with European literature and intellectual currents. Shortly after returning to Tehran in 1930, he published a collection of short stories called *Zendeh be-gur* (Buried alive). The collections *Seh qatreh khun* (Three drops of blood, 1932), *Sāyeh-rowshan* (Chiaroscuro, 1933), *Vāgh vāgh sāhāb* (Mr. Bow-Wow, 1933) and *Sag-e velgard* (The stray dog, 1942) followed, and a longer story called *'Alaviyeh khānom* (1933) as well as books on various literary and cultural subjects. A sampling of Hedayat's short stories appears in *Sadeq Hedayat: An Anthology* (1979). The much-translated story from *Three drops of blood* called "Dāsh Ākol" inspired a major Iranian motion picture in 1970.

Hedayat's fame as Iran's best known novelist and the controversy which still surrounds his career rest primarily on his short novel called *Buf-e kur* (The blind owl, 1937, 1941), Iran's most talked-about piece of fiction, which has been published in several paperback English translations over the last 50 years. Michael Beard traces European influences in his 1990 book, *"The Blind Owl" as a Western Novel*, while the essays in the 1978 collection, *Hedāyat's "The Blind Owl" Forty Years After*, analyze Iranian elements in the novel. In 1995 it was translated into Arabic in Kuwait as *al-Bumah al-amya* and in 2001 into Turkish as *Kor baykus*. In recent years, translated collections of his short stories have been published in France *(L'eau de jouvence et autres recits* and *Madame Alavieh et autres recits)* and Turkey *(Aylak kopek: oyku).*

Hedayat published another novella called *Hāji Āqā* in 1945, which appeared in translation as *Hāji Āghā: portrait of an Iranian confidence man* in 1979. Hedayat's vituperative attack on religious customs called *Tup-e morvāri* (The pearl cannon), written in 1947, remained unpublished for thirty years. Never married, Hedayat left Tehran for Europe at the end of 1950 and committed suicide in Paris the following April.

Abji Khanom

Translated by Ernest Tucker

Abji Khanom was Mahrokh's older sibling, but people who did not know them and saw them together could not believe it. Abji Khanom was tall, thin and swarthy, with thick lips and musky hair—on the whole, a rather ugly girl. In contrast, Mahrokh was short and fair, with a small nose, auburn hair, and beautiful eyes. Whenever she smiled, dimples would appear. They also behaved very differently. Abji Khanom had a nitpicking, quarrelsome, and unsociable nature, to the point that she would not be on speaking terms with her mother for two to three months at a time. Her sister, on the other hand, was sociable, attractive, good-natured, and always smiling. Their neighbor, Naneh Hasan, called her "the Fair Lady." The sisters' parents liked Mahrokh the best since she was the younger and a dear, sweet child. Ever since Abji Khanom's childhood her mother had hit her and picked on her. She would express concern about her in front of neighbors and strangers. She would slap the back of her hand and exclaim, "O, what shall I do about this misfortune? Who will marry such an ugly daughter? I'll be stuck with her forever. She's a daughter without wealth, beauty, or goodness. What wretch is going to marry her?" So many harsh words were hurled at Abji Khanom that she had lost all hope and gave up the very idea of marriage. She spent most of her time in prayer and worship. Once, when they wanted to give her to Kalb Hosayn, the carpenter's apprentice, he did not want her. Abji Khanom would tell everyone, "They found a husband for me, but I wouldn't have him. All husbands nowadays are drunkards and whoremongers. They should all be walled up. I'll never get married."

This is what she said in public. But deep in her heart she actually liked Kalb Hosayn and wanted to marry him. However, because it had been said since she was five years old that she was ugly and no one would want to marry her, and because she figured she was not to share in the pleasures of this world, she wanted at least to reap the rewards of the next through prayer and worship. Thus she consoled herself. Indeed, why lament this transient world if one cannot enjoy its pleasures? The eternal and everlasting world would be hers, where all beautiful people, including her sister, would envy her.

During the months of Moharram and Safar, Abji Khanom would make an appearance. There was not a single martyr's commemoration that she did not attend. She would take her place at the *ta'ziyeh* passion plays from eleven o'clock in the morning, and all the *rowzeh-khans* knew her. They all wanted Abji to sit right at their feet, so that the audience would be inspired by her weeping and moaning. She had memorized most of the martyr's stories. Since she had listened to so many sermons and knew religious questions so well, many of her neighbors would consult her about their problems. She rose at the crack of dawn to wake up her household. First, she would go to her sister's bed. She would kick the bed and say, "It's nearly noon, when are you going to get your lazy bones up and go pray?" The poor girl would get up, perform an ablution while half-asleep and stand to pray. The morning call to prayer, the rooster's crow, the morning wind and the humming of prayers put Abji Khanom into a particular mood, a spiritual mood. She was proud in her heart. She would say to herself, "If God does not take me to heaven, then whom will he take?" For the rest of the day, after attending to household chores and nagging at various people, she would grasp a string of worry beads whose black color had been yellowed with much rubbing and she would send off prayers. Her one great desire was, by whatever means possible, to make a pilgrimage to Karbala and to stay there.

Her sister, though, did not seem to pay any great attention to the spiritual side of life. She was always doing housework. When she turned fifteen, she became a domestic servant. Abji Khanom, at age twenty-two, still remained at home. Deep down, she envied her sister. In the first year and a half after Mahrokh left home to enter domestic service, Abji Khanom did not ask about her or visit her even once. Once every fifteen days when Mahrokh would come home to see the family, Abji Khanom would either get into an argument with someone or go pray for two or three hours. Then, when they were all seated together, she would spout sarcastic remarks about her sister and begin lecturing her on prayer, fasting, ritual purity, and dubious activities. She would say, for instance, "Since these dandy women have appeared, bread has become expensive. Anyone who does not veil her face will be hung in hell by the hairs of her head. The head of the slanderer will grow to the size of a mountain and her neck will shrink to the size of a hair. There are snakes in hell that would drive men to take refuge with a dragon," and on and on in the same vein. Mahrokh felt her sister's envy, but did not show it.

One day toward afternoon, Mahrokh came to the house, spoke with her mother for a while, and then left. Abji Khanom was sitting near the door of the opposite room, smoking a *qalyan*. Because of her envy toward Mahrokh, though, she did not ask her mother what the conversation had been about. Her mother did not say anything to her, either.

At nightfall her father, with his plaster-covered construction worker's cap, came home. He took off his work clothes, picked up his pouch of tobacco and a pipe and went up to the roof. Abji Khanom left off what she had been doing. She and her mother took out the bronze samovar, the small pot of stew, the copper bowl, pickles and onions, and went and sat on the rug. Her mother announced that Abbas, a servant in the same house where Mahrokh was working, had decided to marry Mahrokh. That morning, when the house was quiet, the mother of Abbas had come to ask her hand. They wanted to conclude the marriage contract the next week, and to offer a bride price of twenty-five *tomans*, and to set a dowry of thirty *tomans* plus a mirror, a tulip, a Koran, shoes, sweets, a purse of henna, a silk scarf, culottes, and some cloth with gold thread... Her father, while fanning himself, placed a sugar cube in the corner of his mouth and sipped tea through his teeth. With the tip of his tongue, he said, "Very good, with God's blessing, that is all right!" without seeming surprised, or happy, or showing any emotion at all—as though he were afraid of his wife. Abji Khanom was stunned when she realized what was being said, and she could not listen to the rest of the arrangements. On the pretext that she had to pray, she got up

and went down to the room of five doors. She caught sight of herself
in a small mirror. She looked old and haggard; it was as if she had
aged several years in a few minutes. Her forehead had knotted into a
frown. One of her hairs had turned white, and she pulled it out with
her fingers. She stared at it for a while in front of a lamp, and did not
feel the pain of the pulled root.

A few days passed. All of the household was in a flurry of activity,
going back and forth to the bazaar. They bought two gold-thread
dresses, as well as a decanter, glasses, a piece of embroidery, a rosewater bottle, a drinking vessel, a nightcap, a compact, an indigo-
boiler, a bronze samovar, a printed curtain—a little of everything.
Her mother, filled with excitement, gathered up small things that
were lying around the house, including even the cashmere prayer-
carpet that Abji Khanom had several times asked for (and not
received). She set all this aside for Mahrokh's trousseau. Abji Khanom silently and fretfully observed all these proceedings. For two
days, she pretended she had a headache. Her mother constantly
reproached her. "What is a sister for, at this of all times? I know you
envy her, but envy doesn't get you anywhere. Besides, beauty and
ugliness are none of my doing, they're the work of God. You saw
that I wanted to marry you off to Kalb Hosayn, but you weren't
acceptable to them. Now you are going to pretend to be sick so that
you don't have to do anything! From morning to evening you carry
on with your piety, so I am the helpless one who with these worn-
out eyes must thread the needle!"

Abji Khanom, distraught with jealousy, would reply from under
the blankets, "Fine, fine, at your age don't try to brand a piece of ice!
Men like Abbas are a dime a dozen in this town. Why are you carp-
ing at me? It's enough that everyone knows what sort of a person this
Abbas fellow is, not to mention that Mahrokh is two months pregnant. I have seen her belly protruding, but I overlooked it. I don't
consider her my sister anymore...."

Her mother shot back: "God, may you be struck mute! May the
undertaker carry off your body and may I grieve at your death.
Shameless girl, get lost! Do you want to stain my daughter's reputation? I know that it's your jealousy. May you die since no one will
take you the way you look! Now you slander your sister because of
your own grief. Wasn't it you who said that God himself has written
in the Koran that he who spreads slander is the worst kind of liar? It
is the mercy of God that you are not beautiful, otherwise, since you
leave the house so often to hear sermons, many more things would

be said about you. Go on, all of your fasting and praying is not worth one devil's curse. It's all for show!"

Such were the words they exchanged for the next few days. Mahrokh was perplexed and did not speak until the night of the betrothal. All of the neighborhood women assembled had indigoed eyebrows, veils decorated with coins, made-up faces, hair done in bangs, and cotton culottes. In the midst of all this, Naneh Hasan jumped into the fray and sat with neck bent, playing a drum. Whatever was in her repertoire, she chanted:

Beloved, blessed be your marriage, God willing, blessed be! We come, we come, back we come from the groom's house. All the women are moons, all the men kings, and all eyes almonds.
Beloved, blessed be your marriage, God willing, blessed be! We come, we come, back we come from the bride's house. All are blind, all lame, and all eyes moist.
Beloved, blessed be! We come to carry off the fairy and the houri. God willing, blessed be.

She went on repeating this song. People came and went, and in front of the pool they rubbed trays with ashes. The smell of *qormeh-sabzi* filled the air, and someone shooed away a cat from the kitchen. Another was looking for eggs to juggle. Children held hands, alternately sitting down and standing up, chanting, "Ants in the bathtub, sit down, get up!" Copper samovars, rented for the occasion, were lit. It had been announced that Mahrokh's mother and her daughters would be coming to the betrothal. Two tables were arranged with sweets and fruits, and two chairs placed at the side of each. Mahrokh's father was pacing back and forth, thinking that he had spent quite enough money for this, while her mother insisted that they have a puppet show that night. Amid all this commotion, nobody said a word about Abji Khanom. She had left at two o'clock in the afternoon. No one knew where she had gone, but it must have been to a sermon!

When the tulip lamps were lit and the betrothal had been completed and everyone had left except Naneh Hasan, the hands of the bride and groom were joined and they sat next to each other in the room with five doors, and the doors were closed. Abji Khanom arrived home. She went to the five-doored room to take off her veil. When she got there, she saw that the curtain of the five-doored room had been fastened. Out of curiosity, she pulled away the edge of the curtain, and from the window, saw her sister Mahrokh all made up, indigoed, more beautiful than ever in the light of the lamp, sitting next to the groom, a strapping lad of twenty. They were sitting in front of the table full of sweets. The groom had put his hand round Mahrokh's waist and was saying something in her ear, as if they noticed her. Perhaps he noticed her sister, but because they wanted to make her jealous, they laughed together and kissed. The sound of Naneh Hasan's drum wafted in from the end of the courtyard: "Beloved, blessed be!" A mixture of aversion and envy overtook Abji Khanom. She closed the curtain, and went to her bed, which had been put against the wall. Without taking off her black veil, she put her hands under her chin and stared at the floor. She was dazzled by the flowers and patterns of the carpet. She counted them as if they were something new. She focused on how their colors blended. People came and went, but she didn't raise her head to see who they were. Her mother came to the door of the room and asked, "Why aren't you eating dinner? Why are you so bitter? Why are you sitting here? Take off your black veil, why are you bringing bad luck? Come and kiss your sister, come and watch from behind the window, the bride and groom are like the full moon now. Come and say something. Everyone has been asking where you have been. I don't know what to tell them."

Abji Khanom only raised her head and said, "I already ate dinner."

It was midnight. All had gone to bed remembering their own marital night, and were dreaming pleasantly. Suddenly, the household was rudely awakened by the sound of splashing. At first they thought that a cat or a child had fallen into the pool and, barefoot and half-dressed, they lit the lamp. They looked everywhere, but could see nothing unusual. Just when they were going back to bed, Naneh Hasan noticed Abji Khanom's slippers next to the lid of the water reservoir. They brought the lamp over to it, and saw Abji Khanom's body floating on the water, her black braided hairs twisted around her neck like a snake. Her colorful dress clung to her body. Her face wore an expression of radiance, as if she had gone to a place where there was no ugliness or beauty, no marriage or mourning, no smiling or weeping, no happiness or sorrow. She had gone to paradise.

Bozorg Alavi

1904–1996

Born in Tehran and educated in Germany, Bozorg Alavi is the most famous "leftist" Iranian writer. He returned to Iran in the early 1930s, taught, and published a volume of short stories called *Chamedān* (The suitcase, 1934), for which G.M. Wickens provides plot summaries in "Bozorg Alavi's Portmanteau," *University of Toronto Quarterly* 29 (1960).

Alavi was arrested in 1937 for violation of a 1933 anti-Communist law. He and fifty-two others remained in jail until the Allied occupation of Iran in the fall of 1941. Afterwards, Alavi wrote two books on his time in prison: *Panjāh-o seh nafar* (Fifty-three persons) and a collection of short narratives called *Varaq-pāreh'hā-ye zendān* (Scraps of paper from prison), which appears in translation along with a biographical sketch by Donné Raffat in *The Prison Papers of Bozorg Alavi: A Literary Odyssey* (1985). In the World War II years, Alavi was a founder of the Tudeh (Communist) Party of Iran and edited the party newspape *Mardom*.

In 1952 Alavi published his most famous work, a novel called *Chashmhāyash* (Her eyes) and a collection of stories called *Nāmeh'hā va dāstānhā-ye digar* (Letters and other stories). John O'Kane's translation of *Her Eyes* appeared in 1989. Alavi was in East Germany when, in mid-August 1953, Mosaddeq's nationalist government was overthrown. He remained there subsequently, teaching Persian literature at East Berlin's Humboldt University.

Alavi's novella *Sālārihā* (The Salari family) and *Mirzā*, a collection of six short stories written in the late 1960s and early 1970s, were published in Tehran in 1978. Alavi visited Iran briefly in 1979 and again in 1980. Throughout the 1980s, Alavi lectured widely in Europe and North America.

Several works of Alavi's appeared after his death in 1996, including: *Khāterāt-e Bozorg Alavi* (Sweden, 1997), *Nāmeh'ha-ye Berlin: az Bozorg Alavi dar dawrān-e eqāmat-e Almān* (1998), his last novel *Revāyat* (1998), *Bargozideh-e asar-e Bozorg Alavi* (1998), *Dar khalvat-e dust: nāmeh'ha-ye Bozorg Alavi beh Bāqer Momeni* (Germany, 2000).

Mirza

Translated by Judith Wilks

Hardly a year passes when I don't go abroad. I've traveled just about everywhere in the world, being a journalist of sorts. With this card, all doors open before you. Whenever I happen to be in Europe, I make a point of visiting my friend. We first met on the train from Munich to Salzburg. He had a copy of *Lata'ef ot-Tava'ef* in his hand, so I understood that he was Iranian. I started talking to him. Now fifteen years—maybe even more—have passed since that day. He didn't ask me who I was or what work I did; nor did I ask him. I liked that about him. He wasn't nosy, he didn't want to find out every last little detail about a person's business. Some people are so nosy—first they ask me my name, then they want to know how I came to be so wealthy... God forbid they should find out I just made it through the sixth grade of elementary school.

When I was about to get off the train in Salzburg, I said good-bye to him and added: "It was very nice to meet you. If you have any business in Iran, I'd be glad to help you out with it. My temporary address is such-and-such." He in turn said: "If you're ever in such-and-such a city, ask for Mirza at the Pension d'Orient. You'll find me there." I know him by the name of Mirza. As it turned out, one month later I happened to be in the city where he lived. I telephoned his pension. We got together, and it was then that our friendship began. Whenever I'm in Europe, I spend one or two days with him. We meet in the evenings, and he obviously enjoys my company. But I never would have thought that our destinies would be so closely intertwined.

I've said that he lives in a city in central Europe. Actually, "lives" is a rather loose way of putting it; considering what he has suffered, suffers now, and—God knows—will suffer, it's not at all accurate. The first time I sensed he was a homeless fugitive, I was horrified. You see, I've always been disgusted with politics and its schemes both hidden and flagrant, and now for some years I've been absolutely terrified of it, especially since the time I was nearly dragged into it. When I began to take an interest in him after a few meetings, I mentioned him to my wife, since she understood such matters more than I did and had experienced arrest and interrogation and martial law. She said: "What harm could there be in it? Why, no one's going to find out about your relationship with him. Maybe you can even help him out."

From that time on, whenever I plan to meet him, many emotions come over me. I kid myself, saying: "There should be some goal and purpose to this free and easy life of yours, with the windfall wealth that circumstances have put at your disposal." But if you want the truth, these are ideas that my wife has forced upon me. That's why I say I'm kidding myself. But this time I'm terrified, terrified because at this meeting I must tell him secrets of my own destiny. Until now I have helped him, but at this meeting I'm going to… no, this won't do. I have to shorten the introduction and get to the matter at hand. My name is Jahandideh. Mirza has devoted his life to helping political exiles. He tries to obtain information about the situation of families whose relatives are living in exile. He has spent his time and talent and strength on this so that he could arouse the hopes of the hopeless with promises and good news, making their difficult lives a little easier.

Whenever we met we spoke about people who had grown old and broken in prison or who had lost their lives in massacres. No allusion was ever made to himself or his family. I don't even know why he fled Iran. It would have been easy for me to uncover this secret, but that would have been dishonorable. In that very first encounter in the railroad car, we had tacitly agreed not to ask about each other's lives. In my case, it was pointless; in his case, it might even be risky. The important thing is that I don't want to get involved in political matters. It seems comical that a journalist should be concerned with investigating all issues except political ones.

As a rule, all these people who are now wandering in exile were once either Communists or supporters of Mosaddeq. In any case, they oppose the present regime in Iran. The mere knowledge that there are people who imagine they could fight the ruling regime in Iran is in itself dangerous, and one shouldn't play with fire. How is one to know? Perhaps the people who helped him escape are still under surveillance. As the saying goes, "Fear is akin to death," and I am a coward. Of course, if Mirza asked me to bring him news of his family, I would gladly take the risk, and certainly nothing dangerous would happen. Everyone knows that I was never a Communist or a supporter of Mosaddeq; the secret of my present success and wealth and influence is that I have always supported the government in power. If he asked it of me, I would gladly go and make contact with his family. He only needed to tell me his real name. Mirza is his pseudonym. In our very first conversation, when I started talking about my own family, he let me know that he had no one in the world.

Fate takes many strange and surprising turns. Now I must go and put my daughter's hand in his so he can find her father. Yes, that's right: she is my daughter, and she wants to find her father.

Today I sent Mehri to him. He wouldn't see her. That's just like him. He won't open the door for anyone he doesn't already know. This evening I have to gather my courage and tell him the truth. I telephoned him and we arranged to meet at the Café Landolt.

Mehri went to the Pension d'Orient at nine o'clock sharp. I sent her myself. I wanted Mirza to be forewarned so that, if we saw each other this evening along the lake or at the Café Landolt or someplace else, I wouldn't take him unawares. His landlady, a woman between forty-five and forty-eight years of age but still young and pleasant-looking, let her in. The parlor seemed dark to Mehri. When she said she had come to see Mirza, the lady looked surprised, and the girl explained in broken French that she hadn't ever seen him before. The lady asked: "Have you just arrived in this city? Usually Mirza doesn't see people he hasn't seen beforehand. Do you have an appointment?" Mehri answered no to all the questions and, in embarrassment, fixed her eyes on the embroidery hanging on the wall. The woman didn't even extend her the courtesy of inviting her to sit down. She left the room, and Mehri heard her say: "An Iranian girl is here to see you. What shall I tell her? Shall I send her away, or do you want to see her?"

Mehri couldn't make out Mirza's reply, but the landlady's voice could still be heard, although somewhat lower now: "She knows a little French. She's not from around here. I'm not sure, she must be a student or looking for her relatives in hiding in a country behind the Iron Curtain." Again a short silence. "She can't be more than sixteen or seventeen years old."

The landlady came back and said: "Mirza can't see you today. Phone him in two or three days for an answer."

Mirza was known by this name everywhere. He had a small room in the Pension d'Orient. In the summer he would sit in the little garden of the two-story house, which the guests and residents were allowed to use. Facing the university building, he could see at some distance to the southeast the Café Landolt, said to have been Lenin's hangout during the time of his exile. In the winter he would sit beside a window in the dining room on the second story and work there. His "work" consisted of reading books, making notes on pieces of paper, painting designs on earthenware vessels, and doing miniatures and portraits. He ate lunch and dinner in the same room, not in his own miserable little room where, in his absence, the servants were permitted to change their clothes and do their make-up or iron and patch the bed sheets and tablecloths. For lunch he had soup and black bread and boiled potatoes. He didn't eat meat more than once a week. In the evening he contented himself with fried eggs or an omelet, a salad, and a glass of wine—if he had the money. All the people of the pension—both young and old, from the landlady to the Italian servants—kept a respectful distance from him. They knew him well enough to know that one shouldn't bother him too much. When his face had that certain look, he would neither speak nor answer anyone at all. The interesting thing was that, according to the young Iranians, the landlady, Mme. Isabelle, was fond of him. For instance, if he fell two or three months behind in his rent and yet did not pay cash for his glass of wine at dinner, which was not included in the price of the room, the Italians were not permitted to put any pressure on him; because everyone trusted in his sincerity and extravagance, and they had learned by experience that whenever he was able to sell something to get some cash, he would more than pay off all his debts.

The Pension d'Orient was a center for Iranian travelers and students. They all knew Mirza. If he was in a good mood, he would advise them about their affairs. They would consult with him and he would steer them in the right direction. Sometimes in his tiny little room, and once a year (by special permission of the landlady) in the parlor of the pension, he would present an exhibit of his paintings, enamelware plates, sketches of carpets, pencil-boxes, etc. The Iranian students who wanted to give their girlfriends or boyfriends or professors a gift with an Iranian flavor to it would buy a miniature or a sketch from him—sometimes on credit, and of course at a reduced price. This was how he managed to get by.

Sometimes he would withdraw into his shell and imprison himself in the four walls of his room. Rarely did he even permit the housemaid and servants to enter. The landlady was the only exception. This was why the Iranian kids said that she was fond of him. Madame truly wanted to help this homeless Iranian. When he was sitting in the parlor or the dining room or the garden reminiscing, and some American travelers—who found him intriguing, with his narrow nose and salt-and-pepper hair—would try to bother him, Madame knew how to get it through to them that they should leave him alone.

So Mirza had lived in this pension for thirteen years. Sometimes he would disappear. For six or seven months no one would hear from him, but when all was said and done, this was the place he called home, and everyone—especially Mme. Isabelle—knew that in the end he would come back home.

Her favorite line was: "If he hasn't gone back to Iran, he'll surely be back." His little room, from which emanated the smell of paint and enamel, was never put up for rent; at the most, it was converted into a storeroom for bedsheets and tablecloths and miscellaneous other items.

The landlady was truly and sincerely his defender against everyone—the Iranians, the guests, the police, the Iranian students—against anyone and everyone. Whenever an embassy official came, she really applied herself and went all out. She presented them with all the information she had gathered here and there about Iran. She told them a little bit about Persian carpets and cats, and the oil and legendary wealth and paradise gardens of Iran. And whenever they started asking about Mirza, she would respond so coarsely that their heads would spin. The state officials would take it with a grain of salt and ignore it.

When Mme. Isabelle saw that for several nights in a row Mirza hadn't ordered his evening wine and contented himself during the day with bread and soup, she understood that he was broke. At such times his daily food expenses would fall to five or six francs. Then Madame knew that he was unable to sell anything. She would search here and there, and with remarkable dexterity—either by being frank or on the pretext of past debt—she would get one of the guests to buy at an exorbitant price a candlestick or a book that Mirza had decorated. In this way she saved him from his troubles. Madame had obtained his residence permit in this city. She had presented him as a specialist in oriental cuisine for the foreign guests, and in this way she was always able to get him a residence and work permit from the police. As a result of living in this country and this pension for so many years, he had become one of the sights of the city. At least for the Iranians. Doubtless many of them came to the pension only because of him. They wanted to see this mysterious man. The curious ones wanted to know what was at the bottom of his mysteriousness.

That was why the landlady had been taken aback today when Mehri came and said right off that she wanted to meet Mirza. Other people would come and stay at the pension for a few days and watch Mirza at dinner and, if he was in the mood, they could sit and converse with him a little. It was rumored that some of his works were displayed in great museums of the world. About such rumors he himself would say: "They've blended fact and fiction."

The silliest visitors of all would put on airs of patriotic self-righteousness and wonder regretfully why such a precious person did not live in Iran.

Then again, his encounter with "the Princess" was different from the way it went today with Mehri. That day Mirza was sitting in the parlor. An Iranian woman who had accompanied one of the guests at lunch in the dining room came to the parlor and asked the landlady for Mirza. He was sitting beside the window, reading. He paid no attention at all. Madame involuntarily glanced at Mirza, and the woman, without waiting for permission, went over to the man reading and said: "I've been looking for you. Aren't you Mr. ——? My name is Mina." This was the first time that Mirza's real name had been spoken out loud in the pension. The landlady stood there stupefied. No one had expected this. When Mirza told me about this incident, he ended with a conclusion that I'll never forget.

He said: "What difficulties I've gotten myself into. Where shall I go to be free of the evil of these shadows of death?" At the time I didn't understand the meaning of this sentence. Afterwards, when he told me the story of "the Princess," I was able to grasp a little of it.

In any case, Mirza's permanent residence at Mme. Isabelle's house neither was nor is without benefit to her. So her interest in this man—with his frail body, his sad eyes, and the salt-and-pepper curls that fell forward onto his forehead—was not purely humanitarian. Mirza, despite the numerous headaches he caused the landlady, was not exactly useless either.

The Communists were suspicious of Mirza, the supporters of Mosaddeq thought him a communist, the socialists thought him a decadent bourgeois, the students thought him an upright, honest person who was no longer a revolutionary, and the security people thought him "weird." The municipal police tried to be impartial. They had learned a lesson from the revolutions that had occurred in Cuba and in several African countries in the last ten or fifteen years. Often they would pursue an accused or suspect person and insist on his expulsion, and after a while that same person would return to this country and this city with the title of "special envoy" and "representative of his country." And so it was that they granted a residence permit to this Mirza, despite the fact that he hadn't renewed his passport for years. What was important to the police was whether or not his taxes were paid regularly. Lately it had even happened that, when the police came across a criminal who was an Iranian or Turk or Arab and they didn't understand his language, they would call Mirza to translate and pay him for his services. State officials in disguise came repeatedly to Madame, wanting to find out every last detail about Mirza's affairs. How does he earn his living? Who are his acquaintances? Where does he go? When he's not in town, where does he travel? What people come to see him, and what business do they have with him? Madame was experienced in such things. She knew how to put them off the track. Hadn't she herself at the age of only sixteen or seventeen set out for the mountains to escape Hitler's Germany? One of her brothers had been killed in the war, and one of her sisters, the wife of a German Jew, had told her stories about Hitler and his gang. She knew all the tricks of the trade. She had no actual experience with politics. But all that Madame Isabelle knew was that letters were always coming for Mirza from socialist countries and that he spent a large portion of his time on these matters.

Not a week went by that a visitor from Iran did not come and that Mirza did not arrange a way for him to meet with his estranged or missing relatives. So don't you see why I sent Mehri to him today? Of course, one reason was so that I would have an excuse to bring up my topic with him this evening. We usually met in the evenings. Sometimes he would jokingly call me "Mr. Director of News from Everywhere." He knew that I was on good terms with men of all ranks and stations. Oh, these men! Touch any one of them and he will turn out to be rotten. They all share secret misdeeds, and I was sometimes able to tell him interesting bits of information gathered from their little affairs.

He wrote memos on even these trivial matters, thinking that perhaps some day it could be of some use to some poor soul. I knew him as neither a Communist nor a supporter of Mosaddeq nor a revolutionary nor a "weirdo." All I knew was that either a devil or an angel had thrown a rope around his neck and was deliberately leading him along for a reason. Everything he did, whether wittingly or unwittingly, had a reason. My wife's curiosity as to what it was, what power it was that had set him about this work, encouraged me to maintain relations with him and help him in his affairs. We didn't meddle with each other's beliefs. It was the matter of "the Princess" that first caused us to trust each other.

My wife happened to know "the Princess" and insisted on finding out where she was and what she was doing and how she was. My wife was asking about exactly the same things that Mirza had asked me about. She had met "the Princess" when she was a nurse at the hospital and had been in attendance at her appendectomy. In any case, hers is a long story and I don't want to go into it now. He wanted to know the fate of this woman after she separated from her husband and where she ended up once she returned to Iran. Whatever information I gathered from here and there, the next time I saw Mirza in this city I would tell him about it. I think it eased his mind.

I've said that we generally met in the evenings. We would stroll for a while beside the lake, then we would sit in the café near the fountain across from the Hotel Metropol, and later in the evening I would have my dinner at the Café Landolt and he would drink a glass of wine. I never went to his pension. It's not that I didn't want to be seen with Mirza. Everyone knows me well and respects me. Besides, my wild days are over. No, I had no fear of the government officials. I wanted simply to talk for two or three hours with a man who attracted my respect and interest without anyone else pestering us. Mirza took a special interest in these evening meetings of ours. I suppose he thought of me as a safe source for obtaining information about the exiles' families in Iran. Once he was even overcome with emotion and embraced me, saying: "One little bit of news—one doubt removed—saves a person from death."

In any case, he trusted me, and he knew that our conversations would not leak out anywhere else. On the contrary, I never tried to obtain information from him or cross-examine him, although my wife had pressured me to do so. I thought it would be better if he said something to me himself. I didn't want to arouse his suspicions. It should be kept in mind that these political exiles are skeptical about everything; things are so bad for them that they even mistrust their friends.

And my discomfort this evening is for this very reason. This evening I want to get some information from him. I want to know who is the father of my daughter Mehri. If I seek him out today with some apprehensiveness, it's because I want to play the role he has played up until now. Until now I've never even asked him what work he did in Iran, why he fled Iran, why he can't go back. These are his secrets, and what did I care to find out about these things? They would only give me a headache. On the other hand, my wife was always curious and always wanted to find out who this man was.

We had decided to meet in front of the Hotel Metropol at 7:30. In the municipal park at a short distance from the fountain under the arch, the city orchestra was giving a public concert. "The Persian March" by Johann Strauss attracted my attention. I still had a few minutes before the appointed time. I walked in the direction the music was coming from. I saw that Mirza, too, was standing there. We stood there enjoying the music for almost twenty minutes. It was late July and the weather was warm. The air was so still that the leaves on the trees weren't even moving. The ten-spouted fountain sprayed water around. Instead of walking along the lake as we usually did, we waited until one of the benches among the flower beds was vacated. We sat down on it and listened for a moment to the strains of the violin that could be heard even from a distance.

I sensed that this evening, in contrast to our usual meetings, the conversation was not going to flow easily. Usually it was he who started the conversation. But this evening there was a tension between us.

"Will you be staying in this city for a few days?" he asked.

"I only came here to see you. I thought you might have some business with me. My plane leaves tomorrow afternoon."

"Are you coming from Iran or going back there?"

"I left Iran the day before yesterday. I was in Rome for one night, and now I'm going to London."

"Will you be passing through here on your way back, too?"

"I don't think so. As I said, I'm not here for any special purpose. I just stopped here for one night so I could see you."

Again a silence. The splashing of the fountain was the only sound. I wanted to draw the conversation around to himself.

"Didn't you ever go back to Paris?" I asked.

"How do you happen to know that I was in Paris?"

"You yourself told me that you lived in Paris for a while and that you made good money selling Persian miniatures to tourists."

A faint smile flashed across his lips.

"Why do you smile?"

"The only truth in what you've said is that I lived in Paris and sold miniatures. The rest…"

"…is a lie," I interrupted quickly. "Why do you lie to me?"

"Unfortunately, most of our lives pass in lies. Reality is very ugly, and one can beautify it with lies."

I gathered my courage and, in order to get him going, I said: "Then tell me what reality is. I won't hold it against you. But I heard from someone that you used to do miniatures on the banks of the Seine and that you would put your hat on the ground in hopes that passers-by would throw a few coins into it."

"It wasn't as easy as all that. It's true. One of the students had seen me, and he spread the story around. But the truth is even more bitter than that. He doesn't know the whole story. I had fallen on hard times. I had absolutely nothing, not even anything left to pawn or sell. I was sleeping in the train station at night. I was hungry, and every day I would sit on the bank of the Seine and do miniatures. Some elderly ladies walking by would give me a few coins. On the third day of this a girl and a boy passed by me. They had seen me in the public rooming house. The girl was Cuban and the boy was Algerian. They went on a few steps and then came back and looked at my sketches and paintings. Apparently the girl felt sorry for me. She went and bought a banana and brought it back for me. I ate it so greedily that the Algerian boy went and bought a sandwich from those same stands around there and gave it to me. In the evening they took me to the place where they slept, and there we formed a partnership. Yes, three vagabonds went into business together. I did my painting. The girl would deck herself out and come and sit beside me, displaying her pretty, bare legs. The Algerian—poor thing, he was constantly ill—would buy and cook our food. People came, and this time it was the young men who threw money into my hat. The Cuban girl was even able to sell a few of my miniatures. There was a day when we brought in between ten and fifteen new francs, and this amount had to suffice for the expenses of all three of us. They, too, were exiles. But I won't go into that. Hamid had a chronic stomach ailment and could no longer 'work' with us. We found a place for him at one of the religious missions for only two francs all day long. In spite of this, he got worse every day. One day a man—some sort of poet or musician, I don't know, something like an artist—started hanging around the girl. I can't tell you the girl's name. Today she has become world-famous and you must certainly have heard of her. This fellow would come every day to our stand—he would make a fool of himself, acting like a real jerk. One night the Cuban girl, whose bunk was above mine in the public lodging house, said to me: 'Hamid's in a bad way. If we don't get him to a hospital, he'll die. What shall I do?' I stared at her. If the bald man were a doctor, he would treat himself... The Cuban girl stared at me intently and said: 'That guy who comes to our stand every day wants me to come home with him and be his model; he'll give me a thousand francs a month. Of course, I'll have to sleep with him.' I was on the verge of tears. I said: 'It would be a pity if you did that. Hamid loves you very much.' The poor thing didn't go. She nearly died of anguish..."

"What became of them later?"

"There was a revolution in Cuba. The girl went back and did well for herself there."

"Good, and Hamid returned to Algeria."

"No, Hamid never returned to his homeland. After six months the Cuban came back to Paris with plenty of money. She had also found work for Hamid in Cuba. But she never saw him again. We buried him in the Muslim cemetery."

"So what is it all for? Is this short life worth all the trouble?"

I said this unintentionally and carelessly. Nevertheless, I thought it a good way to approach my subject. I wanted to bring the conversation around to his own life. But he interrupted.

"Don't say that. I have so many of these sad stories in my bag, this is certainly not the most tragic one. In the end, one of them died, the other one returned to her homeland and prospered, she found work and became famous. Think about them, those who live together for years, looking forward to returning to their homelands, always living in hope, and in the end they are ruined. Patriotism is not just a figment of the imagination. You know 'the Princess.' If I'm not mistaken, you've met her face to face and talked with her. Her name is Mina. Do you have any idea what that woman has suffered? God knows, perhaps she's still suffering."

"I met her once in Isfahan," I said. "It was at a formal banquet. I didn't get any impression that she had experienced hardship. On the contrary, she seemed to me fresh and charming, talkative, beautiful, poised..."

"That's what's so amazing about her. Her skill lies in letting no one get even an inkling of what's going on in her heart. I can only tell you stories about people who no longer exist. The boys used to call 'the Princess' the 'Rosebud of Cockaigne,' just to be nasty. Perhaps also because when she spoke, she would purse her lips like a rosebud and try to enunciate every letter perfectly. This woman was engaged to one of the exiles. They had seen each other and liked each other, and the marriage negotiations had even begun between the two households when the mass arrests began. A few months after the 28th of Mordad, she managed somehow to flee Iran. When I say 'somehow,' it's only for the sake of brevity—really, it would take a long time to tell you all about it. This sort of traveling is not without risk. Without a passport or with a forged one, hidden from the members of her family who were known and recognized everywhere in Iran. And we're talking about a young, unmarried woman from a wealthy family traveling around, giving up all riches and comfort and reputation and pretty things and the affection of her mother and father, and going around the world looking for someone who has disappeared. Finally, after a year of running around, one day she turned up in this city; she later found her husband in some European country. Of course, they weren't formally married, but they were engaged. Now do you think they lived happily ever after? No, not so. The tragedy only begins here. As the saying goes, 'The silkworm weaves its own shroud.' This woman appeared like a ray of sunlight in the black pit of the exiled man's life, and she melted away like snow in the springtime sun. From the very first day, they started quarreling. How could a revolutionary live in the same house with the 'Rosebud of Cockaigne,' with her head in the clouds, how could he entrust all his papers and correspondence to a woman he hardly knows? This woman could spend several thousand tomans each month on make-up and beauty supplies—where would this money come from? She was a real prima donna, extremely vain and conceited. Such were the remarks the exile would hear about her. God knows what things were said that the rumor-mongers dared not repeat out of respect for the reputation and moral influence of the exile. The 'Rosebud of Cockaigne' from the very first day was aware of the other exiles' wives' resentment of her flightiness and their envy, but she wouldn't face up to it. The exile could see that Mina was unhappy—from the troubled expression that was always on her face whenever he caught her unawares, from her seclusion from co-workers and friends, and finally from the wrinkles that began to appear on her face. It was as though the wrinkles were silently communicating a message: 'One day you'll all find out that I was sincere and innocent.' The unfortunate thing was that the exile, influenced by his small circle of exile friends, misunderstood the message and interpreted it differently: 'I'll show you all some day.' For four years they lived together as lovers in the same house. But there was always a barrier between them. The exile didn't dare to defend his beloved unquestioningly. He was afraid that the whisperings and rumors might turn out to be true. They never once sat down to talk it all out and remove the dust that clouded their love. People didn't know whether this was his wife or his fiancée or his friend or his mistress. His eyes were only opened when he saw that this delicate being was emaciated, and nothing was left to him but his scruples. With the political and moral influence that the exile had, he could have settled the matter once and for all. But his uncertainty and his indecision, his concern for his reputation and political credibility and other such excuses blinded him to the truth. Heroes, too, are cowards. He imagined that these transient matters weren't worth wasting one's time on. He wanted to solve his own problems quietly. He disliked making a big fuss over private matters. He considered such things insubstantial and silly, and this same mentality that arose from moral weakness caused him to lose the dearest creature in the world to him. 'The Princess' left her lover all alone in exile. One day she got in a taxi and, without leaving the slightest clue, she went to the airport and no one ever heard from her again. But even after she left, the disputes didn't stop. And the rumors took on a different form. The reproaches were replaced by false accusations. They said: 'What did he do to this woman that she preferred returning to the lion's den to living in the same house with him? Why didn't he marry her? He's always thinking about himself. You know how it goes.' She told her family that she had become pregnant and, not wanting to cause her parents shame, had gone away. Now that it was all over, she had come back. Her family told everyone that they had sent her to Europe to study and now she had returned. But does the exile know that she hasn't married yet? The exile killed himself. Keep this to yourself. I was their go-between and I still am. And 'the Princess' still sends sums of money and monthly packages of clothing and cigarettes and rice and nuts and sweets, and on holidays she sends many gifts. The exile never made use of the money. I distribute it among those who need it. Why should I tell her that the exile is dead? Let her still be hopeful. Hopelessness is the worst of afflictions."

Several minutes passed in silence.

"Can one keep such information forever hidden from the person involved?" I asked.

"Of course not. Maybe 'the Princess' herself even knows already. There are plenty of blabbermouths around. Or maybe she's kidding herself. Maybe she has even taken a vow to repay the evil people did her with good. Maybe this makes her feel better."

I saw that it was getting late. If I didn't seize my chance now, how could I know when the proper moment would present itself? I decided to bring up the topic that was on my mind.

"This morning when I phoned you, at first Mme. Isabelle didn't want to give you my message. She said she was sorry, but you weren't seeing anyone these days, I didn't ask why. When I told her I was Jahandideh, she called you to the phone. Today a girl asked to see you, and you told her to call in two or three days for an answer."

"How do you happen to know that?"

"I'm the one who sent her to you. She, too, has a problem like that of the other exiles. She's looking for her father."

"Where is her father?"

"I don't know. You have to find him."

"What's her name?"

"Mehri."

"Mehri? What's her father's name?"

"Please, call her and ask her."

"Why won't you tell me?"

"I don't know his name. Like all exiles, he has assumed a different name. Before leaving for Europe, the girl found out that her real father is living in exile. Until now the girl's family name has been Jahandideh."

"She's one of your family?"

"She's a relative of mine."

"What's her mother's name?"

"You're really cross-examining me. You can ask Mehri about all these things. Her mother's name is Tahereh."

"—Tahereh?"

Unfortunately, I was unable to make out the effect of this name on his face. "Is the name familiar to you? All I know is that she was engaged to someone in exile. I never could find out for certain what the name of this exile was. I only know that because of some bad turn of events they were separated from each other."

He said nothing. We had walked so far that we were tired. It was more than past midnight. The weather was turning a little cool. When I realized that I couldn't watch his facial expressions while walking down the street, it seemed better to me that we should go to the Café Landolt. We were thirsty and hungry. I felt I could use some refreshment. I thought that if he, too, had a glass of wine, he'd loosen up a bit. I wanted to sit face to face with Mirza and see what effect the name Tahereh had on him. Was it familiar to him? Had he ever heard it before? It seemed to me that he had indeed. I suggested: "Let's go to the Landolt. You have a glass of wine, and I'll get myself something to eat."

He always had a light meal early in the evening before our meetings. He said: "It's pretty late, but let's go anyway."

We came out of the park. At the curb we paused and waited for the traffic light to turn green. I faced him, stared intently into his eyes and asked: "Have you ever heard the name Tahereh before?"

I saw no change of expression on his face at all. On the contrary, the mask on his face was even more impenetrable than usual.

The light turned green. We crossed the street. We said nothing to each other until we reached the museum. At the door of the restaurant I put my hand on his shoulder, letting him enter before me. I didn't want to sit on one of the chairs along the street. It was always full of Iranian students there, and besides, it was dark. I looked around inside the restaurant to find a cozy spot, but there was none to be found. In the middle of the restaurant there were still two empty places at a table where two young girls were sitting. At a glance I knew they weren't foreigners. When our table companions saw that both of us looked serious and even a little stern, they turned their attention away from us. I looked at his eyes, which were staring fixedly at the surface of the table. I asked: "Haven't you ever heard the name Tahereh before?"

"Why? I want to know what you know about all this. It's been sixteen years since I've uttered that name…"

Aha, I sensed that the ice was beginning to crack. But it wasn't melting yet. A ray of hope appeared. I didn't know whether it was a good or a bad sign. In any case, I felt very agitated.

Then I told him what I knew—or rather, to be more precise, what I thought I knew.

"Tahereh was engaged to an exile officer. In those days when colorful pictures were being drawn on the plains of Iran with a mixture of red blood and black gold, Tahereh had the chance to act as a liaison between her fiancé and his companions. She was their 'cover.' With her job at the hospital, she could easily make contact with all sorts of people. If someone came to the hospital even in the evening or at midnight, it would attract no special attention... One evening Tahereh didn't show up at the appointed time, and she never saw her fiancé again. That same night the security police raided one of the hideouts and arrested three of the leaders, and three months later they were executed."

I went on: "In the underground newspaper published internally, Tahereh was called a spy for the military regime. I only know that afterwards she got married, and Mehri is her daughter."

"Mehri is Tahereh's daughter?"

"The girl who came to you today and you wouldn't see her."

"Now you say that she's Tahereh's daughter and that Tahereh got married in Tehran, and that was after the 28th of Mordad. So how is it that she's looking for her father?"

"When Tahereh didn't hear from her fiancé for a month, she was obliged to tell her family that she was pregnant. And they, in order to save the family's reputation, arranged to marry off their daughter."

"How does Mehri know that she is not her father's daughter, I mean, that she is not the daughter of her mother's husband?"

"Apparently her mother told her the secret."

"Why did you send Mehri to me?"

"I thought that, if I asked you, out of regard for me you wouldn't refuse. Also, the girl is a distant relative of mine. Her mother asked me to help her in a strange city—at the airport, going through customs, finding a hotel. To tell the truth, my wife, who knows about my friendship with you, asked me to send Mehri to you."

"My dear friend, your story seems a bit counterfeit to me. Now, if I ask you how you happen to know about this secret between mother and daughter, between Mehri and Tahereh, you're going to tell me that, in the interval of a few hours between Tehran and here, Mehri told you all about it. And then you would expect me to believe you. Wouldn't it be better to show me all your cards? Maybe then it would be easier to help Mehri."

I saw there was no way out. Duplicity was no longer of any use. I made no reply. I was afraid I would explode into tears and create a scene. I called the waiter and paid the bill. We both got up, and as soon as we were in darkness I said: "Tahereh is my wife."

"And Mehri is your daughter."

"No, Mehri is not my daughter. The circumstances of my marriage are very commonplace. Now is not the time to talk about it.
The very first time we met, Tahereh told me she was pregnant. Her
very courage made me determined to marry her. Now notice—on
the one hand the hypocrisy and two-facedness of her father and
mother, who wanted to kill two birds with one stone, to be freed
from the problem of a pregnant daughter and from the troubles with
the security police; and on the other hand, the innocence and courage of Tahereh. But enough of this, we were talking about Mehri. I
love her more than life itself. You see what regard I have for Tahereh
that I've come to deliver Mehri over to her natural father. I am her
real father. I'm putting her in your hands. Deliver her to her father."

We shook hands and said good-bye. When he was about to leave,
he turned and said: "Send Mehri to me early tomorrow morning.
And I want to ask a favor of you. Stay here one more day, and let's
get together again tomorrow evening."

It was nearly ten o'clock when Mehri rang the doorbell of the Pension d'Orient and the landlady showed her into the parlor. This time
she looked neither at the embroidery nor at the knickknacks that the
guests had brought with them from all over the world. Her heart was
pounding. Not just because soon she would have to divulge the
secrets of her mother's and her own life to a man she had never seen
before, but more because she was afraid that she might not be able to
explain adequately the sincerity and honesty of her mother, who had
lived with this shame for sixteen years. She had said nothing about it
for sixteen years. If several months ago someone had told Mehri that
her mother had slept with another man before marrying her father,
she would have been deeply insulted and offended. Now, how could
she be sure that this man who was going to appear before her
wouldn't have the same reaction? To avoid faltering, she kept moist-
ening her lips, thinking this would give her courage. This waiting
didn't really last more than one or two minutes. The thoughts and
reflections of the past several months that were now coming to a head
all at once made the time seem very long to her. Since yesterday
evening when her stepfather—"stepfather": she pondered the word.
It left a bad taste in her mouth, the father who loved her more than
life itself had suddenly become her stepfather—since last night, when
she had heard from her stepfather that Mirza would see her, she had
been preparing herself, thinking through how she should begin the
story, how she should describe to him her mother's fate, how she
should make known her mother's feelings. Several months ago when

Mehri had received her diploma from high school and her father and mother had decided to send her to Europe, she had told her daughter all about this secret of her life. And in these last few days, her stepfather had even found out that her mother—under another name, of course—had been named as a traitor in the underground newspaper. Even her husband hadn't known about this disgrace. She also had not told him that she had been blamed for the execution of three people. They accused this woman, who had sacrificed everything for her love, of treachery and murder, and no one had stepped forward to plead her cause. Her mother thought that, now that she had emptied her heart, she could rest easy. Her mother was confident that her daughter would find her father and tell him that there had been no treachery involved. And this was why Mehri had devised a plan for herself—how to begin the story, how to continue, how to conclude. The summer sun peeking out from behind the clouds suddenly struck Mehri's eyes, and for several seconds she didn't notice that a man was standing on the threshold of the south door, looking at her.

Mirza quietly approached the girl. He took her hand and sat down beside her on the sofa. He asked, "Well, Miss Mehri, what's new? How is it that you've come looking for me?"

One glance at Mirza's meek and humble manner wiped away all the preparations she had made in the last several days. Mehri fell completely apart and, sobbing, she said: "My mother did nothing traitorous."

Just then a Brazilian boy and girl came into the parlor with their arms around each other's shoulders. Mirza got up and took Mehri's soft, warm hand. "Let's go to my room. It's not as nice as it is here, but it's more comfortable there, and we can talk. Don't cry. I don't know who or what you're talking about. But it's good if you let me in on it so I can help you."

There was only one chair in the room. Mehri sat on the chair and Mirza sat on the bed. He was still holding the girl's hand. It was as though he just couldn't let it go. Only when Mehri wanted to get something from her purse did he have to withdraw his hand. She had calmed down. Mirza left the room and after several minutes returned with two cups of tea. By that time Mehri had taken her memo-book out of her purse and, using her notes, she started telling her story:

"It was the evening of the 24th of Aban. The weather was getting cold. It had been agreed that Tahereh, wearing a chador, would enter the hospital by a back door and stay in the sentry room for a few minutes to wait for a phone call. Contrary to what she had expected, the lights were on in the sentry room. She busied herself for a few minutes. She took off her chador. The phone call was supposed to tell her where to wait to be picked up and taken to meet her fiancé. When the phone didn't ring after a half-hour, she thought she'd better call someone from outside who might be able to tell her what was going on. She didn't want to phone from the hospital, she knew that to be unwise. She put her chador in a closet and went out the main door of the hospital. A jeep was parked across the street. Tahereh became suspicious. She went as far as the box office of the cinema, but she didn't know what she should do. She had to deliver a message to her fiancé from someone she had seen secretly the night before. Several people were in danger. Not more than ten minutes or so had gone by since she had left the hospital. The same jeep passed in front of the cinema and stopped. Someone got out and said: 'Come with us, miss, we have some business with you.'

"They took Tahereh to the security police. They asked her what business she had at the hospital. 'I sometimes visit the hospital in the evenings and stop in and see the patients.' They asked: 'Why did you leave your chador in the sentry room?' 'Because at home I thought it might snow and I didn't want my hair to get wet. When I saw that it didn't look like snow, I left my chador in a closet of the sentry room. I didn't want to go to the cinema wearing a chador.' They asked: 'Then why didn't you go to the cinema?' 'I was just about to go when you arrested me.' They said: 'You went all the way up to the ticket office, but you didn't buy a ticket.' 'Yes, I wanted to buy a chicken sandwich first and then come back to the cinema.'

"They took down Tahereh's name and address. They took her home in the jeep. They searched the whole house. Since they found nothing, they let her go free.

"From that day on, whenever my mother tried to contact people to get in touch with her fiancé, they weren't very helpful. Then it appeared in the newspaper that Fatemeh was a spy for the military regime and that she was to blame for the execution of three people."

Mirza reaffirmed: "Fatemeh—that is, Tahereh."

"That was the code name between my mother and her fiancé," she explained.

"And now, this man who hurt your mother so deeply and didn't have the courage to defend her reputation and honor..."

Mehri broke in: "Don't speak ill of my father," she broke in. "My mother knows him as a man of honor. Anyone in my father's situation couldn't have done otherwise."

"I'm not speaking ill of anyone."

"The matter seemed clear. They arrest a woman, and after one or two hours they let her go. Then they execute three people. Anyone would think that the woman had betrayed them."

"And now, what is it you want from your father? When your step-father is kinder to you than your father?"

"My mother—but it's not just my mother, it's me, too; we only want to tell my father that we didn't betray him."

Mirza was almost overcome by pain, the pain it had taken him a lifetime to conquer. But he restrained himself. He wanted to take Mehri in his arms and kiss her and say, "My daughter…" But he had learned to control himself.

"And now you expect your father to ask pardon from you and your mother for the cowardice that he showed. Will that cure your mother's sixteen years of suffering and be a solace for her in the future?"

"No, that's not it at all."

"What is it then?"

"I don't know. I would just like to put my arms around my father and cry. Then I would write to my mother and tell her, 'Mother, my wound has healed—you can be happy, too.'"

Mirza's eyes brimmed over with tears. He stood up and placed Mehri's head on his chest and said: "My girl, imagine that I am your father." And he stroked her hair.

For a while they both were silent.

"Go now. I'll make some inquiries and if I find out anything, I'll tell your stepfather."

The truth is, after the wave of emotion that had welled up inside of him, he had again regained his composure. He realized that this delicate creature had disturbed the equilibrium in his life. Even if Mirza intended to live his life alone, his plight would not have been as unhappy as that. He raised Mehri from her chair. He accompanied her to the door. The Brazilian boy and girl were sitting there smoking cigarettes and writing letters. Mirza glanced at them. He put his hand on Mehri's shoulder and saw her out of the pension.

As usual, we met in the garden in front of the Hotel Metropol. There was no concert this evening, and the benches were empty. We walked for a while, then we sat on one of the benches in front of the fountain. We didn't talk much. We wandered until three in the morning through several cafés and restaurants and bars. We didn't have much to say to each other. I'm sure he was wondering—just as I was—how all this would end. We had started a task that we didn't know how to finish.

As Mirza saw it, the solution seemed simple. But a person would have to have nerves of steel to take the tenderest of emotions and crumple them up roughly and throw them away.

"You saw Mehri? What did you think of her?" I asked him.

"Mehri is my daughter. Yes, I am Mehri's natural father. Tahereh and I had agreed that if we ever had a child and it was a girl, we would name her Mehri."

"Did you tell Mehri this?"

"No, I didn't tell her. And if I have my way, I'll never tell her. God willing, I'll never have to tell her. I am her natural father. That's all—no more, no less. Mehri must remain your daughter. I'm used to being alone in this world. I can't take your daughter away from you. Besides, it's better for her that she remain your daughter. The question is: what shall we tell her?"

"What do you think? The truth, of course."

"Which truth? This truth? That I was her natural father and I've been dead for a long time? My love died the day those accusations were printed in the newspaper—with my consent, mind you, with my consent. I renounced all love for wife and child. You, who had the courage to defy tradition and take Tahereh as your wife and raise Mehri as your own child, you are her real father, not I, inept coward that I am. When Tahereh didn't show up for our meeting, I was sure that something had come up. It seemed impossible to me that a woman who loved so unstintingly could give up her lover and all her desires in the course of one or two hours. But what I thought was not enough. The events spoke for themselves more convincingly. If I hadn't feared for my life and had gone to her house the next day or as soon as I heard about the execution of the three people—which was some time before it was printed in the papers—and if I had just talked to her a little so I could find out the truth, yes, then many things would have turned out differently. Perhaps they would even have killed me right then. I would be dead now. But then I wouldn't have become a living corpse. Tell her he's dead."

"No, we mustn't tell her that. I don't have the courage. You know, you mean much more to this mother and daughter than a mere father or fiancé from her younger days. As I see it—rightly or wrongly—you are everything they hope for. We mustn't lie to them. You yourself have always said that one must give people something to hope for."

We spent the whole night this way, without uttering a word, asking ourselves over and over again: "Where shall we find the truth?"

Beh'azin

1915–

Translator, fiction writer, and political activist Mahmud E'temadza-deh, better known by his pen name Beh'azin, was born and raised in Rasht. After high school, he traveled to France on a government scholarship to study engineering. Upon his return to Iran in 1938, he worked in the Iranian Navy and the Ministry of Education, then got involved in the Tudeh Party, and subsequently pursued a career in translation from French into Persian.

Beh'azin's first collection of short stories, *Parākandeh* (Scattered pieces), appeared in 1944. In 1948 a second collection of stories was published called *Be-su-ye mardom* (Toward the people). In 1951 Beh'azin's novella called *Dokhtar-e ra'iyat* (The serf's daughter) appeared. Its tale of class struggle in Gilan during the early years of the twentieth century typifies Beh'azin's leftist views and established him as a major writer in the eyes of engagé critics.

Beh'azin's third and most critically acclaimed collection of short stories was *Mohreh-ye mār* (The snake stone), published in 1966. In 1970 came a fourth collection of short stories called *Shahr-e khodā* (God's city). But by the 1970s, Beh'azin's resolve to engage in oppositionist political activism led to several periods of incarceration and a diminution in his literary productivity. He wrote a book called *Mehmān-e in āqāyān* (Guest of these gentlemen, 1970) about one period of incarceration and *Ān su-ye divār: goftār dar āzādi* (On the other side of the wall: a statement on freedom, 1977).

During the Revolution of 1978-79, Beh'azin was a leading voice for Marxist Tudeh Party views. In the mid-1980s, the Islamic Republic put him and other Tudeh Party leaders in jail, where some of them remained as of the early 1990s.

His latest fictional work is *Māngdim va khorshid chehr* (Māngdim and the sun-faced one), a collection of seven short stories published in 1990. In 1991 his study of Rumi, *Bar daryā-kenār-e Masnavi*, was published, as well as a volume of memoirs, *Az har dari--: zendagināmeh-e seyāsi-ejtemāi.* This was followed in 1998 by another memoir *Sāyeh'hā-ye bāgh.*

The Snake Stone

Translated by Judith Wilks

Golnar was sitting on the ledge in the sun. Beside her she had placed her eyeliner box and indigo case and the bundle containing her rouge and powder. She had in her hand a copper mirror of the sort that women use in the public baths, and was putting on her makeup, feeling quite cheerful.

She had just finished her household duties. After her husband had left for the shop, she had cleared away the breakfast things and taken the teapot and the tray of cups and saucers to the edge of the pool and rinsed them off. Then she had swept the room and washed two or three pieces of clothing. From then on, until late afternoon, when her husband returned from the bazaar bringing, as usual, something for an evening snack—bread and fruit, sesame halva, dried fruits or nuts—bundled up in his kerchief, Golnar was alone at home with nothing to do.

There were just the two of them, man and wife. They had no relatives or friends in that town, either. Their little home was as tiny as a bird's nest: two rooms facing the sun, with a small brick-paved court-yard—no larger than the palm of one's hand—leading to the steps to

the water storage tank. They had no children. In the three-and-a-half
years since Golnar had become Usta Ja'far's wife and had come from
the village with him, she had had three miscarriages. None of the
pregnancies had even reached the fourth month. The advice of the
bathhouse workers and the various remedies of the local midwife had
proven useless. Golnar still had not become a mother. Her husband, a
strong, vigorous man in his forties, didn't seem all that concerned. His
wife was young, nineteen or twenty years old: God willing, they still
had time! But Golnar herself wanted a pastime. She wanted a sweet
diversion to fill her days at home. But, well, until Fate willed it, what
could they do? Golnar kept several chickens and a rooster in a wicker
cage in the tiny courtyard. Her husband had also bought her a pair of
canaries in a cage. These were the companions of her long days. No
one came to see her, and she herself had no comings and goings with
the neighborhood women. She didn't want them to be always giving
her unwanted advice on the pretext of being more experienced in
these matters: Hey, cook this, go there, dress this way... Golnar had
nothing to do with them. All she knew was that she was young and
pretty and that her husband, Usta Ja'far, the shoemaker at the end of
the bazaar, would give his life for her. What more could she want?

Golnar was sitting on the ledge in the sun doing her makeup. She
smiled at herself in the mirror. She bit her lips and was delighted at
their bright, moist redness. She looked at herself seductively. She
raised her eyebrows coquettishly. She narrowed her eyelids. She
smiled. She pouted. She puckered up her lips. She clucked her
tongue in her mouth. She hummed a ribald little tune that was popular at the time. She made faces and turned and swayed to the rhythm
of the song. She was so caught up in this activity that suddenly the
sound of her own voice singing aloud resounded in her ear:

Oh, oh, Dandy Hasan! The mouse has come!

Golnar startled herself. She looked up. She glanced self-con-
sciously at the rooftop of the neighbor, whose children would
sometimes come and peek in. Fortunately, there was no one there.
Golnar, whose upper lip was perspiring, drew a sigh of relief. But just
then her eye fell on the rim of the wall. A long, thin snake, whose
color gradually paled from red on its back to rose on its underside,
was creeping down from the eaves. Although Golnar could not of
course see the eyes of the slithering reptile from that distance, still it
was as though its flashing look split her chest open. Her heart sank in
terror. She screamed, and her terrified eyes remained fixed on the
snake. Suddenly a round object the size of a *do-hezari* fell from above

and rolled noisily on the bricks of the courtyard. And the snake turned its head around and disappeared behind the projection of the eaves. When she had calmed down a little, Golnar got up from where she was sitting and, one eye on the ground and the other on the roof, she started searching around the courtyard of the house. She peered into the crevice of the joint between two bricks and couldn't believe her eyes: a gold coin!

Golnar turned it over carefully with a twig and looked at it from all directions. My, it seemed to be an *ashrafi* fresh from the royal mint. Still, the young woman was afraid to touch it: "What if there's some witchcraft involved!" Golnar said a *besmellah*, mumbled all the prayers she could remember, and breathed on it. But nothing happened: the coin smiled at her with a joyful glint. Golnar stretched out her hand. But all at once she remembered something. She went and filled a pitcher with water and washed the coin ceremoniously three times. Then she picked it up and held it in the sun and amused herself playing with it for a while. A warm and lasting delight welled up within her. Her exhilaration at the reality of this gold *ashrafi* that was here in her hand, that belonged to her, rendered her temporarily incapable of any doubts or suspicions. But anyway, what was this? Where had it come from? What connection was there between this beautifully colored, delicate little round object that rolled so nicely and had such a pleasant ring to it—smiling, Golnar rolled the coin on the surface of the brick pavement, making it ring out—yes, what connection was there between this *ashrafi* and that snake? And really, had her eyes seen correctly? Had there actually been any snake there? Golnar wasn't really sure. Maybe she had seen something else, maybe she was imagining things. But then, what was this *ashrafi*? Maybe someone had been tossing a coin in the street and the coin had gone rolling along the roof and had fallen into the courtyard. But if that were the case, why had no one come knocking at the door looking for it? Golnar pressed the *ashrafi* anxiously in her fist, went and half-opened the door to the house, and furtively glanced up and down the street. There was no noise, no traffic at all. A dog was napping at the foot of the wall with his two paws folded over his head. And far down the street two children were playing in the dirt. Reassured, Golnar bolted the door and came and sat in her place on the ledge. This time, although her eyes smiled in the mirror and a soft veil of powder fell over her fresh face like a halo over the moon, there was a hastiness in her heart that made her fingers work carelessly, without the usual loving attentiveness. She finished her task perfunctorily and then tied up the *ashrafi* in the bundle with her powder and rouge and took it and placed it at the bottom of the chest. But once again, as at first, she felt perplexed. She didn't know what to do. For a little while she played with the canaries, whose cage hung on a column next to the ledge. After that she peeked into the chicken coop, on the pretext of checking to see if her chicken, Beanflower, had perhaps laid an egg. She went back into the room. She brought out her sewing bundle, spread out the contents, and took up her husband's shirt to mend the hem. While she was working with the needle, her thoughts kept constantly turning back to that one image: the gold *ashrafi*! And Golnar imagined making it into an earring, or a bracelet, or a pendant. But really, the matter still remained in God's hands and it was up to her husband, Usta Ja'far, as to how to invest this one *ashrafi* of hers and make its value increase.

That day passed very slowly for her. In the evening when her husband came, Golnar, before she had even opened up the door all the way, asked smilingly as she did every evening, but a bit more warmly, "Is that you, Usta? Good, what have you brought?" And without waiting for an answer, she took the kerchief full of bread and other edibles, and they went in together.

That night Golnar made love with her husband and yielded her body to his desirous caresses more ardently than ever, and she fanned the flames of his passion with enticing little tricks. She put her arms around his neck and pressed him to her chest more tightly than usual. She gave and received kisses freely. She was very talkative. She laughed. She asked how his day had been. All in order to prevent the secret that she held in her heart from unwittingly escaping like a bird from a cage.

They spent the night contentedly in refreshing sleep until morning and began another day exactly like the one before. To all appearances nothing had changed in their lives. Usta Ja'far went to his humble job in the bazaar and Golnar went about the sweeping and housekeeping unhurriedly. And when the sun shone down on the surface of the ledge, Golnar, having finished her work, sat down to do her daily makeup. But now and then her eye wandered over to the rim of the eaves. Of course, nothing happened. Golnar was not so naive as to allow herself unfounded hopes. But at the moment when she was applying the eyeliner to her eyelids, with only one side of her face in the mirror, suddenly a crow on top of the wall cawed loudly and flew away. The young woman's heart was suddenly gripped by fear. She turned and looked. The same snake as yesterday was slithering down in the shadow of the wall like a curling flame of fire. Golnar let out a cry of terror and started to get up. But when she saw that the snake had turned back halfway and was returning in the direction of the corner of the roof behind which it had disappeared yesterday, she calmed down. She sighed in relief and raised her hand to wipe away the cold sweat that had settled on her temples. Just then something like a *do-hezari* rang out with a loud rolling noise on the bricks of the courtyard. Golnar's eyes and mouth opened wide. Her heart started beating rapidly. She felt hot and flushed. And she was afraid. Thoughts of demons and fairies and witches crossed her mind. She involuntarily mumbled a prayer for safety and breathed on herself. But desire was slowly gnawing at her heart. God! Does this mean there is yet another *ashrafi*? Then there would be two, and Golnar could make a pair of earrings out of them! Could it be?

The young woman got up in excitement and set about searching in the courtyard. Beside the step of the water tank a gold coin was looking at her like an alert eye. Again Golnar brought the pitcher and washed it three times. Then she picked it up and looked at it. It was just like the *ashrafi* she had found yesterday. Laughing and humming, she went to the ledge and brought out the first coin from the bundle in which it was tied up and played with them for a while in the sun, jingling them together between her hands.

Truly, this second *ashrafi* was even more splendid. With it, a certain hope was born and nourished and this hope carried Golnar to distant horizons on the wings of her imagination. But with it came also a small anxiety. How would she tell the story of these past two days to Usta Ja'far? Well, should she tell him? Would her husband believe it? Wouldn't he be suspicious? Wouldn't he think there must be more to it than this? Might this not lead to accusations of unfaithfulness, and shouting and beating and weeping? Then what would Golnar do? How would she ever dig out the root of suspicion from her husband's heart? Would she sit him down in the house to wait for the snake so he could see it with his own eyes? Well and good. But, say we do this and the snake doesn't appear. That would be a disgrace. Yes, and everyone who heard about it would say the man is right... No, she should leave well enough alone. She shouldn't say anything.

Darkness fell. Her husband came home and, unaware that anything had happened, he spent another happy night with his wife, and in the morning he went to work. Golnar, as soon as she had locked the door after him, went straight to the chest, brought out the coins and jingled

them merrily in her hands. She laughed and snapped her fingers and
danced, turning her head and body to and fro and humming:

> Oof... little woman, sleep tight!
> For at this time of night,
> All locked is the house,
> In the dark, not a mouse.

Happy and lighthearted, she set about doing the housework. After
that, as she did every day, she brought out her cosmetics, spread
them out, and set about the task of making up her face and hair.

That day and for several days more, the snake flashed out each
time suddenly, from a totally unexpected corner. The woman, as
soon as her eye fell on it, would jump up from her place and let out a
scream, and the snake would go back the way it did every day. And
every time, a gold coin would fall from its mouth and ring out on the
bricks. Oddly enough, each time the young woman's cries of terror
sounded less surprised, there was a certain affectation in them; and
the snake, who at first had been timid and cautious, now came out a
little farther and, when it was time to go back, went a little more
slowly, hesitating from one moment to the next, looking back, and
curling its long, narrow, red body in a most appealing way.

One day, when Golnar was carefully looking around at her customary makeup time, the snake silently appeared beside her and crawled
up on her petticoat that was spread flat on the floor. All at once, a
light humming sound—like the hissing of water trickling from a faucet not quite turned off—reached Golnar's ear. It was as though
someone were saying something very softly, so softly that all she perceived was an indistinct presence. Golnar held her breath and listened
closely; but she told herself it was the wind rustling through the
branches of the neighbor's willow tree, or perhaps it was a cat playing
with some dried grasses on the roof. Suddenly a coin—larger and
newer than the seven *ashrafis* that Golnar had received so far and had
put in a small purse made of purple satin—rolled off the small rug and
rang on the bricks of the ledge. Golnar looked. Her eyes and mouth
opened wide. She quickly put down the small round mirror and the
eyeliner stick that she was about to apply to her eyes and reached out.
She picked up the coin. But just then her fingers were drawn to something soft and warm. She looked. The snake unhurriedly drew itself
back and was raising its head affectionately. Its half-opened mouth
seemed to be smiling. Its tiny eyes were fixed on the woman with a

warm, penetrating glance. Golnar heard, or thought she heard: "My lily-breasted one, my jasmine-legged one, do not be afraid!"

And the strange thing was that Golnar was not afraid. There was no trace left in her of that ancient terror and disgust mankind feels for the creature that caused our mother Eve and her husband to be driven out from God's paradise. It was as though they were two acquaintances who had known each other for several years and had never been apart. Still, Golnar didn't know what to say or do. She sat there motionless, looking at it. Everything was silent and motionless. The canaries weren't even breathing in their cage. Under their wicker coop in the courtyard, the chickens and rooster were totally silent. Even from the street no cries could be heard from a greens or onion peddler or a beggar; not a crow cawed, not a dog barked. The snake coiled beside Golnar affectionately and sometimes put its head forward and stuck out its narrow, sharp-pointed tongue like a spark of fire. Golnar looked at it and felt herself totally transformed. A weakness and pleasant sleepiness enveloped her body. Her eyelids became heavy. She stretched out on her side on the small rug, and as her cheeks glowed in the midday sun and the drops of sweat glittered on her upper lip, she softly caressed the snake's head and said to herself, "If my husband were here and saw me..."

Before her eyes was a large verdant garden immersed in a bright midday mist, with a vast pond on which white waterlilies sat in serene majesty on the smooth salvers of their dark leaves. Everywhere was green shade and half-shade, and there were multicolored flowers whose warm, intoxicating fragrance was borne by the breeze in every direction. And Golnar herself was stretched out on a silken bed upon a platform of ivory and ebony under a tall tent of elms and plane trees. In her arms she held a tall, young man with a broad chest and strong arms whom she had never seen or known before, but who was now dearer to her heart than anyone or anything in her life. What burning ardor flashed out from the young man's black eyes, and with what overwhelming power he embraced her! Golnar had never experienced such a sweet weakness, a weakness that made her totally oblivious of her own existence. All her senses were merged together, and it was as though from each one a window opened up to another: that which she saw and heard and smelled melted away in the pleasure of their mutual embrace and enveloped her completely.

And what delightful little games they played! Golnar jumped up out of the young man's embrace and, half-nude, wearing only a delicate silken shirt, strolled down the paths of the garden, hiding behind the rose and jasmine bushes, imitating the sounds of the turtledove and ringdove, trilling like a nightingale, picking apples and peaches from the trees, and sinking her teeth into them. And the young man, after a while, hurried in search of his beloved; Golnar shied away from him like a young deer, ran away laughing and, in the end, was gladly captured...

And time passed. The garden blazed with the happy colors of autumn. The wind lingered in the leaf-shedding branches. The air took on the pungent smell of earth, and the forehead of the sky became wrinkled with clouds. The fresh love of the two on the ebony platform became heavy and numb...

And the garden was left bare, and the water lilies on the pond withered. The sky wept. It was cold. Golnar pressed the young man ever more tightly to her breast and coiled around him with her entire body, but waves of cold ran through her body one after another. She shivered. Her eyelids closed. Her embrace opened helplessly. A kiss froze on their lips.

In the evening the poor husband was forced to enter his house by way of the neighbor's roof. Golnar seemed to have fallen asleep on the ledge. Beside her were the copper mirror and the eyeliner case and the bundle of rouge and powder, as well as a small purse with seven *ashrafis* in it and a large gold coin that had rolled out of her hand. A snake was coiled upon her marble-like breast, and at the sound of the footsteps of the man and several neighborhood women who had come with him, it quickly withdrew to the rim of the eaves and disappeared.

Just when the man was closely examining the *ashrafis*, counting them and putting them back into the purse, the sharp eye of a young woman fell upon two tiny milky-white beads between Golnar's two cold breasts. She knew what they were. She reached out and eagerly picked them up, tied them up in a kerchief and tucked them into her bosom.

From now on she could be sure that her husband's heart would be forever bound by love for her...

Sadeq Chubak

1916–1998

Short-story writer and novelist Sadeq Chubak was born in Bushire, where his father was a prominent bazaar merchant. After elementary schooling in his home town, Chubak attended secondary school in Shiraz, where his family had moved. He later graduated from Alborz College high school in Tehran, and became a teacher. During World War II Chubak served as an English translator for the Iranian General Staff in Tehran.

In 1945 Chubak published his first book, a collection of short stories called *Khaymeh shab-bāzi* (The puppet show). In 1949, the year in which he became a librarian at the National Iranian Oil Company, a position he held until taking early retirement in 1974, Chubak published a second collection of short stories, *Antari ke lutiyash mordeh bud* (The monkey whose master was dead). By this time critics considered Chubak the leading "naturalistic" short-story writer in Iran.

Chubak proceeded in the 1950s to publish short stories in *Sokhan* magazine and elsewhere, but his next book was the 1963 novel *Tangsir* (Man from Tangestan), which has been translated as *One Man with His Gun* together with four short stories and a play in *Sadeq Chubak: An Anthology* (1982). In 1965 appeared Chubak's third and fourth collections of short stories: *Cherāgh-e ākher* (Last alms) and *Ruz-e avval-e qabr* (First day in the grave).

Chubak's last published fiction was the important novel called *Sang-e sabur* (1966), published in translation as *The Patient Stone* in 1989. Since *The Patient Stone*, except for work on unpublished memoirs, Chubak has apparently produced no creative writing. In 1974 the film version of *Tangsir* enjoyed considerable success in Iran. In the mid-1970s the author and his wife moved to London and thereafter settled in a San Francisco suburb.

In the 1990s, only two of his works appeared in Iran. His translations of love stories from Sanskrit literature into Persian, *Mahpāreh: dāstān'hā-ye āsheqi-e Hendu* was published in 1991, and in 1999, *Gozideh-e dāstān'hā-ye kutāh-e Sādeq Chubak: entekhāb va tahlil-e Ruh Allāh Mahdipur 'Omrāni* appeared.

The Wooden Horse

Translated by John R. Perry

Night was falling when they brought home a wooden horse for the little boy's New Year's present, and he had played with it so long, running his fingers over its nostrils and huge, staring eyes, that he finally dropped like a stone onto the sofa next to his mother and fell fast asleep.

The wooden horse stood in the middle of the room on four stubby wheels painted to resemble tires, with a black varnished bridle and a red ornamental saddle. It was a dull red-brown in color, with tiny specks of dirt protruding like emery from beneath the paint. Its muzzle resting against the boy's face, the horse was staring at him. The boy still had his arms around the horse's neck. It was a big horse, bigger than the boy, so he could sit astride it. Their breaths intermingled; the boy's cheeks puffed out, his lips parted and his warm breath was exhaled into the horse's face.

The woman sat on the sofa, opposite an unlit, smoke-blackened brick fireplace piled with the ashes of assorted paper and cardboard and candy wrappers, staring at them glumly and listlessly. The room was starkly empty. There was nothing in it but this one old, brown leather sofa and a couple of badly scuffed suitcases standing next to each other in anticipation of their next trip. A naked, dusty lightbulb hung from the ceiling, shedding its harsh, insolent glare over the room. It looked as if they had recently moved; the half-inch layer of dust covering the tiled floor had been tracked by footprints and furrowed by furniture legs to reveal traces of the reddish mosaic underneath.

The woman, too, was grubby, like a doll that needed dusting. Her hair was mousy and straggling, her clothes dowdy. Tears had washed the dust, grime, and powder off her face in two dried streaks. From beneath her fine, blond eyebrows, two large, silky eyes stared blankly and unblinking at the ashes.

She was no longer even crying. She was thinking: "What a disaster it was, that night in Montmartre when I promised to marry this animal and got dragged away under this alien sky! I lost everything: my name, my religion, my love, my desires—all were destroyed. How could I know it would come to this? And all for the sake of this child. What a mistake! Anywhere else in the world, I could have had a child by anyone else—and without all this trouble; but I was such an idiot, I loved him as much as I love this child. These people are not human!"

Beyond the bare windowpanes, large snowflakes, whirling and howling, lashed the air. The room was cold; a faded lightweight overcoat was slung over her shoulders. She tried to take the child's arms from around the horse's neck, but he held on tight and bit his lip in his sleep. The woman let him be.

A sudden terror of being alone made her heart sink. She took out a cigarette from her handbag, lit it from the half-smoked one in her hand, and drew on it deeply a few times. Her body was trembling, and she did not care whether she sat or stood or walked.

This was the third Christmas she had spent in Iran. Three years ago, pretty and fresh and carefree, she had stepped from the plane onto the soil of Mehrabad airport. She thought back to her life in prewar Paris. In those days Jalal was a medical student and she was a salesgirl in one of the bookstores on the Boulevard Saint-Michel. Jalal was a dark, bronzed, well-built, shy young man who often came and browsed among her books; he had a lost, fugitive air, blinked continuously, and looked away whenever the woman's eye fell on him. Then they had fallen in love and she had been walking on air; at night they would buy a bottle of tepid burgundy from the liquor store at the end of the narrow, arched alleyway called the Rue de la Huchette, then go down the steps to the Seine and, leaning against a tall, green elm, drink in turn from the upturned bottle; then they would sink into an embrace and kiss passionately, while the clochards near and far lay on the ground swigging their Beaujolais and crooning to themselves. The couple always went to their own special spot, where they could see the lamps on the Pont des Arts reflected in the Seine; and then they would kiss and clinch so ardently that they would start to tremble, their mouths would go dry, their bodies would ignite, and Jalal's expression would become more anguished than ever. Soon they would get up and go to Jalal's small attic room in the Rue Gai Lussac, and strip naked. First he would slip beneath the covers, then their body scents would alter, they would break out in a sweat, start to pant, and fall drunk into each other's arms.

And now, after six years of love and marriage, Jalal had gone and taken up with that dark-skinned, bushy-browed, hen-toed cousin of his, and she would have to hang her head and go back with her child to her friends and relations in Paris. Her past life was now burned to ashes, and the smoking memories choked her. She was heartsick and apprehensive. She had the urge to go out into the street and stand in the snow to cool the heat of her body. Her son's body heat as he lay close by her calmed her. She was aware that her sole worldly possessions consisted of this child and the two suitcases sitting in the middle of the room.

Three years before, when she first alighted at Mehrabad, she had been two months pregnant with Arman. Jalal was with her and she held his arm, aware of her heart beating. It was July, and the sun's liquid glare weighed on her head like mercury. As soon as she landed she was intimidated by the sight of two dark-skinned, helmeted guards, bayonets held high, prowling back and forth outside the aircraft. Then she sat by Jalal's side in the car of one of his friends, whose name was Ahmad. Her husband's brother, Jamal, had also come to meet them, a man with a spiky half-beard and purple lips; when she held out her hand his face split into a broad grin, and in halting French he asked, "How are you?" and then said nothing more, sitting silent and motionless for the whole ride, running his tongue around his dry purple lips at regular intervals and fiddling with a set of dirty worry-beads.

Once they reached home, however, everything changed abruptly, and nothing was as she had expected. As she stepped into the hallway her nostrils were assailed by a rank smell and she was almost sick. The house was cramped and dark, with high, plastered mud-brick walls. It had a tiny courtyard with a silted-up pool in the middle.

The twisted skeleton of a clinging vine was draped over a weather-beaten trellis and formed a canopy, its miserable, mildewed bunches of black grapes dangling over the yard. Suddenly she remembered that this was the very house where Jalal had come into the world. She studied its door and walls with interest; but the stink in the hall-way stifled her, burned her thoughts and roughened her throat.

Jalal's father and mother and three sisters of different sizes were waiting for them in the yard with smothered and tremulous smiles. In Paris, she had seen photos of them, separately and together; only here they were all somehow different. They had pot bellies, their complexions were sallow and grimy, as if the family were cursed with some hereditary disease.

When she took their cold and clammy hands, she shivered inwardly. She knew she was supposed to smile at each of them, say "salaam" and shake hands. Jalal had taught her "salaam" and some other phrases to say after that, but she had forgotten these, and now was embarrassed and tried to recall them, while stammered words seethed in her brain and the stink in the hallway scorched her nos-trils and stopped her thinking. On the way Jalal had taught her to say *"Kaniz-e shoma hastam"* (I am your servant-girl), which she had assumed was a polite cliché without knowing what it meant; now that she had forgotten what to say, she cursed her own stupidity.

Then Jalal took her into a room with sash windows, and went back to bring in the luggage. There was a spindly round table, a bench and one or two Second Empire-style chairs, festooned with tattered fringes and faded tassels, in a corner of the room. On the table was a bowl of black grapes, cucumbers and cherries, over which flies were walking. A brand new hardwood double bed—the smell of varnish and alcohol still permeated the air—together with a plumped-up quilt and a cylindrical bolster, was placed at the far end of the room. There was even a gleaming white icebox in one corner. She liked the room. She liked the little multicolored panes in the sash window. But here, too, there was the same smell that had struck her in the hallway. It was something she had never smelled before; she had not even known that such a smell existed. And now it had her by the throat, ebbed and flowed, squirmed about her stomach.

She was alone in the room. She put her bag down on the sofa and stood waiting for Jalal to return, looking curiously at the door and walls. On the wall hung a picture of a scowling warrior with a bushy mustache sweeping back to his ears, gripping the stock of a Mauser under his arm. This scared her, and the memory of the guards at

Mehrabad flashed through her mind. From the yard the muffled, unfamiliar voices of Jalal's parents and siblings reached her. They appeared to be quarreling. She made out Jalal's voice among the others. She realized that she had been alone in the room for some time. She went back to studying the colored panes in the sash window. It reminded her of the stained glass windows in Notre Dame cathedral.

Jalal came back into the room. His coat was over his arm, he was damp with sweat, and he had not brought the suitcases. He sat down quietly and thoughtfully on the sofa, which creaked underneath him. Disappointment and regret were plain to see in his features. Then he said quietly: "Whatever I do, nothing suits them. I wish I'd never come. They won't listen to a word I say."

"What doesn't suit them? Don't they like me?"

"No, they like you all right. But they're insisting that we have a Muslim wedding."

"But we were married once in church!"

"They don't accept that. They say you have to do it our way."

"Very funny. What business is it of theirs? We already have a child!"

"They say a child born of a Christian marriage is illegitimate. I'm ashamed of them—I wish I had no relatives. I hate myself."

They were both silent. Jalal hung his head and looked at the pattern on the carpet. She stood there, studying Jalal's bowed, miserable form. She felt sorry for him. She loved him. She felt that he was no match for his family and they would have their way. She went and sat next to him on the sofa, took his hand in hers and said, "You know how much I love you. I don't want you to be unhappy. I'll do whatever you wish."

"I know that your coming to this country is a great sacrifice in itself. I'm ashamed to make such a request of you. But so long as we adore each other, what do these externals matter? You know I don't believe in these things."

"It's of no importance. I'll do whatever you wish. I want my life to be for you."

So then a mullah came and performed the Muslim ceremony and she was renamed Fatima, which she didn't like at all, since she knew that all the Algerian women who lived in Paris were called Fatima. After the wedding, when Jalal's mother called her Fatima she shivered inwardly and under her breath muttered "merde."

But that night when she saw the lavatory, then she realized what she was in for. Four steps led down from the yard into a dark pit with a heavy, damp, faded tarpaulin hanging from the door. Suddenly a hot, stifling blast of humid, acrid gas hit her. Involuntarily she held the bit of paper she had brought with her before her nose. The flame of the oil lamp she had with her did not catch beyond the wick, and specks of oil surrounded the wick like tiny blobs of mercury; it was this faint light that nevertheless stirred up the beetles and spiders and gnats. From the bottom of the pit she heard a sound. The scent of the French perfume she was wearing mingled with the smell from the pit; her stomach turned, heaved, and she was sick. She threw the lamp away in fear, and fled. For the rest of the night she was sweating with fever and raving in her sleep.

Next she caught typhoid from Jalal's seven-year-old sister; Jalal's sister died, and she herself lay at death's door, while the whole family averred that this woman was bad luck and her arrival had opened the door to death, and all turned away from her. She was nursed by a Catholic *soeur*. Her head was completely shaved, and when she recovered she was left with a weak liver, a yellowish complexion and sunken eyes. So changed was she that one would think she had been bodily removed and replaced by someone else.

What a long night it was! Christmas Eves were always long. But she had never noticed, because she was always busy rushing about, shopping, putting up decorations, dressing up, dressing the tree, dining and dancing. Now this endless, wretched night was drumming its heaviness and coldness into her head.

She raised her eyes from her wristwatch and stared through gummed-up eyelashes at the ashes in the grate. Everything was cold, distant, blank, lifeless. It seemed to her that she had looked at her watch once before and it had been twelve o'clock; and now it was still twelve. The fingers seemed to be manacled, immobilized.

Christmas never used to be like this. Christmas in Paris was fun. There, life and beauty danced in each other's arms. What a night it was at the Lapin Agile in Montmartre! Colored lanterns hung from the barrel vaults and all the *gars* were gathered there; those overflowing trays of wine, martinis, champagne that the waiters brought around, from which everyone could take whatever he wished, and the singers one after the other sang popular songs, and people held hands and swayed in time to the music and joined in the choruses. In Paris, Jalal had been quite a lad—how well he had danced! How liberal were his views! But once he arrived here, he had changed. His form and complexion were different; he smelled different; the way he looked at you was different. How quickly he forgot the sufferings, the caresses, the love and beauty they had shared. Everything must come to an end one day; now it has. Everything has. My life as it was has ended, she thought.

A burning shiver ran up her spine. Gently she took the child's arm from around the horse's neck, pushed the horse back across the floor and laid the boy's arm over his chest. She had been meaning to do this for some time, and finally she did. Then she took her overcoat off her shoulders and put it over the boy, wrapped it around him and tucked it underneath him. She felt that everyone in the city was her deadly enemy and they were all lurking outside in the snow to harm her child. She stared at the lightbulb. Sharp needles of light landed on her eyes and bored into her brain. In another four hours she would leave this country, without so much as a backward glance. She looked around the room. It was empty and alien. It was the same room in which she had spent the past two years, only now Jalal had taken the furniture away and left it like a looted bomb site.

She got up and stood in front of the wall in which two large, bent nails were still buried. She knew they marked the spots where two prints had hung, a Cézanne and a Manet. Her broken, shapeless shadow fell onto the wall between the two empty spaces—on the wall as far as her waist, and from the waist down, along the floor. Abruptly she turned to go to a spot where a mirror used to hang; she wanted to see herself in the mirror. As she turned her head she saw that the mirror was not there. She had known it was not there. She walked around the room, looking this way and that, recalling the guests she had entertained in this room, the laughter and pleasure and conversation that had been. Her nose and eyes began to smart. She wondered if she had really lived for so long in this room, or if in fact she had never left Paris, married, and had a child, and was really still in Paris. Then she thought that she had never seen Paris in her life, and had been in Tehran for as long as she could remember, and was now somewhere else. Everything around her was strange. She felt she had suddenly forgotten everything, and it seemed to her as if she had never been alive. She fancied she was dead. She went over by the window and lit another cigarette, blowing the thick smoke at the windowpane. Through the window she watched the snowflakes and the black flecks of space in the street that were untouched by the snow. Cars with dazzling eyes chased after one another like scuttling ladybugs. She looked at the city scene, at the dome and minarets of the Sepahsalar mosque. Suddenly she felt sick. She rushed out of the room to the bathroom. Here the unwashed face and bleary eyes and tousled, grubby hair that she saw in the mirror abruptly turned her stomach and she threw up in the sink.

She tossed the half-smoked cigarette in her hand into the sticky white foam, a string of which still adhered to her lower lip. She vomited again. The cigarette did not go out, and a wisp of damp, acrid smoke still rose from it. Then she felt cold. With her head still over the sink, she looked at her watch: it was half-past midnight. She thought, I don't care how long you drag out your existence, or how you creep along like a tortoise—two or three hours more, and I'm leaving! I only wish these three hours were three minutes. I've never wished for anything so much as I wish that my time could go up in smoke like this. But at least I'll take my child away from this ruin, so that when he grows up he'll have no conception of this father, this family, this country! I never want him to know who his father was, I'd prefer him to think that his father was some man on the street and there had been no bond between us. He'll only have this sallow skin and black curly hair for the rest of his life as a mark of shame.

She was getting the chills. She went back into the room. The child was still asleep and the wooden horse was gazing into his face with its serene, untroubled look. She was shivering slightly, and thought the child must be cold too; she sat next to him. The child's body was still hot. She ran her hand over his forehead, and from its warmth realized how cold her own fingers were. The child shuddered in his sleep at the touch of her cold fingers, frowned, and parted his lips. Again she told herself, "I could have had this child by anybody else; in the event, it would have looked different. I wouldn't have been any the wiser. I would have loved him the same as this one. Maybe he is cold; I'm certainly freezing. Everything here is dry and metallic: the sun, the cold, the people, all of them. My life is over. Now I'll have to work my fingers to the bone to bring up this child. A rotten apple for me from the tree of life. But I must plant a seed of loathing in his heart for this country and this heavy sun and its liquid heat, so that he never remembers this place or his father. In order to live, one needs both love and rancor, friendship and enmity. Jesus Christ's time has come and gone. One can't build a life on a basis of love alone. I can never forgive anyone again. No more of that stuff! I live in this world, and here is where my duty plainly lies. True, I can't do anything about it; but I can't simply fold my arms, sit back and watch whatever befalls me and do nothing."

She took hold of the horse's bridle and pushed it back from the sofa. The wheels scraped over the dust on the tilework. The child suddenly stirred. She started and let go of the horse. Her lips were stuck together with saliva. She stood up, tucked the horse under her arm and gently put it down among the burned paper in the grate, then struck a match and held it under the mane and tail.

The horse caught fire. She stepped back, and hoped the flames would warm the child. She wiped her mouth with her sleeve and went and sat down on the sofa next to the child. Her gaze, regretful and unblinking, was fixed on the flames. Her heart raced with anxiety. She wanted not to be there, had wanted for a long time to get away from this country. "When he wakes up, I'll tell him his father came and took it away by force. At least the room will warm up a bit; we're freezing."

The flames embraced the horse; the brick fireplace filled with flames, the horse was big and then shrank, grimaced, stumbled, reeled and fell over. And she watched her own gaiety and nimbleness and liveliness and love and life and extinction there pictured among the flames.

The Gravediggers

Translated by John R. Perry

The children surrounded Khadijeh like a pack of dogs that had cornered a wolf in a strange village and pursued her the whole length of the bazaar, clapping and jeering rhythmically: "She's got a bastard—ho, ho, ho! She's got a bastard—ho, ho, ho!"

The girl, barefoot and wearing a coarse cotton shift with a tear running from shoulder to waist, clutched her heavy, distended belly and made her way fearfully past the shops. Her hair was matted with bits of straw and burrs and hung about her grimy face like strands of fleece.

When she reached the baker's her feet stopped, and her torso lurched forward a little, and her gaze fixed upon the counter. One of the boys behind her grabbed the torn flap of her shift and tore it further. The girl did not look away from the shop. Her back was burning; she put her hand behind her and perfunctorily rubbed the spot where her shift had been torn, her eyes fixed on the loaves on the countertop. They held her spellbound.

The baker stood over his scales, rocking from one foot to the other; his hands busied themselves on the top of the counter. The girl lunged forward with outstretched hands, her face was suddenly pregnant with

bread as she crammed the loaves into her mouth until there was no
room for more and gulped them down.

"Well, when are you going to drop this kid of yours? Why don't
you tell us whose it is, so we can fix things for you? Make him clean
you up and settle you down!" The baker tried to make her say something; every day he asked her the same question, but she never
answered, and now too she was wolfing the bread whole with a
chronic, gnawing hunger while staring at him dumbly.

Her face and neck were speckled with mud, her skin was grimy,
her hands marked with ingrained dirt. The children would not let
her alone: they capered about before and behind, tugging at her,
poking her, throwing stones at her and chanting: "She's got a bastard—ho, ho, ho! She's got a bastard—ho, ho, ho!"

"You're a stubborn one, girl! Why don't you speak? Come on,
who's the father? Is it someone from here?" The baker was lean and
lanky and stood there behind the till, rocking from foot to foot, nee-
dling her to give something away. Khadijeh looked at him without
batting an eyelid. Suddenly someone pushed her from behind and,
as if about to overbalance, she lurched forward involuntarily and
continued on her way, the band of assorted urchins trotting after
her. One of them bit into a carrot-end he was holding and asked the
boy next to him, "What's the girl done?"

"She's got a bastard in her belly."

"What's a bastard?"

"A kid that nobody knows who his father is."

"Whose father?"

"The bastard's."

"How come they don't know?"

"'Cause they don't. 'Cause she's a whore."

Then the boy flung his carrot-end at the girl and hit her on the
back of the head. She bent down to pick up a stone to throw back
and, not finding one, latched onto a piece of pomegranate rind,
which she flung at the urchins, who scattered. She chased them, her
belly bouncing about in front of her and her broad, heavy breasts
pounding against her chest. Then she turned back and went on, and
the kids resumed their pursuit, clapping and shouting: "She's got a
bastard—ho, ho, ho! She's got a bastard—ho, ho, ho!"

A gendarme approached, carrying a rifle over his shoulder and a
bundle wrapped up in a kerchief in his hand. He was joined by a
passer-by, likewise carrying a bundle, and also an unlit lantern with a
smoke-blackened funnel. They walked in silence side by side. The

passer-by observed, "Looks like she doesn't plan on having her kid. Her belly's been way out for quite some time."

"Didn't they ever find out who the father is?"

"He isn't from hereabouts. They say it's a a lad from the village up that way. Funny world we live in!"

"There's no good left anywhere anymore. God willing, she'll not make it through labor and the kid neither."

"I don't want to tempt fate, but sometimes a person doesn't knuckle under to God's will. How many times has this girl been knocked about in town here?—and she hasn't given any sign of losing it!"

"And not only beaten!—why, she was only one or two months gone when Mashti Gholam-Reza, the landlord of Siya-kolah, went and hitched her to his plow and made her plow his field. He said she'd no right to have a bastard getting under everyone's feet. But no matter what he did, still she didn't miscarry. The brat's got seven lives, like a dog!"

"Mashti Gholam-Reza is a god-fearing man, I know him. It's right what he says. Whatever he did was right. So what happened?"

"Well, someone reported to the police post that some girl in Siya-kolah was dying. We went there with the lieutenant and found her lying in a field, bleeding. There were a few villagers standing round her. Mashti Gholam-Reza himself was there too. We made inquiries locally and it turned out that Mashti Gholam-Reza had hitched her to the plowshare. We all thanked God that she'd had a miscarriage. Then we heard she'd gotten up and gone off, and we went back to the post. But it wasn't any use, she didn't lose the kid after all."

When they reached the midpoint of the bazaar there appeared a stocky, thick-limbed peasant leading a bear cub on a chain. At this sight, the children threw whatever was left in their hands at the girl and swarmed after the bear cub. The girl, too, turned round and stared at the bear cub. A tight smile played over her thick lips and involuntarily she moved a few steps toward the cub. Then she stopped, took one last look, and went on her way. The sun sank into the woods and the street lamps and buzzing mantle burners of the shops came on.

In the stable where Khadijeh slept at night were also two donkeys belonging to an old donkey-driver. The stable, which he also owned, was attached to a shack in which he lived with his wife, an old woman with one eye. During the day the old man worked the donkeys, though ever since one of them had fallen sick and could no longer be goaded from the spot, he took out the other one only.

The stable was dark and had no door as such; a gap in the wall served for access. One of the donkeys stood at the manger eating straw. The other was lying on its side, legs outstretched, panting. At first the girl did not see the donkeys. But she could sense them. This was how it was every night when she returned to the stable: one donkey was eating, the other was lying panting heavily. When her eyes grew accustomed to the dark she saw them, and could make out the faded henna-colored patches that had been branded into their hides.

She went straight to the platform of warm dung that lay in one corner of the stable, flopped down on her distended belly, and sat for a while in the still unfamiliar gloom. She could sense the movement and breathing of the donkeys. She was glad they were there. Then she lay down on her back and stared at the cobweb-covered, smoke-blackened wooden ceiling. From the shack next to the stable she could hear the voices of the owner and his wife.

"I'm not having anyone with a bastard in her belly staying at our house; it's bad luck," the old man said. His wife countered: "What bad luck? Have you no thought for God? Why, a dog wouldn't live in that stable! A chit of a girl spends the night on the packed dung in a corner of your stable, and that will bring you bad luck?!" But the old man went on: "It already has—one of my donkeys is dying; why d'you think that is? Any day now she'll drop the brat, then there'll be two of them, and my other donkey will fall sick." The old woman said nothing, and the girl stared at the neglected, rotting rafters and breathed in the acrid smell of the dung.

She liked the smell. It was the smell of oblivion, of sleep. Her bed was warm and soft. She dug her hands and feet into its thickness and soaked up its tingling warmth into her body. The snorting of the sick donkey pounded at her ears. She knew the poor beast was sick and crippled and did not eat anything put before it, that its eyes were always open and it panted continuously. She stared at the threadbare darkness of the ceiling, thinking to herself, Maybe I'll have a furry baby donkey. Donkey foals are so cute, you want to pick them up and kiss and cuddle them. Or I might have a bear cub, like the one in the bazaar. It was so cute! Why did they beat it? Where are its ma and pa? If only I could have brought it here to hold tight and sleep with. It was so cute. If it were mine we'd run away to the woods together. Then the lions and tigers wouldn't bother us. No; first I'd take it to Qasem's house and wake him up. When he'd first set eyes on a bear like that, he would throw a fit! I'd say, "Come on, hurry up, now that you've gotten me pregnant, marry me! If you don't, I'll tell the bear to eat you." But if he didn't, I still wouldn't tell the bear to eat him. Qasem's a good boy.

Hardly had her lips parted in a smile than a sudden sharp pain shot through her lower body. Her heart fluttered in alarm and her head tossed from side to side on the damp dung. The pain soon ceased, leaving a void in her stomach. Her body was wet with exhaustion and she was still thinking about how the pain had suddenly come and gone when it came back; her body broke out in sweat, and she jumped up, then sat down, then huddled up on the floor, rolling from side to side, then again got up and sat down, her body writhing beneath a glaze of sweat. Then the pain went away again, leaving her body battered, and she fell limp onto the dungpile. Her body and insides were wracked with pain. She waited for it to return. She did not know where in her body this pain was located: her whole being was trembling, and her inside had become light— she no longer felt the heaviness of her belly.

Again the pain came, seized her, pounded her, and stayed. She clawed handfuls of the dung and sprinkled it over her face and head. She grated her teeth and lacerated her body with her fingernails. Her face was wet with tears and perspiration and seamed with dust from the dung; the moans within her forced their way out, her body heaved and turned about, loneliness and pain sank their claws into her heart. She moaned; she wept.

A small, quivering oil lamp, its lens liberally coated with soot, lit up the interior of the stable with a reddish glow. Behind it the old man and the old woman stumbled in, the lamp trembling in the old woman's hand. Their weathered, troubled faces turned about in search of the loud, drawn-out, embarrassing cry that rose from the corner of the stable. The old woman saw and understood, and told him, "You'd better stay back—she's in labor."

The old man lowered his head and said, glum and helpless, "I don't care what you say—my donkey's sickness is because of the bad luck that girl brought us. If she hadn't come here, I wouldn't have lost my donkey. And on top of it all she's having a baby!"

The old woman became annoyed. She went up to where the girl lay and said, "This is not the time for that sort of talk. Can't you see it's as if she had a snake coiled round her? You go back to bed; I'll take care of the baby."

The old man nodded, placed his hand on the wall and turned away from the dung bed, spat on the ground and returned to the shack.

The old woman bent over the girl's head as she lay trembling, a desperate appeal in her black eyes, which stared from their sockets as they followed the movements of the old woman and the lamp; her body writhed about, wracked with tremors of pain, her face was white, her belly and breasts protruded from her torn shift. The old woman placed the lamp in a gap left by a brick that had fallen from the wall like a broken tooth, bent over the girl and sat down, and took hold of her hands.

The girl clutched the old woman's hands with painful eagerness and drew them toward her with her youthful strength. Both pairs of hands locked together and the girl's pain transferred itself to the old woman's body. A molten rod ran through the girl's marrow; she keeled over onto the dung bed and her legs opened. Her body grew limp and flaccid, the old woman's hands loosed their grip, and the girl's distraught look died; her struggling and writhing and terror poured out together with the baby and the placenta and the gush of blood, and the baby's cry washed clean the bloody darkness.

The old woman laid the child and the placenta on the dung bed, hurriedly stood up and went to the shack. She was back in a moment with a piece of sacking and a large knife. She cut the umbilical cord and tossed the placenta, warm and bloody and swollen, into a corner. "Another girl," she murmured as she wrapped the baby in the sacking, smiled at it, and carried it into the lamplight. She stuck her broken, gnarled old finger, a mass of flesh and nail, down the baby's throat and freed its tongue from its palate, and the child's cry rang out; and with her toothless mouth she kissed it.

The baby lay in the girl's arms, the lamp was burning, the baby was crying, the red and black shadows cast by the lamp distorted the stable, and the old woman was gone. The baby's crying merged with the snorting of the sick donkey. The beast's fevered panting distended the wings of its flared nostrils. The other donkey had eaten all that the stable had to offer and lay looking straight in front of it.

She was awakened by the sound of the baby's whimpering at her ear, and the warmth and weight and blood-clogged fragrance of the child drew her head round toward it. Her arm was around the baby. She was afraid. She half rose, and stared at the newborn. Her lips remained closed, but her face and eyes smiled. Suddenly a rush of blood welled up inside her and gushed from between her legs; she felt faint and sat down, and heaved a few times; her lips parted and a sticky foam dribbled onto her chin. She looked at the sick donkey, and threw up. Then she hastily turned round and examined the baby. She stood up, her body and legs trembling. She picked up the baby and cradled it in her arm. Its lower legs were red and wet. Its knees were trembling and meconium oozed down its thighs. She wrapped the sacking round the child and went out of the stable.

There was nobody in the street. A cock crowed from the wall next to her ear and her heart missed a beat. She felt cold and frightened, and shivered. Beneath the archway of the bazaar she saw a donkey-driver, two beasts walking ahead of him with swaying loads of manure, while he fought off the dogs snapping at his heels with a long-handled spade. The stench of the mixture of dung and ashes crammed inside the wide-mouthed sacks burned her nostrils. She overtook the donkeys and, once outside the alley, saw the morning star twinkling on the brow of the sky; the broad avenue with its shops shuttered and asleep beckoned her and made a path for her toward the bridge.

A gendarme, rifle in hand, stood rocking from one foot to the other in the wooden sentry box at the entrance of the police post. The girl's slight, childlike form slipped across to the opposite side of the road and approached the bridge through the half light of the mist-laden early morning air.

"Halt! Stay where you are!" The harsh command rang in the girl's ears. She broke into a run. "Stop or I'll shoot!" The girl stumbled, falling forward, overbalanced by the child in her arms; but the stone parapet of the bridge held her, and then the bridge was empty as the forest swallowed her.

The sentry peered along the bridge; its humped back was utterly empty. He poked his head back into the passageway and yelled, "Qorbanli! Qorbanli!" A policeman in an open-necked shirt and no cap, with a bayonet dangling at his backside, came out. The sentry told him, "Quick, go tell the lieutenant that someone—a woman, carrying something—just ran across the bridge like crazy and disappeared into the woods." The policeman in the open-necked shirt, rubbing his eyes and yawning, replied, "If we wake him for that, he'll scream bloody murder. Best not to say anything."

"Then go and wake the duty sergeant and bring him here quick," the sentry said, peering this way and that into the trees. The policeman in the open-necked shirt and no cap went in and soon returned with a corporal. The sentry stood squinting along the bridge and sensed, rather than saw, the corporal coming.

"Who was it? What was he carrying?" the corporal stuttered.

"Looked like a woman. Yes, definitely a woman. With something in her arms. She dashed into the trees. Pretty scared, she was. Looked like someone was after her."

The sentry stared into the forest and would not look the corporal in the face. He did not like him. The policeman in the open-necked shirt and no cap and the corporal went inside, then re-emerged with a third man. The sentry sensed the aura of the lieutenant and stiffened to attention even before he saw him, his rifle held straight by the three fingers of his right hand. The lieutenant had an automatic holstered in his belt. He was in a bad mood, his face awash with sleep, and a freshly lit cigarette clamped between his lips.

"Go and get the flashlight," the lieutenant ordered. The policeman in the open-necked shirt and no cap went off and returned with a long flashlight, and with his collar buttoned and wearing a cap. All three started toward the bridge. The sentry stayed put and watched them, now standing easy. They walked onto the bridge. The clatter of their hobnailed boots punctured the air. The sentry outside the police post could no longer see them.

"If you find anything, sing out. Qorbanli, you take that side and you, Akbar, take this side." The lieutenant indicated the directions they were to cover and stopped to inspect the trees in front of him. Then he too moved on, into the sector between those he had assigned to his subordinates.

There was a sound of drowsy birds fluttering from branch to branch and the hooting of owls. Crickets and beetles buzzed, the leaves quivered and rustled, the winding stream babbled and the sky glimmered between the branches. A triumphant shout rent the forest's stillness. "Lieutenant, I've found her!" No sooner had the lieutenant reached the policeman than they were joined by the corporal. A woman was cowering on the ground in front of them. The lieutenant cut through the still darkness of the forest with the flashlight beam.

"What were you carrying? What did you do with it?" the lieutenant shouted into the girl's face. Then the corporal laughed, "It's that crazy girl who's pregnant with a bastard."

The lieutenant shouted again. "Out with it, you bitch! What did you do with that bundle you had?" The lowest ranking policeman bounded forward, grabbed the girl by the shoulder and shook her, shouting, "Come on, damn you, speak up!" The girl's eyes stared into the distance between the forms of the policemen.

The officer stepped close to the girl, clicked his flashlight off and on again, and searched all around her. The light hurt the girl's eyes, which were staring out of their sockets. The officer's feet sank into a heap of damp, freshly turned earth.

The policemen dug into the loose wet earth and unearthed the baby. The officer straightened up, swallowed hard, and ordered, "Take her to the post." The policemen began to drive the girl toward the police post, one of them carrying the baby under his arm. The officer hunted in his pocket for a cigarette, eyeing the ridges of earth around the shallow pit. He unbuttoned his fly and pissed into the pit, then switched on the flashlight and looked at the resulting pool.

Simin Daneshvar

1921–

The daughter of a physician, Iranian fiction writer and literary translator Simin Daneshvar was born in Shiraz. After high school, she moved with her family to Tehran. Daneshvar worked there for Radio Tehran and a newspaper called *Iran* and completed a doctoral degree in Persian literature at Tehran University. She published her first book, a collection of short stories called *Ātesh-e khāmush* (The extinguished fire) in 1948, the first collection of short stories ever by an Iranian woman.

In 1950 Daneshvar married the writer Jalal Al-e Ahmad (1923–69), thereafter serving as an editor of sorts in his rise to literary prominence. From 1952 to 1954 Daneshvar participated in a Fulbright program at Stanford University, which she credits with nurturing her writing skills. From the mid–1950s to 1979 she taught Persian art history at Tehran University, and published numerous translations, among them fiction by Anton Chekhov, Nathaniel Hawthorne, William Saroyan and Alan Paton. Her fame rests primarily on her 1969 novel *Savushun*, the first novel ever published by an Iranian woman. By the late 1970s, *Savushun* had became Iran's best-selling Persian novel ever and an English translation by M.R. Ghanoonparvar was published in 1990.

Daneshvar's second collection of short stories, *Shahri chun behesht* (A city like heaven), appeared in 1961 and her third collection, *Be-ki salām konam* (To whom can I say hello?), was published in 1980. Translations of five Daneshvar stories appear in *Daneshvar's Playhouse* (1989), together with an essay about her husband called "The Loss of Jalal" and an assessment of her own achievements in "A Letter to the Reader." Six more translated stories are collected in *Sutra and Other Stories* (1994).

Daneshvar's most recent novel is the 1993 epic *Jazireh-ye sargardāni* (Island of bewilderment), which is partly based on her life. Other books published in the last decade include *Māh-e asal-e āft_bi: majmu'ah-e dāstān* (1991), *Az parandehhā-ye mohājer bepors: majmu'ah-e dāstān* (1997) and *Sārbān sargardān: jeld-e dovvom-e Jazireh-e sargardāni* (2001).

The Half-Closed Eye

Translated by Frank Lewis

Sorrow for these who slumber
robs my weeping eyes of sleep.
–Nima Yushij (1895-1960)

Effat ol-Moluk:

Yes, my dear woman, the late doctor Haj Hakimbashi was my uncle, the full-blooded brother of my mother. Everyone called him Haj Hakimbashi the Deaf. Khanom Kuchek was his favorite wife. When she didn't indulge him his matrimonial prerogatives, he'd get very peevish. He'd come to the clinic in Mirza Mahmud Vazir Street, take one glance at the patients and say, "Give them all an enema." Then he'd walk right back out again. And how do you suppose Khanom Kuchek got all her money? Well, it's obvious she got it from Haj Hakimbashi. They say that once, while Haji was prostrated in prayer, Khanom Kuchek got a pillow and sat right down on top of his head. Haji's about to suffocate and she tells him, "I won't get up until you swear you'll leave me all your wealth and possessions and if you don't, I'll just sit here till you croak." Haji had no choice

but to swear to it. But, by and by, she did him in. They say she
ground up some glass and mixed it in with his enema water. Haji,
God rest his soul, was a great believer in purgation.

Yes, my dear, that makes you the granddaughter of my uncle. By
visiting you today, I'm reaffirming family ties, as a good Muslim
should... but, I've disturbed you; good lord, I could die of shame!
You were asleep! I didn't realize you nap in the afternoons; I was
afraid if I came in the evening, you'd be out. I swear by the hair
upon your head, I've come to see you three times before but
couldn't find your house. Today, I said to myself, no matter what,
I've just got to find the house of my uncle's granddaughter. Excuse
me for coming in my house-slippers; my foot is swollen, you see,
and won't go in my shoe... it's my rheumatism. You wouldn't
remember what my late uncle, Haji, prescribed for rheumatism,
would you? Verjuice! In fact, my son-in-law bought eighty bottles
of verjuice from Sar Cheshmeh... I got out of the car at the end of
your street. I asked a gentleman to point out your house, but he
didn't know the way. What a sweet man! He entrusted me to the
neighborhood street-sweeper, who brought me straight to your
door. I've come to say farewell. I want to go on pilgrimage to Mashhad—may it be as much a blessing to you as it will to me—and kiss
the feet of the Imam Reza. I've brought this package for safekeep-
ing in a corner of your strongbox. If I die, give it to my daughter
and forgive me for any wrongs I've done you, or no, give it to Azizollah Khan, he'll look you up. I'll give him a piece of paper so
you'll know it's him. I'll write "May God be with you always, my
dear" on the paper.

In the package? The package contains the title deed to some
property in Khademabad. I had saved up a few pennies and everyone
was saying that in one year the value of this land would increase
from forty *tomans* per square meter to four hundred. You go to sleep
at night, they said, and when you wake up in the morning, the price
of everything has gone up, including land. I went and bought a two-
thousand-square-meter plot. Did it belong to the Baha'is? So what.
Doesn't matter whose it was. May God lengthen the reign of this
government and add to its glory... I've also got a pair of earrings, a
bracelet, two cashmere traveling bags, a cashmere prayer-rug and
my winding-sheet in the package. The sister of my daughter's husband went to Mecca last year and brought this winding-sheet for
me. She washed it in water from the well of Zamzam and circled
around the Black Stone with it. I'll open it. No, no, never even think

of it... I may not be able to rely on my own eyes, but I know I can
rely on you. I'd even trust you with my mortal soul.

The house of my son-in-law? My son-in-law's house is at the head
of the wooden bridge on Shahreza Street. My son-in-law is a colonel.
We have one orderly, a maid and a girl to run errands. On top of that,
a laundry woman comes once a week, for washing and ironing. We
also have a gardener who charges 120 tomans a month year-round just
to come and plant a few petunias and geraniums in the summertime.

...O thank you. To your health! ...My daughter has, may it meet
your approval, two little girls, each prettier than the other, just like
two little dolls. My other daughter has gone to England and is
studying medicine. First the younger sister of my son-in-law went.
She came for a visit last year. My, how she sings the praises of that
place, you can't imagine. She told my daughter, "I'll sign you up to
study medicine, all you need to do is pay for the trip there." They
pay for everything themselves. Nursing?! Who said so?! I bet it was
Aqdas, sticking her nose into everybody's business! Do you think I
just found her wandering full-grown in the desert that I would let
my precious baby clean up the piss and shit of Europeans and tie
shut the chins of their corpses? No, my dear lady, I bought a first-
class airplane ticket and sent her to London, where she is now studying to become a doctor... She studies medicine in the hospital
morning till night. She sent a letter, she wrote, "Mommy, dear, I
want to be the successor of the late Haj Hakimbashi" ...It's just like
Aqdas to say my daughter's become a nurse ... It figures that when
everyone else is dying from honest-to-God snake bites, I go and get
myself bitten by a rank stinkbug! The daughter of one's own sister
going around spreading lies about her cousin! She's jealous. She
came to ask my daughter's hand for Ahmad... I said, "I'm not about
to give the girl to that dim and squint-eyed boy of yours." Now, to
get back at me, she says my daughter's become a nurse... Does she
think Mansureh's not rightfully my child? So what if she isn't really
mine? After all, it was me who raised her, on my hip and in my arms!
If I live to do it, I'll get a passport and go to see my baby in London.
She's in London itself. You don't happen to know where to go to get
a passport, do you? Do I have to go without a veil? Well, I will. I'll
just put on a head-scarf and go. No verse has come down from heav-
en saying that I have to wear a full-length chador.

The house? No, he didn't buy it. My son-in-law paid the
400,000 *tomans* I told you about—did I say 300,000 *tomans*? I can't
remember the exact amount now—in any case, he bought the

land, but the city wouldn't give him a building permit. They say there's no cement, there's no bricks or plaster, and there's no limestone... There's no meat or eggs or poultry or onions, either. All of a sudden the cupboards are bare and the dogs have all the bones. I stood in a long line to buy meat and when it got to be my turn, I found myself at the egg seller's, but the eggs were finished, so I bought sugar... I should go buy cement on the black market? God forbid! Are we common criminals that we should do so? Take to trading on the black market in the autumn of our lives, when we should be donating to charity or doing good deeds?

No thanks, you're very sweet to offer, but I smoke filterless Homa cigarettes ...My son-in-law is fixing to buy one of those apartments across from Sa'i Park, only for the sake of the children, so that they can take some fresh air. I vowed to give Ahmad, Aqdas's son, five thousand *tomans* so he could go to America. They said it wasn't enough and looked down their noses at it. My daughter got indignant and wouldn't let me give it, so I didn't. Now I hear Aqdas has said "My aunt's gone back on her word." Now am I the sort of person to go back on her word? I swear by the hairs on your head, I never promised. I only took a vow that if my daughter gave birth to a son, I'd give five thousand *tomans* to Ahmad. My daughter had a miscarriage during her third pregnancy. In spite of that, I said I'd give it to him; the boy is a descendant of the house of the Prophet, and he'd like to go to America. Now, since I didn't give him the hand of my daughter, at least let him go to America. But they made such a fuss and ruckus about it that in the end, I wouldn't give it. I heard Aqdas said, "Let Auntie go blind, Ahmad's got to go to America!" They sent that one-eyed boy to America just so he could wash the dishes of the Westerners and sweep their floors. I heard he became very friendly with an old lady; this old woman kept him around... God forgive me for thinking such thoughts.

How could they get the money to send him? I don't know, they must have taken out a loan. Aqdas says, "I sold my bracelet and my heavy gold necklace..." I heard she sold her entire trousseau. I know they sent the boy on a military airplane. Do I know who arranged it for them? First they came to my son-in-law, Colonel Asadpur. He told them, "Such arrangements entail certain responsibilities. What if the boy were accidentally to fall out into the ocean or the plane were to crash? Then how could I answer to Aqdas?"

No, my dear, Aqdas is my niece, my sister's daughter. I know her very well, she isn't the type to save up a lot of money or anything like that. She's very sloppy… Once they said it was scissors that went into the child's eyes, once they said something else… I mean Ahmad's eye. His right eye is deformed. The rest of his face is not too bad. He has a very dark complexion, but his features, except for the swollen eye, are all right. Aqdas swears that she wasn't home, but if she wasn't, how come she's so insistent on sending the kid despite all obstacles to America? Huh? Is it for any other reason than that she feels it's her fault and wants to make it up to the kid? The stupid kid is trying to pass himself off as a child of the aristocracy. They sent the son of a vegetable seller to Alborz College! Well, now let them pay for it… I heard that Aqdas went off and became a maid. They hid it from me, but I know she was cleaning houses to pay for Ahmad's expenses. Now he's off to America, and some old lady's hankering for cockerel and brings Ahmad in to live with her. He drives her around town, washes her car, sets her shoes in front of her feet, washes her dishes. He does the gardening for her. Tsssk! God help us! A descendant of the house of the Prophet, in such pathetic circumstances. Now, what law says you have to go to America? You could go to England like my daughter and study medicine. I don't spend a single red cent on Man-sureh; their pocket money is all provided for, they even pay for their baths and soap and everything themselves.

That stupid boy was deficient from the beginning. In Alborz College, he became friends with the grandson of Sadiq ol-Dawleh. What an outrage! The son of Karim, the vegetable seller! Some people say—and let those who say it take responsibility in the next world for the truth or falsehood of the rumor—they say Ahmad's father moonlights as a pimp and a go-between. He found a maid for us and he probably arranged the maid's job for his wife, too. Whenever they're asked, "What does your father do?" they say he works in an office. Like hell he does! Now that the grandkid of Sadiq ol-Dawleh has gone to America, this one's gotta go, too. There's no one around to tell him, "you miscreant of a boy, Sadiq ol-Dawleh owns the whole village of Lavizan, are you trying to compare yourself to the grandson of Sadiq ol-Dawleh?" In a few years Sadiq ol-Dawleh's grandkid will be a member of parliament or a government minister, does Ahmad think he's going to make it to the ministry?… God preserve us.

…I've heard they sent a picture of Atefeh, Ahmad's sister, to the magazine *Today's Woman*, so she could compete in the Miss Iran pag-eant. Can you believe it! My niece is really out of her league on this one! With all the influential weapons I can bring to bear on the contest—my son-in-law, the few pennies I have—even I didn't let my daughter become Miss Iran, though they begged her to enter... I sent her to England. I said, "We are above such tinseled conceits." Who's more beautiful, Atefeh or my Mansureh? Of course my child is the prettier! She's fair-skinned and rosy-cheeked, while Atefeh is dark-complexioned and too tall. Atefeh's never going to be Miss Iran, they didn't even print her picture in the magazine! That got their goat. I said to my niece, I told her, "Aqdas, such things are beneath your dignity." She said Ahmad had bought a camera, took his sister's picture and sent it in. "Anyway," I said, "It just isn't right to send a photo of the legs of a girl descended from the Prophet's family for strange men to inspect." Then she butts in and says it didn't get to that point anyway.

I'd better be going, I don't want to overstay my welcome. Take some chocolate for the kids? No, my dear lady, thank you, though; if you would just be so kind as to keep my parcel, you will have done me a great service. If Aqdas should come to see you, please don't mention anything to her. Don't tell her that the title to the Khadem-abad property is with you. She'd be hurt. She'll say, "Why doesn't my aunt trust me, the child of her own sister?" When I get back from the trip, if I can't come myself, I'll send Azizollah Khan. Deliver my parcel over to him. No, for heaven's sake! I look on him as I would a brother. Anyway, once upon a time he was my son-in-law. He's a faithful man and he comes around to see us. No, there's not even a hint of what you're suggesting. I'm an old woman...

No, really, thank you kindly for offering, though. People are always bringing gifts for my son-in-law; my, how they do carry on—crate after crate of oranges, box after box of dried snacks, with every imaginable kind of fruit and nut in it, some in the shell, some without. They say that people are hired to sit from sunup to sundown to shell sunflower seeds with a little mallet or something. My son-in-law is a postal director; he's in charge of the mails from here clear to Isfahan. He's the director, a real big shot. What of it if he is my daughter's second husband? He was a police lieutenant when he came to ask for her hand, but my daughter brought good fortune upon him and he became the Right Honorable Colonel Asadpur. Azizollah Khan? There was nothing wrong with Azizollah Khan, just that he couldn't have children. He treated little Mansureh like an adopted child. But my daughter—the one he was married to—would say, "I want to have a kid from my own womb, to kick about in my tummy and suck at my breast."

Aqdas:

I was just passing by this way and I thought I'd drop in to say hello and pay my respects, since you, my good woman, do not honor us with your presence. Believe me, since the day that Ahmad left this city, my only sustenance has been the tears I shed. I sit at home and all of a sudden the desire to go out for a walk will possess me, so I step out into the lane and walk down to our neighbor's house, Azar Khanom. I fix her evening meal for her in hopes she'll listen to my woes... I go for a walk in Farah park and watch the people, wondering to myself which of them has a son stuck in a far-off land? Which mother suffers so in longing for her baby? When I see the boys sitting under the trees solving math problems, my heart just melts. How often my baby has paced back and forth beneath these trees memorizing his lessons, how often he would sit here to do his math homework. In the end, he didn't pass the college entrance exam. When I realize how empty the house is without him... No, no, I swear, I'm not crying . . . there's just something in my eye.

...My dear aunt said she made a vow on Ahmad's behalf? What a lie! Let her make a vow on behalf of her skinflint of a son-in-law! The day Ahmad was saying farewell, after I'd knocked myself out to hail a taxi we went from Amirabad to the house of my aunt's son-in-law, Asadpur, in Fawziyeh. He has no shame! He put his hand in his pocket and gave a measly fifty *tomans* to Ahmad as a bon voyage present. He's made millions upon millions by smuggling—Mansureh's told me all about it. I motioned to Ahmad not to take the money, and he didn't. Later on, of course, he regretted it. My boy wanted to say good-bye to everyone by putting his picture in the paper. It didn't work out. He took a picture in silhouette... here, take a look at these. My child is as beautiful as the shining moon! His right eye is half-closed. Scissors? No, it wasn't a pair of scissors that went in his eye. One day he was playing bows and arrows with his sister. Atefeh takes a piece of straw from a reed curtain and fastens a pin on the end of it, aims it at Ahmad and it goes right in the boy's eye. I had gone to the tailor; I'd sooner my legs had been broken! When I got back they were sitting on the doorstep, Ahmad with his hand over his eye... How I begged and pleaded with the doctors, prayed and made vows. His right eye is closed just a pinch. He sees all right, but his eye is deformed. What could I do? It was the hand of fate.

...With what pain and aggravation we sent him to Alborz College in hopes he would pass the college entrance exam, but he didn't. How much money does a fruit seller in Amirabad street make that he can afford to send his kid to prep school? Please do not let my dear aunt know that I was going every morning to the homes of Americans to do their ironing. I've been doing the same job for four years now.

I came here, if you would be so kind, to have you write Ahmad's address on this envelope in the language of the Americans. Mrs. Barbara always used to write it for me, but now she has gone to America to be with her mother. She goes every year for three or four months and brings back with her clothes, books and gramophone records. How these women spend their husbands' money! And the husbands are like little lambs; they don't say a word. I iron for Mrs. Barbara. She's introduced me to all her American friends and acquaintances, and I iron for them too. What wonderful houses and lives of leisure they all have! There's Akram, Mrs. Barbara's housekeeper, then there's the chauffeur, and the cook, who wears a white hat and a white coat, just like a doctor, when he goes in the kitchen. Mrs. Barbara's husband is the director-in-chief of I-don't-know-which ministry. The husband of every last one of them is a director general or an assistant director. They really look after their wives, who don't have to lift a finger around the house. Large sunny gardens, professional gardeners, swimming pools, tennis courts. All this for women who, in their own country, were the children of some janitor or laundry woman. I don't mean all of them, mind you. This loneliness has made me so spiteful. How I do go on...

...One night Mrs. Barbara had company so I went over to help out. First of all we go to buy groceries at this huge supermarket. She takes this buggy, similar to a baby buggy, only made out of wire, and piles it full of meat, turkey, chicken, milk, eggs, sugar, tin cans of every imaginable thing, until it's so full I have to go and get a second buggy. It's no wonder that there's a shortage of everything! That evening I put on an apron and went to work. I counted seventeen Iranian gentlemen, all of them good-looking and muscular, and every last one of them had a foreign wife, from all parts of the globe. They don't mix with Iranian couples. They say that Iranians are barbaric, dirty liars. Well then, my esteemed lady, why did you marry an Iranian? No one dares to ask them... Mrs. Akram was saying, "Look, the gentleman with the glass of whiskey has a Swiss wife and is a senior member of the Bureau of Plan Organization. That one there, smoking the cigar, has an important post in the oil company. The other one over there is a university professor." Despite all this, their wives always have their passports in their hands so that whenever they get tired of it, they can run along home. They're always having arguments over the religion and nationality of the children.

Mrs. Barbara has a copper *aftabeh* and a brass basin which she's put in a corner of her living room! She's got a huge wooden spoon and fork, made in Qazvin, which she's nailed on the wall of the dining room... God help us!

...As for poor old me, I've ironed so much my wrist has swollen up and I can't move my shoulder. Eight hours' work a day, from seven in the morning to three in the afternoon, just to make a few dollars for my boy. These infidels may pay well, but you've really got to work for it. They even iron their sheets and their dish-cloths! But now that Mrs. Barbara is away, nothing's going on. Sometimes I go to iron the shirts of her husband, Gholam-Ali Khan. Now that the lady of the house is away, the man has the run of the place. In the evenings he sits on a rug next to the pool, puts his cloak over his shoulders, smokes the *qalyan*, reads the paper, and does the crossword puzzles.

...Ahmad used to say, "If I get accepted to study electrical engineering at Aryamehr, I'll stay right here, but if not, I'm going to get to America no matter what! All my buddies have gone, the grandson of Sadiq ol-Dawleh, the son of Mofakham." Ahmad didn't get accepted at Aryamehr, in fact, he failed the entrance exam altogether. We bought newspaper after newspaper in hopes of finding his name somewhere. I kept thinking, O God, O God, let him be called for military service, but they wouldn't take him on account of his eye. My boy was so upset he developed a fever. His temperature was three-tenths of a degree above normal in the mornings and a half degree by afternoon. He'd put his head in his hands and cry. His legs hurt so much he couldn't walk. The doctors said he'd contracted Malta fever, some said he just had a nervous condition. As soon as talk of going to America came up and I told him I'd dig up the money from under some stone if I had to, but that I'd send him to America, his fever broke and his legs got better. I sold the quilts from my trousseau, my heavy gold necklace, my earrings, my sewing machine. I took my silver out of hock, my television, I sold them all. I went everywhere, groveling and pleading, nobody would lend a helping hand. I knew they had sent Mansureh on a military airplane, so I went to see Officer Asadpur and fell at his feet. I swore upon all that was holy in hopes of getting him to send Ahmad on a military plane, but he could not be prevailed upon. In the end, Ahmad went to Bushire and took a steamer. Mrs. Barbara arranged it for him, she even got him admitted to a university. She sent all the letters and did all the paperwork herself and even gave him a letter to take to her mother and sister. My boy worked as a crewman on board the ship, cleaning up the barf of the passengers until they got to America. He's been working in America, too, but what jobs! He washes dishes, does gardening, drives old ladies around, washes cars, washes dogs, drags hotel guests' suitcases up and down the stairs. God bless him, the poor thing once wrote me that he only had thirty-seven dollars left. He still hasn't learned the American language real well.

If only he had been accepted to study electrical engineering at Aryamehr, he'd have stayed right here, but now he just suffers, and in a foreign country of all places. Even if he had been accepted at Aryamehr, there was a student strike every time you turned round and the exams were always being cancelled, and my boy would have either had a nervous breakdown or they'd have come to tell me he'd been killed or something. That's just what happened with Azar's boy; he was accepted at National University, but when he'd set off for school in the mornings she was like to die of fear until he'd get back.

...Anyway, thank God that Ahmad wasn't forced to become a nurse like Mansureh and work for peanuts. You know, Mansureh had just turned fifteen when my cousin married Officer Asadpur, and my aunt had to account somehow for Mansureh's presence in her household. She had been whispering to me about marrying Mansureh off to Ahmad, but Ahmad said, "Mother, I won't take a wife until I go off to America and finish my studies." So, my aunt told Asadpur that Mansureh was his wife's sister. Later on they made out that Mansureh was found on the doorstep as a baby, which got the poor child all confused and upset. Now she's gone off to England, where she suffers still. Poor thing, she sits by the bedside of the dead till daybreak, brings bedpans for the patients, changes the sheets.

...That Mansureh's studying medicine!? I bet that's what my dear aunt told you. There's not a truthful bone in my auntie's body. She's busy morning till night weaving herself a tangled web of lies and half-truths. Mansureh herself sent me a letter saying, "Cousin, if you only knew what I go through from sunup to sundown. I was so pleased with myself to be going abroad. Going abroad, huh! I'm rooming with four other girls, three Indians and a Pakistani, and the Pakistani won't speak with the Indians. We've got to scrub the floors each day and play the maid, and on top of that, we're supposed to smile at the patients." She wrote that the people over there wouldn't dream of doing such lowly work, so they lure innocent kids from the four corners of the earth to do it for them. You can't eat the food there, either. It's mostly boiled fish and shriveled-up potatoes. At the end of her letter she wrote: "How hard one has to toil to reach *Behesht-e Zahra*." Do you see what circumstances our precious children have fallen into? Today they're working their fingers to the bone studying and tomorrow, when they get back, who knows what kind of a job they'll be able to get.

I tell myself, O God, O God, let an American girl fall in love with Ahmad so my boy can stay over there. There's a hint of it in the air, too. He works in the house of an old American woman . . . Mrs. Barbara's mother? No, a friend of Mrs. Barbara's mother. Mrs. Barbara's mother is poor folk. After Ahmad went to her house, he wrote that she didn't have a house, just a little room filled with more junk than can be had in a Syrian bazaar, a hodgepodge jumble of furniture. The only thing in the room of interest was a Turkoman carpet that had come from Iran...

...I think—that is I should say, I pray—that the granddaughter of this old woman who is Ahmad's landlord will go sweet on him. One night he saved her from the part of town where the blacks live . . . I'd really love it if a girl like Mrs. Barbara is in store for Ahmad. If you only knew how Mrs. Barbara dotes on Gholam-Ali Khan. I've told you her bad points, it's only fair to tell you about the good as well. Whenever her man comes home from the ministry, she runs out to greet him, gives him a big kiss, hugs him, fixes him a drink and puts it in his hand, massages his temples, sits on his lap. The relatives of Mrs. Barbara's husband are all country bumpkins; Gholam-Ali Khan is the only one that turned out well and was able to go to America. Mrs. Barbara had an artist paint her picture. She's standing in the middle with blonde hair and a red dress, and all around her stand the female relatives of her husband in their chadors, pointing out Mrs. Barbara to one another. It looks like they are all in awe of her great good fortune.

...When my dear aunt despaired of us, she sent Mansureh to England. Now, whenever she sits down to chat, she says, "Ahmad wanted my daughter, but I didn't approve." May I be struck blind if I tell a word of a lie—it was we who didn't approve!

You've finished writing them? A thousand thanks! That's ten envelopes for the next ten letters... Are you kidding? My dear aunt's son-in-law can't read American writing... A colonel!? It's just like her to say that. He's the policeman at the post office at the Dawlat intersection in Qolhak district... I told you what tall tales she tells. They have an orderly and a maid? I've never heard anything so ridiculous... She washes the kids' diapers every day herself while my cousin is slaving in the kitchen. Ahmad used to say that the signpost to Auntie's house was a clothesline decked with diapers. In the autumn of her life, dear Auntie is in league with Aziz, her daughter's first husband, selling smuggled goods. Officer Asadpur lends them a hand too. I've heard that Aziz still hankers after my cousin. He went with my aunt to Shiraz and brought back opium. Heroin, hashish, they smuggle everything. By God, I was afraid they'd get a hold of Ahmad and corrupt the boy. That's why I practically killed myself to send him away.

…My dear aunt brought a package to our house and asked that we keep it for her. She said it was cashmere and some silk brocade and silver and the deed to some property, but I know it was opium. She said, in return for the favor, I'll pray for you when I visit the Imam Reza. But she's not the praying kind. She's going to Mashhad to get some opium. I wouldn't take the package from her. I said, "My husband will come home and give me heck for taking it." She said, "Just keep it two or three days, Azizollah will come and get it from you. You'll recognize him by the piece of paper I'll give him. I'll have my daughter write on it, 'May God be with you always.'" Nothing's sacred, they'll drag the name of God into anything. I wouldn't take the package. I was afraid.

Aqdas: Hello, Auntie dear, it's so nice to see you. You know I worship the ground you walk on!

Effat ol-Moluk: And hello to you; let me kiss that radiant face of yours!

Aqdas: Auntie dear, I dreamed of you last night. May God strike me blind if I'm lying. You were sitting next to a pool filled with water, and it was full of red and gold fish. Your grandchildren were there, too.

Effat ol-Moluk: God willing, it's a good omen. Water in a dream means light.

Aqdas: Where is my cousin? How are her precious children?

Effat ol-Moluk: Your cousin has gone to the public bath, for a ritual purification. The kids are asleep.

Aqdas: Auntie dear, God blacken my face, but I think I may have jinxed your grandchildren in my dream. They've gotten so cute and chubby, I'm afraid of the evil eye on their account. I've come to say you should burn some wild rue to protect them.

Effat ol-Moluk: Consider it done.

Aqdas: May you never know misfortune.

Effat ol-Moluk: Well, dear, you've brightened up my home with your presence. How are you, and what news do you bring?

Aqdas: Well, since you mention it, if I don't tell my troubles to you, Auntie dear, who can I tell them to? Ahmad's no longer working for that old American lady.

Effat ol-Moluk: Didn't you tell me that an American girl had fallen in love with him?

Aqdas: Oh, Auntie, I may have said a thing or two—you sometimes have to in order to keep up with the neighbors, but who's kidding who? What American girl would fall in love with my skin-and-bones son? American women only marry robust Iranian men in perfect health so that they can pop out flawless, good-looking, international children. In one letter he wrote me, "Mother, compared to American guys, I'm a pullet. They sometimes grow to be two meters tall and drink four glasses of milk a day. Once I drank two glasses of milk and got diarrhea."

Effat ol-Moluk: How many times have I told you to take my adopted girl as a wife for your son, that they would live here happily ever after and you can find a job or a source of income for Ahmad? You're very clever, all to no good purpose. You've been to school through the eighth grade, you read the newspapers, you watch television. You should have known better.

Aqdas: It wasn't in the stars, Auntie.

Effat ol-Moluk: Nowadays Mansureh can barely walk, they've got her running around like a dog, eight hours a day of nursing the sick... I'll get up and make some tea.

Aqdas: Don't trouble yourself, instead help me solve my problem. I've got to send some money for Ahmad anyway I can. I can no longer iron—I was hiding this from you—I can no longer iron at the Americans' houses; my shoulder is about to explode with pain and my wrist is swollen. See? I was making eighty to one hundred dollars a month sweating over the iron, but I can't do it anymore.

Effat ol-Moluk: (*Silence*)

Aqdas: Auntie dear, I'll be glad to take your package now, no matter what's in it.

Effat ol-Moluk: Oh, go on! I only mentioned that package business to see how much my niece is willing to do for her aunt.

Aqdas: Auntie dear, you are dearer to me than my own eyes. I'd like to—not be partners, you see, because I have no money in hand to become a partner—work with you and Azizollah Khan, so that I can somehow send a hundred dollars a month for Ahmad. My boy has been reduced to eating bread with hot water and vinegar for the last three weeks and I'm afraid he'll starve to death. What a mistake I made! You know that Ahmad's life is my life, if he… he's dearer to me than all my other children and Karim Aqa put together.

Effat ol-Moluk: Well, I'll tell you, I really can't do anything to help. Aziz and I don't have much business to speak of that you should become our partner. I probably see Aziz about once a year, anyway once a month at the most. After all, he was once my son-in-law. The poor fellow hasn't yet taken another wife and he's fond of his ex-wife's children. What can I do? He buys lollipops for the girls, holds them, takes them for walks on the wooden bridge. Officer Asadpur doesn't have time for such things. He's always saying he's on call. Aziz, well, he takes on the role of a father, the kids call him uncle. Besides that, Mansureh is his daughter, too. If you could see the letters she writes for Aziz…

Aqdas: Auntie, I'm family, I won't say a word to anyone. Remember that day at lunch when you vowed to give five thousand *tomans* to Ahmad if this deal came off without any headache? Azizollah was there, too. After lunch he took his trousers off and put on Officer Asadpur's pajamas. You brought opium for him to smoke. I was clearing away the dishes, his back was to me. My cousin was giving her breast to her baby. Azizollah Khan said, "It's this kind. As long as we don't get caught..." You gestured to him and he stopped in mid-sentence.

Effat ol-Moluk: God strike me down if I'm lying, I don't have any package here that relates to any kind of business transaction. I was just trying to test you...

Aqdas: Do you want me to tell you the truth?

Effat ol-Moluk: You haven't been lying up to this point, have you?

Aqdas: Mansureh told me about the whole thing... She said you bought an airplane ticket for her with the money you made by smuggling. She said, thanks be to God that she was leaving this house of lies, deceit, and drug-smuggling.

Effat ol-Moluk: There's an old saying: "You can raise another's flesh and blood as your own, but you can never win its loyalty."

Aqdas: Thank God I am still young, I'll find work... Even if I have to dig it out of the earth... I'll go and be a housekeeper for the Americans.

Effat ol-Moluk: You mean you'll be their maid...

Aqdas: It's a sight more honorable than smuggling and breaking the law. I'm earning my bread with the sweat of my brow... I read in a magazine that mankind became civilized through the fruits of his labor.

Effat ol-Moluk: I can hear the children, they've woken up. They're so sweet, one like sugar, the other like honey.

Ebrahim Golestan

1922–

From a family of Shi'i Muslim clerics, Ebrahim Golestan was born and raised in Shiraz, where his father served as mayor for a time and ran a newspaper from which the family took its name. After high school, Golestan briefly attended Tehran University and entered into the employ of the National Iranian Oil Company.

From the late 1940s through the early 1970s, Golestan was a photographer, translator, publisher, movie-maker, and writer of fiction. He translated works of Mark Twain, George Bernard Shaw and Ernest Hemingway, and four volumes of short stories: *Āzar, māh-e ākher-e pā'iz* (Azar, the last month of autumn, 1948), *Shekār-e sāyeh* (Shadow-hunting, 1955), *Juy-o divār-o teshneh* (The stream, the wall and the thirsty one, 1967), and *Madd-o meh* (Tide and mist, 1969).

In 1965 Golestan produced and directed an important feature film called *Khest va āyeneh* (Mudbrick and mirror). A second feature film of his reached movie theatres in 1974. Called *Asrār-e ganj-e darreh-ye jenni* (Secrets of the treasure of the haunted valley, 1974, 1978), it parallels a novel by the same name, which exists in two unpublished translations, one by the author and the other by Paul Sprachman, who provides a plot summary in "Ebrahim Golestan's *The Treasure*: A Parable of Cliché and Consumption" in *Iranian Studies* 15 (1982).

In the mid-1970s Golestan emigrated to England. During the 1980s he was reportedly working on a history of modern Iran and the course of modernist Persian literature.

Esmat's Journey

Translated by Carter Bryant

She trembled when she reached the courtyard of the shrine. She had been trembling ever since the start of the trip, ever since that unlucky night when there had been so many customers and she had been tired and weak and not really up to much, and had fallen sick. It had ended up in a fight, and she had been slapped, and finally, in between convulsive sobbing and a splitting headache, she had conceived the idea of running away and doing penance at the shrine. She had been trembling all along the way out of excitement at having made the pilgrimage at all, out of excitement at realizing that she might ultimately reach her goal. And now she had reached it, and she trembled in the courtyard before entering the shrine. She had lost patience and courage, and the entrance hall was so awesome, and the mediating holy glow that would redeem her lay there in the deep, dark heart of the tomb. She was impatient. She had forgotten to ask anyone as to the proper ways of penitence. She went up the steps of the terrace and, in unconscious reverence, knelt down, and wept there on the threshold of the sepulcher.

When she raised her head, her eyes had already grown accustomed to the light, and she felt that everything was washed clean and that there was no one there but herself. The multitude of people milling around the high-domed sanctuary failed to dispel her solitude. It was as if no human being had ever gone beyond that threshold and no glance had ever reached the limits of the sepulcher and it had remained so clean, so untouched, virgin. Now she had reached it, and there she was alone, and whoever else there was nobody but herself; it was she herself alone with the immediate link with being, with the grillwork around the center of sanctity. And she wept.

Kneeling there, caught in this self-realization, it was as if all the years of her life had become inconsequential, as though it had been someone else's life, as if she had returned to the first day of time. She had come to the realization now that no one had really ever loved her, that never had she loved anyone, that never had she really existed. She put her finger through the bars and stroked the polished hardness of them, searching for the sanctified dust screened from her by the grillwork. She ran her finger along the dust and rubbed it over her eyelids. She pressed her lips to the bars, until the pressing kiss turned into a greedy sucking to absorb all that was godly.

"Sister, may your pilgrimage be recompensed." She turned to see a sayyid, tall and handsome, eyebrows thick and full, red cheeks, black beard, and velvety eyes, gazing upon her with solemn compassion and clemency.

The sayyid spoke again. "These tears of yours are pearls, sister." The woman wiped her eyes, brushed the tears from her cheeks and, overwhelmed with awe, gave him greeting.

The sayyid, murmuring a prayer, fixed his heavy, dignified gaze on the back of his hand and the agate gems of his ring and spoke softly, "Your chador has slipped off your head, sister." And he gave her a moment to replace the chador over her head, then said, "Let your good deed be completed, allow me to recite a verse of praise to the Imam on your behalf, worthy of your bitter tears." And he began chanting in a steady bass.

From the moment she had crossed the threshold of the sepulcher, the outside world had faded away, and in her mind nothing remained of names or faces or features and memory, not even thoughts for the future, nothing but her state of ecstasy. Under the shadow of the sayyid's voice, the world once again came into being, one that was a negation of past memories. Memories of the nights at the house were swept away, the smell of sweat vanished, and the terrible bloodstain at the end of her anguish. The drunkenness and the nausea were dispelled. The man whose breath failed him, the man with a heavy body, the man smelling of manure, the man whose manliness under his round, balloon-tight stomach dangled like the last autumn leaf from the hollow trunk of a tree, panting in useless desire, unable to reach her. The man with a knife between his shoulders, who had burst through the door with a single kick, crying, "Esmat!" And when the fellow lying on her, frightened and confused, had jumped up and fled, the man had fallen on top of her, all covered with blood, wiping his bloody hands over her face; he had pressed his lips to her neck and on her breast, and moaned, and she had uttered not a sound. And then she had seen that there was a knife plunged up to the hilt in his back, and that there was blood flowing from the wound onto her breast. She had remained mute, and then the man died. She had remained mute, and then fallen asleep beneath the corpse.

Esmat. Esmat. Esmat.

Esmat was moved to tears. The incantation of the professional reader had the odor of rosewater, and brought warmth to her cheeks. She stood between the sepulcher and the sayyid. She shut her eyes and silently implored, "O Imam, forgive me!"

Behind the grillwork of the sepulcher lay the Grave. The sayyid broke off his holy words and said, "May God recompense your tears. Amen, by the truth of God, by the truth of the sanctity of this sepulcher."

"O God," said the woman, wiped her cheeks with her head-covering, and kissed the metal bars.

The sayyid asked, "Do you know the proper way to kiss the sepulcher?"

"What?" she said, turning to look at him. The sayyid had noble, affectionate, velvety eyes. Beneath the dome echoed murmurs of helplessness and supplication, as people circled the sepulcher with fear, tears and hope.

"All actions are governed by certain rules," the sayyid told her sternly but gently. "You must learn the rules and rituals of pilgrimage. This sepulcher is dear and holy. Do you know the rituals?"

"No," she said, and was afraid lest she had already done something wrong.

"You have to know the right way to do it. Why didn't you ask?"

Helplessly, she said, "I... just arrived today. This is the first time I ever made a pilgrimage."

"May God accept and bless it. Where is your home?"

"I'm just a poor wretch. I don't have a home."

"No. You mustn't say such things. Your home is the abode of bliss. This weeping of yours is the sign of a pure heart. Did you make an oblation? A vow?"

"No."

"Eh! Well, first you must make an oblation for yourself, for your children. Promise something to charity."

"What children? I have no one. I'm alone."

"Alone? Then who did you come on this pilgrimage with?"

"I came alone."

"Alone is God. A woman does not travel alone, especially on pilgrimage."

The woman bowed her head and said, "Well, I'm alone. What can I do? I'm alone." Then she said softly, "It's as if all at once He summoned me." And she was calm, and knew that she had found refuge. There was the smell of rosewater.

The sayyid spoke kindly to her. "You are certainly a woman of great good fortune to have been summoned by the Imam himself."

Near them stood a woman, her back to the sepulcher, staring up at the vault of the dome. The sayyid spoke softly: "Now it is time to circumambulate the tomb." He nudged the woman forward and followed along close behind, reciting the votive prayer. She could hear him praying behind her as she walked along moving her hands from one bar of the grillwork to another, passing among the other people milling around the sepulcher. The sayyid, now walking along beside her, interrupted his prayer with "You are indebted to His Perfection, the holy Imam. You have an obligation to fulfill to Him."

Turning at the first corner of the tomb, the woman said, "How should I? I am so unworthy!"

"Stay here, under the shadow of His Perfection. It is a great glory to serve him here."

"What must I do then?"

"I will show you the rites myself, with His gracious help. You see, many pilgrims come here. For a day or two, sometimes several days, they stay in His gracious presence." They passed another corner of the sepulcher. "These pilgrims have needs. They need mending... and tending. You will make some money out of it, enough to live on. Whenever your heart is troubled, you can come here to the shrine. It's good business, it's performing good deeds, and it's a constant pilgrimage."

They turned the next corner. "What should I do?" the woman asked.

"Come stay with me. My house, my humble little hut, is round the back. Here beneath the shadow of the shrine. There are several sisters of the faith dwelling with me there. Pilgrims come there; pilgrims, students and others of the faithful. They have needs."

They turned the final corner, thus completing the circumambulation. The sayyid said, "And for rendering lawful service, you may rest easy and live as one of the family."

The woman stopped. She saw in the gentle caressing of the velvety eyes the luminous acceptance of all her prayers. She beheld the end of her wandering and the achievement of grace. The sayyid spoke with determining kindliness. "I myself will arrange everything for you."

Close by them a woman was moaning before the grillwork of the holy tomb. When they emerged into the courtyard it was noon, and the clear, high voice of the muezzin sounded through the flapping of pigeons' wings: "Come ye to deliverance!"

Jalal Al-e Ahmad

1923—1969

The son of a Shi'i Muslim cleric, Jalal Al-e Ahmad was born and raised in Tehran. He pursued formal education there to the doctoral dissertation stage in Persian literature at Tehran University. Al-e Ahmad's first collection of short stories, *Did-o bāzdid* (Exchange of visits), appeared in 1946. There followed *Az ranji ke mibarim* (Our suffering, 1947), *Seh-tār* (Setar, 1949), and *Zan-e ziyādi* (The unwanted woman, 1952, 1964). Representative Al-e Ahmad stories in translation appear in *Literature East & West* 20 (1980) and *Iranian Society: An Anthology of Writings by Jalal Al-e Ahmad* (1982). In 1950 Al-e Ahmad married writer Simin Daneshvar (b. 1921) and later acknowledged her important role in his emergence as a leading writer in Iran in the 1960s.

From the mid-1950s, Al-e Ahmad turned to the novel, publishing four: *Sargozasht-e kanduhā* (Tale of the beehives, 1955), *Modir-e madraseh* (The school principal, 1958), *Nun va'l-qalam* (By the pen, 1961), and *Nefrin-e zamin* (Cursing of the earth, 1968). Translations exist of The School Principal (1974 and 1986) and By the Pen (1989), while a plot summary of *Nefrin-e Zamin* appears in *Literature East & West* 20 (1980).

Besides short stories and novels, Al-e Ahmad authored some fourteen volumes of prose nonfiction, chief among them being: *Khasi dar miqāt* (Lost in the crowd, 1964, English translation, 1985) based upon his pilgrimage to Mecca, and his most famous work, the polemical essay *Gharbzadegi*, which has been published in multiple translations with the titles *Weststruckness* (1982), *Plagued by the West* (1982), and *Occidentosis* (1984).

A posthumous volume of Al-e Ahmad stories called *Panj dāstān* (Five stories) appeared in 1971. Ten years later his controversial autobiographical narrative on the childlessness of his marriage called *Sangi bar guri* (A stone on a grave), written in 1964, was published in Tehran, only to be banned shortly thereafter. His short stories have been reprinted in Iran in recent years.

The American Husband

Translated by Judith Wilks

"Vodka? No, thank you. I can't take vodka. If it were whiskey, then maybe I'd go for it. Just a little, enough to cover the bottom of the glass. Thanks very much. No, I can't tolerate water, either. Have you got any soda? That's too bad. That filthy dog's habits have had their effect on me. If you knew how he used to drink whiskey sodas! As long as I lived in my father's house, I never touched alcohol. My father himself still never touches the stuff. Not that he's a holy roller. But, well, it was just never the custom at our house. But the first thing that filthy dog taught me was how to make a whiskey soda. As soon as he would come home from work, there had to be a whiskey soda within reach. Before he even washed his hands. And if I had known what work he did with those hands …Sometimes when he wasn't home I felt like having some of his whiskey. Of course, that was before my daughter was born. And I was so fed up with the loneliness. But I didn't like the stuff. It burned my throat so badly. However much he insisted that I drink with him, I never did. But when I became pregnant, he insisted that I drink beer. He said it was good for my milk. But never whiskey. Until the very end I never got used to it.

But that day when I found out about his occupation, I drank that whiskey straight down, in spite of myself. Then I poured one for myself and one for that 'girlfriend' of his. That is, his former fiancée. Actually, she was the one who came and told me about it. The two of us sat there drinking and commiserating. If that wasn't the time to cry, when is? Just think, a girl with a degree, pretty—you know, from a respectable family, with everything going for her, someone who had learned English—in any event, not in need of taking just any man for a husband, then this? ...Can you believe it? The country's full of these well-educated young Iranian men. All these engineers and doctors... But all those damned guys go and take European or American wives. They marry the neighborhood postman's daughter or the cashier at the local supermarket or the dental assistant who once put cotton in their mouths. And then just look at how they show off! You'd think they were Susan Hayward or Shirley MacLaine or Elizabeth Taylor. Let me describe them to you. The other evening I saw one of these girls. Two months ago she married one of these Iranian guys and she's been here for two weeks. Her husband received a telegram recalling him because he has become a member of Parliament. The landlord called me so that his foreign tenant wouldn't be lonely. So she would have someone who speaks her language to talk to. This was just last week. That girl with that Texas accent of hers... No. Don't laugh. I'm not joking. You should have seen how wide she opened her mouth when she spoke. Her fingernails were still rough. It was obvious that she used to wash a lot of dishes every day. Do you know what she said then? She said, We came and brought civilization to you and taught you how to work with gas lights and washing machines... and things of this sort. It was obvious from her hands that she still scrubbed laundry by hand in a tub in Texas! And then all these high and mighty airs! She was a herdsman's daughter. Not one of those who had discovered oil on their property and become mighty oil barons. No. One of those who looked after other people's cattle. Of course I said nothing to her. But one man in the group spoke up in broken English and said that if that was what she meant by civilization, then the company that sends you to us as a bonus along with the washing machines can just keep it all. Of course, the girl didn't understand. That is, she didn't understand the guy's English. I had to translate for her. Then, instead of answering him, she turned to me and said that I must be an immoral, loose woman for my husband to have divorced me. She came right out and said that. Because I—in order to soften the harshness of that guy's words and to make the girl feel less lonely—I had told her my

story, that I had been in America and had an American husband and
got a divorce. And that I had come back. And when I told her what
work my husband did and that was the reason I had divorced him, do
you know what she said? She said there was nothing wrong with that.
That there was nothing shameful about any occupation... It must be
that his family wanted to get rid of you so your child couldn't get his
inheritance. Or it must be that you're immoral, and things like this. It
didn't matter to her at all that she had just arrived! She behaved as if
we were obligated to her. Well, obviously. Her husband was a member of Parliament. Well, if these damned guys didn't go and marry
such whores, then a girl like myself wouldn't go and put herself
through all that... No, thank you. Don't give me too much. I'll over-
do it. Whiskey on an empty stomach. Just another little bit, enough to
cover the bottom of the glass, that'll do. A little piece of cheese
wouldn't be bad, if you've got any... Thanks. Oh! Is this cheese? Why
is it so white? And so salty! Where is it from? ...Liqvan? Where is
that? ...I'm not familiar with it. I know the Dutch and Danish ones,
but not this one... I don't like it at all. That one with pistachios is better. Thanks. What was I saying now? Oh, yes. I met him at the
American club. I had been going to language classes for a year. You
know how crowded it was. When I got my diploma I signed up for the
university admission exams. But you know how it is. In the midst of
twenty or thirty thousand people, how can one get admitted? That's
why Father had suggested that I go to language classes. It will be fun,
he said, and you'll learn a foreign language at the same time. At that
time that filthy s.o.b. was the instructor. He was tall. Nice-looking.
Blond. A perfect American. And he had such long hands. They covered the entire surface of the workbook. Well, anyway, we liked each
other. From the very first. And he was very well-mannered. First he
invited me to an exhibition of paintings. At the new club in Abbasa-
bad. The type of paintings that show a head without the body, or just
spots of color side by side, or draw a pillow and call it a person and put
a goblet on its head, or two brown spots in the middle of two meters
of canvas. He had also invited Father and Mother, who were overjoyed. He took us home in his own car. And such beautiful manners.
He opened the car door for us and such. And this for Father and
Mother, who still don't even own a car. Well, anyway, you know.
Things really took off after that evening. Then he asked me to a
dance. One of their holidays. I think it was Thanksgiving. Oh! How
could you not know what that is? America wouldn't be America without its Thanksgiving! I mean, it's the day of giving thanks. It's the day

when the Americans got rid of the last Indians. Father gave permission, of course. Why shouldn't he? I had no one to practice English with outside of class. A language is useless unless you practice it. Then, too, we had decided that I would give him Persian lessons. Outside of class, of course. Once a week he would come to our house for this. That's what we had agreed upon. You don't know what a celebration that was. They had carved holes in a pumpkin where the eyes and nose and mouth should be and lit a candle inside it. And what a dance! And now I understood a little English, so I didn't feel left out. And besides, there were many Iranians there. But though he insisted that I drink some beer that night, I didn't. He seemed pleased even at that. When he brought me back home he congratulated my mother for having a daughter like me. I translated it myself. I had already become a sort of translator. Things went on like this for eight months. We went boating at the Karaj Dam, or to the movies. We went to the museum. We went to the bazaar. We went to Shemiran and Shah Abdolazim, and many other places I would never have seen except for him. Then on Christmas Eve he invited us to his house. You know what Christmas Eve is, right? Father and Mother were there, too. Fafar was there, too. You don't know him? That's my brother's name. Fereydun. They had sent him two roast turkeys all the way from Los Angeles... Oh! Don't you know anything at all? It's right in the vicinity of Hollywood. They don't only send them to him. They send them to everyone so they won't feel homesick on the eve of the holiday. When they send a guy like that s.o.b. to Tehran especially for that job, of course he gets turkeys and beer and cigarettes and whiskey and chocolates as well. Honestly, I wouldn't have minded if he were a murderer, a thief, a felon, a gangster—but not someone with that occupation... Another little bit of whiskey, please, just enough to cover the bottom of the glass. It doesn't seem to be American stuff. They drink bourbon. It has an earthy taste. Yes, this is Scotch. It's very crisp. Just like the English themselves. Well, what was I saying? Yes. That very evening he asked for my hand. Formally, at the dinner table. And I myself had to act as interpreter. Isn't that funny? No one had ever found a husband this way. First he carved the turkey and put it on our plates. Then he opened the champagne and poured some for Father and Mother as well. He poured some for everyone. Of course, Mother didn't drink it. But Father did. I myself tasted it, too. At first it was sharp and acidic, but when the sharpness disappeared it left a sweet taste. Then he said, tell your father that I would like to ask for your hand. He insisted that I say it sentence by sentence, very distinctly, that he had done his military service—he was exempt from taxes—his blood type was B—he was in good health—he earned $1,500 a month, which would be $800 when he returned. He has his own house in Washington and wouldn't have to make any rent or mortgage payments. His father and mother are in Los Angeles and don't interfere with his life. And things of this sort. Father was receptive to the idea from that very first night. He had told me, be careful, daughter dear, not one in a thousand girls is lucky enough to marry an American. That's no joke. That is, they can't. I can still hear his words. But you yourself know best. You're the one who has to live with your husband. But ask him for a week so you can think it over. And that's what I did. Of course, the matter was settled right from the start. The whole family knew about it. There were two or three parties and get-togethers and such formalities. And such envy! And how many girls were paraded in front of him! All of my girl cousins stopped talking with me because of this. My father was right. This was no joke. All the girls wanted him. But the guy had asked for me. Would it make any sense for me to be self-sacrificing and recommend another girl to take my place? In the midst of all this, my grandmother was the only one to mutter her objections. She said, We have people from Kashan in the family, and from Isfahan, and even from Bushire. And we know all of them. But we've never had an American before, how do we know who he is? He's the groom, you can't go investigating his family background and asking around about the ins and outs of his affairs… And other such grandmotherly advice. She didn't even come to our wedding. She went to Mashhad so she wouldn't have to be there. As for myself, I was overjoyed. We had notified the officials. The whole family was there, as well as a number of Americans. And so many pictures of our wedding banquet. One of my husband's friends even took movies of it. God save us from these Americans! They wanted to know about everything. They kept coming and asking me all sorts of questions. I mean, I was the bride. But did that occur to them? They'd ask, what's this thing called? Why are they crushing the candies like this? What's written on the cake? Where do they bring the wild rue from? …But in any case, I survived it. At the wedding reception, two family members who had been prepared beforehand were employed as drivers for their departments. And they gave me a dowry of one hundred thousand tomans. He recited the Muslim formula of conversion, 'There is no god but God…,' right there at our wedding banquet. And he had such trouble with it! How we laughed at the way he recited it! …All of that to make our wedding acceptable to the law of Islam! And what about his occupation? Well, he was a teacher of English. And then, too, on the marriage document they had written that he was a lawyer. Two embassy staff members were his witnesses. Just with that lie that he had told me, I could have him thrown in prison. And sued for damages. At least I could have forced him to pay six hundred dollars more in addition to the four hundred he now sends me for my daughter's expenses. But what's the use? I didn't even want to see him anymore. I wasn't even willing to put up with him for an hour. That is why he finally agreed to give me the child, because otherwise, according to their laws, he would have been able to keep the child. Of course, I gave up my dowry. May he take his money to his grave. If you knew how he earned his money! How could one make a necklace out of such money and wear it? Or buy meat and rice and eat it? That girl said the same thing that day. His former girlfriend. His fiancée. What do I know. That was the first and last time I saw her. She had come on a direct flight from Los Angeles to Washington. She had rented a car at the airport and come straight to our house. In the two years I had been in Washington there had been no word from anyone in his family. He used to say, the distances are great, and everyone's busy with his own affairs, and things of this sort. I was more comfortable with things that way, too. With no one looking over my shoulder. Sometimes I would write to them, or they to us. I sent them pictures of my daughter, too. They sent her birthday presents. We sent them her first-year pictures, and after that there was no word from them until that girl arrived. She greeted me and introduced herself. She very politely asked if I wasn't fed up with the loneliness, and she raved about how pretty my daughter was, and things of this sort. I was tinkering with the washing machine, which had some problem at the time. Quite unpretentiously she helped me. We straightened it out and emptied the clothes into it, then went and sat down and she began to tell me about herself. She said she had been his fiancée when he was sent to the Korean War. When the war was over, he didn't come back to Los Angeles. He took a job here in Washington. And she said, God knows what those poor young men had been through in Korea that they would accept such work when they returned. I asked, but what do you mean, 'such work?' She was shocked that I still didn't know what my husband did for a living. Then she said, Of course no work is shameful. But his whole family had disowned him because of his work. And he couldn't persuade them otherwise… Now my heart was filled with dread that he might be an executioner. Or in charge of a gas chamber or the electric chair. Actually, even these jobs could be considered as part of the legal profession, in a way. But that job of his? When she told me what it was, everything went black before my eyes. My reaction was so obvious that the girl herself got up and went over to the buffet, brought out the whiskey bottle, poured a glass and gave it to me, then poured another for herself and continued her story... He had been the third fiancée she had lost in this way. The first one had been killed in the Korean War. The second one was killed in Vietnam, and the third one turned out this way. She said, No one knows why so many of these guys once they come back either take up such weird occupations as this or become halfwits or thieves or murderers... and she wondered why I had not up until now been able to figure out what my husband's occupation was. Well, I wasn't a servant girl's daughter or a foundling or an orphan. I had a degree and a mother and a father, I was pretty and all that... Yes, thanks. One more wouldn't hurt. Your guests haven't come. My throat is really dry. The bad thing was that I really took a liking to the girl. She was a sweet, tidy person. She said she had been in Los Angeles for seven years trying to find a husband or become a movie star. Then we both got up and hung out the clothes, then put my daughter and her stroller in the back of the car and went to look for the place where my husband worked. I still couldn't believe it. I couldn't be convinced until I had seen it with my own eyes. First we went to the office. They greeted us and asked how they could help us. What pictures there were of such parks and trees and lawns. If you didn't know what kind of place it was, you would have thought they were constructing a honeymoon cottage there. And everything had a plan. And dimensions and measurements, and hinges and handles on both sides, and a bouquet of flowers on top of it, made of any sort of wood you might want, with the cloth that had to be drawn over it, and what sort of ceremonies one wants. And the carriage that carries the person away should be drawn by how many horses, or if you wish, we can take it away by car, since that's much more economical, and which car models we have available. And how many people will you need for the honor guard, and what will it cost per person, depending on how sentimental they appear and which absent relatives they substitute for and what clothing they wear and in what church ... I don't know if you're getting my meaning. There were advertising pamphlets and matches and tissues in every corner of their office. They were printed with bright pictures and details with slogans such as 'Eternal sleep on velvet' or 'Such-and-such a park is a second Garden of Paradise,' and things like this.

The employees fluttered around us, asking if we wanted a single plot or a family one. For how many people? It's worth your while to purchase a family plot, since it's fifty percent cheaper and can be paid in installments... My heart was ready to burst. I couldn't believe that this was my husband's occupation. He had said he was a lawyer. A lawyer! That's exactly what he said! Finally we introduced ourselves and found out where my husband was working. We didn't want them to suspect anything. Yes, we told them this lady is his sister who has come from Los Angeles and has to return this afternoon, and has to see him for an urgent matter, and that I didn't know what area my husband was working in today... We came out of the office and we went to the very place where he was working. I couldn't believe it until I saw him behind the row of boxwood trees. His sleeves were rolled up and he was wearing a workman's overalls. He was measuring the lawn. He put markers at the corners, then started up the back hoe and dug from one end of the area to the other. Then he went to the next spot. Then two black men came and first dug up the lawn in square sod and put the sods in a small truck. Then my husband came back and once again began digging with the back hoe, and the two black men excavated the earth and tipped it into another truck. In this manner my husband kept going down and coming up again. Then one of the blacks did the same thing. All three of them wore the same overalls. And how carefully they worked! They didn't let one speck of earth fall on the lawn and spoil it. And the two of us sat in the car and watched them for an entire half hour through the row of boxwood trees along the avenue, crying our eyes out. Trucks kept passing alongside our car, either taking away earth and grass or bringing new coffins that were lined up on the lawn, waiting for the excavators to finish. That was in the days when they were bringing the soldiers home from Vietnam. In small batches. Two or three hundred per day. And they were all so busy. Besides my husband's gang there were about ten or twelve other groups working. Each crew in one area of the park. And what a strange park it was! It's called Arlington. You must have heard of it. If you've heard of the capital, you must have heard of Arlington. It's famous throughout the world. I mean, if you've heard of America, you must have heard of Arlington. The girl told me these things that day. She said the place had been famous since the time of the American Revolution. Kennedy is buried there, too. People go to see it. And there's an honor guard and a big ceremony for the changing of the guard. Everywhere you look there's grass and gentle hills. From one end to the other, every plot has grass and trees and bushes, and above the head of each person there's a white stone marker with his name and essential information on it. The colonels here, the majors there, and the privates over in that direction. The girl pointed out that they were arranged in rows according to their military ranks. I don't know if you're getting my meaning. The girl said, All our efforts as Americans end here at Arlington... She had known such heartache! Waiting for seven years and losing three fiancés! ...She showed me where the two of them were buried, and also Kennedy's grave and the place where the changing of the guard took place, then we went back. I wasn't in the mood to watch it. We ate lunch out. Then we went to a movie, where my daughter cried the whole time, and I didn't understand anything of what was going on. At about four in the afternoon she dropped me off at home and left. She had bought a round-trip ticket at a discount and had to return that same day. Do you know what was the last thing she said to me? She said, They were so involved in the world of war that they forgot about our world... When my husband came home from work that evening I brought the matter up. I mean, after the girl left I just kept thinking about it. I called up my Iranian friends and acquaintances and talked with them about it. I started thinking about the day in Iran when he had insisted on taking me to see Mesgarabad. Before our wedding. As casually as if we were going to see the Golestan Palace museum. At that time I didn't even know what or where Mesgarabad was. I've already said that, if it weren't for him, there are many places here in Tehran that I would never know about. At that time I didn't even know where it was. The chauffeur at his office knew. I kind of acted as interpreter. He asked so many questions about our burial customs. I didn't know anything about such things. The chauffeur was Armenian and didn't know our customs, either. But he went and brought one of the gatekeepers of Mesgarabad, and he told us about it and I interpreted. At the time I didn't think of asking his purpose in asking all these questions. But I do remember that my grandmother used the incident as another reason to grumble. What does this mean, she asked. This infidel comes and asks for a girl's hand, then takes her off to see Mesgarabad? ...I remember that my husband had another American with him that day, and as I was interpreting the gatekeeper's explanations for them, that person said to my husband: See, they don't even use coffins. They just wrap it in a piece of cloth that requires no great investment... I knew the person. He was the adviser at the Plan Organization. I think they even agreed between themselves that they should speak with the Plan Organization on this matter. And look how stupid I was at the time, I couldn't make out any of these exchanges. I remember that when they found out that day that we don't use coffins, he told me that they dress up the people like brides and grooms and put them in coffins. If the people are old, they put cotton in their mouths and curl their hair, and all of that requires a lot of money. At dinner that evening, I talked the matter over with my grandmother, who blew her top. She started grumbling. And then she went to Mashhad at the time of our wedding. But do you think I was aware of anything? Well, you tell me. A twenty-year-old girl engaged to an American suitor, handsome, rich, respectable. Was there even any room for suspicion? And what did I care anyway about the Mesgarabad business? It would be a long time before I started thinking about such things as my grandmother did. When I was in Washington, sometimes it would happen that when he came home from work in the evenings, he would grumble about how the blacks were taking work away from them. I remember asking once if blacks, too, were permitted to be judges. You see, until the very end I believed that he was a lawyer, a judge, or something in the legal profession, somehow involved with the administration of justice. In any case, as soon as he came in the door and I handed him his whiskey, I poured one for myself, sat down facing him, and brought the matter up. I had thought it all over and considered all the advice I had received from my friends. One of my Iranian friends had said on the phone that everybody knows it. All of them have that sort of job. And for all mankind! I retorted, This is no time for slogans, please! Of course, I knew she had a grudge against them. They had canceled her passport. She could neither return nor stay. She was giving up her citizenship in order to become a citizen of Egypt. I really felt like asking her, If this is the way things are, why have you stayed in America? Another friend, who was young and handsome, and whose wife I often wished I could have been, do you know what he said? He said, Oh, man, I think you're just overwhelmed by America's pleasures! That's what he said. And do you know what his job was? He had no job. He had two American women supporting him. Don't think I'm just drunk or just mouthing off. One of his women was a teacher and the other was an airline stewardess. Each of them had a house. And that guy would stay three days in one house and four days in the other. He was living like a king. He neither studied nor had an income. Nor did he have any money coming to him. But he was living like a Gulf sheik. He would insist on taking the Iranians to the house where he lived so he could show it off, simply not realizing how shameless this was. Yes. So it was that I, a young woman of twenty-three, had to take my daughter and come back here. But may God forgive that Iranian's father. As soon as I hung up the phone, it rang again. I picked it up. It was another young Iranian who introduced himself. Yes, he was the friend of the other guy. He was studying law and had heard that I had a problem, and if he could be of any service, and so on. I said, yes, and he came and met with me. We sat for half an hour discussing the matter thoroughly, and I came to a decision. My mind was made up, and when my husband came home, I knew what I wanted. We sat until ten o'clock, with me drinking one whiskey after another, and I informed him that I wouldn't remain in America any longer. However much he insisted that I tell him how I had found out about it, I told him nothing. He thought someone in his family had decided to cause trouble. I didn't say one way or the other. And however much he insisted that we go out that evening for a walk or to a movie or to a club, and resolve the matter in the morning, I wouldn't give in. When I had said what I had to say to him, I went into my child's room, locked the door behind me, and went crazy. I was really drunk. Just like now. In the morning we went to court. It was funny what the judge said. He said that this was an occupation just like any other occupation. And that this was no cause for a divorce... I told him: Your Honor, if you yourself had a daughter, would you want her to marry such a man? He said: Unfortunately, I don't have a daughter. I said: How about a daughter-in-law? He said: Yes, I have one. I said: If your daughter-in-law should come tomorrow and say that her husband, who had claimed to be a teacher, has turned out to be of this occupation, or had just lied to her about it... And my husband broke in and kept interrupting me. He didn't want the judge to hear about his lying. Yes, so it was that he consented. He signed the child support papers for my daughter, and I got the money for the return trip from him right then and there. Yes, that's how it happened. And so it was that I had an American husband. Please, could I have another glass of that whiskey? I wonder why these guests of yours haven't come yet? ...But ... Oh, what an idiot I am! ...What if that girl tricked me? His girlfriend, I mean. Hm?...

Ahmad Mahmud

1930–

Ahmad Mahmud is the pen name of major writer of fiction Ahmad E'ta, who was born and raised in Khuzistan. In his youth he worked as a day laborer and truck driver, and suffered imprisonment for leftist political views and oppositionist activities.

His first story appeared in *Omid-e Iran* magazine, and in 1959 Mahmud began publishing collections of stories with *Mul* (The paramour). Other collections followed: *Daryā hanuz ārām ast*(The sea is still calm, 1960), *Bihudegi* (Uselessness, 1962), *Zā'eri zir-e bārān*(A pilgrim in the rain, 1968), *Pesarak-e bumi* (The little native boy, 1971), and *Gharibeh'hā* (The strangers, 1972). *Modern Persian Short Stories* (1980) features a translation of his 1969 story "Az deltangi" (On homesickness) from *A Pilgrim in the Rain*.

From the mid-1970s Ahmad Mahmud concentrated on the novel. His *Hamsāyeh'hā* (The neighbors) appeared in 1974 and gave him immediate status as a novelist. *Dāstān-e yek shahr* (Story of one city) was published in 1981. *Zamin-e sukhteh* (The scorched earth) was published in the spring of 1982 in 11,000 copies, with a second printing a year later of 22,000 copies. The three novels are a sort of a continuing saga set in Khuzistan during three important periods: the days of nationalization of oil in 1951, the aftermath of the coup d'état which brought the Shah back to the throne in late August 1953, and Iraq's invasion of Iran in 1980.

In the early 1990s Mahmud published three collections of short stories: *Didār* (Visiting, 1990) and *Qesseh-ye āshnā* (Familiar tale, 1991), *Az mosāfer tā tābkhāl*(1992), as well as a novel *Mādar-e sefr darajeh* (1993). 1995 saw two books of his: *Du filmnāmah barā-ye sinemā* and *Hekāyat-e hāl: goftogu bā Ahmad Mahmud* Most recently, his novel *Derakht-e anjir-e ma'ābid* was published in 2000.

The Little Native Boy

Translated by Judith Wilks

By the time Shahru had crossed the width of sun-scorched Nafti Avenue, the soles of his feet were scorched.

He strode along and sat down in the warm shade of the mimosa trees. He immersed his feet up to the ankles in the stream that branched off from the Bahmanshir River, flowed past the rows of young mimosa trees, came out in the salt marshes, and continued up to the small bazaar which spread out under the sun amid the irregular wooden houses.

The cool water rushed under Shahru's burning skin and his spine tingled. He leaned against the trunk of the tree and looked at his footprints, which had sunk into the oily ground. Then his glance ran along the length of the avenue, the end of which was blurred in a mirage. The overseas telegraph lines ran along the avenue, and the wooden poles shimmered in the waves of light that welled up toward the salt marsh and returned and crashed. The surrounding land gleamed white, and the wooden houses seemed to have no shadow at all. Shahru took his feet out of the water, stood up, and wiped the sweat off his forehead with his shirttail. Then he set out in the shade of the mimosa trees in the direction of the even row of wooden houses where the Europeans lived. From the monotonous tapping sound that reached all the way to the edge of the thicket of date trees and mingled with the muted sound of midday, he knew that the fat, short European—the one who was always dripping with sweat and panting and who never smiled—had not yet finished building his chicken coop.

This was the third day they had been working with disgusting slowness on a chicken coop on the withered lawn of the fat European's house.

When it was noon, when the whistle had blown and it was time for the European to come home, the workers got up from the shade of the trees, put their teapots and tea glasses in their bags and busied themselves with the half-finished henhouse.

All the Europeans' homes had henhouses, but the fifth house also had a little green, wooden house where the owner's dog lived. Two months earlier, when the European and his young wife and Betty, their twelve-year-old daughter, had returned from a holiday, they had brought along with them a medium-sized dog that looked rather like a wolf. The next day, two workmen dressed in blue came and built the little house, and when they left, the European's wife had painted it the color of the grass.

Shahru stopped when he reached the front of the fifth house and peeked over the short wall of boxwood trees into the house. Then he went and sat down on the edge of the black-and-white cement bridge over the stream.

The gardener was trimming the boxwoods. When he saw Shahru he said, "Shahru, aren't you tired of it?"

"Of what?" asked Shahru.

The old gardener's bald head was the color of burnished copper, and large drops of sweat were running in channels down his wrinkled forehead.

"Of coming to this house and sitting on the hot edge of this bridge."

"Why should I be tired of it?"

The sound of the gardener's shears stopped. "Tell me, don't you have any work to do at all?" Shahru said nothing. Once again the sound of the shears began. The wolf-like dog was sitting on the wooden swing with his tongue hanging out. The wooden swing was grass-green, and the owner of the house, who was tall and slender, had not yet come home.

The smell of food wafted out of the house—the smell of fried vegetables and hot butter. The doors of the rooms were open, and a gentle breeze ruffled through the fire-red tassles on the lamp and blew through the passageway of the building.

The gardener asked Shahru, "Have you eaten lunch?"

Shahru said, "I've eaten. When I brought my father his lunch at work, I ate with him."

On the ground beside a green trashcan in front of the house lay a half-smoked cigarette. Shahru got up, went over and picked it up, and asked the gardener, "Got a match?"

"What do you want it for?"

"If you have got one, give it to me."

The gardener gave Shahru a match. Shahru lit the cigarette butt and drew the smoke into his mouth.

"Do the Europeans give you these matches?" he asked.

The gardener looked at him, muttered, then said, "Tell me, Shahru, did you learn to smoke at the party meeting?"

"At the party meeting? ...Why, they don't teach people these things at party meetings."

"All right, then who did you learn it from?"

Betty came out of the room. Shahru threw the cigarette into the stream of water and looked at Betty, who waved and then went and placed a dish of food in front of the dog.

Betty was wearing short, close-fitting pants. The skin of her thighs was red from the heat, and her youthful, budding breasts quivered under her thin blouse. Shahru waved to Betty and smiled, and his large black eyes shone briefly.

Betty petted the dog, waved to Shahru again, and went back inside. Shahru's eyes remained fixed on her tousled curly blond hair until she disappeared inside the house.

When Betty was gone, the gardener said, "Seems like you know them, Shahru."

Shahru said nothing. He went over to sit on the edge of the cement bridge once again, but before he could settle down, the whistle sounded over the city.

The gardener said, "Her father will be coming now."

Shahru said, "Let him come."

"He'll scold you again."

"No, he won't."

"You are always sitting around their house like a faithful dog, why, they must be tired of shooing you away all the time."

"Where did you learn to call a person a dog, in the mosque?"

The gardener held the shears and stared at Shahru.

"Ho... harsh words." Then he scratched his little beard and said, "I don't know how things will be ten years from now, the way they are bringing up kids nowadays." He trimmed off some branches of the boxwood and said, "Do you understand what you said, boy? Do you have any idea what you're saying?" He said nothing more. Only the sound of the shears could be heard. Then the sound of the shears stopped, and now there was the sound of Betty's father's gray automobile, which had turned out of Nafti Avenue and was heading toward the cement bridge.

The car came to a stop in front of the house. Betty's father got out of the car and stood face to face with Shahru, looking at him. Shahru looked at the white roof of the car, which was reflecting the sunlight. Betty's father looked at Shahru's black, flashing eyes that seemed to be moist.

Without saying a word, Betty's father strode inside the house. The gardener left the task of trimming the boxwood trees half-finished and got ready to leave for the day.

Shahru asked him, "You'll have work to do here again tomorrow?"

The gardener held up the shears threateningly and said, "If you think you're going to talk to me like that again, I tell you I'll break your neck with these shears."

"I was only asking."

"Now I'll have to tell your father that you spend every day in front of that European's house."

"My father won't give a damn about what you say."

The old man's eyes narrowed. "Tell me, do you think that falling in love with a European's daughter is something any bare-assed hungry beggar can do?"

Shahru burst out laughing. The gardener became irritated.

"Get up, go find yourself something to do... I said get up and get out of here, find some little job and help your poor father out with a few pennies."

Shahru laughed again and said, still laughing, "It's enough that you're slaving away."

The gardner turned red. "Again you're being sassy, you little lizard."

"Old man, will you go eat your lunch?"

The gardener's lips trembled and his voice became hoarse. "This evening I'm going to tell your father everything so he can give you what you've got coming to you."

Shahru interrupted the old man. "Tell him whatever you want... but don't lie."

The gardener clenched his teeth. "All right, you wretch, I feel sorry for you."

"Feel sorry for yourself that you have to live in the sewage pipes like the gypsies."

Now the gardener's face turned amber. He raised his eyebrows and his eyes opened wide. "Still another smart remark? …If your poor father knew what this European has in store for him…"

"He would definitely grab him by the neck and strangle…" Shahru, without finishing what he was saying, craned his neck. Betty had come out again to pick up the dog's dish. The gardener set off, mumbling to himself. "The poor wretch, if he knew that the European was saying, 'I'll have to send that Abdol to Dar Khevin so I can be relieved of that insolent son of his' …If you knew that, you wouldn't sit here glued to this bridge all the time like a tick to an ass's behind…" The gardener had walked some distance now. He was bent over. His head and neck seemed to be weighted forward. He seemed to have come from the earth. He was the same color as the earth, and his shadow mingled with the shadows of the mimosa trees.

When Betty went inside, the European came out. He was wearing shorts and no shirt. His skin was as red as deer meat. First he came and put the car in the garage, then he went and picked up the rubber hose and watered the lawn and the boxwoods. Then he drenched himself with water. Then he pushed the dog aside and sat down on the wooden swing. The hot wind passed over his wet body and evaporated the drops of water. A few moments later, the European got up from the swing and went inside.

Shahru stretched out on the wide edge of the cement bridge and put his feet in the water. He heard the scraping sound of pieces of paper being blown along the ground by the wind and the sound of the rustling of a row of mimosa trees. Shahru's body was wet with sweat. The sharp smell of oil, the salty smell of the sea, and the smell of the wet grass blended together. A mist seemed to rise from the surface of Nafti Avenue. It was as though a tall tank of water had merged with the flat surface of the sky. In Shahru's eyes, there was the sky with white spots, and a grayish-yellow bustard that had opened its wings and was headed in the direction of the date-palm grove. The faint sound of the sparrows made him sleepy. Shahru's eyelids grew heavy…

Toward evening, when the heat of the day had abated, and the moist south wind had subsided and the north wind had begun to blow, the European and his wife set up a table on the lawn, sat on straw chairs, drank coffee, and talked.

Betty took her green bicycle and left the house. She passed by Shahru and smiled, then went down Nafti Avenue and got on the bicycle. Then several girls and boys, wearing colorful clothing, came out from the row of wooden houses. With their bicycles and tricycles they rode around in groups noisily, playing.

Betty's father lit a cigarette and left the house. He stood beside the stream and watched the children. The intense heat of the afternoon had subsided. The coolness of evening had come, and now a gentle sea breeze refreshed the area.

The fat European who never smiled came outside, stood beside Betty's father and lit his pipe. Then Betty's mother came and looked at Shahru and said something to her husband.

Shahru got up from the edge of the bridge and went and stood at the end of Nafti Avenue. He looked at Betty. Her youthful bosom quivered as her legs went up and down on the bicycle, and the wind tousled her blonde hair.

Shahru turned and looked at Betty's father and mother and the fat European, who were looking at him and talking. Then he saw the surly European take a few steps toward him. Shahru backed off a few steps, then ran off and stood under the water tank. He could see the Gulf and the colorful lights of the ships. Behind him he could see the shooting flames of the towers of the refinery, which seemed to burn more brightly as nightfall approached. The ground had now lost the heat of midday and absorbed the coolness of evening. Shahru felt the heat leaving his body. He pressed his cheek against the iron post of the water tank and watched the lamps in the row of wooden houses driving back the blackness of night. Under the lamplight that colored the ground, Betty's shadow came and went along with the shadows of the other children. He could hear the sound of Betty's sweet voice speaking a language he could not understand. All he could see was her smiling green eyes.

Shahru looked away from Betty's shadow and over to the shadows of Betty's father and mother and the surly European, who were walking along the avenue toward the water tank. Shahru inhaled deeply and then started running. In one breath he ran all the way to the little marketplace, where it was as bright as daylight under the strong light of the buzzing mantle lamps. In the square was the smell of broiled liver, broiled *sabur* fish, leftover fruit and watermelon, and trampled melon rinds which had shriveled in the noontime sun.

The smell of fresh bread reached his nose and his mouth watered. As he passed in front of the bakery, he heard Suri's voice. "Shahru!"

Suri, with his watery eyes, thick black hair, careless appearance, and sunburnt skin, was standing beside the bakery shop, nibbling on a rolled-up half-loaf of bread.

"What is it, Suri?"

"Were you there today again?"

"Well, yes... I'm just coming from there now."

"Well?"

"Well what?"

"What did you do?"

"What did you expect me to do?"

"Well, you know, since you don't understand her language."

"I am happy just to look at her."

Suri gulped down a mouthful and said, "Well, yes, but just looking..."

Just then Shahru felt his father's big fingers on his neck and heard his voice. "Tell me, Shahru, what did you say to this old man today that he won't shut up about it?" Then he ran his hand across Shahru's shoulders caressingly and said, "Look, Shahru... you have to respect your elders."

Shahru took his father's wrist and said, "Well, it's all his own fault."

They set off together. Shahru heard Suri's chirping voice calling to him. "Shahru, tomorrow I'll come for you and we'll go fishing."

They left the marketplace. Abdol said, "Look, son, if you go fishing, don't get any ideas about swimming."

They heard the shuffling sound of the gardener's slippers as he came toward them, turning his prayer beads in his hand. "Abdol, don't take this kid along with you." The gardener spoke as he walked alongside Abdol. "All else aside, I'm some ten or twenty years older than you are. I've experienced more than you have..." The gardener slowed his steps when they reached the mosque. "This evening why don't you come to the mosque with me for once?"

The mosque was enclosed with sheets of white metal. At the door were two black flags and a thin cable that came from the Europeans' quarters, passed through the marketplace, and lit up the lamp at the door of the mosque and several dim bulbs inside it.

They stood facing the mosque, their shadows under their feet. The light from the buzzing mantle lamps of the marketplace colored the surface of the street. It was dark behind the mosque. A little farther, beyond some scattered wooden houses, the dim flames of sooty lanterns nestled in the darkness. Beside the flames were steel pipes piled on top of one another, the openings of which were as tall as a man, and inside of which people lived.

Shahru's father said, "Say, old man, why don't you come with us this evening?"

"Me?"

Under the lamplight at the door of the mosque one could see the wrinkles in the old man's forehead deepen. His eyes opened wide, and his lips trembled: "What a weird idea!"

Abdol set off with Shahru. "Look, Shahru, you shouldn't go to that European's house so much."

"But I don't do anything there."

"I know... but the gardener was saying that you're in love with Betty... So who is Betty?"

"She's the daughter of one of those Europeans."

"Is it true that you've fallen in love with her?"

"Dad... I don't even understand their language."

"Well, then, don't go there so often."

Shahru pressed his father's hand and seemed to have trouble speaking. "Well... all right... Dad... but... Dad..."

"What is it?"

Shahru said, "But did the gardener also tell you that . . ."

Abdol took the words out of Shahru's mouth. "...that the European is out to get me? ...Well, yes, he said so, but I know he is lying."

Shahru said, "Well, yes, the gardener doesn't know their language."

They entered the house. Shahru's mother had sprinkled water on the floor and spread a straw mat beside the thick-trunked date palm in the middle of the courtyard. She had lit the small primus stove and placed the kettle on it.

Shahru asked, "Isn't there supposed to be a meeting this evening, Dad?"

"And Arzu is speaking," said Abdol.

At the meeting Arzu was speaking. When night fell, it seemed that the Bahmanshir River roared more noisily. The date-palms seemed to be whispering, and the pungent smell of the date trees and the sharp smell of oil intensified.

Arzu's voice seemed tired. His voice was hoarse but pleasant. "It's all just talk when they say that they dumped the pipes here for sewage... and if so, by now they could have taken care of the sewage. And what's more, they could use all these piled up pipes..." Mosquitoes hummed around the buzzing lamp that threw faint shadows on the corrugated metal walls of the house. Cigarette smoke rose into the air.

Shahru was sitting beside his father. He had his arms around his legs and was resting his chin on his knees, on the border of sleep and consciousness. "...You see, many people have gradually made a habit of living in these pipes. Well, this is another way of keeping the men content... they're content not to pay any rent and have a roof over their heads..." The faces were familiar to Shahru, and now that sleep was settling in his eyes, he seemed to be hearing Arzu's voice from the bottom of a well. The faces seemed to grow larger, and Arzu's thick mustache quivered... Suddenly someone outside ran his fingertips over the surface of the wall of the house. The sound of the corrugated metal wall resounded in the silence of the house and Shahru, who had been falling asleep, suddenly jumped up from his place.

Abdol took Shahru's arm and asked, "Are you falling asleep?"

Shahru said sleepily, "I keep thinking about the gardener who lives in the pipes."

"Look, son, if you're falling asleep, get up and leave, it is not far to go home from here."

Shahru said, "I want to stay and hear what Arzu has to say."

Abdol fell silent and listened to Arzu speaking. Shahru once again rested his chin on his knees and looked at Arzu, who was squatting and speaking excitedly.

"The Justice Party people want to participate in the elections, and there are also the Democrats... in my opinion they are in cahoots with each other... In their own minds they are thinking of fighting us and taking us unawares. They want to cloud the issues in order to get what they want. We're holding a rally on Friday. An election rally... everyone must have this clearly in mind... but, you know, we have to keep cool..." Shahru's eyelashes were getting heavy. His forehead was perspiring, he heard only bits and pieces of what Arzu was saying. It was as though Arzu were far away, at the bottom of a valley, and his words were the sound of the mountain lost in the crevices. And there was the roaring of the Bahmanshir, and the whispering of the date trees, and the rustling of the sharp-pointed leaves. "The Europeans... We have to... the Justice people... the pipes..." The words were muted and inaudible. Shahru's sleepy mind was heavy, and the sporadic words intruded insistently on his mind over and over again. "These Europeans... Europeans... Europeans..." The words were persistent, they attached themselves to his mind like leeches. Sometimes they were clear, and sometimes they were confused and mixed

up, then they became distinct once again. "The leeches... the Europeans... the pipes... the pipe... European... leech... Europe..."
Shahru had fallen asleep.

It was late at night. The north wind rippled the surface of the Bahmanshir, then fell on the tips of the branches in the date grove and
sighed. Shahru moved and opened his eyes. With the edge of his sleeve
he wiped the sweat of sleep from his forehead and said, "Is it over?"

Abdol said, "Get going... this evening you slept through everything."

"I didn't want to sleep, but I fell asleep anyway. I was exhausted, I
guess."

In the street the air was cool. The smell of evening mingled with
the pungent smell of the date grove.

The gardener appeared. "You must be coming from the meeting?"

"And you're coming from the mosque!" said Shahru.

Abdol said, "Why? What about it?"

Before the gardener could take a breath, Shahru said, "He is
always asking this, this is what he always says."

"I know one thing," said the gardener. He paused for a moment,
then he continued, "You know, if God doesn't wish it, no single person can do anything contrary to the will of the Creator."

Abdol asked, "What else do you know?"

"I also know that these meetings and such do nothing but cause a
lot of commotion." The gardener spoke with perfect composure.
"And also that these meetings and things make the servants of God
turn rebellious, and the rebellious one is damned. And that is why he
can never be saved."

Shahru seemed to be muttering, "Old man, did you learn these
things this evening?"

Abdol's voice became stern. "Shahru, I told you to respect your
elders."

The gardener began muttering to himself: "Yes, all right... when
the first brick is laid crooked, the whole wall will be crooked all the
way up to the sky."

The wooden houses loomed larger than life in the dark of the
night. Behind the open ground of the wooden houses, sooty lamps
glimmered here and there in the piles of cast iron pipes.

Abdol stood facing the corrugated iron door of his house, looked
the gardener in the eye and said, "That depends on what you think
crooked is."

Then he said, "Come in now and have a glass of tea."

The gardener shifted from foot to foot and said, "If it wasn't so late I'd really like to come in and speak with you…"

"No doubt to try and convince me," said Abdol.

"And maybe you would convince him," said Shahru.

The gardener hung his head and set off. "Good night."

The town was floating in a heavy mist. The sun looked like a dish of blood floundering in a sea of milk. Suri had his dirty canvas bag thrown over his shoulder and his fishing line and hook twisted around his wrist. The ground was wet, and the soft, moist earth sank beneath Suri's footsteps. He was nibbling on a rolled-up half-loaf of bread.

The large black dog walking alongside Suri sniffed the ground, then ran ahead and stopped and sniffed the ground again. Suri had just left the marketplace. There seemed to be no one inside the houses, and the marketplace was asleep. Suri's large head with its bushy black hair looked like a large ball of wool floating in the mist. His pants and shirt were the same color as the earth, as were his feet. Someone riding a bicycle emerged from between the houses and rode toward the marketplace. Papi, Suri's scruffy dog, shied away until it passed, squishing the moist ground under its tires. Then came the dry sound of the oil seller's cart, and the sound of the iron door of Abdol's house, at which Suri now knocked with a large, rusty steel bearing.

Shahru came out of the house. He was barely awake. His hair was tousled, but in spite of his sleepiness, his large eyes shone in his wide face. "You're here early."

"Is it early? Get away, it's almost noon!"

Shahru yawned.

"You just got up, didn't you?"

Shahru said, "No, I've been up for half an hour."

"Well, then, get your hook and let's go," said Suri.

"Come in, I haven't had my tea yet."

They went into the house together. Shahru had taken his calico bag and fishing hook. Shahru's mother called after them from inside the house: "Boys, don't get any ideas about swimming."

"Don't worry," said Suri.

Shahru's mother poked her head through the shabby rags on the door. "Shahru, come back at noon so you can take your father his lunch."

"I'll come… I'll come early, Mom… Maybe I'll even bring a fish so you can grill it for him."

The sun had risen higher, become hot, and driven off the mist. Now the sun was orange-colored under a tent of pale yellow sky. The heavy morning mist had thinned out, its thickness melted away and settled like dew on the ground. The two boys left the marketplace.

Suri asked, "Tell me, Shahru, where do you think we should go?"

"Above the river branch," Shahru said.

"Why don't we go under the bridge? ...They dump the garbage there and there are lots of fish."

"There are a lot of them, but they're all teeny-weeny little *latak*," said Shahru.

"Well, even if they are tiny, that's not so bad."

"There are big *shanaks* above the river branch."

As soon as they left the cluster of the wooden houses, Shahru turned toward Nafti Avenue.

"Why are you going in that direction?" asked Suri.

"Let's go pass in front of Betty's house," said Shahru.

"But that is out of our way."

"Not too far. From there we can go by the salt marsh to the date grove, then we can come out in the direction of the river branch."

The sun had climbed high in the sky. The shadow of the water tank stretched long over Nafti Avenue and broke off from the Bahmanshir. Shahru pointed at the dog. "Why are you bringing Papi?"

"He just came along with me," said Suri.

"Get rid of him, will you?" said Shahru.

He drove him away. The dog ran over to the water tank and stretched out in its shadow. They started out down Nafti Avenue.

"Suri, you go on ahead to the salt marsh until I come," said Shahru.

"You mean, you don't want me to come with you?"

"Well, it's better, because I don't want Betty to know that you know."

"What strange ideas you have."

"Well, you don't know how stubborn these Europeans are ... If she is offended, I might never see her smile again."

Suri went off left in the direction of the lowlands and salt marshes that extended to the edge of the date grove.

Shahru stopped when he reached Betty's house. The gardener was sitting among the boxwood trees smoking a cigarette. Shahru climbed on the cement bridge and craned his neck. He heard the gardener's voice: "Are you here again, kid?"

"Well, you are just loafing anyway, sitting in the shade, smoking."

"Don't bother. She's not even awake yet."

"Nobody asked you," said Shahru.

Betty came out of the house and waved to Shahru. Shahru waved back and shifted from foot to foot. The shade and the coolness of morning had fallen over the lawn. Betty went and sat on the wooden swing. She signaled to the gardener, who had now stood up and taken the shears and resumed trimming the boxwoods. He put the shears in his belt and went and pushed the swing. The gardener kept looking at the ground, Betty at Shahru, and Shahru at the old man with his head down like that, pushing the swing.

Betty got up and stood on the swing. She took the shears out of the gardener's belt and jumped down and ran toward the hedge of boxwood trees. Shahru jumped down from the bridge and ran toward Betty, and the two of them stood face to face, looking at each other and smiling.

The gardener came and took Shahru firmly by the earlobe. "Lizard," he said, "won't you leave this girl alone?"

Shahru pulled his head away and stepped back and stood facing the gardener.

"What the hell business is it of yours?"

He heard Suri whistling. Shahru turned and saw that Suri was standing at the edge of the date grove, waving his hand. The gardener took the shears from Betty and went toward the boxwood trees. Betty took Shahru's hand and pointed to the fishing hook and said something that Shahru did not understand. Shahru walked away from the house with Betty and sat down in front of the bridge. With his fingertip he drew the picture of a fish on the soft ground. The two of them laughed together.

Betty's mother called from inside the house. Betty flew off like a butterfly. When she reached the porch, she stopped and waved to Shahru. A smile froze on Shahru's lips, and his eyes remained fixed on the door that closed behind Betty. Again Suri whistled, and then the rough hand of the gardener grabbed Shahru's collar and shook him.

"All right now, are you going or do I have to kick you out of here?"

Shahru wriggled free of the gardener's grasp. "Old man, you see that she herself wants to be friends with me." He stepped back and went to the cement bridge, then turned and ran in one breath to the salt marshes. When he reached Suri he sat down and leaned against the rough trunk of a date tree and stretched out his legs.

"Was that Betty?" asked Suri.

"That was her," said Shahru, panting.

"What did she say?"

"She took my hand, then she smiled, then she pointed to the hook."

"Well?"

"We sat down on the ground and I drew a picture of a fish for her. I really wanted to ask her to come fishing with us."

Suri burst out laughing. "You've got some strange dreams for yourself... would her mother ever let her come with us?"

Shahru said, "Wouldn't she let her?"

"Well, everybody knows that..."

Shahru interrupted Suri: "You are older than I am, but you don't know that it doesn't matter to Europeans..."

"What doesn't matter to them?"

"That girls and boys should be friends with each other. They say that their dads and moms even teach them how to be friends with each other."

"Ho, ho... keep on dreaming!"

Shahru stood up, threw his bag over his shoulder and walked on, talking. "You know, Suri... I have to learn their language... I have to take lessons in their language."

Suri jumped over a bush and said, "If you could first go to grade school and learn your own language, then you could think about..."

"I am thinking about going to an adult class..."

"An adult class? ...Where?"

"They say they're going to open an adult class near the marketplace."

"Who knows when that will happen?"

They came out from the date grove into the open. A large lizard jumped out from under their feet and stopped farther away. It reared up on its legs, craned its neck, and stuck out its tongue. With rolling eyes it stared at them. Suri stopped and listened. "Shahru, do you hear the nightingale?"

But the sound of the nightingale was lost in the confused chirping of a flock of sparrows.

"I hear it. If only I could catch it alive."

"For Betty? ...Right, Shahru?"

"Well, yes... for Betty."

"Our neighbor has a big nightingale. Want me to steal it from him?"

"Are you talking about Baba Khan's nightingale?"

"Did you see how big it is and how it sings in the evenings?"

"But that poor thing is addicted to opium now."

There was a pattern in the tangle of the pointed date leaves on the ground. The sun had now driven off the mist and was burning fiercely. The weeds on the ground in the date grove were in light and shadow, and the branches of the Bahmanshir went coursing into the date grove here and there. There was a smell of grass and a sharp smell of newly sprouted thorn bushes. They crossed over the dried trunk of a date tree that had fallen over one of the wide streams and skirted around a tangled heap of leaves. Taking long strides, they went on to the edge of the date grove, then downhill toward the river.

Shahru said, "I'm worried."

"What about?" asked Suri.

"Betty."

"I know you really like her, but what's the use, Shahru... she is not going to be your wife."

Shahru stopped. The soles of his feet absorbed the cool wetness of the sand. He looked at Suri and said, "Be my wife?"

"Well, why, yes."

"You idiot, don't you understand?" And he walked off, with Suri following him.

"What don't I understand?"

"I only like her... I want to talk to her... I want to look at her, so she'll smile at me and wave to me... I don't want her to be my wife."

Suri burst into laughter. "Well, but these things are useless."

"They're useless?"

"If a man loves someone, he has to take her in his arms and kiss her, and then... well, you know... and then..." Suri didn't finish his sentence. He sat looking at the river. The surface of the water seemed made of blue and gold spangles, some areas rippled, some calm, with waves of silver and pale gray and blue.

Shahru asked, "And then what?"

Suri said, "What do I know? ...Baba Khan always says that when a man loves someone, he has to sleep with her..."

Shahru's eyebrows shot up in astonishment, and his eyes opened wide in amazement. "Sleep with her?"

Well, yes... Aren't Baba Khan and Narges...?"

"Don't tell me any more. I know."

Farther up the river branch, they threw their bags on the ground and unwound their lines. Shahru went and stood on a smooth, moss-covered rock in the sand and said, "Suri, give me a piece of that gut, will you?" Then he sat and chopped up the piece of gut and put some on the hook. He whirled the hook and let it go far into the river. Suri squatted beside Shahru and said, "We'll split the catch, all right?"

"Fine."

And they fell silent. On the surface of the river, two sailboats with their sails unfurled glided by side by side. The sound of the water was restful. The sweat was streaming down Shahru's forehead, and the sunlight burned his back.

Suri cleared his throat and said, "If she were a Muslim…"

"Are you talking about Betty?" asked Shahru.

"Well, yes," said Suri.

"What if she were a Muslim?"

"You would marry her… I mean, how should I put it… you would be able to marry her."

Behind them was the murmuring of the date grove, before them were the sparkling ripples of the river, which the wind played with and tossed about, jostling them together, then apart. The silent form of the metal bridge appeared whitish in the heat and the vapor seemed to play on the surface of the river. Sometimes the wind carried over the sound of an automobile horn, which blended with the murmuring of the river and the whispering of the date grove.

"You know what, Suri?"

"What?"

"I'm afraid of the day after tomorrow."

"Of…" Suri started to say.

Shahru interrupted him, alerting him, "We've got a nibble, Suri."

Suri looked at the line, which trembled and tightened and pulled away a little.

"Don't lose control," said Shahru. "Be patient." But the fishing line relaxed and floated loosely in the water.

"I think it snapped up the meat and got away," said Suri. He drew in the line. "Yes, the ungrateful thing… they've wised up." Suri put another piece of gut on the hook and cast it in the river. He shifted and said, "You were saying you are afraid of what?"

"Of the day after tomorrow."

"What about the day after tomorrow?"

"There is a rally… don't you know?"

Suri shook his head. Shahru stared at the fishing line, deep in thought. Arzu had said, "When they spread rumors all over the country that they want workers, that they'll give a good salary and a house and a livelihood, then people from everywhere leave their work and their way of life and set off to find a good job and good food. But as soon as they get here they see that there isn't anything to these promises. And since there are plenty of men, they can make us dance to their tune. When there are plenty of hands, the wages go down. If someone doesn't work, ten other hungry ones are ready to slave twelve hours a day for the promise of food…"

And now Shahru was thinking about Mandal, who had left his farm and had come from Andika, a district north of Khuzistan. He had come to Abadan and worked for several days as a gardener at a house in the bosses' quarter of Braim when, as Suri heard it from his father, "The European arrived unexpectedly and saw Mandal sitting on the lawn smoking a pipe. He took him by the ear and sent him to the office, where they paid him off. Now Mandal had set out, borrowing and pledging money, selling even his *kilim*, to buy a little donkey for the European's son, because he had heard from here and there that the European's son was very fond of little white donkeys. Nobody knows yet whether..."

Suri's piercing cry shook Shahru. "Hey, Shahru, I think your line is moving."

"Yes... it is..." The words froze on his lips as he jerked up the line and the hook flew out of the river, bringing along with it a silvery *shanak*.

Shahru stood up. He removed the fish from the hook and threw it onto the sand. Once again he baited the hook and cast it into the river... Once again he thought about Arzu's words and about Mandal, who had said, "If I were in Andika, by now I could have found a hundred little white donkeys. But in this desolate place one can't find any sort of animals..." And his father had said jokingly, "Animals? ...It just so happens that the only thing one can find here is animals..."

And now Shahru was reflecting. "If only I could get a gun and shoot the surly European like... the damned Europeans... they get up and leave the other side of the world and come here where... If my father would set out again and go into the hills and mountains and be a herdsman like he was in his childhood, and I would set out, too, and I would carry a loaded musket and wear leggings and boots and travel all over the plains... But Betty? ...If I could get hold of a fine horse, one day toward evening I would waylay Betty and take her hand and toss her up on the saddle behind me and set out for the plains... like... like who? ...Aha... like the drunkard. Dad tells such great stories about when he attacked the black tents with his loaded rifle and... but... from what Dad says, times aren't so good now..."

Shahru's mind was confused, and the memories were all mixed up. The memories of his father's story-telling and Betty's smiles and the days and the nights and Arzu and the gardener. "The peevish old man, like *a bowl hotter than the soup*... What would he do if it were his own daughter? ...Some day I'll have to do something terrible to him so he'll realize where things stand... an old man who thinks he knows it all shouldn't intrude in other people's affairs... an old man shouldn't lie. He's always fingering his rosary and picking his nose and poking his head into other people's business... Yes, old man, what do you care if Nasim stole the bolt from the board and sold it and bought a primus stove? ...With those goddamned eyes of yours, can't you even bear to see a primus in the house where poor Nasim lives with his six or seven naked children? ...Isn't there anyone who wonders why you yourself are always hanging around the Europeans, and if he could... But really, Betty's blouse? ...It looked so terrible on the gardener's daughter. It seemed to be weeping and crying ... How could Betty have given this pretty blouse to the gardener? I don't know. Maybe... But when Betty used to wear it... Ah! ...I mean, is there anyone prettier than Betty? ...in the whole world could one find anyone prettier than Betty? ...God, if only Friday would come and go quickly... If they get worked up... If Betty... if..."

Shahru sighed and said, "You know, Suri, it doesn't look good."

"What are you talking about?" asked Suri.

"I'm saying I'm afraid they'll get worked up and they'll harm some of the Europeans."

"Who'll get worked up?"

"The workers, you know... I just told you there's a rally the day after tomorrow."

"Well, what does the rally have to do with the Europeans?"

"You are amazingly stupid, man."

"Well, tell me so I can learn."

"Well, Arzu is always saying that it's the Europeans' fault that we're hungry and don't have proper houses and lives."

"It's the Europeans' fault?"

"Well, yeah."

"What do they have to do with it?"

The wind carried the sound of a dark-skinned boatman who was lying naked on the edge of the boat. "Yoo-hoo... kids..."

The rest of his words were carried by the wind into the depths of the date grove. Suri looked away from the boat and said, "It just so happens that they do go to a lot of trouble for us."

Shahru was curious. "They go to a lot of trouble?"

"Well, yes."

"Who said that?"

"The gardener."

"The gardener?"

"He says that when there weren't any cars, they used to load the pipes on mules with a lot of hardship and suffering. They would go over the mountains and hills to reach Naftun and to drill, and now we owe them something back in return."

"The gardener's mind..." He left his sentence unfinished and said hurriedly, "Look out, Suri!"

And Suri quickly drew in the line from the river, with a dark silver *zobaydi* on it. He took the *zobaydi* off the hook and threw it on the sand. The fish flapped its head and tail on the ground... Suri got up and hit the fish on the head with a rusty bearing he kept in his bag. The fish opened and closed its mouth several times then stopped moving.

Shahru said, "As long as you're up, wet down the bag and throw the fish inside it so the sun won't dry them out."

Suri put the bag in the water and asked, "You were saying something about the gardener's mind?"

Shahru said, "Just now he was pushing Betty on the swing like a servant... He was ashamed to even look me in the eye."

"Then what do you want him to do? If he didn't do it, he'd have to go like Musa in the night and steal wire from the overseas telegraph lines and get arrested and handcuffed and thrown in prison."

"I'm saying he shouldn't act like a servant," said Shahru.

"What else can he do?" said Suri.

"He could manage not to do it," said Shahru.

"Your father works for them too. My brother is a laborer for them, too."

"My father works, but not as a servant."

Suri pulled out the line. A fish had taken the meat and gotten away. "They've really wised up... they steal the bait ten times before one of them gets caught."

"They've wised up, but you're also not hooking the bait right."

"How should I do it?"

"Come here, let me show you," said Shahru.

Suri went and sat beside Shahru. His legs had fallen asleep and were tingling with pins and needles. Shahru knotted his own fishing line with his big toe and pulled it tight. Then he baited Suri's hook, secured it, twisted it, and freed the end. "Come, take it... Now it won't be so easy for them to steal the bait and run off."

Suri got up. Shahru stared at the surface of the river. Calm waves played with the sands of the shore. The cluster of date trees at the edge facing them looked blackish. The wind made Shahru's line tremble, and Suri's line tightened, then loosened, then tightened

The Little Native Boy

again. It was silent for a few moments. There was only the gentle sighing of the wind and the muted, sleepy sound of the river. Suri felt sleepy. His body relaxed, and Shahru's voice seemed to come from the bottom of a well. "I'm worried... I don't know, I've been always this way. Every time something was about to happen, I've felt this way. The time that they brought the news that the Naft-e Sefid well had caught fire and the steel had burned down to something like charcoal, two days earlier I had an inkling that something bad was going to happen... You know, Suri, now I'm more worried about Betty. I'm always thinking about her. It's as though I'll never see her again. I just know that she argued with her father, that the gardener was a tattletale. My heart says that the fat European told Betty's father that Betty shouldn't smile at that boy... Arzu was saying that the Europeans say we're gypsies... I don't know, maybe that surly European told Betty that if she made friends with this barbarian boy, one day he would strangle her. I just want to look at her... You know, Suri, I only like her. I just want to look at her, look into her smiling eyes... but... maybe..." Shahru's fishing line moved and trembled and tightened, then relaxed again.

"It ate the bait and left." Shahru pulled out the hook. The whistle sounded over the city and traveled a great distance.

Suri said, Ten o'clock already!"

"Get up, let's go," said Shahru.

"Oh, let's stay another half-hour."

"But it's getting late, and I have to take my father his lunch."

"But we didn't catch anything much."

"That's all right, you take the *zobaydi*, I'll take the *shanak*."

"No, you take both of them, Shahru," said Suri, "you wanted to grill them and take them to your Dad."

Shahru gathered up his hook and line. Suri quickly drew in his hook, and out came a large, milky-colored *sabur* fish that fell on the sand.

Friday morning, the air was as thick as clotted milk. The flames of natural gas that issued from the tall towers floated in the haze like streaks of blood. It was humid. There was no wind. The lamps were lit in the row of Europeans' houses, as was the lamp at the door of the mosque. Betty left the house. The mist enveloped the whole building. Betty's dog was sitting on the wooden swing with his head on his paws. He craned his neck and stretched his nose toward the sky, and now his wolflike howl wandered through the mist. Then the howling of Suri's big dog could be heard from outside the house. He had stretched out his lean black body on the wide edge of the cement bridge, his nose resting on his paws and his bleary, half-closed eyes fixed on Betty's house. Betty's father came outside and took the car out of the garage. Betty petted the dog. She pressed his head to her chest and ran her hand over his neck. Betty's father got out of the car, went over and took the dog's leash and pulled it. The dog fell off the wooden swing onto the ground. He dug his nails into the grass and howled and wagged his tail.

Betty's mother came out and stood on the porch. Her white linen dress covered her knees, and her lemon-colored belt cinched her waist. Betty's mother signaled to the dog and said something, and Betty' father let the leash go and straightened up and said something in reply. Betty ran up and hugged and kissed the dog. The howling of Suri's dog, Papi, mingled with the wailing of Betty's dog. Betty's father looked around, then strode out of the yard and kicked the dog in the rump. Papi jumped up and moved away. He went and stretched out in the middle of Nafti Avenue, rested his nose on his paws, and howled once again. Betty's father's cheeks were red up to the ears and his earlobes were pale. Betty's mother smiled. Betty kissed the dog, then pulled him toward the automobile. The dog's claws drew lines on the lawn. Then he put his paws on the running board of the car and scratched at the white arrows that were drawn on the fenders, and howled. Betty's father lost his temper. He said something and muttered something. He picked up the dog by the foreleg and hindlegs, lifted him up and threw him in the car. Betty sat beside him and closed the car door.

Betty's dog stuck his head out the car window. His blue eyes were fixed on the green eyes of Betty's mother. He barked, then howled. Suri's Papi, who was stretched out on Nafti Avenue, lifted his nose from his paws, looked toward the sky, and howled.

The large marketplace opened like the mouth of a hungry whale in front of Ahmadabad's First Avenue, swallowing up whole bands of people. Here and there the green city buses and the workers' trailers stopped on Nafti Avenue at the edge of the square and spewed forth workers in blue overalls. The narrow opening of Ahmadabad Avenue spilled waves of people toward the open space of the square like a river emptying into the sea. Banners and colorful flags rose like gentle waves above the heads of the workers. A high platform had been set up on a dark-colored truck at the edge of the west side of the square. There was a microphone on the table and loudspeakers on the roof of the truck. A red cloth banner fluttered above the truck with the inscription: Let's Make the Fourteenth Majlis a Strong Fortress for Greater Victories."

Now the sun was rising. Struggling in the haze, it pulled itself up over the dark, lead-colored horizon. The air was heavy, and there was a hubbub of disjointed talk.

"Arzu is speaking today."

"The weather is nasty."

"It's been decided that he'll talk about the elections to the Majlis."

"And about the workers' wages."

"That they are being exploited."

"What if the weather doesn't clear up?"

"What if we don't get a breeze from the north?"

"We'll all suffocate."

"He'll talk about the workers' houses."

"Which are more like jackals' lairs."

"The Democrats are going to enter a coalition."

"What?"

"We're talking about the Democrats."

"A coalition with whom?"

"Why, with the Justice Party, of course."

"The workers from Central Office are here."

"Those are the warehouse workers."

"Do you think if they form a coalition they'll be able to accomplish anything?"

"It seems you don't know them at all."

Someone's voice roared out from the loudspeakers over the entire square: "Form solid lines, don't let the troublemakers get through." The waves of men moved up, and the murmurs grew louder. The trucks and buses and trailers stopped on Nafti Avenue, and workers in blue overalls spilled out in haste and agitation to join the crowd of men pressed together in the square. Now from one end of the square to the other there was a wall of men in blue overalls with their arms linked and their shoulders pressed together. Every time the mouth of Ahmadabad's First Avenue poured a wave of newly arrived men into the square, the wall would open up and swallow the men, then close again. The sun was high now and had driven off the haze. The heat and humidity beat down on the heads of the men. The muted wave of murmuring in the crowd of workers was rough. Words were confused and voices intermingled.

"Tell the cutters to go to the right of the truck."

"No, no… that's where the electricians are standing."

"Suri…"

"What is it?"

"Where is Shahru?"

"He went toward the truck."

"Keep your wits about you."

Abdol, with his broad shoulders, broke through the ranks of men, and Suri followed after him in the narrow path that opened behind Abdol. The flags and banners waved and mixed together, then separated again. Along the open cement-sided sewage canal closing off the west side of the square, along the entire ridged road down to the rounded Ahmadabad bridge and extending down Nafti Avenue and the narrow throat of First Avenue, there were tight-lipped policemen, dripping with sweat. They were restless. They paced up and down, then stopped. They took their rifles off their shoulders, rested the stocks on their boots and leaned on them, then grew more restless. The murmurs were suffocating, and the slogans issuing from the loudspeakers rose over the crowd. Then there was some applause. It kept getting hotter and hotter. The wave of men was driven forward and settled back.

Arzu's voice came from the loudspeakers, weighty and awesome. "Friends,"—and there was a clamor of acclamation and applause— "Friends, our dignity and our victory depend on our indestructible solidarity. Our ranks pressed together are the surest guarantee of our success in gaining our social and political goals…" The sky was clear and bright now, and the morning mist was completely gone. The sun burned brightly. Here and there the orange color of the flames atop the towers mingled with the blue of the sky. "Friends, we must not allow our enemies to win any seats in the Majlis…" Arzu was foaming at the mouth. His short body was bent forward, and his head moved in rhythm with every word that came out of his mouth. Sometimes he shook his fist in the air and quickly lowered it, he opened it, then closed it tightly. "Friends, we can—and we must, for the sake of those who are hungry and illiterate—win a majority in the Majlis…"

Suddenly from the distance came the sound of a shot, then the sound of another, more muffled, perhaps lodged in flesh. A few moments of silence and fear cast a shadow over the square. There was a question in the furrows of the foreheads, then a murmur and a scream, and the sounds ran together.

"There's been some shooting."

"Where did the shot come from?"

"From far away."

"Did they shoot at Arzu?"

"No, the sound came from far away."

The wave of men became agitated. "They say they raided the party office."

"They say they shot one of the kids in the Party."

"They say it was the Justice Party people."

"Doesn't anybody know what happened?"

"Then, maybe..."

Arzu's voice coming over the loudspeakers dominated all the other voices. "Friends, stay calm..." But the crowd of men began moving, and the banners moved along with them.

"Was it the Democrats?"

"They say it was both of them."

"Who got shot?"

"Nobody knows."

"Maybe it was the Party guards."

A flood of men began flowing, raising the yellow dust of Nafti Avenue. The crowd was driven westward, and the truck moved and pulled over to the edge of the square. Arzu spoke once again. "We are holding a peaceful street demonstration to show our victory... Friends, avoid any sort of deviation from this..."

The policemen, who had grown impatient with calm, were dislodged. Now the men dressed in blue, their bodies drenched with sweat, covered the entire length of Nafti Avenue. There was no goal, only movement. Shahru had reached the truck, and Abdol was protecting the table with his arms. Arzu was standing on the table, the microphone in his hands, foaming at the mouth. His dark blue shirt was drenched with sweat and clinging to his back. Suri was hanging onto the bed of the truck... Shahru clung to the boards of the truck and pulled himself up. The crowd made way for the truck. The truck drove along slowly, and Shahru pulled himself up onto its roof. He saw a wave of colorful flags and banners intermingled haphazardly above the heads of the workers in dark blue uniforms. He saw the crowd seemingly driven forward, then back, then forward again... The smell of the sweat of the men's bodies mingled with the salty smell of the sea and the acrid smell of oil. The entire length of Nafti Avenue was being trampled underfoot, and the yellow dust rose and enveloped the men. A muted wave of murmurs and words filled the space of the square, and Shahru heard someone say in a muffled, rasping voice, "They've raided the Party office."

Shahru turned and saw a short man quickly pull himself up onto the truck. The man's lips trembled and his face was dark. He was foaming at the mouth, and shouted, "They smashed all the doors and windows, they beat the guards with clubs and kicked them... some of them might even be dead..." Shahru saw Arzu turn off the microphone and jump down from the chair, shouting, "No one must know about this."

The short man screamed, "They all must know!"

Arzu shouted, "No... there'll be no stopping them."

The short man yelled, "This is conspiracy! They must all know!"

Arzu gave the microphone to Abdol and grabbed the short man by his wet collar. He stared into his eyes and shouted: "No, no... I said no!" But the short man lunged forward and grabbed the microphone from Abdol's grasp. Before Arzu could make a move to take it, he touched the button and his voice burst over the crowd like a machine gun. "Friends, the Justice Party people and the Democrats have killed several of the Party guards..." Arzu grappled with the short man. The crowd grew noisy and started to move quickly. Arzu's voice sounded from the loudspeakers but was lost in the clamor of thousands of screams.

Abdol grabbed Shahru's sweaty arm and said, "Shahru, get away from here as fast as you can."

Shahru stared at his father. "Why?"

"Jump down with Suri."

"But why?"

Abdol's mouth was as dry as a match. The words scratched his throat. "Things are getting out of hand. Run behind the men toward home."

"But why, father?"

"Get away, get away from the workers!"

Shahru held the broad palm of Abdol's hand and said, "You have to tell me why... you always give me a reason."

"It's getting dangerous."

Arzu's voice again rose from the loudspeakers: "Friends... don't let anyone disturb your orderly conduct..."

Shahru released Abdol's hand. Abdol said sternly, "Faster, Shahru, faster!" And he gently pushed him.

Suri took Shahru's hand and said, "Shahru, your Dad is right."

Shahru hugged Suri. "Suri, I'm afraid..."

"What are you afraid of, Shahru? ...Come, let's go... your Dad isn't saying this without good reason."

"I'm afraid of today, Suri... of today..."

"If we go, there'll be nothing to be afraid of."

"I'm really worried." He let go of Suri. "I'm afraid... because of the Europeans."

He clung to the board on the side of the truck. Suri pulled himself up. Arzu's voice hung heavily in the sultry heat. Now the front ranks of the crowd were heading toward the Democrats' party building. It was as though fire were raining from the sky and scorching the earth. People were foaming at the mouth, there was a confusion of sounds. Shahru, who had pulled himself up onto the truck, saw that from the wide mouth of Zolmabad Avenue a disorderly mob of Democrats was coming out with banners and flags. Before Arzu could shout anything else over the microphone, a clash had begun. Abdol grabbed Shahru's neck firmly with his hard, grimy fingers and shouted: "I said go, son... as fast as you can!" He looked at Suri. "Take him, Suri."

Shahru looked at him imploringly. "No, Father... let me stay... I want to see what happens."

Abdol roared, his teeth clenched. "Go! ...go fast!"

"Please, Dad... I'm afraid."

"Well, fine, if you're afraid, then go!"

"No, Father... I'm afraid there'll be an attack... an attack on the Europeans."

Abdol yelled with all his might, "The Europeans! ...the damned Europeans!"

The microphone picked up Abdol's voice and carried it over the crowd. Every mouth began muttering, "The damned Europeans..."

"All this is on account of the damned Europeans."

"If we don't have any bread to eat."

"If we have no place to live."

"If we're hungry and out of work."

"It's all because of the Europeans."

"The damned Europeans."

"The damned Europeans."

"The damned Europeans."

But the walls of the Zolmabad quarter resisted the crowd of men wearing blue. A compressed, foaming wave broke off from the crowd of men, fell back along the channel, and headed toward Bawarda.

"The Europeans..."

"All our misfortunes."

"All our poverty."

Just then a dull, angry shout from a man in the front row of work-ers twisted in the air: "That car!" And the crowd was incensed. Suddenly, in the circle of men pressed together, a tongue of flame shot up and flickered. A car caught fire. A man soaked with sweat made his way to the truck through the rows of workers. He pulled himself up and shouted hoarsely: "All hell's broken loose! The Dem-ocrats, the Justice people… They killed Hosayn Gazi, they crushed his head like a snake's." He shook the table violently. "Do something, Arzu! …they say they've set fire to one of the Europeans' cars…"

Shahru immediately jumped up on the roof of the truck and craned his neck. He saw that in the midst of the crowd flames of fire were mingling with branches of the mimosa trees, and smoke was bil-lowing up above the mouth of First Street in Bawarda… Arzu grabbed the microphone. "Friends…" Shahru jumped into the crowd and was dragged along with the men toward Bawarda. Anxious to be free of them, he drew toward the side of the wave of men where the sewage channels were. He jumped into the sewage water, which reached up to his hips and splashed up on his head and face. The sweat on his face mixed with the black sewage water. He was looking at the smoke, which rose high, unwound like a skein, and scattered. When he reached the bridge, he pulled himself up and out of the water and ran. He saw that the mob had abandoned the car and was now headed toward the houses in Bawarda. He was out of breath. He squatted down and hugged his knees. He looked at the flames, which were subsiding, and at the smoke, which was getting denser.

Suri caught up with him. "Shahru."

Shahru's eyes were wide with terror and alarm, and his voice was hoarse. "I'm afraid, Suri… I'm afraid."

"Is it their car?"

"No, Suri… but I'm afraid."

Suddenly he stood up and started running. Suri ran after him. Confused voices could be heard. The street was blocked off. Arzu's voice fluttered through the air like a wounded bird and fell: "Friends, disperse! …do not stain your hands with the blood of your brothers!…"

And suddenly another murmuring began: "That car!"

"It belongs to the Europeans!"

"Gasoline!"

"A match!"

Through the crowd of men, Shahru's eyes settled on the car as it slowly came out from behind the wooden store. Shahru let out a piercing scream: "No!" But no one heard him. The mob ran and turned around and gathered in front of the car as it pulled out of the shade of the mimosa trees, its white roof reflecting the sunlight. Before it could turn back behind the store, it came face to face with the mob of men and stopped.

Shahru once again shouted, "No, no, no!"

He saw the door of the car move, and the broad white arrow broke apart and fell off. The door opened and the wolflike dog jumped out and lunged at the mob. A tin of gasoline whirled through the air. Before Betty could get her feet out of the car, it suddenly caught fire. Flames began to flicker, and Shahru screamed, "No!"

He threw himself into the fire and took Betty, her hair on fire, into his arms. Before he could rescue her from the fire, another tin of gasoline came hurtling through the air. The gasoline sputtered all around. It enveloped Betty and Shahru. The flames flickered and flared, and the smell of burnt flesh mingled with the salt smell of the sea and the oil fumes that filled the air.

Jamal Mir-Sadeqi

1933–

Born and raised in Tehran, Jamal Mir-Sadeqi started teaching immediately after high school and while pursuing an undergraduate degree in Persian literature at Tehran University. Besides teaching, his professional career has included librarianship and documentation center work in Tehran. He is married to the poet and critic Maymanat Mir-Sadeqi (b. 1937).

From the late 1950s onward, Mir-Sadeqi published several dozen short stories in the monthly magazine *Sokhan*. His first collection of short stories was called *Shāzdeh khānom-e chashm- sabz*(The green-eyed princess, 1962), retitled *Mosāferhā-ye shab*(Night travelers) in later editions (1963). His steady productivity thereafter resulted in the following collections of stories: *Chashmhā-ye man-e khasteh* (The eyes of tired me, 1966), *Shabhā-ye tamāshā va gol-e zard*(Spectacular nights and the yellow flower, 1970), *In su-ye tal-e shen* (This side of the sand dunes, 1974), *Na ādami, na sedā'i*(Not a soul, not a sound, 1975), *Davālpā* (Bugbear, 1977), and *Harās* (Fear, 1978). His pre-Revolution novels were: *Derāznā-ye shab* (The length of the night, 1970), the interconnected narratives of *In shekasteh'hā* (These broken ones, 1971) and *Shab-cherāgh* (The brilliant stone, 1977), which features multiple narrators.

In the first decade of the Islamic Republic, Mir-Sadeqi published eight or more volumes, among them a short novel called *Ātesh az ātesh* (Fire from fire, 1986), a 362-page novel called *Bādhā khabar az taghyir-e fasl midādand* (The winds told of the changing seasons) which appeared in early 1985, a novel called *Kalāgh'hā va ādamhā*(Crows and people, 1989), and *Pasheh'hā va dāstānhā-ye digar*(Mosquitoes and other stories, 1989). Also during the 1980s Mir-Sadeqi was active as a critic, publishing *'Anāser-e dāstān*(Elements of narration, 1985) and *Adabiyāt-e dāstāni: qesseh, dāstān-e kutāh, romān, bā negāhi be-dāstān-nevisi-ye mo'āser-i Irān* (Narrative literature: the tale, the short story, the novel; with a look at contemporary fiction-writing in Iran, 1988).

Ever prolific, his most recent work includes: *Dāstānhā-ye panjshanbeh* (1997), *Avāzhā: majm'uah-e si dāstān az seh ketāl*(1998), *Vāzheh'n_meh-e honar-e dāstān'nevisi: farhang-e tafsili-ye estelāhhā-ye adabiyāt-e dāstāni* (1999), *Rawshanān: hijdah dāstān-e kutāh*(2000), *Dāstānhā-ye chahārshanbeh* (2001), and the novel *Ezterāb-e Ebrāhim*(2002).

Through the Veil of Fog

Translated by Kinga Markus

Jalal was sitting beside Minu, watching the boys and girls. The boys in shoddy clothes and the girls wearing boyish slacks or short skirts and make-up were cuddled up together. The small round room was full of cigarette smoke. The fast dance music had just stopped. The boys and girls were still hot and excited. Their faces were shining with sweat. Their bodies, half-naked and trembling, were turning around each other and were dancing to the soft tune of the tango. There were small and intimate conversations, soft, light, calm and sweet music. The club was full of boys and girls. It was still early evening. As they had entered the dance room, Peggy was asked to dance, but Minu did not want to dance with anyone. She was sitting silently beside Jalal and refused every invitation. The air was stifling and warm in the room. The yellow lamps that lit up the room were gradually extinguished and now a soft, red light was glowing from the corner. Jalal's eyes fell on a French boy who came staggering toward them and, with his back to Jalal, leaned over Minu, laughed, and talked to her in a low voice. Then suddenly, like a bolt from the blue, something happened.

Jalal became aware of it when he saw Minu jump up from the chair and slap the French boy, and the iron chair toppled over onto the floor with a big rattling sound. The noise of the slap and of the chair falling rang through the room, cut off the music and turned curious eyes toward them. Chewing his lips and wringing his fingers, the French boy was standing in front of Minu, angry and red-faced. Minu was standing opposite him with her face ablaze and was about to slap him again when Jalal jumped between them. Minu's eyes were flashing, and only when Jalal stood between her and the French boy did she turn away her gaze from the latter and stare now at Jalal with eyes overflowing with anger. Jalal pushed the boy roughly aside and took Minu, who wanted to slap the boy again, out of the room. The music started again, but all eyes were on them. The boys and girls kept bowing toward each other and gently and lightly turning around to the fast rhythm of the dance music. Peggy and the French boy went out and an Indian followed them. The Indian boy was grinning. He was piercing them with his grotesque stare. His white teeth showed and his smirk tempted Jalal to hit him.

Peggy was dumbfounded and kept asking, "What happened?" Minu's hands were trembling. Her eyes were ablaze and her face hardened.

Peggy went back and shouted into the face of the boy, "What have you done to her, you idiot?"

The boy shrugged his shoulders. "I don't get it. I've done nothing." He was agitated, but his manner was reserved. His eyes were full of contempt. He put his hands into his pockets and held his head up with pride. Jalal asked himself, Should I hit him? He wanted to beat him. He felt his fingers automatically press together and he clenched his fist. The boy was tall and thin. His cold blue eyes were shining like broken glass. "I am sorry. I only kissed her. She slapped me."

The Indian boy was still smirking. He had been tailing Minu since early evening until he could talk to her privately. "Would you like to come with me to a pub? Would you like to dance with me?" Jalal raised his fist. "Get lost or I'll sock you! What a moron!" Peggy helped with Minu's coat. Both left the cloakroom. The manager of the club, a tall, white-haired Englishman, was talking to the French boy. Jalal quietly told Peggy to go out with Minu and planted himself in front of the manager. He did not want Minu to hear the man's derogatory words. The manager was looking at Jalal with narrow, cold eyes and said: "If such a thing happens in the club again..."

Jalal interrupted him, "I know..."

"That crazy girl..."

Jalal stared into his face. "What do you mean?"

The man withdrew. Jalal muttered between his teeth, "Damned English!" Jalal had been coming to this club for a long time, and the man was looking at him as if he were seeing him for the first time. "Do you know me, mister?" The Englishman only gave him a cold look and did not answer. Jalal went toward the door.

The French boy followed him. "I want to talk to that girl or to you…"

Jalal looked at him. "What an impudent fellow. And stubborn too!" His look was still contemptuous and the smile around his lips was even more so. His clenched fist dropped heavily on his side. It dawned on him that he alone wouldn't be held accountable. They would say, "Well, he is Iranian… Iranian!" He calmed down and politely said, "Sorry. I must go now. Tomorrow at four I shall come to the club."

The doorman, a skinny old Englishman, opened the door of the club for him. He put a coin into the doorman's hand and stepped out into the street. It was cold. Yellow lamps lit the street. He saw Peggy standing with Minu across the street. Rain was drizzling. The street was wet and a dark ray fell upon the hard, washed asphalt. When he approached them, Minu did not look at him. Her eyes did not show any interest in the world around her. Her pretty face was pale. She was standing silently beside Peggy, with her hands in her pocket and the collar of her coat turned up.

She had come to London four or five months ago to study. With her high school diploma in hand she was going from one school to another and writing applications. The answer she received was always, "Sorry." "Sorry." Who cared for her trifling money and her high school diploma? Everybody was looking for secretaries and stenographers to train. Those classes were full of Iranian girls.

They passed through the wet, rainy street and took the tube. Minu was silent all the way. She stared ahead, her face hardened, and she answered their questions abruptly. Jalal and Peggy were walking on either side of her. Jalal saw that Peggy's face was sagging and she kept yawning. Damn it, that her Saturday night got spoiled. Damn it, that the weariness of her six days' work still remained on her face. She should not have pressed so hard to go to the dance hall. Would it have been the end of the world if she had not gone dancing tonight? Jalal liked to look at Minu. He asked himself why he did not blame her. Such a thing could happen to any girl, but he was sure that no girl would react so strongly. He knew the air of London stifled her. She had told Jalal that every boy after only a couple of words wanted to take her to the bedroom. "As soon as they see you alone, they follow you. 'Are you Italian or Spanish,' they ask. 'Do you want to come with me to a pub? Would you like to dance with me? Would you like to come to my place?' They do not know my name yet, but they want to sleep with me."

She befriended some Iranian girls who had boyfriends. She used to say, "You may think that I am a hypocrite; I actually like them. With their tall bodies and big green eyes, they are very attractive. They often make my heart throb. But you know, when they give me that strange look, I feel nauseated. Can't they think of anything but seducing a girl to sleep with them?"

They were good friends. Whenever Jalal felt lonely, he went to her room and had a chat with her. They talked about everything. Minu talked so warmly and so gratefully about her parents, such as Jalal had never heard from an Iranian girl before. Her hands shaking, she would fix her tearful eyes on his face and say, "They sacrificed everything so that my unworthy self could come here and study at the university..."

When they arrived home, they went up the stairs one behind the other. Minu shook Jalal's hand in front of her room and, as always, kissed Peggy on the cheek. Without the usual invitation to take a cup of Iranian tea, she just smiled and went into her room.

One morning, when Jalal came downstairs, he met the old woman caretaker of the house. She was sweeping the stairs. "Good morning, dear. Beautiful sunny day, isn't it?" Pale sunshine fell through the window into the corridor. The old Englishwoman was looking at it with joy. She said, "Do you know, dear, that an Iranian girl has taken room number ten?"

"Really?" He thought that the woman had again took an Arab or a Turk for an Iranian.

"She came yesterday afternoon. Don't you want to drop in and see her?" She winked at Jalal. "She is a pretty girl with black eyes." She winked again. Jalal laughed and came down the stairs. The door of room number ten was half open. Jalal looked into the room and thought that she must have arrived in London only recently, otherwise she would not leave her door open. The girl also saw Jalal. Maybe she recognized him by his looks. Jalal thought the old woman must have told her too, "Do you know, dear, that there's an Iranian boy staying in room number fourteen?" The girl turned her eyes away from him. Jalal walked past her room and went down the stairs.

That evening Jalal was in his room when someone softly knocked at the door. It was the girl, anxious and embarrassed. She started to speak, fast and without formalities. "Sir, are you Iranian?" she asked in English. But she immediately realized that she did not need to speak in English. Her black eyes lit up and she put her hand before her face. She asked in Persian, "Aren't you?"

Jalal smiled, "Yes, I am."

The girl's face now became calm and she stepped closer. "Excuse me, sir, I don't want to impose upon you, but the light went out in my room and I don't know what is wrong with it." Quickly she added, "I did not touch it at all." In the light of the corridor, between the closed doors of the rooms, Minu looked humble and abject, trembling and confounded like a lost child. She was short and frail, about twenty to twenty-two years old, plainly dressed, and her shiny black hair was gathered on top of her head. She did not wear make-up. She gestured with her little white hand and her eyes were shining like black circles in her face. Worried, she said again, "I didn't do anything. It just went out."

"No problem, don't worry!" Jalal pushed the door half-closed. "Wait a minute!" He changed into his clothes and returned. They went down the stairs together. The rooms were silent. Only the lights shone from beneath the doors. From one of the rooms came the sound of soft music, chatting and the shuffling of feet. "Did you put some coins into the meter?"

The girl looked at him. "Coins? Into what meter?"

Jalal smiled. "Have you arrived in London recently?"

"A week ago. I took a room in a hotel. It was very expensive." After he put a coin in the meter and the light went on, the girl burst out laughing. "You don't know how afraid I was. I thought that something had gone wrong with it." She took out money from her purse and pleaded with Jalal to accept it. "I didn't know that I must pay separately for electricity."

"There is a charge here for everything. The heating, the boiler, the bath, the kitchen stove, everything is charged separately."

"It took me one week to find this room."

The room was tight and small, a dove's nest. A bed, a dresser, a table, and a small folding chair were put together so tightly that no space was left in the room. The kitchen burner, the boiler, and the electric stove could not be jammed together any closer. "Shameless of them to rent even this little hole! How much rent do you pay?"

Minu sat on the bed. "Four pounds a week. It is the cheapest room I could find. Rooms are very expensive here."

Jalal returned with Peggy to his room. It was cold in the room. He lit up the stove, filled the teakettle with water and put it on the gas stove. He lit a match. Peggy said, "He was a stupid boy without manners. But Minu should not have hit him. What a scene it was, what a mess!"

Jalal turned away from the gas stove. He was frowning; he did not like Peggy criticizing Minu. "She did very well to hit that bastard. You cannot imagine yourself in the place of an Iranian girl. They are so different from you!"

Peggy's face fell and she looked offended and astonished at Jalal. He realized that he had spoken thoughtlessly. Her Saturday evening had already been spoiled. And now he had offended her with his statement. Minu had not said even a word of apology to her.

One night he and Peggy had been having tea in his room when someone knocked on the door. It was Minu. He had not seen her since the evening when her light had gone out. She was carrying a plate of pistachios and a box of baklava. She said that her mother had sent them from Tehran. When her eyes suddenly fell on Peggy, she became confused. She turned hastily to go back to her room, but Jalal asked her to stay. He knew that the sense of loneliness, the painful loneliness of being in a strange land, had led her to his room. He himself knew too well the bitter taste of this loneliness. Sometimes he would travel many miles on a train in order to spend an hour or two with an Iranian family and to be among familiar faces. Minu entered the room with the plate and the box. She was relaxed and smiling, yet shy and modest. When Peggy complimented Minu on the pistachios and the baklava, she got up and said, "Just a second!" She hurried out of the room and returned with another plate of pistachios and a box of baklava. She had brought them for Peggy. Again, when Peggy admired Minu's brooch, she took it off and pinned it on the collar of Peggy's dress. Peggy was surprised and looked at it full of joy. "Oh, it is so pretty, very pretty!" That evening Jalal liked Minu. "She is an artless, good girl," he said. They took Minu to a movie. Minu very quickly became close friends with Peggy. That night when Jalal took Peggy home she told him that she liked Minu. Afterwards they took Minu along almost everywhere they went.

The room warmed up. The water started to boil. Jalal brewed the tea and asked Peggy, "Would you like something with your tea, dear?" Peggy shook her head. She was sitting on the bed, swinging her white, shapely legs. She did not speak. Jalal sat beside her. He put his arm around her waist and kissed her face. "Dear, you should know us Easterners better. How long have you been dating me?"

"I have never dated any of your girls."

"They are no different from boys. Easterners are Easterners."

Peggy stared at him. She raised her eyebrows. "That is not true at all. You have me."

"Minu does not want..."

"Why didn't you dance with her?" asked Peggy.

"I don't know. It didn't occur to me," said Jalal.

"I know, you always ignore her."

"There were so many men around there if she wanted to dance."

"She would have danced with you."

"How do you know that? Minu shies away from men. You must have realized that."

"From men, yes. But not from you."

"Why not from me?"

"She feels close to you. She can trust you."

"Perhaps you are right."

"You always tend to forget that she is a woman too. You looked at every woman in the hall, but not at her."

"What does that mean? Minu is different from them. Moreover, I have you."

"I didn't say, stupid, that you should look that way at her; I said you pay no attention to her. No woman can put up with that."

"I don't pay attention to her? You are wrong. I have great respect for her. Minu is like a sister to me and I think..."

"You think if you look at her, you have blasphemed your country. I am sorry for Minu. You are all selfish. You do whatever you want to, and when it comes to your women, you want them to remain pure and innocent, like a doll. You only want to respect them. In their place I would spit on such respect."

One day on his way home, Jalal saw Minu. Smilingly she told him, "Can you guess where I am coming from? I went to the movies with a tall, handsome, young Englishman."

"Bravo! Congratulations! Are you becoming more outgoing, Sister?"

Minu laughed loudly. "You know, from the moment we entered the theater, he moved on me and wanted to kiss me. In that crowd, in front of all those people. I almost died of shame. And it was a nice film too."

"Did you leave the theater? Miss the whole film?"

"Oh no! Somehow by offensive-defensive tactics I managed to bear it to the end. Finally the handsome boy got mad at me. You can't imagine how edgy he became. When we left the theater he offered to give me a ride to his home in his beautiful cherry-red car. I told him that Iranian girls marry a man first and then go with him to his house." Jalal burst out laughing. "Do you know what happened?" asked Minu. "He left me standing there in the middle of the street and got into his car. From there he waved bye-bye to me and drove away. The devil take him! I can't tell you how much I fell for him."

Jalal looked into her unhappy face and gave her a friendly pat on the back. "Don't worry, little sister! That is the way they are here." Minu smiled and turned her wistful eyes away from him.

It was late when he and Peggy left the room. The rooms were all silent. Red light shone from beneath some doors.

"She is asleep."

"That's better. She'll get over it," Peggy said quietly. "It is difficult to take. I know how difficult it is for a woman. It makes no difference whether Western or Eastern, a woman is a woman."

Jalal looked at her. Peggy fell silent and went down the stairs. Peggy's words made him think. Sometimes he had noticed that men were hanging around Minu. He had the feeling that this tiny black-eyed Eastern girl had caught their eyes more than those lewd blondes. Wasn't Peggy jealous of Minu? He accompanied Peggy to the train and went home. Heavy fog descended and settled on the yellow street lamps. The street was wet and silent. Occasionally a car's headlights flashed by and, like a golden flower bloomed on the veil of the fog. The pubs were closing, and half-drunk men and women, arms around each other, poured out of them. In front of his place, near the door, a girl and a boy were intertwined. He opened the door. It was silent in the corridor. He quietly went up the stairs and stopped at the door of Minu's room. He thought he heard some sound. He went closer and put his ear on the door. He heard the muffled sound of Minu's crying. His heart sank. He quietly knocked on the door. The sound of crying ceased. It was silent again.

Jalal remembered the night when Minu had come to his room near midnight, her face wet with tears. She looked very pale. Early that evening an Iranian girl had taken her to a party. The guests were Germans, Swedes, Finns, and Italians. They were the only Easterners among them. They had eaten dinner and then started to dance in pairs, at first the tango and then the twist and the "stylish." Then someone had announced, "Kiss party!" Minu described it: "The boys one after the other would switch off the light and dance moving around and mingling together in the dark. Then they would turn on the light again and each boy would kiss the girl next to him." In the first round a German boy turned up next to Minu and started to kiss her. Next came a Swede and a Finn and each of them kept kissing her really hard and forcing his tongue into her mouth and pressing her against his body. "I never imagined it could end up like this. When Manizheh came to pick me up, she told me that it would be a simple party. Her German boyfriend had asked her to take me along. When I realized what was going on, I told myself, 'All right, I shall stay and see what happens.' To be honest, I didn't want to be a spoilsport. I didn't want to restrain myself anymore. I don't know why. I had become sick of all that self-restraint, all that withdrawal. I wanted to see how it would end. I wanted to break free from this damned fear of men which had always plagued me. I don't know how to tell you what fright gripped me, and how I kept resisting when they started on me. At that time, you know, I only wished that I were a boy, and not so timid. I wanted to let myself go and behave like one of those girls. They embraced me and pawed my body. I had let myself go. My ears were filled with music. I kept dancing. I don't know which one of them it was, the German, the Swede, the Italian, or the Finn. It didn't make any difference to me. I had surrendered myself into their hands to do as they pleased. My body was on fire. My head was dizzy. A strange pleasure slackened my body. I became a different person. I did not push away the hand that found its way under my blouse. My lips were kissing. My eyes were clouded, I could not see well. I saw everything through a veil of fog. The other girls were already naked. A German girl was dancing with only her panties on. The boys were pulling those off too. I heard the laughs and the screams. I went limp… I was not afraid anymore. I was not afraid of anything. I was lying in someone's lap. My ears were filled with screams and moans. The entangled naked bodies, the red light of the lamps in front of me. Then, I don't know how, suddenly I felt sick. I saw Manizheh naked in the embrace of a Finn lying on the floor. I saw myself in the embrace of a German boy. My blouse was getting pulled off. My breast, my body. Now I could feel, I could sense the revulsion, I could touch it. It was like an animal, a big animal, moving on my body. Screams, moans, naked bodies here and there, around me. All at once I felt that I wished to die, I wished to…"

When she ran away from that party and got home, she could not fall asleep from the overwhelming feeling of revulsion. For a moment the mad idea came to her to turn on the gas. But then she remembered her parents and, terrified and shaken, ran out of her room and went to Jalal. She was sobbing. "I loathe myself, I do…"

Jalal quietly called her. "Minu, Minu, dear!" He knocked twice on the door, softly. But still no one answered. Then he heard the creaking of the bed and her quiet footsteps. The light went on and he heard the lock turn. Minu's tearful face appeared from behind the door. Her hair was disheveled. She looked confused and troubled.

"Minu, may I come in for a moment?" He sat on the chair opposite the bed. He looked at the bed. She had not been in bed, but the sheet and blankets had the imprint of her body. The pillow was wet. The room was cold. Jalal got up and turned on the electric fire. "Do you want to kill yourself? Your room is as cold as a refrigerator."

Minu was standing at the back of the room near the washbasin, with her back turned to him. The trickling of the water filled up the room. She was wearing the same dress she had on earlier in the evening. Jalal looked at her. Her shoulders were trembling. "Sis…"

Minu wiped her face with a towel and moved away from the washbasin. She sat on the bed. Her eyes were red, her face swollen. Drops of water were still on her face. "I am a rotten person. It was ugly what I did, wasn't it?"

"Sis…"

"I can't tolerate it anymore. I behave like a dog. Wherever I go, I spoil everything. I am fed up with myself."

"Stop this!"

"I like it here, I like it very much. But it seems that I have not been made for it. I have thought of writing my father that I want to go home. I've grown tired. I don't have the strength to hang on."

"You will get used to it, Sis. There are all these Iranian girls here. You are not alone, dear one!"

"I don't want to get used to it. I don't want to get used to being bought with a cup of tea. I don't care about the other Iranian girls. I am not interested to know what they are doing. I loathe it. I can't help it. I was not made for this sort of life. I have come here to study, so to speak! Who would imagine such things? When I first arrived here I felt like flying, out of joy. How many plans, dreams, sweet illusions I had! I've grown tired of writing letters to this school and to that school. I am tired of struggling to get by till the end of the month on my money. This is a lousy life. I'm deluding myself that I am in London. Where are the results of my stay? What have I achieved so far? What have I learned?" She hid her face in her hands and started to cry again.

Jalal scolded her. "What do you expect? It's only been five months since you came. How demanding you are! Did you expect to receive welcome letters from schools right upon your arrival here? You must be a little patient, kid! Everything will be fine."

Minu was crying quietly. Her delicate body was trembling, like a tree being shaken. It was past midnight. No sound could be heard. Everywhere was quiet. Jalal was sitting beside her trying to calm her. Minu's shoulders were trembling. She held her hands clasped together on her lap, her shining black hair fell on her shoulders and teardrops were rolling down her cheeks. Minu's simple, pure face and her tender, red lips reminded him of Peggy. Peggy once told him that she had been using make-up since she was fourteen and still a high school student. Jalal recalled how he first met her in a club. It was in the dance hall. How he felt captivated and excited by a glimpse of her. She was a tall, slender girl, with golden hair falling down her shoulders. Her big blue eyes, delicate lips and mouth, her finely drawn nose and proud, lovely face made Jalal's heart beat faster. She was dancing with an Indian boy, and the boy would not let her go for a moment. He kept whispering into her ears and making her laugh. When the dance ended, Jalal could not help getting up from his seat and inviting her for the next one before she could start to dance with the Indian boy again. They danced together for some time and later they left for a pub. Jalal tried to get her drunk. He took her hand and brought her half-drunk into his room.

He woke up in the middle of the night and looked at Peggy. She had her arms around him and slept quietly. In the faint light of the reading lamp, her lovely naked body stunned him. She had the most beautiful body Jalal had ever seen. He suddenly felt overwhelmed by strong jealousy and foolishly tried to imagine how many men had loved her before. This thought filled his heart with revulsion. Involuntarily, he withdrew himself from her embrace, got out of bed, and spent the rest of the night sleeping on the floor. He now remembered the words of an Iranian girl who married an Englishman who did not mind in the least whether she was a virgin or not. "What a fool I have been," said the girl, "to have restrained myself so long!" Jalal compared himself with that Englishman and Minu with Peggy. How could he be in love with Peggy? He looked with admiration at Minu's plain and lovely face. She was sitting there quietly weeping. Jalal sat next to her and didn't know what to do, what to tell her. The sorrow he saw in Minu's eyes and face made his heart sink. He tried to find a way to make her forget her sorrows... He started playing the clown for her. He grimaced at her to make her laugh. Minu stopped crying and looked at him in surprise. Her face and eyes had the expression of a small child who suddenly stops crying to stare at something interesting. Minu's gloomy face slowly cleared up, her eyes started to shine and a smile was hiding around her lips.

Jalal was telling her the story of the girl who was afraid of men, and her father told her on her wedding night that whenever she was afraid, she could call out to him. When Jalal arrived at the punch line, where the trembling, scared girl called out only once, "Oh, Dad!" and then her tongue slipped because of the pleasure, "Dad - da-da, daa..." Minu burst out laughing.

The room was warming up and the atmosphere was pleasant. Minu was laughing through her tears. Her cheeks blushed in the warm air like roses. Jalal took her by the hand and led her to the washbasin. He washed her swollen eyes and face with his own hands. The cold water awakened a pleasant feeling in his palms as Minu's warm, delicate face hung in his hot, wet hands. Suddenly, involuntarily, he turned and stared at Minu. She had the most innocent and sweet face he had ever seen. With her shining eyes Minu stared back at him and her lips were quivering like two red butterflies. Jalal's heart trembled and he felt weak. His hands dropped on the faucet and water sprang from between his fingers. It shot high and sprinkled into Minu's face. She screamed and laughed. Then, suddenly, she put her hands under the faucet, leaned over and filled them with water and splashed it in Jalal's face. Jalal fought back... then they both leaned over the faucet and splashed water on each other and laughed. Their hands kept touching each other and their bodies got entangled. They were scuffling and throwing water at each other. Jalal was wet all over, and Minu's blouse clung to her, revealing her firm, young body. Big, bright water drops were running down her head and face. Then they both stopped laughing and scuffling and looked at each other, trembling and excited. Her big black eyes sparkled with little flames of fire. Jalal's hands twined around Minu's waist and he drew her to him. He put his lips to her mouth. The softness and the heat emanating from her lips took away his senses. He took Minu into his arms, laid her on the bed and pressed her wet, warm body into his embrace.

Later he got up and his entire body was trembling. His face was burning. He could still see the little white hand in front of his eyes, rising and settling on his face like a piece of fire. Then he was in his own room, turning over in his bed without being able to fall asleep...

Next morning, as he went down the stairs, the woman caretaker was sweeping. "Good morning, dear!"

"Good morning!"

"Nasty weather, isn't it?" Jalal looked out of the window. It was raining steadily. The sky was pitch dark. "Did you know, dear, that the Iranian girl moved out?"

"No. When?"

"An hour ago. She was a nice girl, wasn't she?"

Glorious Day

Translated by Kinga Markus

It was a trip I had to undertake on official grounds. Inevitably, my attention was called to a matter that could, for a destitute young man like myself, be a real treat beside the boring official duties. The words of the boys still rang in my ears: "Don't miss it! Once you get there, don't forget to visit that street, you lucky dog!" When I got on the bus, the boys from the office still kept whispering into my ears and winking at me: "Go on, enjoy yourself! This is a God-given opportunity." When the bus arrived at our destination and I was waiting among the passengers for my turn to get off, these words slowly came back to me again: "Don't leave that out, hey!"

I took a room in the local inn, had a bath, and changed my clothes, then set out for the town. I was impatient, and the words of my pals ran through my mind... I had hardly caught my breath when the old coachman let me off "there."

He stuck out his head over his comically crooked back, like a turtle, and winked at me... just as if he agreed with my pals: "Go on, enjoy yourself!" Then the coachman withdrew his head into his crooked shoulders, whipped his skinny horse and the coach left noisily. I

remained alone in the middle of the dirty street, between low walls
and mud houses. Overpowered with fright, feeling like a lost child, I
looked all around and just for encouragement I told myself, "Here
you are ... Try your luck!" And I stared at the street I had been told
not to forget to visit.

It was empty and stretched out like a lazy, dusty snake in its muddy
nest, and dirty, faded sunshine fell on it. In the middle of this lane a
thick, black stream—like a big worm—stretched out, curving and
flowing ahead. As I followed the route of the stream with my eyes, I
came upon the pit of the canal at the lower end of the street. My body
felt weak. My heart was beating fast, my legs were trembling. My
head was rattling like a box full of gravel. I don't know why, but as I
started forward, following the "street worm," I automatically slipped
my hand into my pocket, took out my glasses, and put them on. All
the time I imagined that someone was following me. I looked back
and when I could not see anyone, I told myself: "Who knows you
here? Don't worry, enjoy yourself!" I was climbing up a steep alley. It
stank and stretched out like a putrid carcass under my feet...

When I arrived at a house which had a relatively pleasing appearance, and whose door, just like that of the other houses on the same
row, was ajar, I bolted in. But after a few steps into the corridor, I
turned back. It occurred to me that somebody was following me like
a shadow. I could even hear his footsteps. I turned back and looked
into the street. Everything was the same; the only people there were
a man sleeping by the side of the road, a grocer licking his greasy
hands, and an old woman sweeping the front of her house. I calmed
down. Then, filled with a familiar sweet desire, I entered the courtyard. "The girls" were sitting in the courtyard, beside the pond,
playing cards. The weather was stifling hot. With my clothes on, I
was choking. The brick pavement of the courtyard had been sprinkled with water. The whole place smelled foul. There were four of
them, all half-naked. A plump old woman was sitting on a small stool
beside them. When I looked at "them," the color of their white sor-
did bodies hit me, as if a fistful of sand had been thrown in my eyes.
The smell that had been hanging over the whole courtyard assailed
my nose. I felt like retreating. But I thought about the pleasure
ahead. "Don't be a fool!" I told myself.

The plump old woman stood up, smiled at me, and came near. She
began to talk to me hurriedly. A birthmark, like some filthy rag, spread
over her face. Then she turned back and shouted. The women at the
pond got up from the mat, so dull and heavy, with such difficulty that

they might have been under a great burden. They came toward me. Because they had to interrupt their game, the women seemed sullen and cross. Yet, somehow or other, when they came near, they were all smiling. When I looked at them, I was astonished. The smiles upon their lips were all identical, just like the one frozen on the old woman's lips. It occurred to me that I was seeing one smile reflected in four or five mirrors. A smile in four or five copies. When they were smiling, their eyes were staring at me and their lips were signaling to me.

I turned my head away to escape the hailstorm of their stares. My eyes wandered to the opposite room. A stout man was stretched out there snoring in the arms of a little girl. He had his big hairy hands locked around her slender nude waist and held the little girl tight as if she were a soft white rabbit.

As I gazed at them the girl moved and, like a cat, shook herself gracefully and slipped out of the man's hold. She was stark naked. She rose and glowered at the man. He was still snoring. The girl threw her shift on and came out of the room to us. When she saw me, she stopped short and inspected me nonchalantly. But, unlike the others, she was not smiling. She was very small, a real girl child, no more than thirteen or fourteen years old, perhaps. But her eyes were like those of a woman. Now she was studying my necktie and my suit. Her curiosity was aroused. My eyes met hers. I turned around and went to the narrow, dark room opposite me. She followed me and closed the door behind her. She no longer showed any curiosity; she was again nonchalant and listless.

In the room a filthy mattress was thrown on the floor, like a bloated carcass. A few steps from it a girl of four or five years was stretching and with her shining languid eyes was staring into the air. She was very similar to the girl who had become my companion. Even their eyes had the same languid, nonchalant look. The little girl blinked her blue eyes a few times, then her eyelids dropped and her breathing slowed.

On the mantelpiece beside the mattress there was a filthy Argand lamp and beside it a clean notebook and pencil. On the walls of the room all kinds of lips—blossom-like and thin, kidney-shaped and fleshy—were drawn, in pairs, or just single, like illustrations in a zoology textbook. I turned back unwittingly to look at the lips of the girl. She picked up the notebook and was turning the pages like a schoolgirl. I took off my clothes and she too—without much fuss, very expertly—leaned down, slipped out of her shift and dropped it over her head to the carpet. I hung my clothes on a thick rusty hook on the wall, and went to her. My eyes were studying her body. It was whiter than mine.

Her body fell under me like a soft pillow on the mattress, and her eyes fixed on the ceiling. I don't know how many times she counted the beams of the ceiling before it was over and I rose. I remembered all the pleasant dreams and plans I had had for the night. I felt nauseated. I went to fetch my clothes. All my pleasant dreams and plans had evaporated. I wanted to say something, but I was in no mood for it. I don't know why, but I thought that my official duties in this town were now over... I almost asked myself: "What should I write in my report?"

The girl put on her shift, stood up and went to the mantelpiece. She was humming to herself:

Slowly-slowly let me in,
In your lap, take me in...

She took the pencil, turned the pages in her notebook and began to write. I leaned over to look into her notebook. Something was written there in a childish hand. She put the pencil in her mouth, then went on writing. "Three in the morning... four in the afternoon... seven yesterday night... one overnight..."

She put her finger to her lips and started to count. I stared at her without understanding a thing. When she saw that I was looking at her writing in the notebook, she was very happy.

She laughed again. My eyes fell on her writing in the notebook: "Since yesterday night: one overnight guest,"and I was stunned by her childish, cheerful face. The girl added with special pride and joy, "You know, I am not like them. I went to school, I am educated... I can write anything. They can't. I can even read the newspapers. They can't read at all..." She paused a little, looked at me with her shining eyes, and went on, "Do you want me to recite 'Glorious Day' for you? Then you could see for yourself that I haven't forgotten it yet. When I used to go to school, you know, I was the only one who could recite 'Glorious Day' by heart. The lady teacher always said, 'Bravo, Shirin Abadi!' Do you want to hear it?" Without waiting for my answer, she began to recite it in a high, piercing tone, while her face was glowed with childish grace:

The night was gone, and came the morn;
My glorious lucky day has been born!
The sun, the king of stars as yet
Has not raised to the sky his head,
When I open my sleepy eyes
To hail the sun as he doth rise.

The girl's eyelids opened up like mother-of-pearl and her big eyes were shining radiantly. She looked like a happy and proud child, standing upright and motionless, just as in the classroom. When she saw that I was listening, she closed her eyes again, and happily went on with the recital:

From one side calls the crowing cock,
The Muezzin from the other;
To hear my father's kindly words,
Sweet whispers from my mother,
I open up my sleepy eyes
To hail the sun as he doth rise.

It was a cheerful verse, but for some reason, her voice broke my heart. In spite of a strong desire to escape from her to the street, I listened to her chanting, to the verses from her childish lips, to their end. It was the saddest song I ever heard in my life. The girl stood like a beautiful, sorrowful picture in front of me.

When she finished her chanting, she looked at me with enthusiastic eyes: "Didn't I tell you I could recite it all…" I nodded and smiled at her. The girl blushed in her happiness and, like a bashful child, bowed her head and put her finger between her lips…

When I left the house, I felt the piercing of a hundred needles in my body. My head was full of rattling noises, like a box of gravel. I was humming to myself:

The night was gone and came the morn;
My glorious, lucky day is born . . .

Gholam Hosayn Nazari

1933–

Short-story writer Gholam Hosayn Nazari was born in Malayer and graduated from dental school at Tehran University in 1962. A year later, he emigrated to Germany to practice dentistry. From 1965 through 1977 he published at least seven short stories in *Sokhan* magazine (1943–79). Four of his stories, including "Moths in the Night," "Adolescence and the Hill," and "Shadowy," have appeared in a German translation by Faramarz Behzad (*Moderne Erzähler der Welt*: *Iran*, Horst Erdman Verlag, Stuttgart 1978, pp. 307–15).

Moths in the Night

Translated by Heshmat Moayyad

I surprised them. When I entered the room, all three of them were sitting around the *korsi*. My mother jumped up and opened her shriveled arms. I realized that I was the same helpless child again who had escaped from school, seeking shelter in her arms. I told myself, "Man, you are grown up now." But I will never grow up. I will never be grown up.

I shook hands with my brother and sister and kissed their foreheads, and we sat down. My mother wouldn't take her eyes off my face.

"Well, now tell us," she said. I gulped.

"Let us hear, where have you been these two years? What have you been doing?"

"Nothing!"

"Are you tired?"

I did not answer. My brother was sitting across from me. He had started growing a mustache, and his eyes... his eyes looked frightened.

"What are you doing?" I asked him.

"Nothing!"

I said nothing to my sister. We just looked at each other, cold and silent, like two hopeless lovers. We only looked at each other.

On the *korsi* the same old oil lamp was burning. A few moths were flying around its shade. Nothing had changed: the doors, the walls, the windows, the curtains, the ceiling-beams. Nothing had changed. Only my mother looked more worn out, and my brother's eyes looked frightened. And my sister... my sister was sitting there like a pretty doll, leaning her chin on the edge of the *korsi*, gazing with her glassy eyes at the lamp's flame.

"Don't you have a tongue left in your mouth?" said my mother.

"What do you want me to say?"

"Tell me where you have been these two years. What have you done?"

"Nothing!"

"You are tired. Let me get up and fix you some tea."

No, nothing had changed. Doors, walls, windows, curtains, ceiling-beams, everything was as before. Only in our hearts, I believe something was broken. Something had been broken in our hearts.

The lamp was burning on the *korsi*. The moths no longer flew; they were clasped to the shade. The samovar was gurgling. My sister's head, like the severed head of a doll, lay on the corner of the *korsi*. The night passed slowly, and we looked at each other in silent sadness.

The Cast

Translated by Heshmat Moayyad

I told my apprentice to get ready to leave, to put things away and… He knows best what sort of things need to be done before leaving. I lit a cigarette and waited near the window. Darkness and silence poured down from the sky over the city like a high black waterfall. I thought to myself, "That is a good sign. In darkness people take some rest—in darkness they charge themselves." And just at that moment I heard steps in the hallway. I turned around. My apprentice looked at me frightened and I understood his message from his eyes. I thought, "Whatever happens from now on, it will be unexpected. From now on I will bear no responsibility for anything that may happen."

The door opened and a broad-shouldered man came in. "Hello, Doctor." And now I remembered that I am a dentist. It was as if I had forgotten it for years: a cheap, miserable dentist in a remote town.

The man sat on the chair and I stood in front of him. What a serious situation! It was as if I were waking up from sleep. It was as if I were hurled from one world into another. It was as if I were growing on my legs, and my legs… my legs, these bitter roots of an imaginary plant. Instantly I decided to tell my patient everything, to tell him that at this time of the evening in this remote town many unpredictable events are lurking in the dark and he should know that I will bear no responsibility for anything that happens.

And so I began: "Well, what can I do for you?"

"I have come for my teeth. Some time ago you made a cast of my mouth. Now I have come for my teeth."

Surely the man was telling me a story, or perhaps he was unknowingly repeating some tale from an old book. In any event it has been many years now since I have made a cast of anybody's teeth. Confused, I went to the storeroom of my surgery. In this storeroom—and in other places, in other storerooms—there are artificial teeth, wigs, glasses, canes, hearing aids, trusses, and other trivia, all small tools of defense against the beckonings and grimaces of death. I picked up a few sets of dentures and returned to the patient. I tried them on in his mouth, one by one, but none fitted.

I felt obliged to tell him the truth: "My dear sir, believe me that for many years now I have not made a cast of anybody's mouth. That is to say that nowadays orthodontical factories are constantly manufacturing dentures, in all sizes. We try these ready-made teeth out in the mouths of interested parties. Usually one of them will fit. If none of them does, with a small surgical procedure we change the jaw to fit the shape of the artificial teeth. In your own case—as you yourself have seen—you must allow us with a small operation to…

He smiled contentedly. My apprentice tied a large white napkin around his neck and handed me the scalpel. The man opened his mouth and I stood in front of him with the knife in my hand. It was as if I were waking up from sleep. What a dangerous situation! My apprentice was weeping bitterly. He is sixteen years old and is still able to cry. I bent over and inserted the knife into the patient's mouth. I had not yet pushed down on it when blood gushed out of his mouth, and it seemed that it would never stop.

Adolescence and the Hill

Translated by Heshmat Moayyad

In my dreams there is always a commander (and that is me, myself) who, clad in the attire of the heroes of old, with a mace and helmet and shield, comes down from a hill and attacks the enemy's army single-handedly. My wounded commander falls in the middle of the field and dies.

I carelessly scrawled a line on the wall and thought that after me another playful boy would continue the line to its intended end. In my dreams there is always a playful little boy (and that is me, myself) who scrawls coarse lines on the walls.

It was from the top of the hill that I saw them. The legs of the woman were bare and the man was making bewildering, incomprehensible motions between them.

After we had seen each other a few times, I decided one day to take her behind the hill in order to give clarity and meaning to those bewildering and incomprehensible motions. As I looked from afar, the hill now looked like the tip of a woman's breast.

In my dreams there is always a little girl, in an elegant litter, in the depths of history, traveling on nameless roads toward an unknown destination.

Uncompleted homework, the litter lost between the pages of the history book, closed notebooks and unsolved problems, and the hill which now looked like the nipple of a woman's breast. At night I cried restlessly.

The little boy scrawled a line on the wall and walked up the hill fast and went down the other side, clad in the attire of the heroes of old, with a mace and helmet and shield. My mortally wounded commander in the middle of the field.

Mr. Hemayat

Translated by Heshmat Moayyad

It was a vulgar film. But Mr. Hemayat was happy that he had wasted two hours of his time. Besides, all films are vulgar: women have well-shaped white legs and big breasts, and the men... the men are either thieves or smugglers, and violent in any case. One such man runs away together with one such woman. The policemen whistle—trains, cars, crossroads, beds, screaming, horns, alarm lights. In the end, the thief embraces the woman, and the policemen whistle no more because the film is finished.

Mr. Hemayat thought that if one night, only one night, one of these women would sleep with him, the policemen could keep on whistling until Judgment Day, he would not pay as much attention to them as to a dog. That evening Mr. Hemayat thought a lot. What about dropping the rules for one night and living voluptuously? he thought to himself. What was wrong with tonight? Nobody had taken tonight away from him.

He emptied half a bottle in a liquor shop and then decided to take one of these veiled women on Takht-e-Jamshid Avenue by the hand and take her home. Half an hour later Mr. Hemayat was walking home together with a veiled woman. On the way Mr. Hemayat told the woman that living in a rented place is full of troubles; one is not free, and Mr. Hemayat in particular does not like to be watched. In the end he asked the woman to take off her shoes when going up the stairs. And the woman agreed to do so.

They walked up the stairs. Mr. Hemayat inserted the key and opened the door and they entered the room. Mr. Hemayat turned on the light and saw that somebody was lying on his bed. Mr. Hemayat seated the woman in such a position that she would not see the bed. Pretending to make the bed, he approached it and lifted the corner of the blanket. Indeed, it was he, Mr. Hemayat himself, who was lying on the bed.

Mr. Hemayat sat on the corner of the bed and told the woman, "It is a nice room if one does not make any noise." The woman looked around the room. Mr. Hemayat thought, Well, we should actually start, and said to the woman, "Well, let's start... But these spring beds make a lot of noise. I am afraid it might wake up the landlord. Let's place the mattress on the floor. And it is even cozier on the floor."

The woman said, "If you are afraid that your bed might get dirty, I have nothing against it."

Mr. Hemayat felt embarrassed. He showed the woman his own self, who was sleeping in the bed, and said, "Look! Someone is sleeping in the bed. But don't worry. He is a friend of mine who is sick and I take care of him. He won't bother us." He then got up and placed the mattress on the floor and told the woman, "Please! please get on the mattress."

The woman sat on the mattress and said, "Please, hurry up a little."

Mr. Hemayat bent down to untie his shoelaces. Right at that moment Mr. Hemayat rose from the bed and, just as he was, in his undershirt and drawers, sat on the bed. Mr. Hemayat was mortified. For the sake of something to do he went close to himself and sat on the bed and told the woman, "My friend and I look surprisingly alike."

The woman said, "Not at all! Your friend looks younger, more cheerful, and more pleasant."

For the first time in his life Mr. Hemayat wished that instead of being his own self he could be his other self. He thought, In reality we are both the same person and can easily change places. He got up and asked himself to move over a little, and sat in his own place. He then asked the woman, "What do you think in this position..."

The woman answered, "Don't be so fickle. Your friend is a little younger. You are not unpleasant either. You are indeed very nice."

Mr. Hemayat looked at himself. How he hated himself! Many times he had decided to get up one night, choke himself with his own hands and free himself from his own evil. But, well, now was not the proper occasion to carry out such intentions. This one night they would somehow have to manage to get along with each other." Then having lost all hope, he asked the woman, "Now, which one of us would you prefer to sleep with first?"

At this juncture Mr. Hemayat saw Mr. Hemayat get up from his place and lie in the arms of the woman. Mr. Hemayat thought looking at such scenes is also pleasurable. He sat on the chair and watched them. It is possible that he fell asleep. Mr. Hemayat became aware when he himself and the woman got up. He went back to the bed and lay down, and the woman picked up her handbag. Mr. Hemayat escorted her down to the street. Before saying good-bye to him the woman asked, "Are you upset?"

"No, just a little annoyed. After all the trouble and…"

"Don't worry," said the woman, "I work on Takht-e-Jamshid every evening. Just come if you like." Mr. Hemayat returned home and stretched out on the floor. Mr. Hemayat was in bed snoring.

This was an awful misfortune. But what can one do? Mr. Hemayat was now convinced that it could not be helped. At lunchtime in the restaurant Mr. Hemayat had just ordered when he himself… yes, right on cue he himself would come and instruct Mr. Hemayat to move over a little and would sit in his own place. Mr. Hemayat would only watch. All his life Mr. Hemayat had only watched. Mr. Hemayat thought, This situation can no longer continue. A remedy will have to be found. With this thought he fell asleep.

The next morning Mr. Hemayat woke up and shaved. Mr. Hemayat was still in bed snoring. At the doorway he turned around and looked at himself as if asking himself for help. In the office many things might happen. Mr. Hemayat went near the bed and sat at his own side. He shook his own self until he woke up. Then, choking with tears, he promised himself that from now on he would order for his own self the most delicious foods in restaurants and take home the nicest of the veiled women from Takht-e-Jamshid every evening. Mr. Hemayat then got up from bed and accompanied Mr. Hemayat to his office.

Shadowy

Translated by Heshmat Moayyad

When we talk of an imaginary city, this imaginary city certainly also has a square which is indisputably imaginary. But the existence of imaginary squares in imaginary cities is a reality that may not be denied, a form of reality which is real but lacks reality. All in all, it appears that imaginary cities, with their shares of reality, are basically imaginary-real.

In an imaginary city that possesses an imaginary square as well (of course, we do not intend to lay out the plan of a city here), the streets lose their extensions in alleys, and the alleys are surrounded by walls and houses, and the houses are filled with people—all imaginary.

From the imaginary center of an imaginary city an imaginary person sets out to walk. You agree with me that it is very difficult to describe the route of this person. We assume that he passes through one of the streets and enters an alley. And we already know that the alleys are surrounded by walls and houses. Normally, this person ought to be living in one of these houses. But the imaginary person does not reside, the imaginary person is not limited by anything or confined within any

place. The imaginary person exists at all times and in all places. Thus
we see that imaginary persons disrupt the order and security of imaginary cities. And since we have no proper picture of imaginary persons,
we can only say that the existence of imaginary persons at least threatens, if it does not deny, the existence of imaginary cities.

I am a real person, there is no doubt about it, even if you may have
forgotten this fact temporarily. I set out to walk from the center of
the city. Everything is real. You agree that my route can easily be
described. But I have never liked homely description or descriptions.
I pass through one of the streets and enter an alley. And we already
know that alleys are surrounded by walls and houses. And a person
like me should, as a matter of rule, be living in one of these houses
on this alley. Unfortunately I do not live in this alley. None of the
houses in this city belongs to me. Even the stone pavements of the
alley do not acknowledge my steps. The city rejects me with a peculiar tone. I am chased away. Politely, I am chased away. On the city's
edge—where the buildings end and the reality of the city merges,
without demarcation lines, into the ambiguity and imagination of
the wasteland at the supposed location of the city gate (would that
cities had gates!)—I get caught in the same dead end that all real
persons in real cities get entrapped in, a sort of forced choice. Fortunately enough, I have no doubts about my own real being. All in all,
it appears that real cities, turning their backs on reality, are basically
real-imaginary and deny the existence of real persons. Real persons
thus have no choice but to migrate to imaginary cities.

In an imaginary city that has no name yet, I lead a splendid life in
our magnificent palace together with my wife Farangis, my son Fari-
borz, and my daughter Katayun. In this magnificent palace we
receive our mutual friends. My wife and I have selected our friends
meticulously and with great care, according to the concept of freedom, the way all of us deeply—and equally—perceive it. When we
give a party in our house, after horseriding or swimming, we sit down
and play games. Our conversations are in remembrance of those
great human qualities that have immersed our small circle in a sweet
dream, neither awake nor asleep. On one unimportant subject alone,
which is not worth even mentioning, I am, not of an opposite opinion, but of a slightly different taste: my friends think that it is the
objective of real cities that becomes subjective. But in the fashion of a
fanatical believer, I deeply believe (my friends are tolerant enough to
know that on this specific subject they should not debate with me)
that it is the subjective of the imaginary cities that becomes objective.

Esma'il Fasih

1935–

An active novelist and short-story writer since the late 1960s, Esma'il Fasih was born and raised in Tehran. In 1956 he traveled to the United States to attend college. With degrees in English literature and science, he returned to Iran and in 1963 began seventeen years' employment with the National Iranian Oil Company, most of it teaching at the Abadan Institute of Technology. Forced into retirement in 1981, Fasih now lives with his family in Tehran and occasionally serves as a technical consultant to the NIOC.

His first novel was *Sharāb-e khām* (Raw wine, 1968). Then came *Del-e kur* (The blind heart, 1974), *Dāstān-e Jāvid* (The story of Javid, 1980), *Sorayyā dar eghmā* (Sorayya in a coma, 1983), which appeared in translation in 1985, *Dard-e Siyāvash* (Siyavash's pain, 1985), *Zemestān-e shast-o do* (Winter of 1962, 1987), and *Shahbāz va joghdān* (The falcon and the owls, 1990). Fasih's novels often treat various members of a fictitious family called "Aryan." Several of these were reprinted in the early 1990s.

Fasih's first short story collections were *Khāk-e āshnā* (The familiar earth, 1970) and *Didār dar Hend* (Visit to India, 1970), followed by *'Aqd* (Wedding, 1978), and *Nemādha-ye dasht-e moshavvash* (Symbols of the shimmering desert, 1990). In the late 1980s, Fasih was also publishing short stories in the Tehran journal *Ādineh*. His article called "The Status: A Day in the Life of an Iranian Writer" in *Third World Review* 9 (1987) sheds light on the situation for writers of fiction living and working in Iran in the 1980s and 1990s.

Nonetheless, his novelistic output has been steadily prolific, including: *Farār-e Farvahar* (1993), *Bādeh-e kohan* (1994), *Asir-e zamān* (1995), *Panāh bar Hāfez: yak hasb-e hāl* (996), *Koshtah-e 'eshq* (1997), *Tasht-e khun* (1997), *Lāleh bar afrukht* (1998), *Bāz'gasht be-dar khungāh* (1998), *Tarāzhedi/Komedi-e Pars* (1998), *Dar entezār* (2000), and *Nāmeh'i beh dunyā* (2000).

Love

Translated by Camron Amin

The sky over the small covered bazaar was wounded by the setting sun. When the evening call to prayer was raised, it was as though the sword of Islam had split the horizon and set it bleeding. At the onset of evening, black clouds appeared, the wind began to blow, and then it began to storm. By the end of the night the wind had set upon the branches of a grapevine in Showkat Khanom's courtyard and was blowing dried branches into the window of the rented room upstairs. (A window pane was broken. Behind the broken glass, pages from a newspaper were taped up.) In the room, a woman and her husband were sitting by a kerosene stove.

The woman, needle and thread in hand, was hemming the sides of some white cloth for swaddling clothes. But her thoughts were some-where else tonight. One moment she would cast a glance at her husband out of the corner of her eye. Another moment she seemed sunk in thought. She knew misfortune was in store again. For two weeks this one, like the other one that had miscarried after three months, had not stirred. Her lower abdomen hurt. But she didn't want

223

her husband to know anything yet. She feared the hospital and the tearing open of her stomach.

She was twenty-one years old and from the north. Her husband was thirty and from this same small bazaar. He was a shopkeeper in one of the uptown bookstores: a small business, a small life. They rented two upstairs rooms. The building on this side of the court-yard had its back to the *qebleh*—it was one of those courtyards that, like the caravanseries of thirty years ago, had a single room for each tenant. Just recently the house acquired electricity, a stone-brick front, an iron door, a bell— everything. But it still belonged to old Showkat Khanom. The storm howled behind the upstairs windows tonight. Both wife and husband were withdrawn and tired from the inside out.

The woman sighed and said, "I hope God'll make it rain and give us some relief."

The man lifted his head from a magazine, tossed a perfunctory glance out the window and said, "It'll come."

Again they were silent for a long time.

The woman said, "A few nights ago, when it was raining and stormy like this, you wanted to talk about something…"

The man yawned and said, "It was the story about my sister."

"Leyla?"

"Yeah."

"How did she die, anyway?"

The man stretched his legs. He took a deep breath. Just as he was ready, there came the sound of rain against the glass of the window. A minute later, a heavy downpour spilled over the whole bazaar. He got up and closed the windows, which the force of the wind had opened. Then he brought his shoes in from just outside the door to the balcony. Again he went out and gathered up the shirt, socks and other pieces of clothing that his wife had washed and spread out on the balcony banister.

Derisively, he said, "The rain makes the rich happy."

His wife said, "Yeah. It's good for them, bad for us. Give me those."

She put the ragged swaddling clothes aside, got up and took the rumpled clothes from her husband and spread them around the wardrobe one by one.

Nothing happened. The dank smell of wet clothes began to per-meate the room. The man was deep in thought. The woman saw in his eyes that he was reviewing old events—no doubt distant, bad and bitter events. After spreading out the clothes she returned to the stove. A teapot and kettle were on the stove. The woman's bare feet scuffed against the thin, coarse wool carpet. A small electric bulb shed a yellow light onto the room. The ceiling had only beams and matting. It was ugly, all rotted wood beams with brown and protruding ties. The plaster on the walls was matted and dirty. Framed pictures and icons hung on the walls: a picture of the young Prophet Mohammad with angels over his head; a portrait of Princess Farrokh-Laqa; Abraham preparing Ishmael for sacrifice and the intervention of the angels; a colored drawing behind glass of The Five—Mohammad, Ali, Fatemeh, Hasan and Hosayn—with angels behind them on shafts of sunlight; a large foreign portrait of a holy woman, naked on a throne in a garden with nymphs and angels in attendance. On all the frames, added to the dust of time, lay the grime of neglect. The woman brought the tea service on a tray from the windowsill and set it down on the floor. She poured two cups of tea. She put one in front of her husband along with sugar cubes. She took some cubes for herself, took her teacup, and returned to the ragged swaddling clothes. She sat and took some cloth and a needle in her hands.

"What was the story about your sister? You've never told me," she said.

It was now that the man lit a Homa cigarette and amidst the dank smell and sound of the rain began to tell his story. Besides his wife, it seemed that all the people, saints and angels in the frames were listening.

He said, "We were a brother and sister. My sister Leyla was three years older than me. There was another older sister who died when she was a baby. My dad was a sayyid and Koran reciter who died of consumption when I was three years old. After Dad's death our life was not good. We went on living in this same room. Mother washed clothes and cleaned houses. Sometimes the rent was two or three months late. This same Showkat Khanom was the landlady. She gave us some consideration out of respect for my father. My mother liked this room. She didn't want us to leave here. We were familiar and protected here. My sister and I were always the children of Aqa Sayyid Abolfazl Khan.

"My sister and I spent our whole childhood in this room. South Tehran, during the years 1320 to 1330 (1941-51). Our lives passed in want and misfortune. My sister was not sick, but she had sort of a great sensitivity to everything, and a kind of strange happiness. She always used to talk of love to me, used to tell me stories about the love of angels, and she really loved me. Days would pass with her cradling me in her arms, talking and telling stories. From the window, from this same window, we would watch the bright blue sky over the pine trees and the bazaar. Sometimes I had the feeling that there was a sadness in my sister that was not in the rest of the people of the bazaar. She was also very beautiful. I wish we had a picture of her.

"My sister (as far as I can remember, from when she was six or seven years old) used to talk of the angels in the sky and the beauty of heaven's garden. When she was ten, this talk had gradually turned into a beautiful madness or maybe a kind of melancholia. When she would talk of the angels and of heaven she could take a person with her into a dream. She loved it: a beautiful place, far from these stern people, peaceful and solitary. Sometimes Leyla would point to the angels in the pictures and marvel at how small and delicate they were, how they could fly amidst the clouds and shafts of sunlight. Sometimes she would want us to pack up and leave this room and this place, and go to a place that had trees and flowers and streams and freedom. And slowly, with the passing of the years, this wishing and talking took the form of dreams and fantasy for my sister.

"But Showkat Khanom's courtyard was a reality right outside our window. During the day we used to hear the sound of our neighbor's fights by the shallow pool, the filth of the courtyard and the outhouse. At night there was the noise of drunks and knife-wielding thugs under the archway, the sounds of weddings, funerals, the cries of 'There is no god but God,' and the children cursing in the street. But this was no life. It was not good. The sighs and moans of Mother, who would always come from the laundry tired and bitter and say that whoever died was at ease and in the end we would all lie under six feet of earth, were not good either. It was no life. My sister would say God did not bring us into the world to be sad for no reason and in the end be laid under six feet of earth. God created us so that we would have free souls, like angels. And like the angels we should love everyone. Life was good and untainted. Just before each dawn, she would tell me of her dreams of heaven. Sometimes I was in her dreams, sometimes not. But the dreams were always there.

"I said Dad was a religious man, and he was not a bad man. I heard he was very fond of Leyla. Some of the loneliness of my sister's soul sprang from my father's death—right in this very room. I don't remember my father's dying. I've heard that near the end he suffered a lot. I don't remember the night of his death either. I have a confused half-memory that it was here that they drew a white sheet over my father. Later I understood how painful the scene of Dad's death in this little room must have been for my sister, and how deep the pain was. As long as my father lived he used to tell her stories—right up to the last night. Stories from the Koran: the story of Adam, the story of Joseph, the story of Noah and the story of Mary. Part of Leyla's other-worldliness and her obsession with angels was because of my father's stories. And then the scene of my father dying in this same room in front of Leyla's eyes!

"Sometimes it was difficult for me to believe Leyla's talk of angelic love. For me, the fights, the shouts, the jealousies, the grudges, the altercations and the harshness were pieces of real life, of our life—here in Showkat Khanom's courtyard. Especially Showkat Khanom's son, 'Brainless' Abdollah, who was a thug and very mean. Each time he was in the house he would beat his orphaned younger brothers and sisters. One day he beat the husband of one of the neighbors who had not paid the rent for two months, then lifted him up and threw him into the pool... but with all this Leyla would never let me lose heart. She would not let me doubt the hidden goodness of people's natures, nor her stories and her vision. She said people, even this Brainless Abdollah, didn't know themselves what they were doing. If they knew, they would understand each other, be kind to each other, and like each other. One unspoken question was always in my head: why, with all that angel-like talk and love, was she alone in this world? Why was she scared? Why did she hide? Did she suspect otherwise in the depths of her soul? There were times when I fearfully thought that Brainless Abdollah's world must be the real world and my sister's the imaginary one.

"One night, when I was passing through the courtyard, I heard sounds from within Showkat Khanom's rooms. I came quietly and watched. Brainless Abdollah was in a corner of the room sitting in front of the mirror. A knife was in his hand. Showkat Khanom was standing next to her son, crying and hitting her own face and head. Brainless Abdollah was enraged over something. He kept striking himself with the knife, but not very hard. His mother would entreatingly offer herself as sacrifice or pray to heaven and say, 'So go ahead and stab me once too!' The rest of the children hid under the quilts from fright. It was rumored that Brainless Abdollah wanted a wife. He was acting up this way so they would get him a wife.

"In short it was in the midst of such chaos and such people that we lived: in this same closed room and with these same framed pictures of saints and angels. And my sister had dreams—or an obsession in the form of dreams and fantasies — that people are angels, or ought to be angels. And when the soul of a girl is filled with dreams and fantasies what can be done?

"Then Leyla got sick.

"The event that caused my sister's illness happened on a summer morning in the courtyard in this same house. I remember that morning. I was eight years old.

"My sister woke me up hurriedly. She tugged my hand and brought me to the window. She pointed to something in the courtyard, by the edge of the pool on the bricks next to the cesspool. Day or night, everything and anything happened in Showkat Khanom's house. Today something had fallen to the floor of the courtyard. It was wrapped in a white rag. Something resembling the swaddling clothes of a child, and it was bloody. Showkat Khanom and the wife of a neighbor were standing by the swaddling clothes and talking. We could not hear them. I asked Leyla quietly, 'What is it? A baby?' Leyla said, 'I don't know.' 'Is it alive or dead?' Leyla said, 'I don't know.' Later I found out that it was 'Blind' Fatemeh's baby.

"Blind Fatemeh was Showkat Khanom's maid. We had seen that she was pregnant. Blind Fatemeh was small and thin and blind in one eye. An orphan maidservant. No one knew where she came from. No doubt she was an abandoned child. Blind Fatemeh had been Showkat Khanom's maid for as long as I could remember—and later Showkat Khanom turned her out. Blind Fatemeh was the same age as my sister, a little older. In the final months of Blind Fatemeh's pregnancy, all the residents of the bazaar took to cursing at her, swearing at her, and ridiculing her. I didn't understand why. The other thing I couldn't understand in those days is why Showkat Khanom hadn't turned Blind Fatemeh out. No doubt it was from fear of, or for the sake of, Brainless Abdollah. That monster was capable of anything. Of course, something had been going on and the baby was Brainless Abdollah's. But that day I didn't know and I didn't understand. Blind Fatemeh's shame was that she had gotten herself pregnant.

"My sister said, 'Yes, it's Blind Fatemeh's baby.' I asked, 'What are they gonna do to it?' Leyla said. 'I don't know.' My sister's lips trembled. A tear had started to roll down her face.

"Showkat Khanom ended the discussion—she bent down and picked up the bloody swaddling clothes. She headed towards the outhouse. She held the bundle away from herself as though it were something unclean and shameful. What can be done with a bastard child, alive or dead? I had become so absorbed in watching that now I was not looking at Leyla, who was standing next to the window.

Showkat Khanom went down the outhouse stairs. The old woman from next door stayed by the pool, biting her fingers. I thought, in one lost second, I heard something like the cry of a baby from within the outhouse. Then the sound of the baby was cut off. Then Showkat Khanom came up the outhouse stairs—and only the empty rags were in her hands. The old woman from next door sat by the pool and prayed. Showkat Khanom threw the rags in the footbath—then she bent over and took two ewers near the cesspool and filled them with water. She went back into the outhouse. Then again she came and filled the ewers and went back. Then I heard a heavy thud next to me. It was my sister."

"She was bedridden for a year, more or less. It was never clear what her illness was. In the midst of all the misfortune and chaos of life at Showkat Khanom's house, nothing was important. Once or twice my mother would take Leyla, put a chador over her head, and take her to the hospital which was by Amiriyeh and the market of Aqa Shaykh Hadi during those times. Then, because she had no time during the day, there was mostly homemade medicine and prayer. At first they thought my sister had become epileptic. Then they said she had malaria.Or hepatitis. Some said she got consumption from Dad. My mother used to say there was nothing wrong with her, since the doctors only gave her medicine to keep her strength up. In the end, nothing. My sister's illness blended into the lives of ourselves and others.

"The fall and winter of that year I was going to school and I saw very little of my sister during the day. In the eyes of the residents of the house, my sister was now always the poor sick daughter of Aqa Sayyid Abolfazl Khan. Everybody liked her. Her purity and chastity were the talk of the house—but no one used to see her. Even after she was no longer bedridden she very rarely came down into the courtyard. I remember that only just before dawn, before anyone else would wake up, she would go down to use the outhouse and to perform her ritual ablutions before prayer. And that's it... her eleventh year was not yet over.

"Then my sister's fate was sealed with a woman's rite of passage in this world."

"I don't remember exactly when or from where the question of marriage cropped up. They had been wanting to get a wife for Brainless Abdollah for some time. A good girl, chaste, deferential—above all, chaste. I think it was near the Nowruz holiday when the rumblings and talk began. Leyla had just got out of bed, but she was thinner and paler than usual. And alone and quiet. More of a disillusioned and resigned silhouette in a corner of the room.

"I was scared and heartbroken. I didn't know where this business would lead. When we were alone we talked and she'd comfort me. I mustn't be scared or sad. But I could see that she had a new secret, a new torment.

"Sometimes I'd seen weddings in Showkat Khanom's house. They were celebrated with music and drums and dancing and merriment. I couldn't believe Leyla would also dress up like other brides, have sweets scattered over her head, sit on a bridal throne, get married, get pregnant and become submerged in the life of the local bazaar. But, fine, a girl has to go to the house of her destiny.

"We had an old aunt, Khaleh Khanom, jovial and very shifty. During these days Khaleh Khanom would come and freeload. She caused most of what happened. She said if Leyla would take a husband her health would improve. My sister's youth was no problem. Khaleh Khanom would bring up a tradition from the Prophet that a girl could marry at nine years of age. Anyway, my father had not obtained an identity card for Leyla. (After the death of his first daughter Dad had not voided her identity card, and out of laziness had kept that same card for Leyla.) Therefore, according to the existing identity card, Leyla was seventeen. Khaleh Khanom and Brainless Abdollah's mother were not the sort to give up easily. So the business went through after all. Especially since the husband's family was higher socially, and the pressure greater.

"My mother softened. The solicitation ceremony took place. Then perhaps for no other stupid reason than 'before Moharram and Safar have come,' they set the betrothal party in motion.

"It was decided that the betrothal and wedding would happen all at once.

"It was a week before the betrothal party. Showkat Khanom came and gave mother a handful of money. Mother went and bought my sister a mirror, a lamp, clothes, toiletries and some household furniture, and odds and ends. Talk of the engagement and marriage ran through the whole house. Mother didn't go to work. She stayed home. Khaleh Khanom came for the depilation ceremony. I don't remember the agreements reached about the engagement and marriage settlement. I just remember that both sides were dissatisfied; Mother and Khaleh Khanom claimed it was too little, Showkat Khanom grudged even the little bit that she had given. Every time Brainless Abdollah came into the courtyard, Showkat Khanom and the neighbors would clap for him. 'King Bridegroom, King Bridegroom,' they would chant. My sister was silent.

"For the party, Showkat Khanom had them plaster the walls with grout and whitewash them. They emptied the pool, fixed the fountain, which had been broken for years, and refilled the pool. It was decided that the party be held in the courtyard. I don't remember all the little details of those ill-omened days.

"For a few days before the party, starting each morning, neighbors we didn't know would senselessly make merry, beating drums and tambourines. Near noon on the day of the party they brought several trays of fruit, sweets, and wedding decorations. In the afternoon they brought a cleric to officiate. A beautician came. They sat Leyla down and fixed up her hair and face. My sister became a heavenly face amidst white clothes, lace, and chiffon. I was happy for her. With that small beautiful face, she looked like those angels in the pictures she was always talking about.

"In the evening, meaning the evening of the wedding, Showkat Khanom had been entertaining the male guests in the courtyard and the female guests in the rooms since dusk. A platform over the pool, a musician, buzzing mantle-lamps, clapping and stomping, applause in honor of the bridegroom, the pouring of coins and sweets on the heads of the bride and groom, and so on and so forth. Everyone was happy. Every hour Showkat Khanom would come to the doorway, pour money and sweets over the head of Abdollah Khan, and call for a hearty round of applause for the health of the bridegroom. There was rejoicing and cheering. I looked at my sister a few times. She just seemed tired, or maybe it was something more than tiredness. I couldn't tell if her health was failing again or not. I was tired and sleepy myself, and the musician over the pool and the thrill of collecting silver money turned my attention elsewhere. When I looked at my sister near the end of the party she looked as though she'd fainted. Her eyes were opening with difficulty. I wished they would come to help her, to take her to a corner of one of the rooms and to put her to sleep. But everyone was caught up in the merriment and joy.

"Then I remember it rained all of a sudden—a downpour, like tonight. The whole gathering fell apart. Everyone got up and left the yard. Showkat Khanom and the rest rushed out and took the sweet-dishes and carpets into the rooms. A group of the male guests left. The ones close to the families came inside and the women threw chadors or scarves over their heads. Then I heard them singing a wedding song, and commenting that the bride was just a little girl and it was past her bedtime. Then Showkat Khanom and some of the women came and lifted up Brainless Abdollah and my sister—in order to join the bride's and groom's hands. Everyone clapped and cheered.

"Brainless Abdollah's large frame was monstrous beside my sister. Leyla was eleven. But a tiny and sickly eleven. What did they want with her? The women went, 'Lee, lee, lee, lee!' They showered sweets... they showered rosewater. They brought the bride and groom to a bridal chamber they had prepared for them. And where was this bridal chamber? This same room; they had fixed up this same room for them. I had been in the room since the afternoon, I was enjoying the wedding party. Now I came and looked inside. New bedding was spread out on our old, coarse wool carpet in the middle of the room. There was a Koran and a mirror and tulips on the windowsill. Two new kerosene lamps burned on either side of the mirror. When the women brought my sister and led her into the room I was happy, because I saw my sister turn back from the doorway, her eyes found mine in the midst of the crowd, and she flashed a hopeful smile. I won't forget that look and that smile.

"Showkat Khanom shut the door of the room after the bride and groom. The gathering was over—most of the guests had left. Only a few of the women came and sat in front of the door of the bridal chamber. According to custom they did not allow my mother to come into the room. I saw her once in the courtyard. She sat at the top of the stairs, away from the rain. She wasn't doing anything. Maybe she was even crying. Here in the room it was as though everyone was waiting for something important to happen. There was a kind of naughty chattering back and forth. No one thought of putting us children to bed, or picking up the children who had fallen asleep in the middle of the room. Everyone became talkative. No sound came from within the bridal chamber. For half an hour, nothing happened. I was thinking of my sister and of the angels. In the depths of my heart I wanted God to have them protect her. Then the door of the bridal chamber was opened from within.

"Brainless Abdollah came out of the room. There was a mocking leer on his face. A huge frame, a white shirt, green striped pajama pants. The women cheered, 'Lee, lee, lee, lee!' when they saw him. They clapped. They poured sweets and candy over his head. Now my mother had also come into the room. Mother, Auntie, and Showkat Khanom hurried into the bridal chamber. I also got up and went after them. But I had not yet reached the doorway when Showkat Khanom pushed me back and came out with a proud and victorious air. A bloody cloth was in her hand. Showkat Khanom held it up as though it was something sacred and pure. She showed it to everyone. My sister was a virgin. The women cheered and cried, 'Lee, lee, lee, lee!' I still didn't understand. But at the sight of the blood an awful fear coursed through my body. I prayed to God for my sister to be all right. God didn't answer my prayer. My mother's cry came from the room and I ran in... it was a frightful sight..."

The man fell silent. The telling of his sister's story had made both himself and his wife sad. Again he got up and closed the window that the wind and rain had opened. His wife said, "Why did they give an eleven-year-old girl who was sick to a husband like that?"

"How should I know?"

"She died that same night?"

"In the bed of the bridal chamber."

The woman sighed, "There is no god but God. What a crazy world."

Rain was beating at the window.

The woman said, "It's as though in this world there's no comfort or happiness in store for anyone." Now her thoughts were again of the dead baby inside her. "There's no meaning or point to it."

Her husband yawned and said, "Even if it had meaning or point, they wouldn't be cause for happiness. They'd be cause for something else."

"Cause for what?"

He was silent for a moment, then said, "How should I know? Get up, let's go to sleep."

The woman put the ragged swaddling clothes, needle and thread into a bag and set it aside.

She had become sadder. She had sorrowful and bitter thoughts herself at the beginning of the evening; now the words of her husband's tale had given her a more intricate sorrow. What things had gone on in this room! The icons in the room were watching her silent distress. They were also silent, at a loss for words. The picture of a young Prophet Mohammad with angels over his head, the portrait of Princess Farrokh-Laqa, Abraham preparing Ishmael for sacrifice and the intervention of the angels, the glass-framed colored drawing of the Five and the angels on shafts of light behind their heads, the portrait of a naked holy woman on a throne in a garden with nymphs and angels in attendance—it was as though they were all silently watching this pregnant woman in this silent room. Only they believed the story of Leyla.

The woman said, "It's in the hands of God—what can we do?"
She got up and laid the bedding.

She decided that instead of going out into the courtyard in the rain,
she would perform her ablutions right there in the room. And she did.
Then she put on her prayer chador and stood and prayed. While she
was performing the evening prayer, her husband got up and left,
returned, closed the door, undressed and came and got into bed. After
prayer the woman turned off the light. She also came to bed.

In the darkness, her thoughts were more weary than ever. Prayer
had not healed the bitterness and ambivalence in her soul. The
thought of her husband's dead sister cast a new shadow on the situation of her and her baby. What would have happened if her
husband's sister had not died and had stayed alive and become pregnant? I've become pregnant twice. What happened? What's the end
of it? Her husband was silent.

They slept back to back. The dank smell of the hanging laundry
twisted through the room but their noses were now used to it. The
woman listened for a long while to the sound of the rain against the
window and in the gutter. She thought her husband had fallen
asleep. But then she heard him speak.

"Say, if this baby is a girl do you know what we're going to call her?"

The woman sighed in the darkness. She knew. She started, "If —"
She was choked by tears.

She wanted to tell her husband about the dead baby right away.
Then she thought, no it was better for her to leave it for tomorrow.
A dank smell was in the darkness of their room. The dead baby was
pressing against her stomach. She stayed awake.

Rain beat against the window all night.

Gholam Hosayn Sa'edi

1935–1985

Writer of fiction, dramatist (under the pen name Gowhar Morad), editor, and political activist Gholam Hosayn Sa'edi was born and raised in Tabriz of an educated Azerbaijani Turkish family. He graduated from the medical school at Tehran University, specializing in psychiatry. For most of his career as a physician he was in general practice in South Tehran, charging his patients whatever they could afford, that being in keeping with older Iranian tradition.

Sa'edi published six collections of short stories in the 1960s and early 1970s: *Shabneshini-ye bā-shokuh* (The splendid soiree, 1960), 'Azādārān-e Bayal (The mourners of Bayal, 1964), *Dandil* (1966), *Vāhemeh'hā-ye bi-nām-o neshān*(Unidentifiable worries, 1967), *Tars-o larz* (Fear and trembling, 1968), and *Gur-o gahvāreh* (Grave and cradle, 1972). A story from the last named collection inspired the important motion picture *Dāyereh-ye minā* (The blue sphere; distributed as *The Cycle*, 1977). Sa'edi also published a novel in 1968 called *Tup* (The cannon) and numerous stage plays during this period. *Tup* is still popular in Iran, having been reprinted in 1999. He also founded and edited the important journal *Alefbā* (nos. 1-6, 1973-1976). Owing to government censorship he left Iran in the late 1970s and ended up in Paris, where he died.

Much of Sa'edi's work is available in translation, for example: *Dandil: Stories from Iranian Life* (1981), *Fear and Trembling* (1984), and *The Cow: A Screenplay*, based on a story from *Mourners of Bayal*, which appeared in *Iranian Studies* 15, a volume dedicated to Sa'edi. His stories "Chatr" (Umbrella) and "Gedā" (Beggar), first published in *Sokhan* in 1962, appear in translation in *Literature East & West* 20 (1980). His story called "Zanburak'khāneh" from *The Grave and the Cradle* is translated as "The Wedding" in *Iranian Studies* 8 (1975). Translations of several of his plays appear in anthologies called *Modern Persian Drama* (1987) and *Iranian Drama* (1989).

Long after his death books by and about him are still being published, including: *Gharibeh dar shahr* (1991), *Tātār khandān* (1994), *Yādnāmeh-e Doktor Gholām Hosayn Saedi*(Germany, 1995), *Saedi be-revāyat-e Saedi* (Paris, 1995), *Ashofteh'hālān-e bidār'bakht: majmu'ah-i dāstān* (1998), *Shenākhtnāmeh-e Gholām Hosayn Saedi*(1999), as well as numerous reprints of his stories and plays.

The Two Brothers

Translated by Steve Meyer

The younger brother was plotting and scheming day and night to get rid of the older brother. As he saw it, the older brother was self-indulgent, averse to work, silly and scatterbrained, and a consummate idler fit for nothing. He was always sitting in the sun, drinking tea and reading a book, and emptying his pockets of the melon seeds he'd stuffed them with, leaving the room full of the shells and cigarette butts that he flung wherever he felt like it. The younger brother wanted the older brother to change, to grow up, to go out and look for work, to get his life in order. But he knew that the older brother was not about to change, that he just didn't have the intellect to understand such matters, to react to the younger brother's advice without getting annoyed. And the only thing the older brother did was to become lazier and more perverse each day.

The younger brother left for work every morning before sunrise, and the older brother, who got up later, would set off on his rounds of aimless wandering, neglecting to gather up the bedding, wash the teacups, draw the curtains, or sweep up the cigarette butts. Toward noon, when the sun had warmed up the room, he would come back and light the samovar, set out his packs of cigarettes and bags of melon seeds, wrap himself in a blanket, pick up a book, and go off into his own world. To all appearances, he was without a care in the world, completely free. With his belly full—for he always ate some bread and salami down at the end of the street—he would listen to the warm, pleasant sound of the samovar and read. But it wasn't long before the younger brother would come in all clean and tidy, straighten his glasses, and let out a roar. The older brother would close his book, get up and, in an attempt to calm things down, gather up the seed shells in a sheet. But the younger brother would snatch the sheet from the older brother's hand and throw it off to the side, take off his glasses and gather up the blankets. Then he would turn off the heat under the samovar and open the window to let some fresh air into the room. Next he would sweep out the trash of the past twenty-four hours onto the balcony of the floor below, causing the old lady who owned the house to grumble and complain. Then he would turn on the light and fix some fried eggs in a pan, eat his meal standing up with his back to the older brother, take off his clothes, spread out the blankets, and lie down. The older brother would get up and relight the samovar without fear, knowing that this time the younger brother would not turn it off. He was extraordinarily fond of tea after fried eggs. Some evenings when the younger brother was in a good mood, his frowning expression would soften and he would sit and chat with the older brother, and the frost of disapproval in the room would gradually thaw. The younger brother would turn on the radio and listen to the news. The two of them would drink tea and call each other by name. But when it was time to go to sleep and they were about to unfold the bedding, the recriminations and abuse would begin again. They would stand up and lock horns, and the younger brother would not be able to rest until he'd flattened the older brother's nose and drawn blood. The younger brother was constantly complaining about the older brother's impudence and ingratitude and loafing, while the older brother complained of the younger brother's unkindness toward him. The older brother, unable to forget anything that had happened, would pull open the curtains of the large window and, staring up at the moon which was framed in all its immensity by the window, would fret and fume as he listened to the peaceful breathing of the younger brother, who was sleeping comfortably in his bed. But the older brother always imagined that the younger brother was not asleep, that he was only pretending to sleep while he plotted; plotted, not because the older brother was stuck to him like a leech and had ruined his life, but because he disliked him, because he despised him and was at the end of his rope with him.

And one night the younger brother had a dream that the older brother had come up the stairs with a bundle of books and had spread them out in the middle of the room and had filled up all the space around himself with packs of cigarettes and bags of melon seeds and had lit the samovar and had befouled his entire existence. And when he sees this, he begins to scream, "Get up and pick up all this garbage, or else I'm gonna sweep it up along with your filthy body and dump it out the window." And he goes to shut off the samovar, but the older brother, grown bolder, grabs his ankle and shouts, "What are you doing? Get the hell out of here, you bastard!" The younger brother is furious and picks up the bag of seeds and smashes it into the older brother's face, and the older brother falls down unconscious. The bag tears open and the entire place is full of seeds. The younger brother bends down and looks into the older brother's eyes, which are open and staring up at the moon. He gets up hastily and tries to hide the corpse in a corner, but he can't find room for it. The only solution he can see is to hide the body under all the books and seeds. But no matter what he does, the older brother's feet keep sticking out, and the old landlady shows up and starts screaming, "You can't hide him, you murderer!"

The younger brother woke up with a start and let out a shout and the older brother, who was awake and listening to his uneven breathing, got up and opened the door, but as he started to run away, he suddenly slipped and tumbled down the stairs. The old lady and the downstairs tenant came out apprehensively, and the old lady began to shout in a voice that trembled with fury, "You will leave this house tomorrow, and I mean tomorrow! You'd better be the hell out of here by tomorrow morning before I call the police. Get it through your heads—I mean it, tomorrow!"

2

The next day the old lady was set on getting the brothers out of the house as soon as possible. First she repeated her warning of the previous night via the downstairs tenant, who was a dark-complexioned woman. The following day the warning was again repeated in a notice that she had had someone write to them. And when the brothers still didn't give in, she came up the stairs in person and said that she couldn't put up with them any longer. They had disturbed the peace of all the residents of the house. They were always pissing on the stairs and the whole house smelled like a toilet. And worst of all, they would sweep up whatever garbage they had and throw it onto the second-floor balcony; wherever you looked in the house there were melon seed shells and cigarette butts. The house was turning into a regular dungheap. As she grew angrier she screamed, "It's not just us! You're disturbing the neighbors too. There are melon seed shells from one end of the street to the other. How do you find room in your stomachs for all those seeds? And you don't even get sick so that we might at least have a couple of days of peace and quiet."

The older brother shrugged off his blanket and said, "Why don't you put a lid on it? You think this dump is the Taj Mahal? Give us two or three days and we'll be out of here and everyone'll be happy."

The old lady was madder than a wet hen. "Shut up, you worthless lowlife! You'd better be out of this house in three days, otherwise I'm tossing out all your stuff."

When the younger brother returned home, the older brother told him what had happened from beginning to end, how the old lady had come up and what she'd said and what he'd heard. The younger brother listened to everything and shouted, "What's all this got to do with you, you ass? As if you've got something important to do that you ask her for a grace period. Who told you to put up a fight? If they throw us out it's on account of you. Everything that I have to put up with is because of you. What right do you have to get mixed up in this? If I told you once I told you a thousand times, don't come home drunk at night, don't piss on the stairs, don't crack all those seeds."

He lost his temper and turned off the samovar and picked up the bag of seeds and threw it out the back window onto the vacant lot and said, as he straightened his glasses, "Since that's the way things are, you'd better bust your hump and get out there and look for a place to live. What do you know about what I have to go through to keep us alive? How I sweat, and the bigwigs I have to grovel in front of so that I can pay the rent. And you, you eat and you sleep and you bum around without a care in the world. Whatever dad sends us, you spend it on booze and melon seeds. I'm at my wit's end with you. I'm about to lose my mind."

"How is it my fault that you're at your wit's end and about to lose your mind?" asked the older brother.

"Then what son-of-a-bitch's fault is it?" said the younger brother. "If it's not your fault then whose fault is it? It's your carrying on and your loafing and your weird cronies."

"What cronies?" said the older brother. "I broke off with all of them for fear of you."

The younger brother said, "So much the better, they were just an extra expense for me. What did you think, that they liked you for your looks? They only hung around because they liked your booze and cigarettes. And where did the money for all that come from, out of your highness's pocket? No, I'm the poor sucker that had to take care of everything."

"Fine," said the older brother. "But why don't you mention that in exchange for that, you've sent me off on your errands at least a thousand times. Aren't I still washing your shirts and polishing your shoes every day?"

The younger brother came over and, instead of answering, clenched his fist and punched the older brother hard in the face. The older brother let out a cry and slumped to the floor, blood pouring from his nose.

The old landlady and the downstairs tenant came up and peeked in through the crack in the door.

He got what he deserved, the miserable wretch," said the old lady gleefully.

When the older brother heard the old lady talking, he got up and opened the door. The old lady and the downstairs tenant were frightened and backed away, and the older brother burst out laughing.

3

The next day, the younger brother put the older brother in charge of finding a place to live. By the time the older brother left the house, he had already forgotten what he was supposed to be doing and set off on his rounds of the streets without giving it a second thought. He stopped by the newsstands, in front of the antique dealers and the booksellers. He had a bag of seeds in his hands, and covered the road with shells in between smoking cigarettes. And he watched the autumn sparrows that sat weary and dejected, trying to keep themselves warm in the trees. When he got tired, he sat down on the curb and took out his book and read a few pages or smoked another cigarette.

At noon when he was about to go home he remembered the reason he had gone out. He killed a little more time and when he got home, the younger brother had already come back and was ironing his clothes. Without even raising his head, he asked, "Well, how did it go?"

The older brother sat down on the floor, searching among the melon seed shells for a whole one, and said, "There's not a vacant room to be found. I'm at my wit's end. I looked everywhere, I must have trudged through the entire city. There are no one-room apartments available. They're all three-room, four-room, with telephones and baths and all the conveniences."

"Whereabouts did you go?" asked the younger brother.

"Just down there," answered the older brother. "There was only one place where I found a single room, but it wouldn't be any good to us."

"Why wouldn't it be any good?" asked the younger brother.

The older brother said, "First of all it's not in a good neighborhood; second, the owner of the house is another foul-tempered old witch; third, it doesn't have running water; and most important of all, it was so small that two people couldn't fit in it. If even one person wanted to sleep there, he'd have to hang his feet out the window into the garden."

The younger brother said, "So?"

The older brother said, "What do you mean, so? It's so stuffy and so dark that you couldn't sit down and read a page of anything."

"Get any thoughts of reading out of your head," said the younger brother. "It was reading that made you so useless and good for nothing in the first place. You've got to go out and find a job. To hell with being educated and reading lots of books. They're no use to a hungry belly."

"I know," said the older brother.

The younger brother said, "Tomorrow, no matter what, you're going to go and make arrangements for taking that dump so we can move."

The older brother said, "The problem is that..."

"I don't want to hear about any problems, understand?" shouted the younger brother. And as he got angrier, he started cursing and pacing up and down the room. Then he coughed and cleaned his glasses and ate his fried eggs and went to sleep. The next day and the day after that went by. The older brother went out every day and watched the sparrows and smoked the cigarettes he'd swiped from the younger brother and nibbled on melon seeds and came home at noon with bizarre stories he had concocted. He would give an account of his labors, how much running around he'd done, how far he'd gone, how much money he'd spent on bus fares and real estate agents, the bad luck that he'd had, and how he hadn't managed to accomplish anything. And how the old lady who had the room wasn't willing to rent it to two single men, because she had two grown daughters and didn't want to create any headaches for herself. The younger brother listened to everything and shook his head and didn't say a word.

The three days' grace period went by in the same way. The younger brother had foreseen everything. He was furious and just biding his time until the last day to take revenge on the older brother.

At nightfall on the third day the old lady came up the stairs coughing and banged her fist on the door. The younger brother, who was sitting on a chair, indicated to the older brother that he should give the old lady an answer. The older brother opened the door. The old lady said, "So?"

"We're going," said the older brother.

"When?" asked the old lady.

"Tomorrow," said the older brother.

The old lady said, "The three days' grace period is over. I came to lock the place up."

The older brother said, "The three days' grace period is over. We're not disputing that. We're moving out tomorrow. Don't lock the place up yet so that we can get out."

The old lady didn't say a word as she went off down the stairs. "What are we going to do?" said the older brother.

"How should I know?" said the younger brother.

"Think of something," said the older brother.

"I should think of something?" said the younger brother. "You think of something, with that sick, twisted brain of yours. Do whatever crazy thing you want."

The older brother closed his eyes and raised his eyebrows.

The younger brother asked, "What the hell is this ridiculous face you're making?"

"I'm thinking," replied the older brother.

"Get out of here, you stupid ass," said the younger brother. "You're just acting like an idiot."

With his eyes closed and his mind in a muddle, the older brother saw nothing but cigarettes and salami and stale bread and melon seeds and empty bottles, and heard nothing but the sound of the sparrows.

"For God's sake, hurry up," shouted the younger brother.

The older brother opened his eyes and said, "I've got it. One of us has got to get sick."

"How's that going to help?" asked the younger brother.

"That way the old lady can't kick us out," said the older brother.

"You can pull whatever crazy stunt you want," said the younger brother. "If you want to get sick, get sick. I'm praying to God that you croak."

"Great," said the older brother. "I'll get sick and lie down in this corner and go to sleep. All I need are some cigarettes and melon seeds and a few novels and I won't budge."

"I see, you're up to one of your tricks," said the younger brother.

"What trick?" said the older brother.

And he stared helplessly at the younger brother. The younger brother paced up and down the room and finally nodded his head in agreement. When the older brother saw this, he spread out his bedding and arranged his novels above his head and got under the covers with a bag of seeds and began to groan. The older brother had fallen sick.

4

When the old lady came up the stairs toward noon to lock up the room, she knew that they still hadn't vacated, but she played dumb. When she got to the top of the stairs, she heard the whining voice of the older brother; she listened for a few moments, then knocked on the door, and said, "You still haven't left?"

The younger brother didn't answer, and the older brother moaned, "I'm dying, take pity on me. How can we move out when I'm in this condition? My heart is palpitating, my legs are swollen, I can hardly breathe."

"Don't play possum with me," said the old lady. "I don't want to hear about it."

"I swear to God and the saints and the prophets I'm dying," said the older brother.

"What's it to me?" said the old lady. "You're always sick."

The older brother groaned, and the younger brother, who was boiling mad, began to pace. He kept looking back and forth between the door of the room and the older brother. His eyes were glazed, and he would have liked to pick up the older brother and ram him into the old lady's face and send the two of them to the lowest pit of hell.

The old lady said to herself, "If he's really sick, God won't like it if I throw him out." And she went a couple of steps down the stairs.

The younger brother and the older brother listened carefully and heard the old lady go down the stairs. The older brother stopped his moaning. The old lady, still on the stairs, became suspicious and thought, I wonder if he's trying to pull a fast one?

She came back upstairs and stood outside the door. The sound of moans could be heard coming from inside the room. She knocked on the door again and said in a serious voice, "You'd better get well soon, understand?"

"Okay," said the older brother.

The old lady went down the stairs and the older brother didn't move a muscle, not wanting to spoil everything.

Five days and nights passed in the same way, and the older brother didn't stir from the spot more than a couple of times over a twenty-four-hour period. He slept under the covers and read voraciously. He had unleashed such a passion for reading that he had even lost the desire to nibble on melon seeds. At noon and at night when the old lady went to sleep and her snores shook the entire building, he would get up quietly and go out to eat some bread and salami. He would take his shoes in his hands, and when he was about to go out through the courtyard door, he would grasp the clapper of the bell that the old lady had hung above the door and pull the bell down so the old lady wouldn't hear the door being opened; then he would run down to the end of the street and tuck into a salami sandwich and then take a look at the newsstands and pick up some cigarettes before hurrying home. He would take off his shoes in front of the door and lift up the bell clapper with his hand and enter the courtyard and creep cautiously up the stairs.

In all the five days he never once got caught by the old lady, although the downstairs tenant had seen him a few times and had laughed soundlessly. But the older brother wasn't worried by this; he was certain that she wasn't going to expose him. The old lady came up every day making a commotion and threatening them and wagging her finger. As for the younger brother, he came home every day with a couple of eggs and half a loaf of bread, his face set in a permanent scowl; he would eat his fried eggs and then proceed to raise hell, spoiling the peaceful atmosphere of the house. He repeated what the old lady had said, that he had to find a room as soon as possible so they could move, and how long was he going to lie under the quilt and take this abuse?

At sunset on the fifth day the old lady came up and banged on the door and opened it without waiting for an answer. She had brought

with her a short man who had a small bag in his hand. The younger
brother had not yet come home. The older brother gave a startled
look at the old lady and the newcomer. What was going on? Without
opening her mouth, the old lady waved her hand and indicated the
older brother. The man with the bag in his hand smiled confidently
at the older brother. The older brother took out the book he had
under his arm and started to read, paying no attention to either one
of them. The old lady looked at the man and said, "Please, doctor,
give him a thorough examination. If he's sick, make him better as
soon as possible. If he's not sick, let me know right away."

The doctor nodded his head and went up and sat down next to the
older brother and opened his bag. He took out a stethoscope, a
blood-pressure gauge, a mirror, a thermometer, a hammer, a number of test tubes, and a handful of papers, and with a kindly face said
to the older brother, "What is your problem, sir?"

The older brother did not answer and kept on turning the pages
of his book.

"Are you ill?" asked the doctor.

"Yes," said the older brother softly.

"What's wrong with you?" asked the doctor.

"I'm dying," said the older brother.

The doctor nodded his head and said, "Fine. Let's see how you are."

"What are you going to do to me?" asked the older brother.

"I'd like to examine you."

"What for?"

"So you can get better."

"Who are you?"

"I am a doctor, sir," said the doctor. With a wave of his hand he
indicated the various medical paraphernalia that he had taken out of
his bag.

"Nobody asked for you," said the older brother.

"I didn't come on my own account," said the doctor. "This lady
called me in."

"That was a useless thing to do. Nobody asked her to do it," said
the older brother.

"I didn't just fall off the turnip truck," said the old lady. "Nobody's
going to pull a fast one on me. Doctor, you will give him a thorough
examination. If you're not strong enough to manage it yourself, I'll
call in some people from the neighborhood to hold him down."

"I swear to God, you could bring the entire world in and I still
wouldn't let anyone lay a hand on me," said the older brother.

"Why?" asked the doctor.

"I don't care for doctors," said the older brother.

The doctor smiled and said, "Ah, I understand. Very well, ma'am, if you would be so kind as to step outside for a few moments. He's embarrassed to talk in front of you."

As the old lady was going out the door, she grumbled, "How come he's not ashamed to piss on the stairs right in front of me every night, but he can't even say what's wrong with him?"

The doctor got up and shut the door and came over and sat down next to the older brother. He smiled as he placed his hand on the older brother's shoulder and said, "So that's the way it is."

"Yeah, that's the way it is," said the older brother.

"Now what do you want to do?" asked the doctor.

"I don't know, I'm all confused," said the older brother.

"This just isn't going to work," said the doctor.

"Then what should I do?" asked the older brother.

"In the end you're going to have to leave here, right?" said the doctor.

"That's how it looks," said the older brother.

"Do you want me to bring her around?" asked the doctor.

"What for?" asked the older brother.

"So that you can stay here and get her off your back," said the doctor.

"It's not just the old lady," said the older brother. "You'll have to bring my younger brother around too. He's my sworn enemy. He thinks I'm an albatross around his neck. And that I'm a worthless, good-for-nothing being. He's always criticizing me. Criticizing the fact that I don't have a job, that I'm a bum, and lots of other things. He's really steamed at me for not going out and looking for work. He doesn't realize that I just don't have what it takes to get a job. And it's not as if I spend that much money. A couple of loaves of white bread and a few ounces of salami are plenty for me. Plus I need some melon seeds and cigarettes, and I won't say no to some booze if I can get my hands on it, especially if it's somebody else's treat. He beats me up a couple of times a day, just like that, for no reason at all. Now that I've been sick for a while he's not bothering me too much. It's the old lady—she really doesn't like me. She thinks that I piss on the stairs out of spite, and that I eat melon seeds on purpose so I can throw the shells on the ground. She thinks I'm the most ridiculous person in the world. Things aren't too bad between her and my brother. It's mostly on my account that she's throwing the two of us out. And my brother knows that it's all my fault. I've got to be prepared at any moment for a first-class beating and one hell of an argument."

As the doctor was arranging his equipment in his bag, he asked, "Aside from all that, what do you want now?"

"A glass of *araq* would really hit the spot," said the older brother.

"That's not important," said the doctor. "The real question is the question of the house. I know of a house where the custodian left and the ground floor is vacant. You could live there. I'll arrange everything tonight."

"Where is it? What neighborhood is it in?" asked the older brother.

As he wrote down the address of the house on a piece of paper, the doctor said, "The best neighborhood in the city, Mobarakabad, number forty-one." And he gave the piece of paper to the older brother.

"Now what do we do?" asked the older brother.

"Tomorrow morning you move, and one of these days I'll be along to see you; maybe I'll bring you some good news," said the doctor.

And he got up, took a handful of melon seeds from the older brother's bedside, put them in his pocket, and went out the door. When he got outside, the old lady, who had been standing on the steps, said, "Doctor, is he really sick? "

"Yes, ma'am," said the doctor. "He's really sick. He's suffering from an unusual disease. But I wrote him a prescription that'll definitely make him better by tomorrow morning."

5

The younger brother went home, having decided to really let the older brother have it that evening. When he entered the room he stood rooted to the spot with astonishment. The older brother had gotten out of bed, taken down the curtains, packed up the books and suitcases and arranged them side by side. The younger brother said with amazement, "What's up? Did something happen?"

"We're moving tomorrow," said the older brother.

"Where?" asked the younger brother.

The older brother showed the address of the new house to the younger brother. The younger brother repeated it a few times under his breath, "Mobarakabad, number forty-one… Mobarakabad… number… forty-one."

"How does it sound? Okay?" said the older brother.

"How did you find it?" asked the younger brother.

"That's one of my little secrets," said the older brother. "I can't tell you."

"What do you mean, one of your secrets?"

"Don't give me the third degree, I won't tell no matter what you do to me," said the older brother.

The younger brother thought for a few moments and then said, "Fine, don't tell me. But I've got to inspect all this stuff. Let me go through your suitcases in particular. I'm not about to live in the midst of all this garbage in the new house." And he reached out and picked up the nearest suitcase and opened it. The suitcase was full of books, and on top of the books a coiled rope had been placed. "What the hell is this?" asked the younger brother.

"Don't touch it, it's a gallows rope, one of the kids gave it to me," said the older brother.

The younger brother threw the rope out the rear window onto the vacant lot and said, "If you ever become a policeman or a hangman, I'll buy you a new one, even better."

And he opened the second suitcase. It was also full of books, and next to them a large flask wrapped in a black cloth had been placed. The younger brother opened the flask and sniffed it. Inside the bottle was a viscous liquid that smelled like bitter almonds and naphtha. The younger brother said to the older brother, "This must be a bottle of hemlock, right?" and he wrapped the bottle in the black cloth again and threw it onto the vacant lot. And he picked up the third suitcase and opened it. The suitcase was full of melon seeds, and on a piece of cardboard was written in the older brother's handwriting: "Reserves for days to come. The month of Mordad of the year thirty-two."

"Days to come?" repeated the younger brother, "What days to come?" And as he picked up the suitcase to throw it out the window, the older brother raced over and grabbed his hand and said, "Don't do it, I'll be damned if I don't smash your glasses."

The younger brother set the suitcase on the table and said, "That was a stupid thing to do!" And as he raised his fist to let the older brother have it, the older brother rushed at him. The two of them went at it full tilt, hitting and punching each other so that the entire house began to shake. After a few minutes the old lady and the downstairs tenant came up and threatened to call in the patrolman if they didn't stop fighting. And the older brother, who was writhing under the kicks of the younger brother, shouted, "What's it to you? Don't we have the right to fight in this house?"

6

The next day they moved to the house at number forty-one Mobarakabad Street. They were expected. Two communicating rooms with one small window a few steps below street level swallowed up the two brothers. They arranged their furnishings and suitcases around the trash that was piled up in the back room and lit cigarettes. The younger brother said, "Before we even get settled in, you've got to swear that you're going to change, that you're going to pull yourself together and look for work; do it for my sake."

An old man appeared and showed them around the house. There was not a pleasant or comfortable spot in the entire place. Moisture was dripping down the walls, and the smell of damp and rust and rat poison was everywhere. Only the courtyard of the house had a certain charm, with a garden full of yellow and purple flowers and a small pool that stared up at the sky like the eye of a corpse.

The other floors of the house were vacant, except for the top story, which had a large sunny balcony where a young woman would sit and hang her underwear out to dry on a line.

There were vacant lots on two sides of the house and on the other side was a broad dirt road where dusty, broken-down bulldozers were swarming around like sand fleas, busy at some unknown task. At the end of the dirt road was a cemetery with very large upright tombstones the size of a tall man; from a distance they looked like a congregation standing in prayer. The older brother decided right then and there that he would go and inspect the cemetery the first chance he had. He said to himself, "On Thursdays and days of alms-giving I'll eat to my heart's content, they'll be giving out dates and *halva*; and on the other days I'll be able to find some privacy there. Maybe one day they'll bring the old lady's body there and really make my day."

The rooms were full of tiny brightly colored insects, thousands of spiders with furry legs, large colorful beetles that would whirl about and secrete tiny white young from their anuses, misshapen old flies that walked around and could no longer fly, and green worms like matchsticks that crawled side by side in pairs.

"This is a strange house you've found," said the younger brother. "Do you plan on sleeping in the middle of all this filth? Until you clean this place up and kill all these vermin, we're not unpacking our things."

The older brother had no choice but to do as he was told. He didn't want to start things off in a new house with a fistfight. Taking off his jacket despite the cold weather, he resignedly set about killing the insects. The spiders were easily caught and quickly killed; by the time they realized the danger and curled up with their legs drawn in, the blows had already landed, leaving only small, dirty stains with dark furrows on the walls. The beetles would scurry away, and the older brother would laugh and imitate them, scurrying after them and attacking them with his shoe. As for the worms, nothing would get rid of the pairs of worms. After being injured by a blow, they would remain motionless and wait a few moments, and the wound would gradually swell and puff up; then they would continue slowly and determinedly on their course. Where they were headed was anybody's guess. If they came across one of the ancient flies, they would moisten it by secreting a fluid all around it, devour it together and continue on their way. The older brother said, "I'm just like them. I'm a paired-off worm. I'm aimless too. I wander along like them and never get tired and never get squashed."

When he had finished sweeping, he sat down and looked around. The house was extremely sick. The doors and walls made tired sounds. Something damp and dark was taking possession of every inch of it, causing the older brother to leap up and rush out of the narrow door in a panic. The younger brother was standing by the side of the road watching the bulldozers wallow in the dust and dirt. The older brother gently took the younger brother's hand and said entreatingly, "It's impossible to live here. Let's get out of this place."

The younger brother pulled his hand away from the older brother's hand and said, "Why? Why should we go?"

"There's something funny going on," said the older brother. "I'm scared. Those worms, there's something strange about them. I think they're flesh-eaters."

"How do you know?" asked the younger brother.

"I know, I just know," said the older brother.

"Quit fooling around," said the younger brother.

"Listen to what I'm saying, this house is definitely bad news for one of us. Let's go somewhere else, to another house," said the older brother.

"Where, for instance?" asked the younger brother.

"Let's go back to the old lady's house," said the older brother.

"Get out of here," said the younger brother. "The old lady's house! You think it's that simple? The old lady's house is not a hotel that you move out of one day and go back to the next. How can you even think of going back there after all the fights and quarrels?"

Just then an ambulance with its siren blaring appeared in a cloud of dust and raced past toward the cemetery. A man who was sitting next to the driver thrust his hand out of the ambulance and waved in their direction.

"Who the hell is that?" asked the younger brother.

"He must know us," said the older brother hesitantly. "But I can't remember where I've seen him."

The younger brother said, as he wiped his glasses with his handkerchief, "What are they in such a hurry for? Why do they want to bury him so quick?"

7

"Either you or me, one of us is going to die very soon. This place smells funny, I'm sick of this house, of this dusty street and this cemetery and this house."

"That's the way it goes. You found it, you picked it out and you're just going to have to get used to it. I can't move out of one dump and into another every day of the week," answered the younger brother.

"If I thought I wasn't going to be able to find some way to get out of this hole, I'd put myself out of my misery right here and now," said the older brother.

"The quicker the better, that way we'll both be out of our misery," said the younger brother.

"Too bad there's no rope around here," said the older brother. "If you hadn't thrown my rope away, I'd show you that I'm not kidding."

As he went out the door furiously, the younger brother said, "A rope's not a hard thing to find. If you can't get hold of one, let me know and I'll buy you one."

The older brother sat alone for a while and thought. It was getting dark outside and a melancholy sunset filled the house. The older brother said to himself, "There's something heavy weighing on my heart tonight. I've got to find a way out."

He went out of the house and headed down the dirt road toward the cemetery. By the time he entered the cemetery, night had fallen and a few stars had come out here and there in the sky. The faint glow of a lantern was approaching him from a distance. The older brother remained waiting. The light came nearer and the older brother saw a hunched old man with a shovel on his shoulder, contentedly swinging his lantern back and forth in the air.

When he saw him, the old man asked, "Young man, what are you doing here at this time of night?"

The older brother became flustered and said, "In the last couple of days, did they bring in an old woman, around sixty or seventy?"

"What do you want to know for?" asked the old man.

"She's somebody I know," said the older brother.

The old man shook his head and said, "Go visit some living acquaintances, there's nothing to be done with the dead ones."

"Who should I go visit?" asked the older brother.

"Go visit whomever you want, go live your life," said the old man.

The older brother turned away without saying good-bye and headed back down the dirt road. The sound of bulldozers could be heard coming from all directions, and the night seemed to vibrate strangely. He was no longer afraid of the new house. When he reached home and was about to open the door, his foot struck something. He bent over and saw that someone had propped up a huge bouquet of flowers against the door. They were enormous sunflowers that had been tied together with a note placed among the blossoms. He picked up the bouquet and went inside. He turned on the light in the corridor and opened the note, recognizing the doctor's handwriting:

"My dear friend. I hope that you are comfortable and content in your new home, and that no one is keeping you from enjoying the sun, eating melon seeds, and reading. The yellow flowers in the garden are not unlike sunflowers. I'll come and see you again with some good news. I also would advise you not to worry about the presence of the pairs of worms. They have nothing to do with the living. I hope that you'll be happy and content among the flowers and sunshine and young women."

Young women have nothing to do with me, thought the older brother as he picked up the flowers and went into the courtyard. In the courtyard, a light shone through the metal bars of the railing, falling on the opposite wall, upon which the shadow of a woman was moving. The older brother went to the back of the courtyard and saw a young woman on the balcony of the upper story; she had a little puppy in her arms, and was taking him for a walk in the bright moonlight. As he stood watching his neighbor, the older brother said contentedly, "Among the flowers and young women."

8

"Well? Couldn't you get hold of a rope after all?"

The older brother didn't answer. He was watching a rope with a box tied to its end as it slowly descended into the garden.

The box reached the ground, and a small, furry puppy jumped out and began to run around the courtyard. "What's going on here?" asked the younger brother.

"It belongs to the lady upstairs," answered the older brother. "I've seen her carrying the puppy."

"Who is the lady upstairs? We've hardly arrived at this place and you've already met everyone," said the younger brother.

"She carries the puppy like a child and takes it for walks on the balcony," said the older brother.

"Great," said the younger brother, "you sit there all the time and watch her! Melon seeds, books, unemployment, liquor, and the lady upstairs, that's just terrific. What a stroke of luck for us."

The older brother laughed happily. The lady upstairs was being counted among his occupations. From that day on, whenever he came back from his afternoon stroll, he would sit under the balcony until the box came down and the lady's cute puppy ran out into the garden and peed and got back in the box so she could pull him up. As long as the box was on the ground, the older brother would be tempted by a strange desire to touch it. But he was afraid, and always restrained himself. Finally, one day he picked a small yellow flower and threw it into the box. A small yellow flower that looked like a sunflower. The next day, the box did not come down; the older brother sat waiting until the middle of the night, but there was no sign of the box. The older brother was heartsick and depressed that a flower had been the cause of the box's sulking and vexation. The next day, the box came down hesitantly, and the older brother, who was sitting by the window nibbling on melon seeds, pretended not to notice. The puppy went around the garden and peed in the middle of the flowers and sniffed a couple of cigarette butts and then, without looking at the older brother, got into the box and went back up. From that day on, the older brother became even more self-absorbed, and the younger brother secretly observed him closely, occasionally directing sarcastic remarks at him. When he went out in the morning with a bowl to collect the cigarette butts from the pool, he would raise Cain, shouting that the older brother had no right to spend his afternoons sitting in the courtyard, filling the pool with garbage and spying on people. But every morning and every evening when the lady upstairs came down the stairs or went up the stairs, both brothers fell silent and listened to the delicate sound of her footsteps, like the chirping of sparrows.

Keeping an eye on the older brother made the younger brother fidgety and angry. The older brother had never seen the lady upstairs. But the younger brother had run into her on the stairs a couple of times, and they had become acquainted and would exchange greetings. Their acquaintanceship had gotten to the point that they would ride the bus together in the morning. The lady upstairs lived alone, and had invited the younger brother up for tea several times. And the younger brother had gone up to her room without the older brother getting wind of it. While the older brother waited in the courtyard for the box, the two of them would sit on the balcony and have fun sending down the box earlier or later than usual. The young woman had told the younger brother the story of the yellow flower. They had both laughed and joked about it.

One day as the older brother sat waiting, the box came down containing a beautiful flower in place of the puppy. The older brother picked up the flower and looked at it. His hand became wet, and an acrid odor made his nose burn and his eyes water. He crumpled up the flower and threw it back into the box. The box went up and then came back down again. In it was a note asking: Hey you miserable excuse for a human being, who gave you permission to ruin my flower?

"Once again a flower has screwed everything up," said the older brother in response.

That night when the younger brother came down he saw the older brother collapsed in a corner, asleep with his head resting on his knees.

9

The next day, the box kept coming down, carrying little letters for the older brother. In each letter, he was asked something. And the older brother didn't know what else to do except answer them. The older brother was being interrogated again.

Q: Hey scum of the earth skulking around down there, introduce yourself.

A: Scum of the earth is exactly what I am. I have no other name or fame.

Q: How do you keep alive?

A: I'm unemployed, and at the moment I'm an albatross around the neck of my dear brother.

Q: Why do you make a habit of self-indulgence and not looking for work?

A: I like self-indulgence, and so I don't look for work.

Q: Are you attached to anything in this world?

A: I like melon seeds and the sun. I'm also extremely fond of drinking and pretty women.

Q: Rather like Beauty and the Beast. You have a refined appetite. Are you going to go on the same way forever?

A: The end is not too far, don't worry.

Q: Take pity on your brother and get out of the poor guy's hair.

A: I'll do as you say.

Q: Take heart and get to work.

A: You can rest assured.

10

For three days cigarettes and drink had not touched his lips, and he had not nibbled on a single melon seed. In the afternoon he would sit by the side of the dirt road and wait, and when it grew dark he would come in and sit beside the empty garden. The younger brother had uprooted all the flowers and thrown them out. The box no longer came down. There was only the shadow cast on the opposite wall of the courtyard by a woman and a man sitting on the balcony joking and laughing. The puppy would come to the edge of the balcony and peek out into the courtyard and bark and try unsuccessfully to stick his head through the bars, and then scratch on the floor of the balcony.

At sunset on the fourth day, the lady upstairs was sitting by herself on the balcony, holding the puppy in her arms and waiting. The older brother could see her shadow on the wall, as well as the outline of her hair, which was very curly and had sketched a pleasing silhouette on the wall. A few moments later the woman got up and came over and looked into the courtyard. The courtyard was dark, and she didn't see the older brother sitting at the edge of the garden. A few seconds later, the box came down and the puppy flew joyfully out. The box was still dangling. The older brother looked up. The woman had tied the rope to one of the railings of the balcony and gone inside, as the puppy contentedly dug up the dirt in the garden. From the upper story came the sound of a door slamming, followed by the voice of their neighbor: "Where were you all this time?"

The voice of the younger brother could be heard saying, "I couldn't come any earlier. He was sitting by the door without moving a muscle until the sun went down."

A few moments later, the older brother saw their shadows on the opposite wall. They were hugging and kissing, then drew apart from each other and went into the room. The older brother said to himself, How many more days are left until winter? How many days until the end of winter?

And he started to think. An ambulance came up with its siren blaring and stopped in front of the house. Someone got out and slammed the door of the ambulance and came over to the door and pressed the doorbell. Nobody opened the door. The bell rang again. A few moments later something heavy thudded against the wall. The sound of the ambulance was again heard as it went off in the direction of the cemetery, its siren blaring. The rumbling of the bulldozers, silent since before sunset, was audible once more.

"The sandflies are here," said the older brother to himself.

The bulldozers drew near and rumbled in the vacant lot behind the house. The older brother heard the sound of the nuts and bolts of the ancient engines as they ground against each other. The older brother took a stool that was in the corner of the courtyard and set it down beneath the balcony and climbed up on it. The sounds became clearer. The sound of a man and a woman laughing in the street and the sound of the bulldozers quietly moving off into the distance and the sound of the pairs of worms that were approaching their goal.

Something resembling a spark was visible in the interior of the room. "What's up?" said the older brother to himself.

A man was striding impatiently on the other side of the wall of the house. In the street, an old lady said, "What kind of people are they, deceiving your child for no reason at all?"

And on the balcony, they tossed a withered flower into the air and let it float down into the garden. The older brother had calmly untied the box from the rope and was making a big knot in the rope as he said to himself, "Too bad there's no light to turn on, you shouldn't make a knot in a rope in the dark, it's bad luck."

He had finished making a noose and was putting his head through it when the ambulance came up and stopped again and someone got out and came toward the door. By that time everything was ready, and the older brother could feel the noose around his neck. He took a peaceful breath and said, "Good night."

He kicked away the stool and remained hanging in the air. Someone was ringing the doorbell. This time they were ringing loudly and urgently. The younger brother came tiptoeing down the stairs and went up to the door and opened it. It was the doctor, who said, "I have business with your brother."

"What business do you have with him?" said the younger brother.

"I have very pressing business with him," said the doctor. He looked at his watch and said, "It's getting late, please call him as quickly as possible."

"Who are you?" said the younger brother.

"I'm a friend of his," said the doctor, "and I'm going on a business trip. I need an assistant. After a great deal of effort, this afternoon I was able to secure the position for him. I came by a few minutes ago and knocked, but no one was home. I went around thinking he might be outside but I didn't find him. I have to get going now. As you can see, I've prepared everything necessary for the trip. I even picked up some melon seeds and books for him."

Overjoyed, the younger brother said, "Are you serious?"

"Yes, yes," said the doctor impatiently, "it's getting late, and I've got to stop by the office and then get moving."

The younger brother, smiling happily, grabbed the doctor's arm and said, "Come in, come in, he's probably asleep. I'll just wake him up. My God, what a piece of luck."

He took the doctor by the hand and pulled him inside. He slid his hand along the wall and found the light switch and the hallway lit up like day. And the younger brother shouted in a loud, enthusiastic voice like a clarion, "Hey, buddy, where are you, Brother dear? A great job has turned up for you, hurry up, step on it, it's getting late, it's getting late!"

The lady from upstairs, who was eavesdropping inside the doorway, thought that the younger brother would come back to her after the older brother left. She shut the door and went out onto the balcony to pull up the puppy in his box.

Mourners of Bayal

Translated by Paul Losensky

When Kadkhoda came out of the house, the landlord's dog, Papakh, began to bark from the top of the garden wall and leapt into the street. The other dogs sleeping on the low roofs of Bayal raised their heads, snorted, and watched Kadkhoda as he walked by, casting a long shadow in the moonlight. They laid their heads on their paws and went back to sleep.

Kadkhoda stopped and listened: the sound of little bells could be heard from outside the village. A muffled, agitated sound, sometimes far away, sometimes nearby, all around the village. All the windows were dark. The people of Bayal were sleeping. Even those who were awake sat in the darkness and watched the moonlight.

Papakh came up, stopped beside Kadkhoda, and sniffed. Kadkhoda stood still, listening, until the sound of the bells grew distant. He continued toward the pond with Papakh behind him. When they reached the edge of the pond, a small window opened, and a man's head came out of it.

The head moved in the darkness and said, "Kadkhoda, it's midnight. Where do you think you're going?"

Kadkhoda stopped, and Papakh stopped too. Both looked at the head.

Kadkhoda said, "Ramazan's ma is ill. I'm taking her to town."

Another window opened. The head of another man came out. "She was all right this afternoon, wasn't she?"

"This afternoon she was fine, but not anymore. She's not well anymore. Can it be the old woman's going to die? What will I do? Huh? Eslam, what will I do? What will I do with the boy?"

"How's she doing now?" Eslam asked.

"She's turned round. She's lying with her head toward the *qebleh*."

The first man leaned over and said to Eslam, "He wants to take her to town." Then he turned to Kadkhoda and continued, "Isn't it better to wait till morning?"

Kadkhoda said, "I'm afraid she won't make it till morning. Ramazan concerns me more. The old woman is done for. I'm afraid the child will do himself a mischief out of grief. What can I do for him? Huh? He is sitting beside his ma, crying and moaning and groaning."

Eslam asked, "How will you take her to town?"

"I'll take her to the edge of the road in your cart and find a truck."

Papakh saw Kadkhoda talking heatedly. He sat down beside the pond, laid his muzzle on his paws and shut his eyes. All at once Kadkhoda turned around and looked back. Papakh also raised his head and looked into the darkness.

"What's the matter?" Eslam said.

Kadkhoda said, "Do you hear it? Bells ringing. Isn't it?"

Eslam and the first man listened, but they didn't hear the sound of the bell.

"Kadkhoda, I'll come with you and bring my cart."

He pulled his head inside. He lit a lantern, put on his hat, and came out through the window. The first man closed his window. His wife came up, and the two of them stood behind the window and watched the feet of Kadkhoda, Eslam, and Papakh, illuminated by the lantern.

"What about your affairs in the village?" asked Eslam.

"I leave them in your hands. All I'm thinking about is Ramazan. I'm afraid if his mother dies, he will do himself a mischief."

When they arrived near the pond, the lantern's light fell on the water. The fish came up to the edge of the pond and looked at the men.

Papakh bent down so he could see the fish. But when his eyes fell on the moon, he turned around and ran up behind the men.

Kadkhoda said, "I'll take my little Ramazan with me. If I don't take him..."

The sound of their footsteps echoed through the street. When the people of Bayal saw the lantern, they thought Ramazan's ma had already died. They poured out through the windows. The old men who couldn't get out of the house stuck their heads out through the openings in the roofs.

When the cart was ready, they brought it to the end of the street. Everyone stood about quietly. Eslam, Mashdi Jabbar, Abbas and Red carried Ramazan's ma wrapped up in a quilt and put her in the cart. They waited. Ramazan, buttoning up his waistcoat, appeared happy and mirthful. He came on the run, got onto the cart, and sat beside his mother.

Naneh-Khanom and Naneh-Fatemeh came up to the cart with holy water. Naneh-Khanom opened Ramazan's ma's mouth, and Naneh-Fatemeh poured a spoonful of holy water down her throat. Standing on the other side of the cart, a mullah wearing a large turban prayed hurriedly.

Eslam and Kadkhoda sat on the driver's bench and packed their pipes. The people of Bayal came alongside the cart to the edge of the pond and stopped. Ramazan turned around and looked at them. The people of Bayal were praying quietly under their breath.

As they came out of the village, the road was bright and clear. Papakh ran about a hundred steps behind them, suddenly turned around and went and hid under a tree, his eyes fixed on the cart. The sound of bells was heard from afar. When they had gone some distance, the moon began to set. It sank lower and grew large. Ramazan turned around and looked back: Bayal had raised its hands and was praying for them.

2

Eslam and Kadkhoda were sitting and letting the horse follow the way on its own. Ramazan had stretched out alongside his mother and had put his hand under her head. Every few minutes, he bent over, shook her and asked, "Ma, Ma, are you better?"

And as a vague ache gripped her chest, and she winced with pain, she would say, "I'm better." And Ramazan would cheer up.

Kadkhoda rode along, comfortable and relaxed, and reflected that not much of the night remained. Suddenly, Ramazan's ma raised her voice, "Lift my head up, lift my head up!"

Ramazan raised his mother's head. With her eyes wide open, she looked into the desert and the darkness.

"What do you want? Ma, dear ma, what do you want?"

She said, "I want to know what it is, that's what!"

"What what is?" he asked.

Eslam and Kadkhoda turned around to look.

Ramazan's ma said, "That sound coming from out there."

They stopped the cart. The sound of bells could be heard from afar. Kadkhoda poked Eslam in the side with his elbow and asked, "Do you hear it?"

Eslam said, "The sound? The gypsies are coming round the other side of the mountain. The anklets on their feet make that sort of jingling."

Kadkhoda said, "It's not the gypsies; they won't be showing up for a long while yet."

Eslam said, "Ah, it's the *Purusis*—listen! They're passing along the bottom of the valley, and they're taking along the sheep they've stolen."

Kadkhoda said, "The *Purusis* never make noise when they pass— they come like a shadow and return like a shadow."

Ramazan said, "I know, it's Papakh coming. There he is."

And with a finger, he pointed into the darkness.

Haltingly, Ramazan's ma said, "It's not Papakh... since... Papakh... has no bell."

The sound grew distant and stopped. Kadkhoda raised the whip, and the horse started out again.

Again they traveled some distance. Eslam wanted to talk and said, "I have heard this sound many times. I'm lonely, you know. I used to go up to the roof at night and sit and listen. Then, I heard that sound many times."

Ramazan put his arms around his mother's neck and said, "My dear ma, don't worry. Mashdi Eslam has heard this sound many times. It's nothing serious. Soon we'll get there, and you'll be better."

The old woman groaned and said, "I'm dying."

Ramazan burst out crying and hugged his mother tighter. "I won't let you die, I won't let you, ma."

Eslam turned around and said, "Don't make so much racket. We're coming up on the edge of the road now, and we'll find a truck."

He turned back again and asked Kadkhoda, "Kadkhoda, how old is this Ramazan of yours?"

"He's twelve."

Eslam said, "God bless us, a big man like this and still crying. And now isn't even the time for it. What are you crying for?"

"I'm afraid my ma will die."

Eslam said, "Your ma's not going to die, don't worry... But in the end she has to die. What're you going to do then? All of our mothers have died. My mother, Kadkhoda's mother. Isn't that so, Kadkhoda? Isn't that so, Ramazan's ma?"

No one replied.

Eslam said, "Kadkhoda, when you've returned from the city, you must get a wife for him. The village is full of girls. There's Mashdi Baba's daughter, plump, rosy, and bright..."

He didn't finish what he was saying. The sound of bells came nearer and nearer. All four listened carefully. Kadkhoda stopped the cart.

Eslam said, "Damn Abbas's father! He's tied bells underneath the cart."

He dismounted and went under the cart. Although he felt around in every corner, he could not find the bells.

After they had started off, Eslam said, "Don't worry. When it gets light, we'll find out where the bells are."

They went on and on. When it grew light, the sound of the bells stopped, and they could see the road in the distance.

3

At the side of the road, Eslam sat waiting on the cart until a truck with passengers appeared. Then he raised his whip and started off toward Bayal like the wind.

Kadkhoda and Ramazan put his mother on the truck and laid her on some bags of rice. Her condition had worsened. The pupils of her eyes were not visible, and her breathing was forced and broken. Kadkhoda was worried that she would meet her end in the truck. He wanted to get Ramazan away from his mother's side by any means possible. But Ramazan had taken hold of his mother's limp and feeble hands and would not move aside. Sleep filled his tired eyes, and his ears heard only with difficulty. He saw neither his mother, nor the dust and dirt of the road, nor heard the sound of the bells that grew louder around the truck.

At noon, beside a curve in the road, they stopped the truck in a patch of shade cast by a cut in the mountain. They spread out the tablecloth in the truck. Ramazan cut a piece of bread and filled it with wheat stew. Forcing open his mother's lips, he poured the stew on her teeth.

Kadkhoda said, "She can't eat—Leave her be!"

The driver came up and looked on with swollen eyes from the corner of the truck and asked, "What's wrong with her?"

Kadkhoda said, "She's sick."

The driver said, "Where are you taking her? To the hospital?"

Kadkhoda said, "Yes. What else are we supposed to do?"

The driver said, "They don't take care of you in hospitals. You should let her meet her end quietly in the village."

Ramazan and Kadkhoda looked at one another. Her breathing had grown shallower. Dust and dirt filled her eyes. A handful of green flies were sitting around her lips.

Kadkhoda said, "If only we'd picked up a Koran."

Crying, Ramazan said, "No, no, she's not dying."

"I know, I know."

"Is that her son?" the driver asked.

While he was gathering up the tablecloth, Kadkhoda said, "Yes, he's her son; he's also mine."

The driver shook his head and said, "These days boys don't often grieve over the death of their mothers. I, too, was like this boy. It's been more than ten years since my mother died. But I can't forget her."

Then he turned toward Ramazan and said, "Don't worry, it won't turn out that way. She won't die. I'll take her to a good hospital where they'll take care of her. She'll get up and walk again."

Ramazan got up and sat down, fighting back his tears. The sun just then slanted over them, and below them a large valley opened up, covered with slabs of black stone. Ramazan said, "See papa! Do you hear it? There it is!"

Kadkhoda listened to the sound of the bells. The driver said, "What's he saying?"

Ramazan said, "Don't you hear it? Don't you hear the bells?"

The driver said, "Bells? I've never heard that sound around here. Sometimes the crickets come out alongside the road and join in together. But that's at nighttime, and now it's high noon." When the truck started off, the sound of the crickets ceased.

4

When Eslam entered Bayal, the men were assembled around the pond. Eslam dismounted from the cart, went toward the group and said, "They've gone."

Mashdi Baba, who was sitting under the willow tree, said, "The old woman will die, of course, but Kadkhoda has thick skin, it won't bother him, and he'll come back to the village. But as for that child, God knows what will befall him."

From amidst the men, Baba Ali said, "She'll get better, if they get some prayer charms for her."

Mashdi Ja'far, son of Mashdi Safar, said, "Nothing will happen. After all, that boy can make his piss foam. In the wink of an eye, he'll forget her and start thinking of other things."

Eslam said, "No, Mashdi Baba, we all know that Ramazan's ma will die. Afterwards, Kadkhoda will take his boy's hand and return to the village. Ramazan will be restless for his mother. Then Kadkhoda and I will come to your house, and we will ask for your daughter's hand in marriage. When we get a wife for the boy, he won't grieve for his mother anymore."

The women around the pond whispered. Mashdi Baba's daughter, who had just returned from a pilgrimage to the shrine of Nabi Aqa, hid behind the others.

Mashdi Baba asked, "Did Kadkhoda say this himself?"

"No, I said it, but he agreed. As soon as they return to the village, Kadkhoda and I will come to your house."

"These things are in the hands of God," Mashdi Baba said.

Eslam mounted his cart, prodded the horse and left the village. Mashdi Baba filled his pipe and drifted off into thought. The women sat down in a circle. His daughter went running along the wall toward home. She stood in front of the mirror and put on eyeshadow.

5

The hospital doorman opened the door. Kadkhoda was holding his wife, sitting on the ground. Ramazan had been leaning on the door, and as soon as it opened, he went flying inside.

"Well?" asked the doorman angrily.

"My wife, the mother of this child, is dying."

Ramazan began to cry. They were covered with dirt and grime from head to foot. The doorman opened the door wide. They entered the vestibule, which was dark and dank. With her eyes still open, the old woman was drawing her last breaths as they spread her on the bench.

The doorman said, "It would've been better if you'd taken her someplace else. Hospitals don't accept people in this sort of condition."

Ramazan cried louder.

Kadkhoda said, "What do you mean someplace else?"

"You know. Our hospital has nothing to do with hearses or that sort of thing. All together there are a few rooms and one doctor. If she doesn't get better, what will you do? How will you get her there?"

Both Kadkhoda and Ramazan begged him to admit her.

"All right," said the doorman said.

They picked up Ramazan's mother, and from the vestibule, they entered a large courtyard. They arrived at a second vestibule, and from the second vestibule they went up some stairs. The sheets, cotton, filth, and iodine were scattered on the stairs.

A thin woman in a white blouse was standing at the edge of the stairs with two children, holding another in her arms. As soon as she saw them, she asked, "Why are you bringing up this corpse?"

Kadkhoda said, "Let us bring her up—she's still alive."

Ramazan cried louder and louder. The woman came forward and looked into the old woman's eyes and said, "She's dead."

Ramazan's mother drew a noisy breath, and the woman said, "All right, bring her up. You always bring your sick when there's nothing we can do for them." They opened the door, and a room came into view. A lantern hung from the ceiling with a small candle burning in it. A dim lamp had been placed in a niche. Three empty beds, filled with sheets and stained cotton, had also been set in three corners of the room.

The doorman said to the nurse, "Why'd you light the candle again?"

The nurse said, "I'm afraid the oil will run out and leave us in the dark."

They placed Ramazan's ma on the bed. Ramazan and Kadkhoda went back and sat beside the door.

The doorman said, "Why are you sitting there? Get up! Let's get the doctor and tell him what's going on."

Kadkhoda got up and went out with the doorman.

Ramazan got up and went over to his mother and looked at her eyes, which were fixed on the suspended lantern. He said to himself, "There now, she's getting better. She's looking at the lamp."

The nurse asked, "How long has she been sick?"

"I don't know," Ramazan said. "We brought her to the road's edge in Mashdi Eslam's cart and from there we brought her here in a truck."

The nurse's children stood beside the door and looked at the old woman and her son and at the old woman's hands, which hung quietly and peacefully over the edge of the bed.

6

Kadkhoda and the doorman entered the first vestibule. They climbed the stairs that were situated in another corner of the vestibule and arrived at a square waiting room with a round window set in the middle of one of its walls that looked out over a large courtyard. The doorman knocked on the door.

Coughing, a man asked, "Who is it? Well, who is it?"

"A patient has been brought in." said the doorman.

A thin man with tattered cotton shoes and a white smock came out. A large stethoscope was crumpled up and stuffed in his pocket. He was crunching on some roasted melon seeds. When he came out, he stared at Kadkhoda. "This one's not sick."

"The sick one's downstairs in Azar's room."

The doctor furrowed his brow and scowled. "Why did you take her there?" he asked. "I can't stand going into that crypt every minute."

Then he went downstairs. Kadkhoda and the doorman both followed behind him. They passed through the vestibule, the courtyard, and the second vestibule and went up the stairs. Azar, who was standing in front of the door holding her child, moved aside. Her other two children, who were in the middle of the room sucking on bones, turned around and looked. Ramazan was frightened and went over by the window.

The doctor said to Azar, "You've brought these whelps to the hospital yet again? Get them out of here." Azar pointed a finger at the children; they threw the bones on the floor and went out in the hallway. Azar went out too and stopped behind the door, and through the crack of the door, she looked at the suspended lantern. The doctor went forward and drew back the quilt from Ramazan's mother. He saw the familiar flies lined up on the sick woman's face. Her eyes were dried out. The mist of the final hour floated in the old woman's silent gaze.

The doctor said to Kadkhoda and his son, "You two should also leave."

Ramazan, Kadkhoda, and the doorman went out.

"She's pretty bad," the doorman said.

Kadkhoda drew the doorman aside and said, "If the old woman dies, my boy will kill himself. This much I know, but what can I do for him?"

"You really think so?" he asked.

Kadkhoda said, "Yes, for ten days he hasn't left his mother's side. I know the old woman is finished. I beg of you, do something so the boy won't find out."

"All right," he said.

Having emptied the room, the doctor opened the sick woman's shirt. The old woman's greenish body was growing cold.

The doctor placed his stethoscope over the sick woman's heart. The heart had stopped beating. But a muffled, incoherent sound could be heard, and the doctor turned around angrily. He opened the door and said to Azar, "How many times must I tell you not to let the children get their hands on their toys when I'm looking after patients?" Azar pointed a finger at the children, who were sitting quietly on the stairs, waiting. The doctor returned again and placed his stethoscope over the heart. The sound of bells softly faded away, and… fell silent at the end of the desert.

7

Mashdi Baba's daughter put on eyeshadow and came and sat on the roof. Not one of the people of Bayal was out. Papakh sat on the wall of Kadkhoda's house and slept with his head laid on his paws.

Mashdi Baba, stretched out in the room, toyed with his henna-dyed beard and looked at his daughter's red camisole through the hole in the ceiling.

Riding on his cart, Eslam came into the village and went to the edge of the pond. He filled a pail and put it in front of the horse's mouth. The horse drank. Eslam's black goat came out of the window and went up alongside the cart and licked at some crushed alfalfa that clung to the cart wheel. The night came on. They all waited. They put their heads out of the windows and listened.

The road was silent.

Mashdi Baba's daughter sat sadly on the roof's brick ledge.

8

In the doorman's room, Ramazan contentedly ate bread and yogurt. His mother had grown quiet and was not moaning. A sheet was drawn over her. The doorman had said she would have to have an operation so that she could walk and that, for this, they had decided to take her to another hospital early the next day.

All three stayed in the doorman's room. After Ramazan finished his dinner, he stretched out and fell asleep. But the doorman and Kadkhoda sat talking half the night. The doorman taught Kadkhoda the ins and outs of this sort of thing.

They put out the lamp and stretched out. Outside a wind was blowing and scraped the branches of the almond tree across the windowpane until morning.

The doorman and Kadkhoda got up. They left the room quietly and stealthily. They carried Ramazan's mother down from Azar's room and set her on the bench in the vestibule. They opened the door and went out on the street, and they were waiting for the car to take the corpse to the cemetery when Ramazan awoke and came out.

The doorman said, "We need to send your mother to another hospital so they can operate on her."

Ramazan said, "I'm going with her too."

The doorman said, "They won't let you in."

"If they won't let me in, I'll turn around and come back."

A black taxi appeared. The doorman started bargaining. Kadkhoda put his arms around Ramazan's mother, carried her into the car and sat down. Ramazan sat beside him.

The car started out, as the doorman watched them. When they reached the end of the street, the sun rose, and the driver turned around and said, "Why are you crumpling up the patient that way? She isn't... is she?"

Kadkhoda said, "We'll get off at the end of the lane it's on, at the end of Violet Garden Lane."

The driver said nothing, drove on and on, and stopped in a small, deserted square. They got out. A long lane covered with dust and dirt was visible opposite them. A slab of black stone lay on the corner of the street. A small banner had been planted on top of the stone, on a pole topped by a copper hand.

Kadkhoda said to Ramazan, "You sit right here. I'm going to take ma in and come back."

Ramazan said, "I'm coming with you too. I want to see my ma." He reached out to grasp the hand of the corpse wrapped inside the sheet.

Kadkhoda said, "Don't touch her. If she wakes up, she won't get better again. Stay right here. If you come, they won't let us in. Then what will we do?"

Ramazan sat on the stone slab. He set a bag of bread and yogurt on his knees. Kadkhoda entered the lane, dragging Ramazan's mother backwards. Her blackened feet stuck out of the sheet. Her long, spread toes dug furrows in the soft dust of the lane.

Ramazan watched the furrows that grew longer with every step his father took. The sun was hot and scorching. A fetid wind blew, and the banner over Ramazan's head fluttered. The sound of wheels and bells reverberated through the street. Ramazan moved aside. A black carriage appeared, drawn by two healthy-looking horses. Small bells were hanging from the corners of the carriage. The carriage entered the small square and stopped. The horses rested, then strode toward the main street, making the bells jingle.

As the carriage was leaving the square, a large, green candle fell on the ground from behind its curtains. The wheels rumbled past it.

9

Eslam and Mashdi Baba were sitting on the cart. Mashdi Baba's daughter, wearing eyeshadow, sat on the end of the cart. They had come to the edge of the road and stopped.

Eslam said, "I don't think they'll be long now. The old woman was in pretty bad shape. When they put her on the truck, she was on the verge of death. In any case, they'll show up."

Mashdi Baba said, "Kadkhoda is a man of God. He won't return until the corpse is properly buried."

The road was empty and deserted. Mashdi Baba's daughter looked toward town with expectant eyes.

All at once Eslam turned around and stared at the road's surface. Two large rats were approaching. Eslam got off the cart. The rats changed course and detoured around them toward Bayal.

Eslam went toward the rats, whip in hand. The leading rat had a large, green candle in its mouth.

Laughing, Eslam called out to Mashdi Baba. Mashdi Baba went over to Eslam. They bent over and looked.

Eslam said, "Look at those sons of bitches! They're taking the candle to Bayal."

Mashdi Baba said, "They bring one candle and in exchange they eat two cartloads of wheat."

Eslam began kicking the rats. The first rat dropped the candle and fled, but the second rat was crushed and broken under Eslam's feet.

Mashdi Baba picked up the candle, looked at it, sniffed it, and asked, "What do I do with this?"

"Let's take it and give it to the girl. She can keep it for her wedding night, all right?"

"Good idea."

They returned and gave the candle to the girl. They packed their pipes, sat down, and got high.

10

No matter what Kadkhoda did, Ramazan would not consent to return to the village. He just sat on the stone, saying, "Wait! Bring ma, and then we'll go."

Kadkhoda said, "Ma will not come for a long time. She'll come in another ten days."

"We'll start in another ten days."

"What about affairs in the village?"

"Go if you want to. I'm going to stay and wait for her."

Kadkhoda sat down and mopped his brow. The old woman's clothes were under his arm. All at once, he stood up and said, "Listen, we can't sit here. Let's go to see the hospital doorman, and we'll wait for her there."

They stood up and went to see the doorman. The doorman had swept and watered down the hospital entrance. He was sitting on a chair in front of the door, eating lettuce.

Kadkhoda said, "We got her to the hospital." He winked and continued, "They said she would come out in another ten days. But Ramazan doesn't want to go back to the village."

Ramazan said, "You go—I'll come with my ma."

The doorman said, "Very well, Kadkhoda, you go. Ramazan will stay here and help me. After a week, I'll send him off."

Kadkhoda picked up Ramazan's mother's clothes and gave Ramazan's car fare to the doorman and obtained his promise that, at the end of a week, he would send Ramazan to Bayal.

Ramazan and the doorman went inside. The doorman said, "You'll stay right here in this room near me until your mother comes back."

Ramazan put the bag of bread and yogurt under the doorman's bed and sat on the window ledge. The doorman hid Ramazan's car money under the lantern and went to bed and fell asleep. Ramazan went out and sat on the chair in front of the door and began eating lettuce.

11

When Kadkhoda entered the village, Eslam was washing his cart at the edge of the pond. Papakh leapt down from the wall, ran out barking to meet Kadkhoda, and sniffed at him. Mashdi Baba's daughter went up on the roof and saw that Kadkhoda had come and was talking with Eslam. She went back down, gathered up her dishes, and hurried through the streets. She went to the edge of the pond and got busy washing and rinsing her dishes.

Eslam said, "Why didn't Ramazan come?"

Kadkhoda replied, "He said, 'I'm not coming until my mother does.'"

Eslam stopped and, struck with consternation, he watched the fish. "When will he finally come back finally?"

Kadkhoda said, "The doorman said he'd send him after a week."

Mashdi Baba's daughter calculated the number of days in a week and tears filled her eyes.

"I wish you'd brought him! Don't you know that some people are waiting for him?" He pointed to Mashdi Baba's daughter.

Both of them turned and looked. Mashdi Baba's daughter stood, picked up the dishes, and left.

When she entered the street, she saw Papakh and Eslam's black goat standing looking at her in surprise.

12

The doorman slept at night, and when the sick came and knocked at the door, Ramazan would get up and go and open it. The doorman had promised Kadkhoda that he would send Ramazan to Bayal at the end of a week. On the sixth day he said to Ramazan, "I've been to the hospital. They won't be discharging your mother quite so soon.

Your father hasn't given me any more money or board for her. Tomorrow, go to the village and fetch some money."

Ramazan agreed, and it was arranged that he would set off in the morning before sunrise. Night fell earlier than usual. The doorman and Ramazan also went to the room earlier and shut the door to go to sleep. A wind rose. They heard Azar leaning out over the window sill and saying to her children, "Do you see what the wind is doing?"

The wind was picking up the garbage and soiled cotton from the courtyard, lifting it up and carrying it out.

Without eating dinner, the doorman pulled the blanket over himself and went to sleep.

Ramazan sat beside the wall and watched the branches of the almond tree scraping against the windowpane.

The noises merged into each other. Every few minutes, the sound of the doctor opening the door and coughing and cursing in the hallway came from the floor above. Ramazan fell asleep listening to these noises.

It was the middle of the night when he awoke. The sound came. A familiar sound. The sound of the bells came on the wind. He listened. The sound came nearer and nearer and stopped in front of the outer door and then a hand picked up the knocker and softly knocked on the door. Ramazan looked. The doorman had not awakened. He opened the door of the room and went into the vestibule. He heard the sound of the doctor coughing in his bed.

Ramazan went on, and the sound of someone breathing came from behind the door. When he opened the door, he saw his mother wearing brand new clothes. Ramazan went out happily and took his ma's hand. They both hurried away. The wind blew more strongly and drove them forward. From afar the sound of other bells was heard.

Ramazan asked, "Where are we going, ma? Are we going to Bayal?"

She said, "We're not going to Bayal, we're going to the Field of Violets."

13

The next morning, Kadkhoda, Mashdi Baba, and Eslam mounted the cart, went to the edge of the road and waited.

Papakh and Eslam's black goat went along and stood beside the cart. Every few hours, the people of Bayal came out all together, looked at the road from the edge of the pond and went back in.

Around sunset, Mashdi Baba asked, frowning, "Isn't he coming? Didn't you say he was coming?"

Uneasily Kadkhoda answered, "He said he'd send him but he still hasn't come."

When night fell, Mashdi Baba's daughter came down off the roof, picked up the large, green candle and went out. She went toward the hill to light it at the lookout point.

Nader Ebrahimi

1936–

A prolific short story writer during the 1960s, Nader Ebrahimi was born in Tehran and raised there and in Gorgan. He graduated with a degree in English from Tehran University, where he also attended law school.

Supporting himself and his family in various occupations, Ebrahimi published numerous collections of short stories from the early 1960s onward, chief among them: *Khāneh'i barāye shab* (A house for the night, 1963), *Ārash dar qalamrow-e tardid* (Arash in the realm of doubt, 1963), *Masābā va ro'yā-ye gajerāt* (Masaba and the Gujarati dream, 1965), *Makānhā-ye 'omumi* (Public places, 1966), *Afsāneh-ye bārān* (Tale of rain, 1967), *Dar sarzamin-e kuchek-e man* (In my little land, 1968), *Hezārpā-ye siyāh va qesseh'hā-ye sahrā* (The black centipede and desert tales, 1969), *Tazādhā-ye daruni* (Internal contradictions, 1971), later renamed as *Dah dāstān-e kutāh* (Ten short stories). His *Ghazal-dāstānhā-ye sāl-e bad* (Ghazal-stories of the bad year) appeared in 1978, followed by the collections *Jang-e bozorg az madraseh-ye Amiriyān* (The great war from the Amiriyan school, 1980), *Ātesh bedun-e dud* (Fire without smoke, three vols., 1981), *Chehel nāmeh be-hamsaram* (Forty letters to my wife, 1989), and *Fardā shekl-e emruz nist* (Tomorrow is not like today, 1989).

Ebrahimi's novels include *Bār-e digar shahri ke dust midāshtam* (Once again the city I loved, 1967) and *Ensān, khiyānat va ehtemāl* (Humankind, betrayal, and probability, 1972). A sort of autobiography called *Ebn-e Mashghaleh* (Workaholic) appeared in 1975, in part a response to criticism that Ebrahimi did not exhibit adequate social or political commitment in his stories.

In the last decade, his books include: *Birā'at-e estehlāl: yā, khosh'āghāzi dar adabiyāt-e dāstāni* (1990), *Lavāzem-e nevisandagi* (1991), *Tārikh-e tahlili-e panj hazār sāl-e adabiyāt-e dāstāni-e Fārsi* (1991), *Mardi dar tab'id-e abdā: bar asās-e dāstān-e zendagi-e Mollā Sadrā-ye Shirāzi, Sadr al-Mutaallimin* (1995), a children's story, *Sahargāhān, Humāfarān, edām mishavand* (1997), *Bar jādeh'hā-ye ābi-ye sorkh: bar asās-e zendagi-ye Mir Mahnāye Dughābi* (1997) a historical novel about Khomeini, *Seh didār bā mardi keh az farā'su-ye bāvar-e mā āmad* (1998), *Hekāyat-e ān azhdahā: majmu'ah-ye dah dāstān-e kutah* (1999), and *Kuchah'hā-ye kutāh: majmu'ah-ye qesseh'hā-ye kutāh* (2001).

Sacred Keepsake

Translated by Marion Katz

I wasn't in top form, but I wasn't fed up, either. Although outside there was wind and the weariness of the afternoon air of early spring, I was reading a book and not feeling gloomy or sad because of the wind or the weariness. My wife opened the door of my room, came in, and asked whether I felt like talking or not. I said, "Why shouldn't I?" She made herself small, sat down on a small footstool next to my couch and sighed.

I asked, "Are you feeling well?"

"Yes, I'm fine," she said.

"You aren't tired?"

"No, no... I'm fine. I just wanted to see... really, to see about New Year's, *Nowruz* that is."

I asked, "What am I supposed to do?"

She answered, "Something that... really... Do you know? There're only five days left."

I was a little surprised that there were only five days left until *Nowruz*. I remembered how, before, I used to sense its approach, its smell and taste, its difference and bright colors. *Nowruz*—I remembered, too, how it used to bring glitter, luster and freshness into things: the shoes, the golf pants, the Lami fountain pen, the briefcase, the pistachios, and the tangerines. I remembered how caressing and glorious the voice of the new year was. I remembered and I forgot. Not a single image was an image of *Nowruz* anymore.

"What do you want me to do?" I asked.

"Don't you feel like talking?"

"I do. I said that I did."

"Then talk. Say what you want to do."

A twinge of pain started in my left leg and spread through the left side of my chest. Involuntarily, my hand clutched at the area where the pain had spread and pressed it.

My wife said, "It's started to hurt again?"

"It's not important. Don't throw my pain in my face so much that I become an addict. We were talking about the new year. You know that I can't stand, can never stand the people of *Nowruz* week; and I'm not one of that crowd myself. Haven't I told you this before, Mehri?"

"Yes, you'd told me; but, if you remember, for the last three years we went to Gorgan. All three years. Didn't we?"

"I suppose we did."

"And this year, they'll certainly come and knock on your door. Either don't be home or open it!"

I started to laugh, felt a twinge, and kept my hand away. My wife said alertly, "It hurts," and I laughed again. She got up from the footstool, held my shoulders, and asked why I was laughing. I told her that her rule, her rule of "either don't be home or open it!" had so much malice in it, and not a speck of humanity. She admitted it and said, "After all, things are how they are. This is the way our life has been settled. What can we do?" She went back and sat down when I said, "I'll stay, but I'm not obliged to open the door to anyone I don't like or don't know."

She said, "That won't do, it just won't do."

I turned my back to her, laid down, and said softly: "It will do. See how it turns out."

I sensed that her voice was becoming harsher, mixed with the acid and bitter substance of the soul's pain. It was no longer possible for her to ask, "Does it hurt or not?"

"That won't, Mahmud. It won't do. You have to understand. You have to be a little closer—to everyone and everything—to be able to talk about them. To be able to write about them." And again, louder, more sadly and more angrily: "I—Mahmud! Are you listening? I left you free to choose, and gave you a chance to ruin our life with your good taste, with books, with thinking and with pain. And I never protested. I never said that I wanted my share from this partnership. I never said that I, too, have the right to think, the right to be happy, and the right to express myself... I never protested how tedious this reclusiveness of yours, this closing the door and turning the back of yours, this suffering and making others suffer of yours have made our life, how monotonous, monotonous, monotonous, and tiresome... But you..."

"I what?" I had turned halfway around, and my hand was outstretched towards her; her hand, which was gesturing "you," together with my hand and the empty space between the two, was like a bridge with the middle of the span demolished by a bombing raid. "I what? Eh?"

"You—you have to turn around."

"Turn around where? Around to these people who, in place of humanity, have Volkswagens? To these people who..."

"No... no... I mean that you have to turn around properly so we can talk. You have to sit and listen and say why we don't take trips and why we don't fix this place up. Everything has gotten worn out, Mahmud. The decor of this house has to be changed. The curtains, the chairs, and the paint on the doors and the walls. It's these things that offend your eyes and make them tired."

"Mehri! It's as if you want to hear I don't have money. Do you want to hear that? Do you want me to talk to you about something they talk about in the bazaar and in the square?"

"No. I don't want you to say that. I want you to keep your cheeks rosy with slapping, slapping, slapping, but never to say that."

The pain twisted, and the voice rushed from my mouth like the swift blows of the wrestling arena.

"Mehri! This thing you want from me—a thing many women want from their husbands—is something I'm simply not capable of. This hand—Mehri! Do you see it? It wasn't made to slap the face of its owner. These people who keep their own faces ruddy and cheerful, and their children's and their wives' by slapping them, have a mania for trading slaps. If someone hits these people they take it, and if someone doesn't hit them they hit him, and if there's no one to take it they hit themselves; but for me there is no reason to raise my hand to give color to my colorless life. I can't make sweets for the gluttonous *Nowruz* guests by slapping. Do you understand, Mehri? This person that you want, I never was, am not and can never be."

Before the curtain of pain was drawn I saw my wife come to my side and heard her say, "Mahmud... Mahmud... Don't get upset, Mahmud..."

When I opened the door of the sitting room, the smell of oil from the sweets hit me. She had prepared something, after all.

The dim and faded color of the curtains depressed me a bit. I closed the door and went back to my room. The doorbell rang, and I heard the sound of Mehri's feet. I locked the door from inside and lay down on the floor. It was my old buddies, my former trench-mates, who now came to see me once a year.

"Come in, he'll certainly come. He'll be very glad to see you. He was a little unwell; he said he was going to drop in on his doctor."

I heard my buddies' footsteps and their laughter. I imagined them saying "happy new year," and then heard the sound of the sitting room door. I listened to their words as a thief listens to the untimely footsteps of the master of the house.

"He's still sick, is he?"

"Yes, he's not well."

"What does he have?"

"Nobody knows. They say he has fainting spells."

"Where do we go next?"

"According to the list, first Doctor Shayesteh's house, then Mukhtarzadeh, and then..."

"Let neither of them be home, we're just fine."

"All right, boys! Are you all ready?"

"Yes."

"I'll scout the terrain. If I see hide or hair of the enemy, I'll report back. Be ready to attack!"

They hadn't changed. They still had the courage to attack. They still entrenched themselves and stood watch. No... they hadn't changed at all.

After they left, my wife knocked on the door of my room. I opened the door and saw that she had the empty pistachio dish in her hand. Laughingly and woundingly, she said, "The boys played a trick. They took away all the pistachios."

"I know," I said. "They haven't changed."

"Are you still upset?"

"A little, just a little."

"Don't you have anyone you can visit and talk to a little? I think you'd feel much better."

"You're right. I'll go and see Mehdi. His wife had better not have ruined him."

I remembered the nights when I used to wander the streets with him until morning. I remembered the night watchmen and how their suspicious looks bored through the night. And how afraid we were and yet, amidst the fear, what things we used to do. I remembered how we wanted, by hook or by crook, to cross the high wall of the night. And how well—even after his marriage—we were able to talk and to show our addiction to pure thoughts.

All the way, I was thinking about those years: defeated years, abject and desolate years.

His wife opened the door to me.

I said, "Do you recognize me?"

"How could I not recognize you?"

I said, "Then, happy new year. A hundred years better than these years. Is Mehdi there?"

She said, "No, but he's coming. He's definitely coming. He'll be very happy to see you."

I said something and followed the woman into the sitting room. We hadn't sat down yet when a little girl came in and wished me a happy new year. I gave her my hand and thanked her. The woman said to her, "The gentleman is your 'uncle.' Don't you recognize him?"

The little girl looked at me closely and then said softly into my ear, "Uncle, won't you give me a present?"

"What?" I said.

She said, "A present."

"Are you Mehdi's daughter?"

"Yes, I'm Papa Mehdi and Maman Farideh's daughter."

"You're a very good girl, but remember not to ask anyone for a present again. It's bad for a person to say to people, 'Give me a present.' It's very bad."

She opened the flap of her little purse and took out a handful of new bills. "I got these as presents."

The woman brought tea. She sat down and talked to me about the state of her husband's work. She told me he had become director of an advertising firm and that his business was the advertisements on television. She said, "Haven't you seen him on television at all?"

"No," I said. "I don't watch television."

The little girl had taken the corner of my jacket and was shaking it and saying under her breath, "Uncle present, present uncle." When the woman went out on some pretext the girl insisted more. She had taken hold of the edge of my jacket—which was pale grey—and her hand was clutching the corner of it; I knew, when she removed her hand, how crumpled and grimy that whole corner would be.

"Uncle present, uncle present."

She said it in such a way that I thought "Uncle Present" was supposed to be my name. I began gently with her, "What's your name, my dear?"

She said, "Uncle present!"

I continued rancorously, "I'm not your uncle. Do you understand? Your uncle died. Your uncle got cancer. They took him to the graveyard and buried him. Your uncle, just like you, was a tick, a louse, a bedbug they took and cut its head off. The dog ate your uncle. Your uncle, your uncle was chopped up. Like this: chop, chop, chop…"

The door opened, and the lady—my friend's wife—came back in. I saw that one of my hands was chop-chopping the other. I laughed and said, "Yes, we reached the place where they ran chop-chop; they ran up to the mountain top. They rushed through and through, and they saw preachers too."

The little girl said to her mother, "This man is saying very bad things. He says he's not my uncle at all."

The woman didn't look at me; but she said to the little girl, "Yes, he is; Mister Mahmud is your uncle. He's even closer than an uncle."

"See, you lied. See, they didn't take my uncle and bury him. Liar, liar!"

The woman said, "Nasrin, don't tease your uncle," but there was no insistence in her voice. When I opened the little girl's hand I saw how crumpled and grimy the corner of the jacket was. I tried to make the woman see the corner of the jacket, but she was looking at the table and I imagined she was very pleased with herself. For a moment my heart burned for my wife, then it burned more and my stomach turned. I looked at the carpet—machine-made, and solid beige. Only its corner had a plume pattern. I became more nauseated. I asked, "Where is the bathroom?"

"Nasrin, show your uncle the bathroom!"

I went to the bathroom, put my finger down into my mouth and tried to throw up. It occurred to me that I hadn't eaten anything in the morning, either. The little girl came into the lavatory behind me and said, "Uncle! If you don't give me a present, I'll tell Mama that you said they took my uncle and buried him." I didn't answer, stuck my finger in again and kneeled. I made myself remember the sugared

mulberries and honeyed *sowhan*, and the table—which was full of little dishes with the pungent scents of oils. My stomach was empty and
it was no use. I came out. I had just clutched the wall when the doorbell rang; I think the woman knew her husband's ring, because she
went and opened the door. I even thought that she was seeking her
husband's protection. She had become afraid of me. I sensed she was
afraid of me by the way she stood behind her husband and said, "Mister Mahmud has been waiting for you for quite a while."

I saw my "former trenchmate," who had a flowered handkerchief
sticking out of the corner of his breast pocket and a gold pin glitter-
ing on his tie. His wife was right. The face of the old fighter was like
those that tout paper handkerchiefs, undershirts and shirtfronts on
the cinema screen. I said hello or I didn't, I don't know; but we
shook hands and went and sat in the living room. The woman also
came and sat down, and the little girl stood next to me. My friend
said, "How are you?"

"Not well," I said.

He repeated, "How are you?"

"Not well, not well at all."

My friend offered his European cigar to me. I refused and he lit
one himself. He inhaled and said, "Honestly, how are you?"

I got up.

The woman asked her husband, "When will you get it back?"

He answered, "It needed a general overhaul. There will be three
days' delay," and then he explained to me, who had stood up, "I took
my Volkswagen to the shop—so as to be ready for the thirteenth."

"Good thinking. You should definitely have it overhauled."

"You still haven't bought a car?" he asked.

I said, "No. I don't like them."

He laughed and said something, of which I only caught the word
"grapes." The woman also laughed.

I said good-bye and was about to be on my way when I saw that
the corner of my jacket was stuck in the little girl's hand.

"Uncle present, my present?"

My former trenchmate said, "They've gotten spoiled; but, well,
Nowruz is for children." I fished in my pocket, brought out a bill and
put it in her hand.

When I got home, I threw myself into an easy chair and lit a cigar.
Mehri came, said hello and asked, "How are you?"

"Not bad," I said.

"Did you go to Mehdi's? Did you talk?"

"Yes, he asked how I was. Honestly, what kind of begging is this that they've taken up? They teach their children to cling to the corners of people's jackets and ask for presents to fill their savings books and provide for their futures. This is begging, armed begging. They're using their children instead of guns. To hell with them and their sacred customs."

Mehri knew my language by now. She understood, she understood well. I said, "Bring me a cool milk from the refrigerator." She brought it, and I drank it off.

"He received you badly, didn't he?"

"No. He didn't receive me at all. He'd taken his Volkswagen in for a general overhaul."

Mehri still imagined that if the decor of the house was changed I would feel better; she was very caught up in the notion.

"Mahmud, you're tired. Your eyes are tired, tired of these curtains and chairs. The decor of this place has to be changed. It will be very good for you."

"There's nothing wrong with me. Don't make me addicted to pain, Mehri. The decor here doesn't need changing, either."

My son tugged the corner of my jacket and said, "Papa, Papa, dedor! Oh, my, dedor! Mama want dedor."

When I saw the corner of the jacket in my son's grasp, a pain suddenly shot through my head. Darkness poured into my eyes, and with the back of my hand I hit my son hard in the face. His face puckered up, he closed his eyes, he broke away from me, cried, and clung to his mother's dress. Then he bawled and bawled. I groped for the chair and sat down on it.

I heard the voice of my wife saying, "Slapping, slapping, didn't you say yourself that you weren't made for slapping? Mahmud... Look! Look!" And I—I couldn't see, couldn't see. I said, "I can't see." My wife took me under the arm, lifted me up and led me among the dim colors, colors that were changing places, revolving, and stretching, and between which there were no boundaries. And she put me to bed.

I said, "Stop his racket!"

She said, "I'll stop it; but don't forget."

"I won't forget... Leave me alone, leave me alone."

It was late afternoon, and the air of early spring was swirling in my room. I wasn't reading the book, I was leafing through it. Salt was making the edges of my lips briny and the pillow was making my ear damp. Someone knocked on the door of my room. I said, "Come in." It was Mehri.

"Do you feel like talking?"

I said, "Very much so. I want to talk."

She came and sat on the small footstool and made herself small.

"Say it, Mehri!"

"Do you want me to remind you of something?"

"Remind me!"

"Do you remember that you said that it's better for children to like someone than for grown-ups to respect him?"

"Yes, I remember; but that little girl was just begging. She had gotten on my nerves."

"I'm talking about your son, Mahmud."

"I'm sorry, Mehri. I'm very sorry. I've never done this before. For a moment, just for a moment I thought that he was much stronger than me when I hit him. I thought that he wanted to break me."

"Ah... Do you think you've grown old, Mahmud? So old that this child can break you?"

"No... no... I don't feel that I've grown old at all."

"Mahmud! Are you afraid that you've fallen without getting anywhere?"

"No, Mehri. I'm the same person I used to be. Believe me!"

"Good, then we had decided, we had decided things wouldn't get this way. Isn't that so?"

In the door, I saw my son's black and languid eyes, which he inherited from me. I called him kindly. He didn't look at me, but ran toward me and buried his head in my body. His breath was warm and moist.

I said, "We're going to Gurgan, and we're coming back. Then maybe we'll give some thought to this place. Anything wrong with that?"

My wife said, "No, it's very good."

As I smelled the soft hair of my son, I said, "I'm going to change my underwear."

Bahram Sadeqi

1936–1986

Born in Najafabad, Bahram Sadeqi graduated from medical school at Tehran University in 1967. He began publishing stories in 1956 in *Sokhan* magazine (1942–79). In 1958–59 Sadeqi served on the literary board of *Sadaf* magazine, but was otherwise disinclined to participate in activities of the Tehran literary crowd. The literary crowd, however, did not ignore him, as critics considered him an important satirical voice in Iranian fiction, a tradition to which such other writers as Abbas Pahlavan and Khosrow Shahani contributed. The short-lived Tehran journal *Mofid* (November/December 1987) featured a portrait of Sadeqi on the cover and several articles asserting his place in Iranian fiction.

Sadeqi's only published longer fiction is a novella called *Malakut* (The kingdom of heaven), which appeared as a special volume of *Kayhān-e hafteh* in 1962. His only collection of short stories appeared in 1970 and was reprinted over 30 years later in 2001. A volume of twenty-five stories, fifteen of which had appeared first in *Sokhan*, *Sangar va qomqomeh'hā-ye khāli*(The trench and the empty canteens) also included a slightly revised text of *The Kingdom of Heaven*. Two Sadeqi stories are readily available in English translation: "Bā kamāl-e ta'assof" (With deepest regrets) in *The Literary Review* 18 (1975); and "Tadris dar bahār-e del-angiz" (Teaching in a pleasant spring) in *Modern Persian Short Stories* (1980).

In the years following his death, reports promised other volumes of short stories from Sadeqi. Finally, in 1998, *Khun-e ābi bar zamin-e namnāk: dar naqd va moarrefi-e Bahrām Sadeqi*was published.

The Trench and
the Empty Canteens

Translated by Alexandra Dunietz

1. Identity Card 1

First name: Kambujiyeh; Surname——; Parents:——; Date of birth: 18 Dey, 1290 Hejri solar; Place of birth:—— (Unfortunately, years later the stamp of the Sugar Office had been placed either intentionally or inadvertently in the spaces where his surname, the name of his father, and his birthplace were written. To put it another way, in front of each space might be written: illegible.) Nothing had been written on the pages concerning marriage and death... Mr. Kambujiyeh resides in Tehran.

2. A Day in the Life of Mr. Kambujiyeh

Once again, the same as always... but no, possibly you say to your-selves: Why "once again, the same as always?" Why, in saying a few general things, do they want "once again, the same as always" to leave unsaid all the parts worth saying? In order to prevent you from saying this, I will try to describe to you accurately and precisely the awakening of Mr. Kambujiyeh. So now listen accurately and precisely.

One delightful spring morning, when sparrows were flirting with sparrows, fish arranging dates with fish, boys dreaming of girls and girls of boys, Mr. Kambujiyeh tossed noisily in his cot, turned from one side to the other, and opened his amiable eyes... That is, he simply awoke. He looked at the ceiling for a while, and a while longer passed before he understood that this activity was futile. Then he turned his face to the window and saw the sun, which was smiling poetically, but even he himself did not understand why he was annoyed by the sun's laughter. So he drew his head under the covers and said: Since things are like this, let me think. A few minutes passed without any thought entering his mind. He said to himself: How about reflecting on planets and fixed stars? He answered: That's very good. Afterwards this short conversation took place in his brain:

—Planets and fixed stars?

—Yes...

—Yes, of course. Some stars are fixed—that is, they don't move from their places, and some stars revolve—that is, they do move from their places.

One or two more minutes passed and Mr. Kambujiyeh was still struggling to find something that would compel him to think about it: Ah! I've found it! I'll think about God. He thought: God... very good; God, God is great... of course, and a number of people believe that instead of "God," one must say "nature." Very good, we shall say "nature"...

Under the covers, on a spring morning and in the brain of Mr. Kambujiyeh, another conversation began.

—Mr. Kambujiyeh, your opinion about... about...

—Ocean liners?

—Wonderful! Oh, wonderful! What do you think about ocean liners?

A while passed in silence and only the tick-tock of the clock echoed in Mr. Kambujiyeh's brain. It was clear that when Mr. Kambujiyeh thought hard, the answer would be well-considered and perfectly impartial. Fortunately, the conversation continued.

—On this subject, I have no particular opinion.

Once again an utterly dark, blind alley, the dreariness of which was apparent from a distance—a blind alley of conversations. Under the covers, Mr. Kambujiyeh forced himself and, like a desperate drowning man who thrashes wildly around in all directions in order to lay hands on a piece of wood, he leapt from one branch to another, ran after various subjects, and stretched out his hand, now roughly and hastily, now gently and calmly, in order to take firm hold of a thought and not allow it to escape. Finally, success, however relative, was his:

—I'll think about love.

—You'll think about love?

—He will think about love.

Near panic, Mr. Kambujiyeh was about to shout. In every corner of his brain, he conjugated one of the various tenses of the verb "to love." Kambujiyeh makes love! Kambujiyeh has not made love! Kambujiyeh, do you make love?

Mr. Kambujiyeh decided to put an end to this confusion. In a firm tone, which is the sign of incontrovertible intentions, he exclaimed in his brain:

—Yes, I make love!

—How, for example? No, we are amongst ourselves, we have been given reason in order to understand. You judge, because your own judgment will admit no mistake... For example, do you make love under the covers?

—It is indisputable that no one makes love under the covers. That is, in the first stages, love begins under rose bushes, and of course it finishes under the covers.

—Oh, Kambujiyeh!...

Yes, "Oh, Kambujiyeh!" ...It was winter. What a harsh winter it was. This story happened several years ago—several years ago when I was quite young and was just beginning to understand the meaning of beauty... It was raining that evening and, so as not to be frustrated, we went to her house. For the first time I saw "her"...

—What a raging love it was, the end of which remained unknown...

—Accurately and precisely, it was a tragedy.

—Oh, what an exaggeration! It was a comedy.

Mr. Kambujiyeh pressed into the bed so hard that all the springs groaned aloud.

—It wasn't a comedy! It wasn't! It wasn't!

Now invisible men began to cry out from within all the chambers and behind all the little windows of his brain: "It wasn't! It wasn't!" Mr. Kambujiyeh clenched his teeth so tightly that the thread of his thought suddenly snapped. Only the sound of the clock broke the silence of the spring day and under the covers something moved. Judging from the circumstances, everyone is right to imagine that thing to be Mr. Kambujiyeh, but I prefer to say: No, respected friends! This was the insides of Mr. Kambujiyeh which, shaken and uneasy, sought a new subject for thought. It might be better if we said that it was not even the insides of Mr.Kambujiyeh, but rather the need to think. One could say that it was the need to think in order to live. Actually, here is one of the places where everything can be inverted without changing the situation. For example, we are right in saying: The thing that moved under the covers was the need to live in order to think.

Whatever the case, one cannot split any more hairs. For if we did, our sin would be comparable to that of priests who, in the midst of a destructive battle between friend and foe, debate over the number of angels on the head of a pin (something which is a far cry from patriotism). Furthermore, we would be deprived of witnessing the defeat or victory of Mr. Kambujiyeh. Fortunately, Mr. Kambujiyeh began to think again with complete success.

—Now, what was the last subject I thought about? The tick-tock of the clock? No, I don't think so. Actually, why did I recall the tick-tock of the clock? Then, it was about God... God was great and some people wanted to say "nature." No, it wasn't that. Some stars are fixed and others move... Of course, no doubt about it, just as some stars move faster than all the others and are called meteors. Then what was it? Ah! Good Lord above! I don't have any particular opinion about ships either—that is, I really don't have any opinion at all, because it is pretty ridiculous that someone whose job... what is his job?

—To eat, sleep, and not to think about life.

—Indeed, this is also a question, whether man should always and everywhere pursue his work or not... I mean, should he, like me, accept as sufficient an elementary life or should he undertake every kind of task, amass money, and buy big and little houses? This must be thought over accurately and precisely on a proper occasion. Well, I for one abhor this life. do I abhor it? Yes, utterly. Just as my friend said, I want to live—not, like him, in the world of imagination, but in this very real world: in some remote spot, on the banks of a tranquil stream that dries up in winter and fills with water in summer. Let me state this quickly: in a metropolitan area—I have gone crazy from all the commotion—I'll build a house just as I like with several gardens where I'll grow flowers and green lawns. I'll water them in the morning and look after them. Then this house should have one room that is very big—after all, I am tired of these matchbox rooms—sunny, and I'll line it with shelves and fill them with new books. I'll carpet the room with a beautiful rug, place several cushions on the sides and in the corners. Then when winter comes, I'll light a heater and draw all the curtains (yet through the glass I'll still be able to see the snowflakes falling gently to the ground). I'll have a few friends to stay—each month one of them will come to inquire after me. Starting in the morning we'll sit together in the room. A brazier will be before us, full of fire-red coals, so responsive that if I want to blow on them, a thin layer of ashes will settle on them. A couple of pots of boiling water for tea will always be ready, the glasses always clean—so clean that they sparkle. From inside the cupboard that won't be installed too far away—in fact, right at hand so no one will have to get up—we'll take out glasses of *araq*, lean the mouth of the opium-pipe on the edge of the brazier, and chat till evening. We'll talk all the time, about whatever we want. Sometimes we'll take a book (the friend who is my companion for the month must make that effort, for I will not be in a state to move at that moment) and we'll read quietly. We'll spend the winter that way till spring arrives. In springtime, we'll draw back the curtains so as to see the blossoms from the room, and start putting the refrigerator fairly close, and...

The point here is that when Mr. Kambujiyeh got this far, his thoughts gave him no peace. Now the scene changed completely, and Mr. Kambujiyeh tossed under the heavy covers (only now did he realize how heavy the covers were), looking for a way to escape the grip of these various thoughts. He raised himself, brought his head partially out of the covers, and almost threw himself from the bed to the ground. Yet thoughts pounded in his head with such speed and force that a moment later, in his soft and comfortable trench, he stretched out, peaceful and immobile, and covered himself up with the covers from head to toe. Once again, the same as always... (Oh, I forgot "once again, the same as always." Never mind.). The tick-tock of the clock slowly erased the silence and everyone is right to imagine that Mr. Kambujiyeh—God forbid!—had died a sudden death or fallen asleep. But I believe I should speak more poetically. For example: "Mr. Kambujiyeh surrendered in the trench. Fortunately his canteen was completely empty and the enemy could not seize any spoils—meaning, any water." But you are right, the official report cannot be called poetic. It is better to say: "Mr. Kambujiyeh lay down in bed with a pleasant apparition. After kissing it, he got out of bed. Outside the room, a beautiful boy waited for him. The boy, who was not yet fourteen, wore garments that made him more beautiful than ever—as if he had come from the depths of centuries past. The boy stroked the gold-embroidered cap that sat at an angle on his head. Upon reaching him, Mr. Kambujiyeh stopped, put his hand under the boy's chin and lifted his head. The boy blushed in embarrassment and smiled. Unfortunately, as soon as he smiled, someone knocked at the door of the large house built on the banks of the river and Mr. Kambujiyeh had to let the boy go open the door. Just as you and I cannot guess who it was who had come to see Mr. Kambujiyeh, no matter how he tried, even Mr. Kambujiyeh himself under the heavy covers could not remember where he had seen the newcomer. In any case, he approached him:

—Yes, sir! What can I do for you?

—Sir, aren't you Mr. Kambujiyeh…? (the stamp of the Sugar Office is on the rest of his name).

—Why yes, that's me.

—Oh! Kindest of kind men and most wonderful of friends! I am that one of your companions whose turn has come.

Mr. Kambujiyeh thought it best to be very serious:

—The friend who is to spend an entire month with me is at this moment smoking opium in my room. Consequently, you will not be officially recognized.

The newcomer did not have time to present his papers before Mr. Kambujiyeh cried out:

—Boy, get him out of here!

All at once, from doors seen and unseen, thousands of beautiful boys leapt out—some beautiful like the rays of the sun and others like the full moon, with gold-embroidered caps and baggy pants, or else with golf trousers and cowboy shirts, and henna-stained fingertips. With utter scorn and contempt, they flung the newcomer into the river, leaving him stupefied in amazement. Now is the time for everyone to admit his error, both he who thought Mr. Kambujiyeh dead and he who believed him to be asleep—even I, who provided an untrue report and recited meaningless poetry. The truth of the matter is that Mr. Kambujiyeh had not surrendered during this time. Instead, he wanted to bring his opponent to his knees with a military trick (to pretend to be asleep or, even better, to play possum). His opponent (thought, penetrating thought that was like a torrent in drilling a passage for itself) was now bent over, just about to fall. From innate cheerfulness, Mr. Kambujiyeh wanted to deal gently with him in these last moments.

—Really, it was ridiculous. I just now recognized that fellow. That poor guy wasn't lying when he said he's one of my close friends. Now what should I do? I swear, once I build the house and get everything set up, I'll spend the first month with him to make up for this disrespect...

—But think about it, wouldn't it be better to get a wife? In the evening she could make a nice soup for you and for lunch fry potatoes and carrots so that you won't upset your poor stomach anymore with sausage and white bread. She'll wash and iron your clothes every day, bear you a child like a peach. Don't worry about its name, just don't worry. Just leave its name alone, some damned name, for it will inherit yours and perpetuate your memory among men. Every year, won't you add another to the assembly of heirs, like the beads of a rosary, so many that there won't be room for you at the dinner table? They'll raise a ruckus and snatch each other's food, and you'll be so surrounded by horseplay that you won't think about anything. Instead of opium, alcohol, and friends of a month, wouldn't it be better for you to drug yourself with your wife and children, a soup pot, and the debts at the start of every month?

It was the alarm clock or heavenly affliction or divine generosity— whatever it was, it so shattered Mr. Kambujiyeh's drowsiness that he sat up in bed remarkably quickly. The alarm clock went on ringing and Mr. Kambujiyeh remembered that he had left the alarm on out of forgetfulness. Gradually a terrifying scene took shape before his eyes: to get up, wash his face and hands, use the toilet, stroll about the streets, and to eat breakfast and lunch in one, calling it dinner.

Calmly and gently he stretched out again in bed. Then, reaching out his fingers, he took a pot from under the bed, slipped it under the covers and after a while removed it, put it back in its place, and said happily—That takes care of that.

Then he again reached out his hand and took a tablecloth from the heater. He spread it on his stomach and began to eat (unfortunately, it is not known what Mr. Kambujiyeh ate because the room gradually grew dark).

On a delightful spring day, the crows flirted, the fish parted from each other and Mr. Kambujiyeh, his eyes wide with elation, thought:

—God bless the days in the office. All the vacation days pass this way. It's clear... However, what was the last thing I was thinking about? Aha! Now I remember: the difference between comedy and tragedy... Right, tragedy is when a person is killed. That person must be in love, and comedy is when the bride's family doesn't give their daughter to someone in love who asks for her hand. In light of that, what was that winter's love of mine? Since they didn't kill me, it wasn't a tragedy. Since I basically didn't ask for her hand, so we could know whether the bride's family agreed or not, it can't be a comedy either. Perhaps one could say...

—There's no perhaps about it. It can be said with certainty that it was ridiculous.

3. Identity Card 2

First name: Sakineh; Surname: (Sugar Office stamp); Parents: (Sugar Office stamp); Date of birth: 19 Bahman, 1300 Hejri solar; Place of birth: (Sugar Office stamp). Nothing has been written on the pages concerning marriage and death. Miss Sakineh lives in one of the cities.

4. An Evening in the Life of Miss Sakineh

Seven o'clock—Miss Sakineh got up crossly from in front of the mirror. Picking up her hair ribbons, she went to her mother. Her mother—may she rest in peace (for it is possible that she eventually died)—looked up from under her glasses and gradually her wrinkled face took on the shape of a question mark. Miss Sakineh pursed her lips into a half-opened bud and answered her mother's question aloud.

—Maman, from sunset till now I have been vexed over trying to tie my hair in a ponytail. But every time, because no one helps me, I make the knot too loose. Instead of looking like the tail of a proud charger with its head held high, it's exactly like that of a horse fleeing the battlefield in disarray. Now I want you to help me do it right.

The folds of Miss Sakineh's mother's face gradually relaxed and this time her face turned into an exclamation mark. She said, — What did you say—dearie?

Miss Sakineh repeated what she had said for the benefit of her mother's deaf ear. But don't imagine that the affair concluded so easily. It was already half past seven before the pious old lady finally understood her daughter's request. Tying the knot and all that took till eight.

Eight o'clock—trying as much as possible not to move her head Miss Sakineh with her proud ponytail sat on a wooden chair, picked up the magazine *Ladies of the Future*, and raised it to eye level in order to read. But since she didn't have the patience (several days before in her diary she had written: I wasn't made for reading), she began to leaf through it. She read fleeting phrases on every page:

—Message of the famous preacher to the future ladies of Iran: Yes, Ladies, these prime roses in the bouquet of society who... who wear short skirts and tight-cut dresses may not expect their bodies to grow perfectly... Otherwise "Robert" knew that he had worked for many years in the field of physical beauty... his failure was tied to the fact that instead of reading books filled from cover to cover with advice and counsel in the guise of fine arts, he had occupied himself with misleading books, and for this very reason, the poor man has lost his life.

Yes, o maidens fair of face!
How long will you pine for husbands?
"Either greatness, glory, wealth, and honor,
Or stand like men face to face with death."

...The reason I participated in this contest, sending in my photo and writing an article, is to explain to all the people in the world that, in the shadow of ever-increasing changes, we, the women of Iran, have stepped out from behind the ancient veil to set up newspapers, clubs, institutions, organizations, and publications. Hand in hand with all segments of society, such as men, children, youth, and the focus of industry and public order, we drive the vehicle of history... Congratulations! Dear young lady, we are pleased that our sisterly advice which is published regularly on the "Question and Answer" page has been so effective that you have given up this unnecessary habit... So that the same thing does not happen to you as happened to the crow. Listen now, children, as we discuss the crow...

Miss Sakineh continued reading in this fashion until nine o'clock.

Nine o'clock—again, the same as always (...but with reservations) Miss Sakineh opened the door for her father. (A while before she had written in her diary: Why do I call my mom "Mother"—she who nurtured me day and night and expended her very heart's blood and the tears of her eyes for me? Why do I deal so formally with someone who treats me with such love and sincerity? No! I am a sensitive girl who cannot act contrary to the call of my heart. I shall call her "Maman." The opposite is true for my father. He is someone to whom I must demonstrate the utmost respect, as far as I can. Yes— first respect, then love. Thus how ugly, unmannerly, and vulgar it would be were I to call him "Dad." Only by using "Father" can I clarify and prove the degrees of my respect for him who in fact is the second of my progenitors.

When Father, Maman, and Miss Sakineh sat down to dinner (fortunately, since the electricity had gone on again after having been cut off in the early evening, everything was lit up and it could be seen that this fortunate family was eating bread and sheep's head soup) they began the serious conversation that was repeated each evening and that took more time than it should have because of Maman's dull ear, Father's stuttering, and Miss Sakineh's Talmudic cavilling:

—Father, I no longer have the strength to endure this decayed environment. How long must a person survey unsympathetic surroundings and hold his peace? I cannot witness all this corruption and injustice anymore. The lies, oppression, and disrespect for the current laws of the state drive every upright Iranian to the limits of his patience. Consider, too, that in addition to all that, I am one of the girls of this country, in gender created female. Certainly, I do not wish to raise myself above others, contrary to the inclinations of my heart, and claim to be more sensitive than they. No, actually, I shall leave this part unsaid. My point is that I want to enjoy equal rights with men, preserve my self-respect, and exercise my right to education and instruction, to be able to develop my hidden talents that have withered in the nooks and crannies of my existence and put them at the disposal of all. These observations bring me to the proposal I made to you previously—namely, that you send me abroad. Tonight I renew my request with the same persistence and I hope that you will give the matter more consideration.

—Father (the manners of the younger generation had been transmitted to the older, such that Maman did not permit herself to address her husband as "little man" as she did formerly), what did my daughter say?

During the communal meal, Miss Sakineh and Father patiently and methodically tried to explain to Maman the request that had been made. When they had finished, Father spoke thus:

—My daughter... as for me... there is no happiness greater than that the unique fruit of the ni... the night of my wedding should continue her education... and for a while be sent ab... abroad, away from un... unpleasantness. But what can I do with my heart and the heart of your Mo... Mo... your Mother (you will notice that respect had become general practice)? We cannot bear to be separated from you. Could you not re-examine your proposal and go... go... go to

Tehran for the completion of your higher education? It is true that your perceptive soul... and your lofty thoughts are troubled there, but what is to be done? Our homeland must flourish under your hand and mine, that of your M... M... Mother and of those like us and your children (knock on wood). The foreigner's heart never feels for us. And then, if you cannot work in your country, how much the more will any work ab... abroad...

Since the danger of apoplexy was imminent, the conversation was broken off. But Maman shook her head philosophically and, as she hadn't heard a thing, it is unclear why once again, as always, she imagined that Father had agreed to Miss Sakineh's trip abroad. So she laughed and said:

—Saki dear (that was a sign that Maman had the very best intentions), now, God the Merciful willing, when will you be leaving?

After they had exhausted themselves trying to explain to her that agreement had still not been reached, futile and serious discussions continued until eleven o'clock. The only result of the night was that Miss Sakineh changed the course of her life. Instead of planning to complete her knowledge of sewing, she will pursue her reading in the field of housekeeping.

Eleven p.m.—five a.m. Sleep. Miss Sakineh never allowed diabolical dreams about sleeping with men, marriage, or pure ones such as having children, enjoying holy matrimony, getting pregnant, lullabies and the like to pass through her brain. Perhaps to that end, she took two sleeping pills every night.

Four a.m. Miss Sakineh went to the bathroom and, after swallowing another pill, slept from then until morning.

5. Several Sentimental Remarks

Time passed. Years after we had inspected those two identity cards, we came across another I.D. that lifted the veil from an important secret. In addition it showed that, contrary to what is rumored abroad, our institutions and particularly that of birth statistics work very well, for on the last I.D. there was no trace of the Sugar Office's stamp.

6. Identity Card 3

First name: Arastu; Surname: Zanjabilian; Parents: Kambujiyeh and Sakineh; Date of birth: 20 Esfand, 1335 Hejri solar; Place of birth: Rayy. (Nothing had been written on the pages concerning marriage and death.)

7. A Day and a Night in the Life of Mr. Arastu

The events that occurred to the unweaned Mr. Arastu during one day and one night, together with those that are likely to occur, can be summarized in a few words: Sleep, Tears, Thoughts. But what a great crime it would be if we were to wish to grasp his great loneliness just superficially and merely allude to it (the records will amount to seventy pounds of paper)... When Mr. Arastu came into the world one year before, he had not been alone: he began his journey through the evanescent world with a fellow traveler, with a brother like himself whom, one or two months afterwards, during a family party of the sort held in the evening only at such times, they named "Ashkabus." Ashkabus and Arastu... Afterwards these two friends of like mind who, even though wrapped in separate swaddling clothes, were one in heart and soul, cried together, screamed together, fell asleep and woke up together, and experienced life. But what can be done when the days work for separation? A week ago, without any preliminaries and with indescribable speed, dear Ashkabus died. His heart-rending death was so sudden and enigmatic that it elicited contradictory opinions from everyone and every competent authority accounted for it differently. The coroner wrote his report with deadly hesitation: "I testify that Mr. Ashkabus, age one year, son of Mr. Kambujiyeh, died due to a weak constitution and internal illness. Although there is no reason to prevent his burial, in order to relieve all doubts, it is advisable to proceed with an autopsy." The local news section of an evening paper notified its readers of the deceased's loss as follows: "According to our special children's reporter, last night a one-year-old child named Ashkabus, as he was lying in the arms of his mother, suddenly threw himself into a pool and died instantly. Mothers must..." In these moments of crisis, Mrs. Sakineh took her diary out of the trunk in which were stored the mementos of her unmarried life and in a blank corner wrote: "Oh... this hostile environment, these sufferings that rain through the doors and walls, these erroneous regulations and requirements, these coarse and ill-bred men caused my Ashkabus to set off for the next world in order to flee them and this age of commonplace, vulgar lives." A day or two later, when the waves of grief had subsided, she added another line in her handwriting: "Yes... tomorrow, if possible even now, I must at least save Arastu... I must send him abroad."

During all that time, Mr. Kambujiyeh was silent and the activities of his fertile brain remained unknown. Finally, on a warm afternoon, he found the time to think about the death of his beloved son (who was an heir to his name). At midnight of that day he reached this conclusion: "Various factors sent my darling son to the world of nothingness. He did not rest for a single minute. He was obliged to be active and pour out his sweat during every hour and every minute of his short life. He didn't die—rather, he committed suicide. He vacated the trench of life, while I flee with several empty flasks from this spot.

8.

Among them all, only Arastu still has no personal opinion about the death of the unfortunate Ashkabus. While men who know nothing about his world and the extent of his perception might have attributed this matter to his stupidity, youth, or lack of sensitivity and affection, the truth lay elsewhere. Behind Arastu's forehead traces of intelligence are apparent and one is able to see quite well that the salient characteristics of his father and mother are combined in him. Unfortunately, it is still much too early for us to predict his future. Our duty now is to sympathize with him and to share his grief and pain: the grief and sorrow of thinking in loneliness, sleeping in loneliness, and screaming in loneliness.

Hushang Golshiri

1937–2000

Fiction writer, critic and editor Hushang Golshiri was born in Isfahan and raised in Abadan, one of a large family of modest circumstances. From 1955–74, he lived in Isfahan, where he completed a bachelor's degree in Persian at the University of Isfahan and taught elementary and high school there and in surrounding towns.

Golshiri began writing fiction in the late 1950s. He published short stories in *Payām-e novin* and elsewhere in the early 1960s, and established *Jong-e Esfahan* (1965–73), the chief literary journal of the day published outside of Tehran. Golshiri's first collection of short stories was *Mesl-e hamisheh* (As always, 1968). Then came his first, and most famous, novel *Shāzdeh Ehtejāb* (Prince Ehtejab, 1968). Translated in *Literature East & West* 20 (1980), it is a story of aristocratic decadence, exemplified through the memories of a dying prince. Shortly after production of the popular feature film based on the novel, Golshiri was arrested and imprisoned by Pahlavi officials for nearly six months. An autobiographical and less successful novel called *Keristin va Kid* (Christine and Kid) came out in 1971, followed by a collection of short stories called *Namāzkhāneh-ye kuchek-e man* (My little prayer room, 1975), and a novel called *Barreh-ye gomshodeh-ye rā'i: (jeld-e avval) tadfin-e zendegān* (The shepherd's lost lamb, volume 1: burial of the living, 1977).

In early 1979, he married Farzaneh Taheri, whom he credits with editing his subsequent writing. In the 1980s he published *Ma'sum-e panjom* (The fifth innocent, 1980) which was made into a film, *Jobbeh-khāneh* (The armory, 1983), *Hadis-a māhigir va div* (The story of the fisherman and the demon, 1984). Following a visit to Europe in 1989, many of his works were published overseas, including the short story collection *Panj ganj* (Five treasures, 1989), novels, *Dar velāyat-e havā: tafannuni dar tanz* (1991), *Ayeneh'hā-ye dardār* (1992), *Jenn'nāmeh: rumān* (1998), and *Bar mā cheh rafteh ast?; va, Fathnāmeh-e Mughān: du dāstān* (199?). In 1990, under a pseudonym, Golshiri published a novella in translation called *King of the Benighted*, an indictment of Iranain monarchy, engage Persian literature, the Tudeh Party, and the Islamic Republic. At the same time, however, books of his were still being published in Iran right up until his death, including: *Davāzdah rokh: filmnāmeh* (1990), *Khābgard* (1990), *Dar setayesh-e shir-e sukut: dar' āmadi bar naqd-e she'r-e mo'āser va hāshiyeh'i bar she'rhā-ye awji* (1995), *Dast-e tarik, dast-e rawshan* (1995), *Bāgh dar bāgh: majmuah-e maqālāt* (1999), and *Hadis-e māhigir va div* (2000).

The Wolf

Translated by Paul Losensky

Thursday noon I was informed that the doctor had returned and that he was sick too now. There was nothing the matter with him. The doorman at the clinic said that he had slept straight through from last night until now, and when he awoke, he just wept, choking on his sobs. Usually on Wednesday or Thursday afternoons he set out and went to the city with his wife. This time too he had gone with his wife. But when the truck driver had brought the doctor, he had said, "Only the doctor was inside the car." It seems he was numb from the cold. He had left the doctor at the door of the coffeeshop and gone on. They found the doctor's car in the middle of the pass. At first they had thought that they would have to hitch it to a car or something and tow it to the village. They had gone with the clinic's jeep to do this. But when the driver got behind the wheel, and several others pushed, the car moved. The driver said, "It's because of last night's cold—otherwise, there's nothing the matter with the car." Since there wasn't even anything wrong with its windshield wipers, no one thought of his wife until the very moment the doctor said, "Akhtar, so where is Akhtar?"

The doctor's wife was short and thin, so thin and pale that it seemed as if she'd collapse any minute. They had two rooms in the clinic. The clinic is on the far side of the cemetery, that is, exactly one block away from the settlement. His wife was no more than nineteen years old. At times she would appear in the passageway by the clinic door or behind the windowpanes. Only when it was sunny would she leave the side of the cemetery and walk about the village. She usually had a book in her hand and sometimes a packet of sugar candy or even chocolate in the pocket of her white blouse or in her handbag. She loved the children very much. For this reason, she usually came out along the path to the school. One day I suggested to her that if she wished, we would be able to assign a class to her; she said that she didn't have the patience to deal with the children. The truth of the matter is that the doctor had suggested it to keep his wife occupied. At times, too, she would go to the canal bank together with the women.

After the first snow fell, she disappeared. The women would see her sitting beside the heater reading something or pouring tea for herself. When the doctor would go to pay calls in other villages, the driver's wife or the doorman would stay with the lady. It seems Sadiqeh, the driver's wife, understood first. She had told the women, "At first I thought she was worried about her husband because she'd start suddenly, go up to the window and pull back the curtains." She would stand next to the window and gaze into the white, bright desert. Sadiqeh said, "When the wolves start howling, she goes up to the window."

Anyway, in the winter, if the snow falls, the wolves come closer to the settlement. It's the same way every year. Sometimes a dog, a sheep, or even a child would disappear, so that afterwards the villagers would have to go out in a group to find, maybe a collar or a shoe, or some other trace. But Sadiqeh had seen the wolf's glistening eyes and had seen how the doctor's wife stared at the wolf's eyes. One time she didn't even hear Sadiqeh call out to her.

After the second and third snows fell, the doctor was unable to visit the outlying area. When he saw that he would have to stay in his house four or five nights a week, he was ready to join in our social rounds. Our get-togethers were not for the women, but, well, if the doctor's wife came, she'd be able to join the women. But his wife had said, "I'll stay home." Even on the nights when it was the doctor's turn to host the get-together at his house, his wife would sit next to the heater and read a book, or would go up to the window and look at the desert or, from the window on this side of the house, look at the cemetery and, I think, the bright lights of the village. It was at our house, I believe, when the doctor said, "I must go home early tonight." Apparently he'd seen a big wolf in the road.

Mortazavi said, "Perhaps it was a dog."

But I myself told the doctor, "Wolves are often seen around here. You have to be careful. You should never get out of the car."

My wife, I think it was, said, "Doctor, where is your wife? In that house next to the cemetery?"

"That's why I must go early."

And then he said his wife was fearless. And he admitted that one night, at midnight, he had wakened with a start to see her seated next to the window on a chair. When the doctor called out to her, his wife said, "I don't know why this wolf always comes up, facing this window."

The doctor had seen the wolf sitting right on the other side of the fence in the dim light of the moon and howling occasionally at the moon.

Anyway, who would have thought that a wolf, large and solitary, I believe, sitting opposite the window and staring, would little by little become a problem for the doctor and for all of us besides. One night he did not come to our get-together. At first, we thought his wife had fallen sick or the doctor at least, but the next day his wife came herself to the school in the office car and said that, if we would give her the children's drawing class, she was ready to help.

The truth of the matter was, there were so few students that there was no longer any need for her. When we gathered all of them in one classroom, Mr. Mortazavi alone was sufficient to handle them. But, anyway, neither Mortazavi nor I could draw well. We settled on Wednesday morning. Later I brought up the matter of the wolf and said that she shouldn't be afraid, that if they didn't leave the door open or go outside, for instance, there was no danger. I even said that if they wished they could come to the village and take a house.

She said, "No, thank you. It's not important."

Then she admitted that at first she was frightened, that is, that one night when she heard the sound of it howling, she felt that it must have jumped over the fence and was just then sitting behind the window, perhaps, or the door. When she lit the lantern, she saw its black form leap over the fence and then saw its two glistening eyes. She said, "They were exactly like two burning coals." Then she said, "I myself don't know why, when I see it, see its eyes or that stance... you know, it's exactly like a German shepherd, sitting upright on its front legs and staring for hours at the window of our room."

I asked, "So, why do you?"

She grasped my meaning and said, "I told you, I don't know. Believe me, when I see it, especially its eyes, I can no longer budge from the window."

We talked of wolves in general, I believe, and I described for her how, when wolves get very hungry, they sit in a circle and stare at one another for hours, that is, until one of them rolls over out of exhaustion; then the others pounce on it and eat it. I also talked about the dogs that get lost occasionally, and only their collars are found. The doctor's wife talked about them too; it seems she had read Jack London's books. "I now know wolves well," she said.

The next week when she came she drew a flower or a leaf for the children, I believe. I didn't see it, just heard about it.

It was a Saturday when I heard from the children that they had set a trap in the cemetery. At the third bell, I went myself with one of the children and looked. It was a big trap. The doctor had bought it in the city and put a side of beef in it. Later that same afternoon, my wife informed me that she had gone to look for the doctor's wife. She said, "She's not doing well." She said, I believe, that the doctor's wife had told her that she was afraid she would not have children.

My wife had consoled her. They had been married for a year. Then my wife brought up the subject of the trap and said, "They're usually skinned here and the skins taken into town." My wife said, "Believe me, all at once her eyes opened wide, and she began to tremble and said, 'Do you hear? That's its very call.' I said, 'Really, madam, now, at this time of day?'"

It seems the doctor's wife ran to the window. It was snowing outside. My wife said, "She pulled back the curtains and stood next to the window. She completely forgot that she had a guest."

The next morning the driver and a few farmers went to inspect the trap. It hadn't been touched. Safar said to the doctor, "It certainly didn't come last night."

The doctor said, "No, it came. I heard its call myself."

To me he said, "This woman is going crazy. Last night she didn't sleep a wink. She sat next to the window all night long and looked at the desert. At midnight, when I was wakened by the wolf's call, I saw my wife fiddling with the door latch. I screamed, 'What are you doing, woman?'"

Then he told me she had a flashlight, switched on, in her hand. The doctor turned pale, and his hands were trembling. We went together to inspect the trap. The trap was intact. The side of beef was still in place. From the footprints, we realized that the wolf had come up to the side of the trap and sat right next to it. Then the trail of footprints went straight up to the fence around the clinic. I saw the woman's face at the window. She was looking at us. The doctor said, "I don't understand. You at least say something to this woman."

The woman's eyes were wide open, staring. Her pale skin had become paler still. She had gathered her black hair together, and it spilled down over her chest. She seemed to have no make-up other than eyeshadow. If only she had at least put lipstick or something on her lips so that they wouldn't be so white! I said, "I've never before heard of a hungry wolf passing up all this meat."

I also described the footprints for her. She said, "The driver said it wasn't hungry. I don't know. Perhaps it's just very intelligent."

The next day they brought news that the trap had been pulled up. They had followed the trap line. They had found the wolf; it was half alive. They killed it with a couple of shovel blades. It was not all that big. When the doctor saw it, he said, "Praise God." But the doctor's wife said to Sadiqeh, "I saw it myself this morning at the crack of dawn sitting on the other side of the fence. This one that they caught was surely a dog or a badger or something."

Perhaps. It's not unlikely that she said these very words to the doctor, for the doctor was forced to get the police. One or two nights afterward, policemen stayed in the doctor's house. It was the third night when we heard the sound of shots. The next day, when the police and several farmers, together with the clinic driver, followed the trail of blood as far as the hill on the far side of the settlement, they saw wolf tracks and a disturbed patch of snow in a ravine behind the hill. But they had been unable to find even a single piece of white bone. The driver said, "The godless bastards, they even ate the bones."

I didn't believe it myself. I said so to Safar. Safar said, "When the lady heard about it, she only smiled. The truth of the matter is that the doctor himself told me to go and inform her. The lady was sitting next to the heater and seemed to be drawing something. She didn't hear the knock on the door. When she saw me, the first thing she did was turn her paper over."

There's nothing special about the woman's drawings. She'd drawn only that wolf. The shining red eyes on a black page, a black ink sketch of the wolf sitting, and one too of the wolf howling at the moon. The wolf's shadow was greatly exaggerated, in such a way that it covered the entire clinic and cemetery. One or two as well are sketches of the wolf's muzzle, greatly resembling a dog's muzzle, especially the teeth.

On Wednesday evening the doctor went to the city. Sadiqeh said his wife was ill. The doctor had told her so. I didn't believe it. I myself had seen her Wednesday morning. She came on time and taught the children drawing. She drew one of those same sketches of hers on the blackboard. She told me so herself.

When I asked her, "But why a wolf?" she said, "However much I wanted to draw something else, it wouldn't come to me. I mean, when I put the chalk to the board, I drew it automatically."

It's a pity that the children erased it when the bell rang for recess. In the afternoon, when I saw one or two of their drawings, I had expected the children wouldn't be able to draw it properly. But in the event, the children's sketches, all of them, turned out to be just like German shepherds, with ears drawn back and tails that wrapped around their haunches.

Thursday noon when I found out the doctor had returned, I thought surely he had left his wife overnight in the city and gone back to work. Still, he had no patients, that is to say, none had come from the other villages. But, anyway, the doctor is a responsible man. Later, when he went to look for Akhtar, everyone went to the pass in the doctor's car and the clinic jeep. The police went too. They found nothing.

The doctor, though, didn't say a word. When he woke up, if he wasn't weeping, he just stared at us, one by one and with his wife's wide open, staring eyes. I had to give him a couple of tumblers of *araq* so he would start talking. Perhaps he didn't want to talk in front of the others. I don't think they'd had a quarrel or anything. But I don't know why the doctor kept saying, "Believe me, it's wasn't my fault."

When I asked my wife, and even Sadiqeh and Safar, none of them remembered the wife and husband ever having raised their voices to one another. But I had told the doctor not to go. I even told him that there would surely be more snow in the pass. Perhaps the doctor was right, I don't know. Finally he said, "She's not well. I don't think she can stand it here. But after all this, why these pictures?"

Later I saw them. She had drawn several sketches of wolf paws, one or two of their drooping ears. I said, "I believe…"

The doctor was not able to speak properly. But I gathered that snow was falling heavily in the middle of the pass, so that it covered all the windows. Then the doctor noticed that the windshield wipers were not working. He had to stop. He said, "Believe me, I saw it, I saw it with my own eyes, standing in the middle of the road."

Akhtar had said, "Do something. We'll freeze to death here."

The doctor said, "Don't you see it?"

The doctor even put his hand out through the window, thinking he might wipe the snow off with his hand, but he saw there was nothing he could do about it. He said, "You know yourself that it isn't possible to turn around there."

He was right. Then, the motor shut off, I believe. When Akhtar shone the flashlight beam about, she saw that the wolf was sitting right at the side of the road. She said, "It's the same one. Believe me, it's completely harmless. Perhaps it's not a wolf at all, maybe it's a German shepherd or some other dog. Get out and see if you can fix it."

The doctor said, "Get out? Don't you see it?"

Even as he said this, his teeth were chattering. He turned pale, exactly the same sickly color of his wife's face when she stood behind the window and looked at the desert or at the dog. Akhtar said, "Should I throw my purse out for it?"

The doctor said, "What good would that do?"

She said, "Well, it's made of leather. Besides, while it's eating the purse, you can do something about it."

Before she threw her purse, she said to the doctor, "If only I had brought my fur coat."

The doctor said to me, "Wasn't it you who said that you shouldn't go out or open the door, for instance?"

When Akhtar threw her purse, the doctor did not get out. He said, "By God, I saw its black form, standing there at the side of the road. It wasn't moving or howling."

Then when Akhtar turned the flashlight to follow her purse, she couldn't find it. Akhtar said, "Well then, I'll go myself."

The doctor said, "Why, you don't know anything about it," or perhaps he said, "You can't fix it." But he remembered that before he knew it, Akhtar had gotten out. The doctor did not see her, that is to say, the snow prevented him. He did not even hear the sound of her scream. And then, I believe, out of fear, he shut the door, or Akhtar shut it. He didn't say.

Friday morning we started off again in a group from the village. The doctor did not come. He couldn't. It was still snowing. No one expected us to find anything. It was white everywhere. We dug everywhere we could think of. We found only the leather purse. On the road, when I asked Safar, he said, "There's nothing wrong with the windshield wipers."

Me, I don't understand. After all this, when Sadiqeh brought the pictures for me, I was still more confused. A hastily written note was pinned to them, saying something like "As an offering to our school." When she was about to go, she entrusted them to Sadiqeh, saying that if she didn't get better or if she couldn't come on Wednesday, she was to give the drawings to me so that we could use them as a model. I couldn't tell Sadiqeh, or even the doctor, but after all, what appeal could sketches of dogs, such ordinary mutts, have for the village children?

Portrait of an Innocent

Translated by Frank Lewis

The gamekeepers had seen him going up a goat path. At first they probably saw his motorcycle parked in the shade cast by a boulder. After that it would not have been much of a problem to find him, as they could follow his footprints and the marks left by his walking stick in the soft soil of the sharp incline. He wasn't aware that hunting had been forbidden on this mountain as well, he had said as he gestured toward the summit. The summit could be seen beyond the delicate veil of fog. In the knapsack slung over his shoulder he had an ax, a few rolled-up pieces of paper, some plaster and wax, even a tape measure. He also had a pot full of *kebab-e shami* and five or six pieces of bread, which would have been enough food for only about two days.

They had come to his house as well. His wife knew nothing about it. She thought he had gone to another town on a job. "He sold his motorcycle," she said, "picked up his tools and took off."

His wife had cooked the kebab for him, as we later learned. A couple of days afterwards, when the mourning cries of his children could be heard, the neighbors had come to visit her. She said, "They broke into his strongbox and made off with everything he kept in there." She showed the strongbox to the women. It was one of those old freezers with brass nails and galvanized iron washers. The lock was still in place, but the hasp was broken. She said, "He always kept the key with him. And he never opened it in front of me."

They found his work tools, too. They were behind a bunch of little knickknacks and other junk in the cellar. My wife said, "He had the sketches for his plasterwork designs back there. Paisley shapes, flowers, bushes, that sort of stuff, and a thin man that seemed to be clad only in a loincloth. There were a few sketches of birds and deer, too." Then there was a bricklayer's plummet, a cord, and a trowel.

I had seen him. He was thin and tall, with a narrow chin, slightly prominent cheekbones and eyes that never looked straight at you. His clothes were always covered with globs of plaster. The saddle-bags on the back of his motorcycle were made out of finely woven pieces of carpet. The design on it was a banquet scene of some kind that you couldn't quite make sense of. He would greet you with a nod of the head. The neighbor's wife had said, "When he worked in our house he was always reciting poetry."

He would recite loudly, she wasn't sure what. They had hired him to do plasterwork around their guestroom, the molding in the corners near the ceiling and the heater. He did good work. He did paisley shapes on the framing edges and filled the background with gazelle, deer, rabbits, birds, and flowers. In the foreground you can see the skinny man my wife was talking about, with his loincloth. He is sitting on the ground, using his left arm as a pillar for his chin.

He insisted on doing an entire banquet scene in plaster above the heater. He had even brought the sketch for it with him. They didn't like it. Later on they built a cabinet with some boards and added a glass door with a handle on it to cover up the plasterwork. They set out their bric-a-brac behind the goblet on top of the cupboard—colorful dolls with long eyelashes, some asleep and some awake; a few china deer and one or two rabbits; a couple of wooden horses, one black and one auburn—that sort of thing.

His apprentices heard the news. There were two of them, their clothes covered with globs of plaster. They had come on Friday morning and left their bicycle leaning against the wall. We came outside when we heard them ring the doorbell. No one opened the door for them. My wife said, "Maybe there's no one home."

"No, they're home all right. I can hear them." I couldn't tell which one of them had said it.

My wife knocked on the door as well, but no one opened it. First she rang the bell and then she banged on the door with her fist. His apprentices were the same height, both with big dark eyes. A wisp of hair hung out from under their caps onto their foreheads. You could only tell that the one was not the other by his left cheek. The one who had no plaster on his cheek said, "We've come to see if they need any help... money, or if there's anything we could do for them."

My wife said, "Their kids are crying, they're just sitting on the other side of the door crying."

"What about his wife?" I asked.

"I don't believe she's home," she said.

The one with plaster on his chin said, "I saw her myself through the keyhole."

The other one said, "She's got something against us, that's why she won't open the door. She's told her kids it isn't their daddy, just Asghar and Akbar, don't you see?"

The man next door asked, "Where's the sculptor now?"

They started to answer at the same time, "We just heard about it..." One of them continued on his own: "We heard about it in the coffeehouse. We simply couldn't believe it." Then he took some money out of his pocket. It was a fistful of crumpled bank notes, damp with sweat. The other one said, "Give this to the sculptor' wife when she opens the door. We can't stay here forever." Then he wiped the two globs of plaster from the cheek of the first one. After one of them had mounted the bicycle and put his foot on the pedal so that the other could climb on the back, my wife asked, "What will you do now?"

The one sitting in back said, "We don't know."

The neighbor's wife asked, "Do you know why he went to the mountains with an ax and a tape measure and that other stuff?"

The other one said, "No, but I swear to God it's not our fault. Tell the boss' wife we told him over and over again not to go, but he wouldn't listen." He said this quite loudly so that the boss' wife would hear if she was listening at the door. Then he started to pedal. They hadn't reached the turn in the lane when the man next door yelled, "If you hear anything, don't forget to let us know."

The one in back waved his hand. My wife had the wad of money in her hand and I thought she was about to bang on the door again when all of a sudden, it opened. One eye was all you could see at first. It was black with lashes so long they cast a shadow on her cheek. As she stuck her hand out to take the money, we saw the oval of her face.

Her mouth was small and red, so small, in fact, her lips looked like a tightly pursed rosebud. We saw the mole next to her lip later, of that I'm sure. But we heard her name that very day, from my wife, only I've forgotten it now. Maybe because I didn't think it was important.

"Why didn't you open the door?" my wife asked her.

She said, "You heard, didn't you? They knew about it. But would they tell me? I was their auntie, I raised them. It's not like I was a stranger, that they couldn't confide in me."

"Well, what was it he was going to do, anyway?" I asked.

"He went to the mountains, that's all," she said. She had her chador on, and we could only see the one eye now.

"Don't you know where he is?" I asked.

"They didn't say. How should I know, anyway? But he must have gone a long way away. He went with his motorcycle and there aren't any high mountains hereabouts."

After she closed the door, the neighbor said, "Surely he can't have gone to that mountain there." He was pointing toward Mount Soffeh. You couldn't see it, behind the buildings, but it was certainly somewhere in the direction of his outstretched arm. "I've been there," he said. "Not recently, of course. It's not more than two hours to the summit, that is if you go up the steps. You've seen the steps, haven't you? They've cut steps into the mountain face so you can go up all the way to the top on horseback. You can get there quicker by a shortcut. Of course, it's forbidden to go, now. I believe they've recently carved an inscription on the summit."

Then he pointed farther into the distance, toward the southwest. "The tallest peak in the Shahkuh range is over thereabouts. I've never been, but I think it would take about three hours by motorbike to reach the foot of it."

"Maybe that's where he went," I offered. "Hunting is forbidden there, too. To protect the game. Mountain climbing's forbidden, as well."

"Why would they forbid mountain climbing?" he mused.

"I've never been," I replied.

Just then, the woman opened the door again, the same chador still covering her head. One paisley-shaped wisp of black hair, only finer and somewhat longer than a paisley, had fallen across the white background of her forehead. When she closed and locked the door behind her, you could hear the cries of the children. Through the keyhole she said to them, "I'll be right back."

"They can stay at our house, if you like," my wife offered. "It's not their fault this has happened. They'll play with our kids."

"They won't be afraid," she said. "They're used to it." The woman was tall, even taller than her husband.

The old lady living on the other side of their house said, "We're good neighbors, you know. At least let us know if we can do something. Maybe my boys can help him out."

I had just noticed the old lady. She was sitting on her doorstep. It was like she was waiting for something, whatever it might be, to play itself out. The sculptor's wife said, "I don't know. I don't know anything about it. You heard for yourself everything they said."

The old lady said something which I didn't hear. I was staring at the sculptor's wife. I've never seen a gazelle walk, with its soft, spritely, prancing steps, gently hopping over a plant or brook or something, just as the old poets used to describe it, but I imagine this must have been just the way a gazelle walks, with her shoulders gently swaying like that and the chador now and then taking on the shape of her rump and the hidden curves of her waist as her legs moved.

The next afternoon I heard he had come back. Mr. Maqsudi gave us the news. "Do you think we should go over and see him?" he asked.

"I don't think he would appreciate it," I said.

"We'll find an excuse to go see him," he said. "If you want to, you could... No, no, I will... I'll tell him to come do a plasterwork design on the space above the heater in our family room, that banquet scene he wanted to do."

"Don't you think it would be better to send the women over first and let them know we want to come over?" I asked.

When my wife returned she said, "His wife says he's got a fever. He was delirious. He's just now dropped off to sleep. Asghar's gone to get the doctor."

"Did you see him?" I asked.

"No," she said, "I heard his voice, though. He was yelling. His wife said, 'Do you hear that? He's awake now. Maybe he's delirious. His whole body is black and blue, like he was hit by a falling rock or something.'"

Mr. Maqsudi asked, "What was he saying?"

"I couldn't hear him properly, but I thought he was saying, 'I can. You'll see that I can!'" My wife wasn't sure what in the world he meant. We couldn't figure it out either.

I saw him the next day. I pulled up in the lane next to him. He had a big watermelon under his arm and in the other hand, his right hand, he had some bread. His head was shaven. "Thank God you made it through all right," I said to him.

"It will grow back, it will soon grow back," he said.

"What?" I asked.

He gestured toward his head with the bread in his right hand. The nails on his hand were neither chipped nor broken. "If you've got time, I'd like you to do one of those designs for us," I said.

"You mean the kind that Mr. Maqsudi didn't like?"

"I don't know what you did for him," I said, "but I'd like to have that scene of Shirin bathing in the spring, where it says in the poem:

> Her limbs with travel's toil were wearied,
>   Her clothes were caked with dust from head to toe.
> She circled for a time about the spring,
>   And, spying no sign of life for mile on mile,
> Dismounted, tied her charger to one side,
>   And put aside her fear of prying eyes.
> At sight of her, that fount of light, approaching
>   The spring to bathe, tears welled in heaven's eyes...
>
> Her waist she tied around with sky-blue silk,
>   Entered the water, and set the world afire.

I couldn't remember the rest of the lines just then, or maybe it wouldn't come to mind because I thought he wasn't paying attention. He was staring dazed, not at me or at my eyes, just staring, and if I hadn't been there or if someone else had been there in my place, it would have made not the slightest bit of difference to him.

"Will you do it?" I asked.

"Do what?" He was blinking like someone who had just been awakened from a deep sleep.

"Didn't you hear what I said?" I asked.

"I never heard that poem before, but there is something or other like what you said. I don't have a sketch of it, but I can find one somewhere. I'll find it for you, if you like."

That night I told my wife about our conversation. She said, "Asghar came over. The sculptor had told him to ask us if he could borrow that book for one night."

"Was it Asghar or Akbar?" I asked.

"How do I know?" she said. "Don't go asking philosophical questions. Will you give it to him or not?"

"Why didn't you give it to him?" I asked.

"I didn't know which book he wanted," she said.

"Didn't he say?"

"No," she said. "He said, 'Your husband knows which book.'"

My copy of Nezami's five romances is very old. It's a leatherbound copy, lithographed, foolscap size, illustrated by artists of the Qajar period. I thought he must want it for the illustrations. I put a bookmark next to the black-and-white drawing of Shirin bathing in the spring with her round face, round as the full moon, just the way the old poets would compare and describe it, with a cute, full chin and full eyebrows that run together, like two hunting bows. The long tresses behind her ears curl together and fall like little lassos on her throat and shoulder and then twist down to cover her breasts, but not so much that you can't see anything, or maybe they drew it to make it look like Shirin deliberately left half of her left breast—shapely as the silhouette of the first-quarter moon—open to view. You can only see Khosrow's head, with its royal diadem, behind the branches of a tree.

I gave the book to my son to take over and then we forgot all about it. It just slipped my mind. Even though they had the book for over two weeks, I didn't remember it. I had to get up in the morning, shave my face, brush my teeth and go to the office. You can't go on foot, and even if you've got a car you still have to rush. No matter how much I plan to wake up a little earlier and get in a few Swedish exercises or at least bend over and touch my toes a half-dozen times, it never works out. Every two or three months I've got to let my belt out another notch, and there're only two more notches left before I reach the end. When I do manage to get up early and have the presence of mind to remember the exercises, I get tuckered out after two or three counts and lose my breath. And you'd think I could stop smoking—I'm not talking about quitting, but couldn't I just not smoke in the mornings? My teeth are all yellowed, too, and one of them's got a cavity, but where do I find the time to get it fixed? I've also got two matching holes on either side of my mouth between my front teeth and my molars. I have to chew with my front teeth and it's getting harder to sleep with each passing night. "For God's sake," says my wife, "cut it out. Didn't you promise you were only going to smoke just one?"

When I want to talk to her, she's asleep. She sleeps with her eyes open and talks in her sleep. She's cut her hair short and dyed it. She's been dyeing it for a few years, a different color every time, some color that you only know won't be black by saying it isn't black, black and long and wavy with a wisp or ringlet dangling over her forehead or over her ears. Her stomach has stretch marks, little white lines. With every child, she gets two or three more. You can see them even in the faint nightlight. And she always forgets to wash her hands with soap or something. She knows I don't like the smell of fried onions or whatever it is, but she still forgets. "I forgot," she says. She sleeps so lightly that you can't even tell whether she's been asleep or just staring at the ceiling. You can never be sure enough to strike a match and light up. And it's really annoying to have to read silently all the time. Sometimes you feel like reading out loud. There are some passages that you have to read out loud properly, as if you were a professional reciter of poetry and the author of the verses is sitting at the head of your gathering on a silver chair of honor, listening to your recitation of his work.

And if I get an opportunity to stay at home for an afternoon or evening and sit in my room sipping a bottle of *araq* and reading something, do you think those kids will let me? Either they've got the TV turned way up or there's the clinking of the dishes being washed or the water dripping from the faucet, or there's my wife worrying about some man who's in love with this woman and he... oh I don't know... he doesn't know that she's really his sister and her hair... Will they let me not worry about it, or not know what happens next?... her hair is short and her big eyes are wide with surprise and her body is limp and flabby, as if she'd always driven everywhere and never walked. And her brother, the very lover who will surely later be revealed as her brother, is so ugly that... Do they listen, if I tell them to turn the TV down? And so you forget what you were reading in the previous chapter and the *araq* doesn't hit the spot anymore and the cigarette tastes like smoky straw that just sets you to coughing. And then if you lend a book to somebody in hopes that he'll come tomorrow or, let's say, a week later, and talk about it with you or that maybe you'll be able to sit quietly sipping *araq* and read a few pages of the book together, the person either keeps the book for so long that you forget all about it or he himself forgets to read it. And when he brings it back or you send someone to fetch it, there are these stains on the cover or, even worse, on the pages, where he has spilled gravy on it. Or maybe the first few pages are marked by his wet thumbprint and the rest of the pages are just as clean as they used to be.

Then my wife said, "The sculptor is at the door and he says he wants to see you." I thought... I don't remember when it was. Anyway, it doesn't matter. I only remember thinking that maybe he'd come to borrow some money or ask me to do him a favor or something the next morning, I don't know… My wife said, "Didn't you hear me? The sculptor's at the door."

"Okay," I said, "tell him to come in." His hair had grown out, not too much, just about an inch or so. Not quite long enough to cover the front of his head, not just yet. That night I understood. He was standing at the threshold of the room with the book underneath his arm. It was the collected romances of Nezami. "Please come on in," I said. "Why did you go to the trouble yourself? You could have sent the book over with one of your boys."

He stood in the middle of the room, holding the book in both hands the way you would hold a tray and offer tea or something to somebody. "Put it over there on the table," I said.

"I don't understand it. No matter how hard I try, I just don't understand it. There are a lot of parts of it that are really hard for me," he said.

Well, if my hand accidently hit the liquor glass and knocked it over onto the floor where it broke, it wasn't anybody's fault, but the sculptor got very embarrassed. He had bent over to collect the broken glass, and I wanted him to stop looking for the little pieces, because it was delaying us from our purpose. I wanted him to sit down somewhere as soon as possible, on the chair at the table or even on the ground, next to me, leaning on a pillow. That's just what we did in the end. We sat next to each other on a pelt-covered seat, our backs resting on two pillows. We began on page one. Next to every line that he hadn't understood he had put a faint mark in pencil. We turned the pages, reading. I had to read the whole page or the whole section in order to understand or remind myself what was going on. There were some passages I didn't understand either, so I had to go get a couple of dictionaries.

When my wife said, "Why don't you drink your tea?" I had a notion. "Bring us two glasses and a plate of yogurt and cucumber salad. Put some pennyroyal and dried sweet basil in it, something to make it smell nice. Bring some ice, too."

The sculptor said, "Just bring one glass."

"Just one? Come on," said my wife.

He didn't respond. After my wife left, I said to him, "Don't you see how Khosrow used to drink glass after glass of wine?" I brought two turquoise wine cups with crystal bases out of the cabinet.

"Farhad didn't drink. I'm sure that Farhad didn't drink," he said.

Then we talked of love. I was drunk. I badly wanted to read the death scene of Shirin for him, the part where she goes to the funeral tower of Khosrow and pulls the dagger out of his heart and stabs it into her own heart, dying right there next to him. The sculptor said, "I've not gotten to that part yet. Read this part first. You read it, and I'll listen. If I don't understand it, it doesn't matter."

He had separated the pages with a bookmark. I imagine it was in the place that he especially wanted to read over again or have somebody read and explain for him. We read where Farhad the stonecutter, in love with Shirin, has been challenged to tunnel through a mountain in order to win her hand. The sculptor said, "If Farhad hadn't listened to that false messenger and had opened a passage through the mountain, do you think he would have won Shirin's hand?"

"No," I said. "I'm sure that they would have come up with another plan to trick him. And anyway, Shirin is in love with Khosrow."

"But Khosrow was in love with Maryam at first and later on with Shakar, the courtesan from Isfahan. On top of that, every night he had a different dish, one virgin after another. That's not being in love! Besides, he swore an oath to Farhad that if Farhad could split the mountain in two, he'd win Shirin's hand."

I didn't remember whether Khosrow had sworn an oath or not. I read on. I believe that when we got to the death of Farhad, he began to cry. I cried too. I even kissed the sculptor, on his hand. He protested, "I should kiss your hand. You are my teacher."

In the morning I realized I had fallen asleep. I'd gotten so drunk that I just nodded off. My wife said, "The sculptor said he wasn't sure if he had your permission to borrow the book again."

"Why didn't you give it to him?," I asked.

"He wouldn't take it. He said he ought to get your permission directly."

I had a headache. It wasn't from the *araq* or anything. Drinking was nothing new for me. We drank more of the stuff at our weekly get-together of co-workers. But this time, this morning, I was so tired that it seemed to me like I'd been walking for years carrying a heavy boulder on my head. I couldn't remember what else we had talked about. I seemed to remember he said something about his strongbox, the designs he kept in it. "They were my father's," he said. "Nowadays you can't find them anymore. They're like the designs you see on carpets."

He said that they'd even taken his sketches. He talked about some sketches of scenes he had had in which, instead of a man, an old woman brings the false news of the death of Shirin to Farhad.

I had heard this version of the story, too. But in Nezami's account, it is a man. I read it for him and told him why, for example, Nezami couldn't stick up for Farhad and place the blame for his death squarely on Khosrow's shoulders. As the poem says, it is fate:

Who can tell the age of our time-worn earth,
    Can see the ancient past and how it was;
Once every hundred years an age begins,
    One cycle ends another starts anew.
To no man's given life beyond his age
    Lest he should fathom time's deep mystery . . .
Each age deals us the cards, both fair and foul;
    In this has God, the Knower, cloaked a mystery.
Unless you seek an increase of injustice,
    Keep every age's secret from the next.

He didn't understand. I had to explain to him that there were tyrants in Nezami's days too, and Nezami himself was a Farhad trying to split the mountain with his hands and his pen instead of an ax. I told him about Afaq, Nezami's wife who had died, how Nezami had modeled the character Shirin on her, on how Nezami may have been buried next to Afaq. Now I remember that Nezami has a line describing the man who gave the false message to Farhad—this in spite of Nezami's fear of the tyrants of his day—and the line is later repeated about Shiruyeh, the murderer of King Khosrow:

One brutal, like a butcher, reeking blood,
    One spitting sparks, like instruments of war.

After that, I think I must have fallen asleep, that is when the sculptor started talking about himself. All I remember is that he was talking about moonlit nights and the round disk of the full moon. He was saying he was afraid that one of these moonlit nights, with the full moon shining bright, he would do something to himself. Why, he didn't know.

My wife told me that he had invited us over that night, if we could make it. "All of us? The kids, too?" I asked.

"Yes, of course," she said. I wanted to see him, but without the wife and kids. I couldn't make it.

Actually, we had one of our weekly gatherings. All of us co-workers get together for an *araq*-drinking session. Everybody tries to tell some new tidbit or joke and then we play a friendly round of poker. And now and then, it might come about that you see the beauty spot next to a pair of lips and you try to forget that this one's hair is blond because she dyed it and forget that her eyebrows are so thin that she looks like someone's accidently made a mark between her hairline and her eyes, or her lips are so huge and red that you're afraid that if she kisses you with those big red lips their outline will forever remain upon your neck or cheek. So it's enough that you squeeze her hand beneath the table and accidently pass her in the hallway or in another room and, in honor of those lips, kiss her beauty spot. It's because of moments like these that you try not to let your belt bulge out to its last notch and you shave your face with double strokes of the razor and stand before the mirror fiddling with the knot of your tie. It was about this time that I got to know one of those types. She's a secretary at the office. It didn't take a week before I said to her, "I love you." It's come to be real easy to say, almost no different from saying, "Hand me that glass," or something. The thing developed to the point that I pretended to be on a business trip so we could spend the night at a friend's house. She was a virgin. She said so herself. I don't like to fiddle around with boys; but I pretended that's what the girl was, so she was still a virgin in the morning. Her beauty spot was rubbed off, my head was throbbing, my mouth tasted bitter and I had a toothache. The girl had thrown her arms around my neck, with her short, shoulder-length hair and was saying to me, "Call me 'my sweet' again."

I couldn't remember why I'd called her 'my sweet,' but I did. Several times. I didn't even remember why as I kissed her beauty spot. When I returned home, I was so giddy that I didn't remember that I was supposed to have been on a trip for three days. When I remembered, it didn't matter anymore, for my wife, I mean.

"They brought him home last night," she said.

"Who?" I asked.

"The sculptor. He had gone to the mountains."

"With his ax?" I wondered.

"What would he be doing with an ax?" she said.

"Well, it's obvious. When that man who brings the false message—or let's say it's an old woman who tells him—of Shirin's death, he has to throw his ax to the top of the mountain. The blade of the ax goes into the soft earth up to the handle. After a while, the handle sprouts and grows into a miraculous tree. I don't remember it or I'd recite the story for you."

"You don't look too well," my wife said.

I had a fever and I dozed off after a little while. My wife said, "Did you have to come back in the middle of the night like this?"

"Did I say something in my sleep?"

"I don't know what you were saying," she said. "You were saying something about boys and girls and you kept going 'Shirin, Shirin.' Then you started sobbing."

"I must have been dreaming about the sculptor. Don't you remember that night?"

They had brought the sculptor's body. His face was all bruised to a pulp; you couldn't recognize him. They said he had fallen down the mountain.

By the time I got up, put my clothes on, and made it over to the cemetery, the local villagers were carrying him on their shoulders from the mortuary. They had been unable to wash his corpse, and had just wound the shroud around his blood-stained clothes. They were saying that the blood had seeped clear through to the shroud. The twins were taking turns as pallbearers, one in front of the coffin the whole way, holding the right-front handle on his shoulder, the other walking behind the coffin crying.

His wife sat at the side of his grave wailing. "I told him over and over not to go," she was saying. "'Don't go,' I kept saying, 'You can go tomorrow night.' You saw yourself how big the full moon was, how white it was."

My wife took hold of her by the arms to lift her up. "Please, Afaq, stand up. Think of the children."

"Please," said Afaq, "just bury me here next to him. He said himself it would end like this." Her chador had slipped off her head and fallen down around her shoulders. Her long black hair had fallen over her breasts. It was then that I saw her beauty spot. It was just under her left cheekbone. She had five or six bracelets on her left wrist. "It was my fault, I did it! He kept begging me to open the door, imploring and imploring, and I did!"

She told my wife about it. "He said I should lock the door. He made me swear not to open the door no matter what. For a week he had been working in the evenings on the design for our living room. Then, the night before last, he started begging me to look at the round face of the moon, how it had come right in front of his window.

'Open the door, for God's sake, I beg you to open the door,' he said. 'If you don't open the door, I'll split my skull right here with the ax.'"

"You hadn't locked the door on him, had you?" my wife asked.

"Yes, I told you. That's what he wanted me to do. He said, 'Tonight is the fourteenth of the month. I'm afraid the moon is going to make me do something crazy again. Put this lock on the door. Don't open it, no matter how much I beg you.'"

"Who?" I asked, "Who was going to make him do something crazy?"

"I don't know, he didn't say."

The twins didn't know either. They sat on the ground on opposite sides of the grave, drawing in the dust. I sat down next to one of them and said, "A martyr goes to heaven." Either Asghar or Akbar said, "He knew himself it would end like this, but he couldn't do anything about it. It came to him in a dream, or maybe he was awake when it hit him. He thought that if he went to the mountains, if he— I don't know—if he exerted himself, he could break the spell. 'Every hundred years it happens like this,' he said. 'Somebody has to go.'"

"Where?" I asked.

The other one said, "To the mountains, of course."

"He went to Mount Soffeh," they both said together as one of them pointed to the peak, or maybe to the stone inscription that had recently been carved there.

"What in the world for?" I asked.

"His ax is missing," one of them said. "It wasn't with his other tools. We looked all over for it."

"He wasn't a stonecutter," I remarked. "He couldn't carve a scene in the rock of the mountain."

The other one said that he had sculpted a scene before he left. "He did a plaster cast of it. You should see it."

I did see it. It had nothing to do with the full moon or an old woman bearing a false message. After the customary week had gone by, we went to see his family to offer our condolences. It was then I saw it, when we came back to their house from the cemetery.

On his grave they had laid a stone with the outline of an ax surrounded by a few paisley designs. But as for the design in their living room on the piping above the heater, that was one of Khosrow's royal banquets. I believe it was still unfinished, not quite complete. I say this because there is just one layer of plaster in the place where Khosrow's face would be. He had finished Shirin, with her long, curly locks, the little lassos of her tresses twining about her neck and then falling over her bosom and coiling around her small, round breasts. She is sitting on the throne next to Khosrow. The minstrels are sitting in a half-circle around the throne. A harp player with hair hanging down to her shoulders and ringlets curling about her ears is sitting on the left-hand side at the front of the semicircle.

You can see her profile. Two other women are sitting facing the throne. A harvest of curly hair spills over their backs. Their shoulders, arms, and wrists are unfinished, maybe on purpose, so that they look as though they are covered with white sequins. Only the edges of the *tonbak* and *santur* they are playing are visible. On the right side of the semicircle, in the front, a singer is standing in profile. The outline of her face appears to be the same as the outline for the face of the harp player, except that her lips are parted. The harp player's mouth is small and pert, but white. There is a dancer in the middle of the semicircle, half-naked, next to the throne. Her breasts look like two round, white lemons, and her hair is hanging in a lovelock over her left shoulder. Her knees are resting on the ground, her arms joined in a circle above her head. Her large thighs are bared. Her face has the same features as Shirin, almond-shaped eyes and eyebrows arched like a bow, with a black mole on her left cheek. The mountain is off in the background and you can see a thin blue line running down its side. Farhad, the same height as Khosrow, is in profile, but without crown or sequins, his ax in hand. He seems to be sitting closer to the banquet than to the mountain, which is off in the distance. The stream of milk he carved out for Shirin is hard to make out. A few boulders have fallen off the mountain and rolled down near the throne. Farhad's forearms and wrists, still grasping the ax, are drawn as though he is still digging up the mountain, as though with but one more blow, he will shift the whole mountain out of the way.

Fereydun Tonokaboni

1937–

From the Caspian littoral town of Tonokabon, Fereydun Tonokaboni has university training in Persian literature and is a teacher by profession. His first publication was a novella called *Mardi dar qafas* (A man in a cage, 1961). Then followed a steady output of short stories anthologized in the following collections, among others: *Asir-e khāk* (Captive of the soil, 1962), written under the pseudonym F.T. Amuzgar, *Piyādeh-ye shatranj* (The chess pawn, 1965), *Setāreh'hā-ye shab-e tireh* (The stars of dark night, 1968), *Yāddāshthā-ye shahr-e sholugh* (Notes from a hectic city, 1969), *Rah raftan ru-ye rayl* (Traveling on rails, 1977), *Sarzamin-e khoshbakhti* (The land of happiness, 1978), and *Miyān-e do safar* (Between two trips, 1978). One printing of his *Dah dāstān va neveshteh'hā-ye digar* (Ten stories and other writings) took place in Berkeley, California, in 1978. His *Notes from a Hectic City* was reprinted in Tehran in the spring of 1979.

A quintessentially engagé writer of his generation, Tonokaboni challenged the limits of censorship during the 1960s and 1970s. His incarceration in the late 1960s became a cause for united action on behalf of the Association of Iranian Writers, which he helped found. Tonokaboni was a major participant in the "Ten Nights" meetings in October 1977 at Tehran's Goethe Institute; the "Ten Nights" meetings, published a year later as a book, signaled the revitalization of the Association of Iranian Writers.

In early 1979, Tonokaboni complained in print about censorship of his writing, wondering aloud what differences existed between the Iranian National Television Organization under *Qotbi* (during the later Pahlavi era) and *Qotbzādeh* (during the early Islamic Republican era). No works of his have appeared since.

The Discreet
& Obvious Charms
of the Petite Bourgeoisie

Translated by Cyrus Amir-Mokri and Paul Losensky

And the spell that the putrid corpse of a dead life, like a grave,
casts on everyone...

And everyone is afraid
that this solid mass of sewage
will not bring water from its dark, swift stream to their lips,
or its mud in a collapsed wall...
will not cast
broken shadows on their heads.

Everyone of them is afraid
that a she-devil's putrid body,
whose whitewash covers lies,
will not embrace them.
—Nima Yushij

"Some friends you are, starting as soon as you got here! You couldn't
wait for me to get here, could you?"

"You might not've showed up until midnight. You're so busy sell-ing vacuum cleaners that you forget everything."

The cheerful and boisterous man who had just arrived hugged everyone, then picked up a glass and poured himself some vodka. One of his friends asked, "Seriously, are you still pushing vacuum cleaners? I guess you've really got a taste for it."

Another answered, "No, man, now he's the boss; you should go see his office. And his secretary."

Another one said, "Do you play the farmer's daughter with her or not?"

Then he added, "This weasel's never really told us whether or not he's given the same treatment to her that they gave to the farmer's daughter."

Not all of the guests had arrived yet. It was just the beginning of the party. The old friends had come before the others and had start-ed up as soon as they arrived. They had taken up their posts around a table which the host had set up in a corner especially for them, and now, with drinks in hand, they were busy chatting about the old days, laughing, and joking around. They were happy to see each other again, but they were shocked at how much everything had changed, especially themselves and the lives they led. Perhaps deep inside they were longing a little for days gone by.

The one who had arrived later than the others had started out as a traveling salesman for a drug company twenty years earlier. Now he supervised product distribution for the same company. For many years, his friends had honored him with the nicknames "the travel-ing salesman" or "the farmer's daughter."

The traveling salesman finished off his drink and said, "Ahhh! That warmed the cockles of my heart!"

Then he sighed, nodded his head, and looked his friends over one by one, as if he were seeing them for the first time. He said: "O fate! Just like we used to write in our compositions in school: O treacher-ous fate, O wicked world…! How time flies. It's been twenty years— it feels like it was only twenty minutes ago. We were all students, happy and carefree, to hell with the world. If we had money left over after buying books, we'd buy a couple of beers and have a ball. Some easy money and a shot of gin, and we'd be on the top of the world. Day and night, every day of the week, we were inseparable, running back and forth between each other's houses. Do you remember, Mr. Ambassador, one night the two of us got on a bicycle and rode from one end of Tehran to the other and back again? Why? So you could tell your mother that you wouldn't be coming home that night and would be staying at our house. Oh, what a world we had! Now we all have wives, children, and homes. We're important, we make good money, but we only see each other once a year."

The ambassador, who got this nickname because he worked at the foreign ministry, said, "Yes sir, it's working and taking care of the family that does it to you. Early in the morning, you've got to go to Karaj Road and stand in line to get purchase orders for a *Paykan* sedan or cement. Then you've got to pick up the little bastards, take bastard number one and dump him in front of his school on Abbasa-bad and then take bastard number two and park him up at the far end of the Parkway. Then you've got to take the wife to Pahlavi Street and drop her in front of the department store. If you don't take her, well, she'll ask for the car and drive you up a wall. Then you've got to go to the office. In the evening, you've got to go to Jajrud or Rude-hen to get fresh meat: the frozen meat you find in Tehran isn't worth a damn. At night, well, there's usually an office party or a family get-together, or we invade the homes of our aunts and uncles, or they invade ours. The funny thing about it is that they all hate each other's guts, but they still put up a good front and act like the best of friends. Late at night, I go to bed exhausted, dead tired..."

The traveling salesman interrupted him, "That's when his real duties begin. It takes a man to carry out his duties. And it takes a man to have enough courage to abdicate his duties!"

"Anyway, in the heat of carrying out your duty, you're still think-ing of your bad luck: you've to got to get up early tomorrow... another day, and more misery. With such a life, where's the time to see your friends? What happened to those long talks, that enthusi-asm, that heartfelt laughter? Now a man can only dream about it."

"By God, if there isn't an engagement party from time to time, or a wedding, or a birthday party, or a farewell party, or something like that, we don't get to see each other even once in a blue moon."

They had been given such an opportunity that night. The son and daughter of one of them had returned from abroad for summer vacation, and he had thrown a party for the occasion and gathered his old friends as well. Of course, there were many others besides them: the son's and daughter's friends—the son was fourteen years old, the daughter twelve—relatives, colleagues, his wife's friends, and other acquaintances.

The host, an expert accountant—or, as he would put it, a certified public accountant—had begun his career as an employee of the Ministry of the Treasury. Now he headed one of the ministry's tax receipt divisions. A few years before, with the help of a few other accountants, he had started up an accounting firm and did work for some import-export businesses. He was firmly established and had a substantial income. Critics pointed to the not-so-clear relationship between his governmental and private business and talked about it openly everywhere. But since they did not have any proof to back up their allegations, most people figured that it was only jealousy that made them talk this way.

Besides, the host was not in the habit of paying attention to such nonsense and worrying himself sick over it. Otherwise, he would not have looked like a young man in his thirties when he was actually now forty-odd years old. Quite the contrary, he was as happy, outgoing, and fun-loving as you could want. Among his friends, the parties at his house were famous for their liveliness and hospitality.

The host approached his friends and asked, "Have you seen this?"

They all asked, "What is it?"

After they had seen it, they all burst out laughing.

It was a statuette of a monkey sitting with its hands between its legs. When a little lever on the back of its head was jiggled, the monkey's hands would move up and down.

When the men laughed, their wives, who were sitting close by, asked curiously, "What was it? What was it?"

The ambassador said, "It's nothing."

The traveling salesman said, "It's an impolite monkey doing naughty things."

Her curiosity piqued, one of the wives said, "Let me see! Let me see!"

So the host held the statuette in front of the wives and started jiggling the lever. The woman who had been most curious said, "Yuck, what sort of obscenity is that?"

The woman sitting next to her, who drawled when she spoke, said, "My, it's so cute!"

The host proclaimed, "I have things even cuter than this."

The woman replied, "Don't get cute with me!"

The traveling salesman asked, "Where did you get this?"

The host replied, "My son brought it back from England."

"Did he bring back anything else?"

"Yeah, I'll get them later. The devil brought back a porno movie which even I hadn't seen before."

"It's not surprising—like father, like son."

"Don't let anyone else know anything about it; then, one night, you should all come and take a look. It's a world in itself."

The traveling salesman said, "Dear Doctor, what do you think? I don't think it would be good for your glasses prescription."

The doctor replied, "Man, an inanimate thing won't do anybody any good. I go for animate stuff."

The traveling salesman said, "Doctor Doolittle, you hang out with animals all day long anyway. What's your worry?"

The doctor was a veterinarian. His friends used to tease him, calling him "Doctor Doolittle" or "The Savior of His Race." Whenever they introduced the doctor to someone, they would say, "The doctor really sacrifices, devotes himself to serving his race."

It seemed as if the doctor himself was somewhat uneasy about being a veterinarian, for after a short time, he left this line of work and got himself transferred to a bureau which had nothing to do with his expertise. Then, with the help of a few physicians and investors, he created Birdfeed Production and Distribution, Inc. He always had customers waiting their turn, and he made a huge profit.

The doctor turned to his friends and said, "Man, you should've been there. I had to go on a business trip to England and Germany. I did some detailed 'studies.' My children's mother wasn't there to watch over me, so I really got to study."

The ambassador said, "You bum! Even when you have a private library, you still go study in a public one?"

The traveling salesman said, "Do you remember when we were young, and the doctor and I had gone on a trip? We called you guys from the public telephone exchange and told you, 'We haven't succeeded in getting any studying done. We haven't even found the library around here.' You said, 'There's no need for a library. You can get your books from the peddlers themselves and study.' As you were saying, dear Doctor..."

"Yeah, a careful and comprehensive study. I studied morning, noon, and night. They don't send us on business trips for nothing. One has to do one's duty conscientiously."

"Did you present the findings of your study to the boss?"

"Yeah, I told him that after intensive study, I have come to the conclusion that, contrary to widespread belief, England is better than Germany—its libraries are better equipped."

The traveling salesman pointed with his head and said, "That is also a subject worthy of study."

Everyone turned around and looked at the guests who had just arrived. There were four of them, two Iranians and two Americans. The Iranians were thin and slender, while the Americans were fat and well-fed.

The ambassador asked, "What zoo did you net these animals in?"

The host replied, "They're distant relatives of my wife. Those two are brother and sister. The plump girl is married to the guy, and that gorilla is the other girl's husband. Their story is long and amusing. To be brief, the brother and sister go to America, apparently to get an education. After a couple of years, the guy married an American girl, but since he didn't feel like studying and didn't have the gumption to get a job, he returned to Iran. Now he lives comfortably off his father and shuttles back and forth between Iran and America. The sister, who either didn't want to stay there or couldn't, returned to Iran right after her brother. Going to America had the sole benefit of enabling her to meet a few Americans here. After weighing her options a while and changing her mind several times, she finally chose the giant you see to be her husband."

The traveling salesman remarked, "He's not a giant, he's gargantuan."

"Whatever he is, the lady really wanted him. She longed for an American husband, especially after her brother had married an American woman."

"So, what does the little guy do?"

"He's in the oil business."

"No kidding! You mean he has some oil well or he's a shareholder in an oil company?"

"No way! Stop dreaming! He's a driller pure and simple. He has a tough job. He goes to sea every week, to the floating rigs. He doesn't make bad money, but he works his tail off."

"What I can't understand is how someone like him could make her mouth water so."

"Are you kidding? First of all, he's an American. Second, it makes her happy to hear her parents introduce her little man as a petroleum engineer wherever they go."

"But the American girl, she's truly ripe for study."

"I didn't invite them just for the hell of it. I have some studies planned. I'm thinking of improving my language skills, learning English."

"If your wife gets wind of it, she'll skin you alive."

"The good thing about it is that she invites them herself. She likes having Americans over. Americans are the life of the party these days."

"It's a book packed with information. No matter how much you pore over it, you'll never be able to exhaust it."

The doctor asked, "Is that guy's reading ability up to studying such a weighty tome?"

"No problem. I, who am far more literate, will study it and acquaint him with what I have learned."

All four of the guests had gone to the drinks table as soon as they arrived. The men poured whiskey for themselves and vodka with Pepsi for the ladies. The American woman finished her drink and poured herself another. Her husband looked at her askance and said quietly, "You'll get drunk again. You'll get sick."

The woman let out a laugh and said, "Who? Me?" Then she laughed again and added, "It doesn't matter."

When the host came to the living room, he was greeted with a burst of laughter. He was wearing a mask that made him look silly. His head was as bald as could be, with only a few strands of curly red hair on the sides. Round, dark glasses covered his eyes, and a huge red nose stuck out from underneath.

The men tried the mask on first, one by one. When they put the mask on, each one looked ridiculous in his own particular way, depending on his figure and the clothes he was wearing, and made the others laugh by gesturing and making funny faces. Then it was the ladies' turn. With their trendy, fancy clothes, their low-cut necklines and short skirts, the women looked even sillier with the mask than the men did. Acting like a child, the woman who drawled insisted, "It's my turn, it's my turn!"

Then she looked at herself in the mirror and said, "My, it's so cute!"

Then they put the mask on the American woman, who was already tipsy. Without looking at herself in the mirror, the woman began to snap her fingers and dance. The others were clapping and laughing. In the voice of a broadcast announcer, the host intoned, "Ladies and gentlemen, the famous American dancer will now perform for you the finest Persian and Arabian dances." Then he went and put on the "Baba Karam" tape.

The cassettes lay in a heap next to a large, imposing, and expensive stereo with a tape recorder.

The traveling salesman looked over and exclaimed, "What an incredible stereo this rascal has!"

The ambassador, who seemed to be bothered by something—perhaps the crowd and the noise or someone specific—said, "Yeah, in those days—what dear memories—we'd find some cheap record player, bought in installments, and we'd listen to Beethoven and Brahms. Now we all have a cabinet stereo and listen to Nush'afarin or Leyla Foruhar. And this is what they call progress!"

When the "Baba Karam" song started, the woman took her shoes off, raised her arms, wiggled her buttocks, and ogled. And as she did this, she sang, "Baba Karam, I love you," in Persian with a foreign accent.

The traveling salesman said, "The little vixen, she really dances well!"

The doctor said, "It'd be worth one's life to study her. She's something a man could devote his full attention to studying."

When "Baba Karam" was over, they started playing Arabic music. The American woman started shaking her belly. However, both because she did not know Arab-style dancing well and because she was out of breath, she moved off to the side and dragged herself to the liquor table to refresh herself.

The host made a beautiful, slender woman get up and said, "She dances Arab-style like a pro. She's out of this world."

The woman was a little coy at first, but then she said, "You rat! At least give me a stick or a cane or something to hold in my hands. I can't do it like this, dry and empty-handed."

"It's not polite for me to give it to you in front of everyone. Dance first, then we'll both go to a corner, and I'll put the cane in your hands."

There was a burst of laughter. But without missing a beat, the woman responded, "Oh dear, it turned into a cane so quickly? I'm sorry, I truly am sorry!"

The laughter was louder and harder this time. The host went and brought an umbrella that was in its cover. The woman raised it over her head, holding it like a stick dancer, and she started to dance and laugh and flirt and make eyes at everyone. A bit later the host made the other women get up to dance. The men started too, and after a while everybody was dancing.

A young woman came into the living room and stared at the crowd in bewilderment for a moment. When the doctor caught sight of her, he asked, "Hey, what's she doing here?" He went up to her. "Hello, what are you doing here?"

The girl laughed with a warm laugh that lit up her whole beautiful face and replied, "Hello, how are you? I came in last night."

"I won't forget your kindness in England. I'm very happy to see you, very happy."

"Where's your wife?"

"She's around here somewhere. As always, she's giving herself and everyone else a fix. You know that she's a natural-born bartender. So what are you drinking?"

"Vodka."

"With what?"

"With water."

"Water, Seven-Up, or soda?"

"Water."

"Do you want ice?"

"No, just water."

"God, what sort of creature are you? The girl's become completely English."

The doctor went and brought back a vodka with water for the woman and a vodka and Seven-Up for himself.

As they drank their vodka, the doctor offered her a Winston cigarette. She said, "I don't smoke those. Here, why don't you smoke one of these?"

She took a pack of Rothmans out of her purse.

"I said you'd become completely English. So where do you work now?"

"At the Oil Company."

"Didn't you used to work at a British company?"

"I quit. The British were stingy. With the terrible situation of their economy, they've become even stingier. It's really hard to work with Iranians; it's unbearable, you know. But they pay well, they really shell out, and the vacations aren't bad."

The host came up and asked, "Hello, how are you? Haven't you hooked a husband yet?"

"Are you kidding? Where can I find a husband?"

"Don't worry. Just wait, and in the end, I'll bite you myself."

The doctor said, "What, are you a dog that you want to bite her?"

All three laughed. The host showed the woman something that he was holding in his hand. It appeared to be a deck of cards in its box with one of the cards pasted on the outside of the box. It was a picture of a naked woman.

"You see this? This is what they call porno cards. This is a just a sample. There's better merchandise inside the store. Step right up and watch."

He then held the box out to the woman. Without thinking about it twice, the woman reached over to take the cards out of the box. Suddenly her hand shook, and she pulled it back. She said, "Damn you! That gave my hand a shock."

The host was laughing heartily. The others who were looking on were laughing too. The host winked and pleaded, "Keep quiet about this."

And he went off to track down another woman.

A few moments later, a woman shrieked loudly and chased after the man, "I'll get you now! I'll rub my hands on the lenses of your glasses!"

The woman rubbed her hands on one of the lenses. The man held her white, chubby forearms and squeezed. The woman was struggling to free herself, moving every which way in the process. The man would not let go of her, on the pretext of not letting her touch his glasses.

The others were busy watching this scene and laughing.

The man was saying, "Listen, we aren't on such terms that we can joke around about important things. Touch me anywhere you want, touch me in the worst possible place, but don't touch my glasses. The hardest thing in the world is cleaning my glasses."

"That's why I want to smudge them. I've found your weakness."

"I have a lot of weaknesses. I have bigger weaknesses than this. Why are you stuck on this one?"

They finally let go of each other and went to track down another of the guests with the trick deck of cards.

Everybody was dancing now: women and men, young adults, teenagers and children. The children were constantly under foot, getting in everyone's way.

They played Persian and foreign songs, one after the other. They started with fast songs, but as they went along, the songs became slower. In the end, they were putting on only quiet tangos and turning off the lights. They sank into one another's arms and kept bumping up against each other.

During the interval between two dances, the doctor's wife came over to him and said, "You've found a nice-looking dance partner."

"What can I do? You know how choosy I am."

"You're really pampering her."

"Are you jealous?"

"No, but you haven't danced with me once in front of all these people, just for the sake of appearances."

"I saw you were infatuated with that American gorilla, so I didn't want to be a nuisance."

"Now you're jealous."

"No, but when someone is constantly in someone else's arms, they become the object of attention."

"What did you want me to do? Sit and watch you and your little darling?"

"Dear lady, would you mind if we played out this family drama at home? Please don't get started tonight. I beg of you."

The woman looked at her husband with obvious hatred. The man turned his back on her and went over to his friends.

Now seven or eight in number, the old friends were busy laughing and joking and talking away.

"What really happened to your plans to leave?"

"If you want to know the truth, they've decided to give me a two-year fellowship. I'm waiting for the fellowship to come through and be finalized. Then I'll sell everything I own, take my wife and kids, and get out of this dump. After two years, if I think that I can stay and have it made without any problems or worries, then I'll ask for an unpaid leave of absence for a couple years, just to be on the safe side. During this time, I'll have really learned the ropes. I'll get started on some job. If I see it's worth the trouble and I can continue, then I'll ask for retirement. If, on the other hand, I don't think I'm up to it and I long once again for the diesel fumes and *sangak* bread, for beef stew made in stone pots and *araq*, then I'll come back to this dump and start all over again. So what's happened with you?"

"By God, they just won't leave me be. They won't agree to my retirement. Otherwise, my plans were about the same as yours. Now I think I'll take a leave of absence for as many months as they give me and go. After all, better a little than nothing at all."

"It's strange. Everybody's leaving. No matter who you come across, they're either leaving or thinking about it."

"They should leave. This dump's no place to live. You can't find meat or chicken or eggs or potatoes or onions or an empty street to drive down or any place to park your car. The way things are, everyone ought to leave."

"This is what they call a brain drain."

"No, my dear friend, this is what they call a gold rush."

"Hey, Mr. Teacher's found his tongue."

"This is just the beginning—wait till he gets rolling."

"Our Mr. Teacher is quite a character. He'll be silent for hours on end, but once he starts talking, nothing will stand in his way."

"It's only because he had the feedbag strapped on that he hasn't said anything up until now."

"He's just like the old musicians. First he gets himself made up, and then he starts his act."

The person they jokingly called Mr. Teacher had not budged from the liquor table since he arrived. In his youth, when all his friends had gone to the university, he had attended junior college and become a teacher. He used to say he was interested in this vocation because it was lively work. He used to say that he was bored with the formalities of office work. Perhaps the poor financial situation of his family was not without influence on his decision. Whatever the case, he had taught enthusiastically for fifteen years. He was not as well off as any of his friends, and his main distraction was staying at home and reading. When he started a family and had children, his financial situation deteriorated. To bring in more money, he was forced to teach forty hours a week. He also used to teach remedial and exam preparation courses during the summer and New Year's vacations.

Then suddenly he had had enough. One summer he talked a few people into transferring him to administration. He used to tell friends, "I'm slowly turning into a tape recorder." He would smile and add, "Ever since television was introduced to this country, these sons of bitches no longer have any use for us."

He got himself transferred to one of these bureaus that have fancy-sounding names, but where nothing useful ever gets done: The Bureau for the Study and Appraisal of the Country's Educational Stages, or The Bureau for Innovation in the Teaching of Newly Literate Adults.

After a month, he started to comprehend how he had had the wool pulled over his eyes during his fifteen years of teaching for such a paltry salary. Now, in addition to his regular salary and bonuses, his overtime pay and holiday bonuses, and the money he got for being the office handyman, he also received good money from the budget that the Plan Organization had allocated for research and study, if he prepared, translated, or edited reports. It was enough to prepare only one report a month. Since there was nobody to evaluate the reports, only the preparation or translation of a report was important, not its quality.

His main task was to edit reports that others had hastily and frenziedly translated. At his leisure, he was supposed to put these reports in a form that was at least somewhat readable—assuming there was someone to read them.

His work took him two hours a day, at most, and afterwards he had absolutely nothing to do. After a couple of months, this lack of work was driving him insane. The first few days he took books along with him to read, but he could not concentrate. There were two or three others in the room besides him, and they talked incessantly, from morning till evening. He was dragged into their conversations whether he wanted or not.

When he got bored, he would get up and go to other rooms and visit with his colleagues, drinking tea or coffee here, smoking a cigarette there. Then he would go back to the cage again—he had named his room "the cage."

He had become cranky. He was constantly grumbling, griping, and ridiculing. When he saw his friends, he would whine and complain. He did it in such a way that he seemed to be consulting with them, seeking their guidance to find the best and quickest way for him to open the door and escape from "the cage." But at the beginning of the month, when he drew his paycheck or received a few checks of greater or lesser value for the various jobs he had done, he felt a peculiar happiness and contentment deep down inside.

Once when his whining had gone on much too long, the ambassador had said to him, "I don't agree with what you say. One can't live on a teacher's meager income these days, true enough, but if you don't like working in administration, you'd better leave it and get back to the classroom before it's too late. It's easier to pass up a couple of thousand tomans now; when it gets to be seven or eight thousand, it becomes difficult, indeed impossible."

But Mr. Teacher wavered for so long, weighing his options, putting money on one side of the balance and peace of mind on the other, that the lure of the money, which increased once every few months, joined forces with habit and completely defeated his already weak willpower. What little was left of his will was dissolved and washed away by alcohol. Now he drank like a madman, day and night.

Mr. Teacher had once again withdrawn into his shell. The conversation, however, continued.

"So, Doctor, what are you doing?"

"Nothing. I run around like a dog all day long. In the morning, it's the office. At noon, I sneak out and spend a few hours at the busi ness. Then it's back to the office until five or six o'clock. Then I go to the business again and stay there until God knows when—nine, ten, eleven at night. Marshal, what do you do? You're not like us. You have it easy."

The friend who was so named had had a tremendous passion for Field Marshal Rommel and his battles and adventures since his youth. He read every book and went to every movie about Rommel. For this reason, his friends kiddingly called him "Marshal Rommel" or "the Desert Jackal" (instead of the "Desert Fox").

"Give me a break. The only time I have it easy is right now, when I'm drinking with you guys. What do you mean 'have it easy?' This isn't what I'd call living. I hope it never happens to you, this dog's life. Work in the morning, work in the evening, work at night. Unlike yours, my job doesn't go by the book. Sometimes they keep you until midnight. You don't dare complain. 'Do this'—yes, sir. 'Do that'—yes, sir. 'Go to Zabul'—yes, sir. 'Go to Khash'—yes, sir. What kind of life is this? I'll have it easy as soon as I croak."

"Come on, Marshal, what are you saying? God forbid. You're still young—you have a lot to accomplish in this world. We have to go drinking together! We have to study!"

"God knows, the only thing that makes me happy in this world is drinking with the few like-minded friends I have. I swear by my life, by your life, by all our lives, if I didn't think about the children or worry about them, my hope would be to croak and end up in Behesht-e Zahra cemetery."

"My dear Marshal, you're bullshitting me! I've read your palm. You just want to be promoted without having to work for it. There!" And he suggested that the marshal do something else instead.

The marshal finished his drink, smacked his lips, and told a youth passing by him, "Please, I'll do anything you want. Pour me a drop of vodka, with Seven-Up. Please add some ice, too. Heavy on the vodka, light on Seven-Up. God willing, I'll come to your wedding and serve people drinks myself."

Then he looked over to his friends and said, "No, believe me, it's not like that at all. What on earth do I need a promotion for? When I'm not happy, what good would a promotion do me? Let's assume I stay alive—when the tables are turned, they'll come after me first and say, 'You son of a bitch, you so and so, your looks betray the fact that you're a son of a such and such. Then they'll send me to join my father, God rest his soul."

"My dear Marshal, you're bullshitting again! You mean you're that important?"

"I'm not kidding. Important? If I were important I would either escape or join the other camp. In the end, it's the wretched, unimportant guys who get the worst end of the deal."

"My heart bleeds for your wretchedness."

"Come on, leave me alone... screw the world, don't give a damn. Whatever happens, happens."

The marshal was fat and completely bald, although he was not very old. His face and head were shining and flushed red with alcohol. He said this and began to snap his fingers, dance, and sing:

These with blood, sweat, and tears were bought,
Don't believe that they're all for naught.

The others accompanied him, laughing and dancing, clapping and singing.

The host asked, "Marshal, has the dragon pill taken effect?"

As he was dancing, the marshal's face lit up even more and he said, "It worked. Boy, did it work. It got the machine running so smoothly that the darned thing didn't think of shutting down!"

Mr. Teacher asked, "What's a dragon pill?"

"Something as big as a hazelnut and as black as India ink."

"I mean, what good is it?"

"Now there's a good question. It's good for those whose eyesight fails because they study too much. Recently the marshal's eyesight had become really poor. The poor thing had completely stopped studying. When the engineer returned from Japan, he brought back a few dragon pills for him. His eyesight improved so much you wouldn't believe it. You could put the book at one end of the room, he'd read it from the other."

With an air of innocence about him, the marshal said, "No, believe me, I don't study much."

"If you don't, your wife will bring the house down around your ears!"

The marshal danced until he was out of breath and stopped. Large beads of sweat stood on his red forehead and bald head. He turned to the hostess. "Dear lady, you're so kind. I thank you so much. Would you be so kind as to get me a clean handkerchief? Wet it, wring it out well, and give it to me. You're so kind."

When he took the handkerchief, he said, "You're so kind. Thank you so much. I really like you very much, you know? Come, let me kiss that beautiful forehead. So your children finally came. You can rest easy now."

The woman said, "Do you know what the first thing Parvaneh said was? She threw herself into my arms and said with a lump in her throat, 'Mom, I'm never going back to England! I want to stay with you.'"

With a drunk's coarse and violent emotions, the marshal frowned, put both hands on his head, and said, "Oh my, oh my, I'm so sorry. But my dear, why do you treat your children so unmercifully?"

The woman said, "I don't feel like taking care of the kids and neither does their father. It's better for everyone like this."

In order to escape his drunken sermonizing, she turned around and left.

The marshal was wiping the large beads of sweat off his brow and head with the wet handkerchief. When Mr. Teacher caught sight of the marshal's bald head, he sang:

Its head has no hair, but it's nice nonetheless.
This is the description of... oh, my goodness!

Everybody started laughing. The traveling salesman said, "My dear Marshal, you're full of shit!"

The marshal responded in a meek tone, "All right, all right, I'm no good anyway, a loser, down and out. I take it from everyone, I might as well take it from you, too."

"I love how you're so meek and miserable. You could've fooled me."

"Here, I got you a drink. I take it all back."

"You take it back? Where did you stick it in the first place?"

The voice of another of the friends could be heard saying, "I'll drink this sherry to the health of my friends."

Because he didn't drink, everybody turned their heads in amazement. The man had picked up a cherry from the fruit tray and was holding it up.

Everybody laughed. As he was laughing, the host said, "Such insipid jokes at your age? Isn't your six months up yet?"

The marshal asked, "What do you mean, six months?"

"His stomach's screwed up. He can't control his stomach—it's ripped to shreds. He drinks for six months and when he's at death's door, he quits for six months and goes on the wagon. He's on the wagon now."

The traveling salesman shouted, "Oh Lord, help me! He's taken out his infamous calendar again."

While laughing and holding his calendar, the man situated himself between the men who were standing next to the table and the women sitting down and asked, "Say, have you heard the one about that guy? A man went home and saw some gorilla fooling around with his wife. He said, 'You poor wretch! I have to do it, what's your excuse?'"

Everybody started laughing. One of the women asked, "Oh yeah, so you have to do it? Then why are you always begging?"

The ambassador said, "To be honest, I have to go to the office, but I don't like it at all. At the same time, I'm always begging my boss to give me some work to do, so I won't be at the mercy of the personnel office."

The men roared with laughter.

The woman who drawled said, "What? You have to? You should be craving for it."

A few of them proclaimed in unison, "We are! By God, we are!"

The woman blushed and said, "God, how tactless."

Another woman asked, "Remember how you used to court us in the beginning?"

With a chuckle, the ambassador said, "My beautiful lady, that was just in the beginning. Every road comes to an end, and every malady has a remedy."

With a scholarly air, Mr. Teacher said, "One writer states, 'And this was how love endured eternally for two who were married . . . not, of course, to each other.'"

When the laughter subsided, the marshal told the women, "Leave them alone. They don't understand. They're dolts. I'm the humble servant of all you beautiful women, at your service."

The traveling salesman remarked, "I didn't know it was also called 'service.'"

The doctor said, "Especially with the dragon pills he's been taking recently."

Amongst the sounds of laughter, the voice of the man with the calendar could once again be heard: "One day an Englishman goes to the wrestling arena. He sees one of the wrestlers doing push-ups. The Englishman turns around and tells the wrestler, 'She's gone.'"

The men and some of the women started laughing. The other women were looking at the men in bewilderment. One of them asked, "What does it mean?"

The doctor said, "You nitwit, the meaning is obvious. It means that the girl had left."

The woman who drawled asked, "What do you mean, girl? There was no girl."

The traveling salesman said, "God, you're so dumb. The Brit thought the wrestler was studying and he was continuing his study even though the girl had left."

The woman said, "Ooh." And after a moment, she added, "How tasteless!"

The doctor retorted, "Did you have a nice nap?"

The host said to the man with the calendar, "By the way, check to see if Wednesday is a holiday. If so, we'll go up to the Caspian and stay there through Friday."

The man opened the calendar and flipped some pages. He looked up and asked, "Who can tell me what the difference is between a condom and a parachute?"

Everybody started laughing. The traveling salesman said, "Man, that's enough. We're going to choke on that calendar of yours."

The man said, "I brought the calendar hoping I might hear a few new jokes from you people and note them down. You're such a stingy lot."

The doctor said, "Look at them!"

On the other side of the room, a woman holding a drink in her hand was standing next to a man. She was a young and very beautiful woman, tall and slender, wearing an attractive, eye-catching, expensive blouse. It was open all the way down her back and was low cut in front, revealing her arms, shoulders and half her breasts. Only a thin string running around her neck and tied behind it held the blouse in place. She talked very loudly and laughed boisterously. She was a real doll. But unlike the cold, dead beauty of a doll, her beauty was alive. Her radiant, dark eyes were laughing. Her ravishing smile lit up her whole face. Her speech was accompanied by such flirtatious mannerisms that it made her listener hot with desire—assuming he were the sort of listener she usually had—for she would twist and turn her body seductively as she spoke. Her beauty and coquettishness resembled that of a very expensive, well-known call girl who had just entered the profession.

The young man standing next to her was handsome and well built. He was clean-shaven, but his hair covered his ears and hung down past his neck. He was wearing a striped pink shirt and a plaid suit. His tie was so wide it would have made the woman another blouse like the one she was wearing. The young man's face betrayed a sense of pride and self-confidence mixed with stupidity. Indeed, his pride and self-confidence were not the products of intelligence, but of ignorance.

"Look at them!"

The ambassador shook his head and with concealed regret but evident jealousy, he said, "Yeah, I see."

"She's beautiful. The bitch is some kind of beautiful."

"Her beauty took care of everything. It may even have caused her some trouble."

"Do you know her?"

"Yeah, I know her real well. She was very young when she got married, and what a husband! She was playing with fire and got burned. You see, she's always horny. Her husband, unlike herself, was a tub of lard like you've never seen. I'm surprised she wasn't hurt. Heaven forbid, it would be like sleeping under a steamroller. Besides, the guy was a cross between a gigolo and a redneck. A few years and a couple of kids later, the lady got fed up with family life and got a divorce. Then she became her husband's mistress! They lived like this for a year until the guy went abroad, and the lady got married again. Her new husband is loaded, and she snared him with her good looks. Now she goes abroad alone several times a year and reunites with her ex-lover every time."

"Wow! Doesn't her husband say anything?"

"Well, you know, they say that a husband only enjoys his wife's beauty from a distance. He's just happy to have a very beautiful wife and show her off. But he doesn't have the strength to forsake the road of chastity. They say he lives in peaceful coexistence with his wife. He's at her beck and call and gives her all the money she needs. He doesn't bother her. The lady snares one handsome young man after another. That jerk who's dressed like a hillbilly and has that stupid, arrogant look is her latest catch."

"Huh. Some people really luck out."

With a calm and serious look, Mr. Teacher said, "Therefore, the husband and the lady's boyfriends have formed a corporation—he supplies the bucks, and they supply the fucks!"

The friends exploded with sudden laughter. Accounted a marvelously funny joke, his comment passed from one person to another until it got to the woman herself. The host went over and delivered the comment to her without the slightest embarrassment. As if she'd heard a funny story, the young woman died of laughter. In her usual coquettish manner, she tilted her head, wrinkled her nose, half closed her eyes, and moved her body in her familiar seductive manner.

A pompous smile came to the young man's lips, and he held his head high with arrogance. After all, he was the major shareholder.

The marshal said, "Boys, I'm suffocating. I'm going to pass out. I'm going to fall flat on my face. Let's go out on the roof and catch a breath of fresh air."

The marshal had drunk and sweated so much that he was going crazy. Anyone in his place would have vomited three times already. But the marshal was no willow that would shiver in the face of such winds. He was an old hand at this sort of thing.

When everybody was drinking before dinner, he, the doctor, the traveling salesman, and a couple of other close and trusted friends had quietly gone to one of the remote rooms in the house and locked the door behind them. Then the marshal had taken out a small case he had kept hidden throughout the evening in the closet behind some clothes. He took a delicate opium pipe, a pair of tongs, and a canister containing some opium out of the case.

The doctor had asked, "Where are you going to get a light?"

His eyes twinkling with joy and contentment, the marshal had responded, "Wait, today's advanced science, modern technology has made everything easy."

Then his bookish tone had turned familiar once again. "All problems have been solved, or alleviated, except the problem confronting my miserable soul. Nothing can make it happy or content or bring life to it. I don't know what's wrong with it."

Then he had shown them another canister. "Do you see this? Despite its small size, it's capable of great things."

He had taken a square, metallic object out of the container and had opened it up. The object turned out to be a simple, miniature burner that had a flat surface supported by two legs. The marshal had placed the burner on the table and taken some white tablets out of the container.

"Do you see these? It's crystal alcohol. It's awesome. As small as they are, it's unbelievable how much heat they generate. It's also very tidy. It doesn't make any mess at all."

Then he had shown them some small, black cubes and said, "This is the charcoal: industrial, modern, and clean."

He had placed the tablets on the cooker and had lit a match. The pills burned with a beautiful blue flame. He had put a couple of the pieces of charcoal on the tablets and had heated up the opium pipe. They all smoked opium to their hearts' desire. After they were done, they had put away the paraphernalia and rejoined the others. They had resumed drinking either vodka or whisky until the marshal had begun to feel ill.

The friends went to the roof. The marshal took off his coat and tie, unbuttoned his collar, and cooled down his head, face, and neck with the wet handkerchiefs that he had brought along. Then he said, "No, this isn't going to do. Please do me a favor. Open up that air conditioner."

The roof was covered with smokestacks and air conditioners. The traveling salesman removed a small panel from one of the air conditioners. The water that had been circulating inside the air conditioner now poured out freely. The marshal held his head under the water and exhaled with pleasure and relief. The traveling salesman shouted, "Watch out! Be careful that the air conditioner doesn't circumcise your head!"

The marshal said, "I'm being careful. I've got everything under control. It's not my first time, you know."

He held his head under the running water several times until he began to feel like himself again. Then he dried his neck, face, and head with a handkerchief and said, "This is the only solution."

The others were talking.

"Engineer, we have a plot of land. Come build something on it."

"How much are you willing to shell out?"

"Five hundred, six hundred grand, maybe more. It's not a problem."

"I'm sorry. You'll have to forgive me, but we don't take jobs that cost less than a few million. It's just not possible for us. It's a waste of time. But let me see, maybe I'll find a friend or something."

"God, Engineer, you're gradually getting to be one of the big shots."

"You call me a big shot? You haven't seen a big shot. A big shot is one who's completely at ease with himself, who has peace of mind."

"Hey, your company is doing pretty well for itself. You must have peace of mind."

"No, my friend. What do you mean peace of mind? True, our company is one of the top ten construction companies in this country. But gathering sixty or seventy engineers into one company isn't easy. We're a construction company, not a consulting firm. A consulting engineer presents a plan and takes his money. Lots of money. Moreover, road-building companies are doing better than we are. They only have to deal with two or three items. We poor bastards have to deal with thousands of items, from cement and steel supports to switches and electrical outlets. We have to deal with dumb, harebrained idiots from dawn until dusk. No sir, it's not as easy as you think. Our job involves thousands of worries, anxieties and miseries."

"Come on, Engineer. Why are you complaining? What's the matter with you? You have a home in the city, you have a resort home by the sea, and you've bought a garden near Damavand."

The ambassador said, "Ever since the engineer bought that garden, my respect for him has doubled. I've already gone there a few times. You should've been there. He really treated us well."

The engineer was glad that the conversation had veered away from his job, money, and wealth. He said, "Believe me, I bought that garden only for my friends, so we could get together for at least a couple of days and enjoy reminiscing about the good old days without anyone looking over our shoulders. We really had an easy, happy-go-lucky life back then. We didn't even have money. What a pain in the ass money is!"

The doctor said, "If you don't like money, give it to me."

The engineer ignored his remark and continued. "This isn't what I'd call living. I go months on end without seeing my wife and children. I'm just back from Shiraz and I have to go to Rezaiyeh; just back from Rezaiyeh and I have to go to Mashhad; just back from Mashhad, and it's off to Bandar Abbas. I've turned into the wandering Jew."

The traveling salesman said, "You're just back from America and you have to go to Japan, and then it's off to Europe."

The marshal said, "God, you guys are always whining."

"And you don't whine at all!"

"My situation is different from yours. You have good jobs, you make good money, and you control your own destinies."

Mr. Teacher, who had been quiet thus far, broke his silence. "It's not a matter of money. To hell with jobs. For my part, there's something missing in my soul. I can't fill this hole with money, nor can I fill it with junk like homes and gardens and whatnot. I say this now so that no one can say, 'The fox can't reach the grapes, so he says they're sour.' I've got the grapes, and now it doesn't matter whether they're sour or not. But I'm not content, I'm not happy. How can I put it? I feel empty deep down inside. It seems as if deep in my soul a voice is saying, 'All this stuff is empty, meaningless, trivial, banal.'"

The traveling salesman said, "The discussion is becoming philosophical. O Great Buddha!"

The doctor continued, "Maybe what you're lacking is faith."

Then putting one hand on his chest and extending his other arm forward, the traveling salesman shouted out in an emotional and sermonizing tone, "O faith, O faith, thou Iron Maiden . . ."

Mr. Teacher interrupted him, "For God's sake, don't make a mockery of the memories of our youth. Don't drag everything down into the gutter. Let us hold on to something."

The traveling salesman said quietly, "Mr. Teacher has heated up. Just wait—he'll boil over soon."

The ambassador said, "As for faith, well, I don't have faith in anyone or anything: not in heaven, not in earth, not in the communists, not in the capitalists, not in the socialists, not in the fascists, not in the leftists, not in the rightists, not in the government, not in the nation. To hell with all of them. Especially the shit people of this shit nation!"

Mr. Teacher asked, "What have the people done wrong?"

"They're behind the whole problem. When the people are so stupid and dumb and idiotic, they only deserve to have someone hit them over the head and kick their butts. These people have never been human, and they'll never be human. These people have ruined their own lives and ours too."

"You've heard the story of Sodom, the city of sinners. God wanted to forgive the inhabitants because of the righteous and devout old men and let them all go unpunished. He listened and heard one of the old men telling the other that he wished a pretty young boy were there so that, as the doctor puts it, he could study intensely. God didn't lose any time and leveled the city. Now we're the righteous and pious old men of Sodom. We ourselves know what we are. Why should we expect anything else from the people? What have we done for the people to give us the right to bad mouth them. Since the people haven't seized us by the neck to make us answer for what we've done, do you think that they must owe us something? Be serious!"

Again quietly, the traveling salesman said, "Didn't I tell you?"

The ambassador asked, "Do you yourself have faith in the people that you should pound your chest in defense of them? Do you believe in anything at all? Do you believe in the government that you should be obliged to defend it?"

"I'm just like you. I'm cut from the same cloth. What I'm getting at is something different. It's all right for someone like you to not believe in left or right, or in any Tom, Dick, or Harry. Our misfortune is that we don't believe in ourselves. If we did, we wouldn't have ended up here. The other misfortune is that we aren't ignorant asses. If we were, we'd be content. We'd have the life of contentment that we don't have now and only wish we did. We drink night and day to forget, yet we never do. We drink night and day and drown ourselves in such a variety of pleasures and problems, and all so that the damned voice inside of us will be silenced, but it isn't—so that the emptiness will be filled, but it isn't."

The host said, "I think the solution is for us to see each other more often. If nothing else, friendship is soothing."

Half seriously and half mockingly, the traveling salesman said, "Moreover, you can drink more when you're in a group than when you're alone."

Mr. Teacher let this comment pass and said to the host, "Do you know why we see each other only once a year? Whenever we call each other or run into each other, we complain about why we don't see each other more often like we used to. Yet nobody takes any steps to initiate our getting together. Do you know why? It's true that we're all tied up. It's true that we don't have time to scratch our heads. But I think there's something deliberate in all of this. In our youth, our friendship was a mirror that reflected our joys and aspirations. Now this mirror shows the distortion of those aspirations. It makes us face our utter defeat. In this case, it's only natural that we don't like to look at it."

The traveling salesman suddenly blurted out, "Look, I suggest we throw out everything we have or sell it and go to a corner of some village or small town, lead a simple life, and escape this misfortune."

Mr. Teacher said, "That isn't our misfortune. Our misfortune is that we've substituted the means for our ends and ideals. Let's not assign our guilt elsewhere. It's not the fault of money, homes, gardens, or cars. They are the means of life. Our problem is that we've bought these means at too high a cost, at the cost of the ideals and goals of our youth. This is why we feel shortchanged. That's what I meant when I was talking about the emptiness and the insistent voice that won't be silenced. Our greatest misfortune is that neither do these meaningless toys make us happy, nor do we have the guts to let go of them. As silly and irrational as it is, your suggestion would at least be something, if we could put it into effect. Alas, we cannot. We don't have the power or the will. We know this very well ourselves."

The doctor said, "We can't live in a village. It's ridiculous. The solution is what everyone is doing. We have to leave this dump, to go somewhere where we can live like human beings. It's no wonder that people are leaving by the hundreds. They take their families and leave this place for good."

Mr. Teacher said, "Where would you go? What do you want to run away from? Who do you want to run away from? Yourself? Wherever you go, your accursed self will go with you. Our misfortune has nothing to do with the time or place, although it's brought about by the time and place. Our misfortune is being lax and passive. Our misfortune is our incurable laziness. When we shouldn't have accepted the time and place, we did so, because we were lazy and we wanted to be comfortable. Now we're running away from it."

"Did you see that young, beautiful woman who netted the young man? She has peace of mind, she enjoys life, she does whatever she pleases, and her conscience is completely clear and at ease. Now inject her with, as the doctors say, ten cc of a fifty-fifty solution of 'intellectual-bourgeois.' Her life turns into a living hell. She can't stop what she's doing, she doesn't like what she doing, and her damned conscience doesn't leave her in peace for a single minute. She turns into an insufferable creature, both to herself and to others.

"Our misfortune is that we're caught in the middle. If we were a little more to either side, either all black or all white, we'd be all right. Our misfortune is that we want to be both saints and sinners. Our misfortune is that we have no strength, no willpower. We're weak and languid, lazy, indolent, and slothful. At the same time, regrettably and unfortunately, we are intelligent, quick-witted, and sensitive. Yes sir, we are afflicted with Hamlet's historical malady, with this difference—we are cowardly on top of everything else. We are cowards down to our bones and maybe even rotten to the core."

The ambassador said indignantly, "You're going too far. Coward! Rotten! These discussions and conversations, precisely these criticisms, are proof of our honesty. Honesty is itself a sort of courage."

Mr. Teacher continued, "Yes, undoubtedly. But we aren't courageous. We're clever. We're very clever people, clever and calculating. We stuff ourselves with food, but when we come across the hungry, we genuinely want to prove that a full stomach is worse than hunger. We're addicted to the automobile, but when we come across people on foot, we honestly tell them that pedestrians are better off than motorists. We add a story to our homes every year, but we innocently complain that the carpenter and the mason have driven us crazy and ruined us. Yes, we are clever people, very clever. The best way to prevent others from blaming you is to blame yourself. These comments that cross our lips from time to time serve only to ease our conscience, so we can prove to ourselves that we're still good people. Incidentally, talking hasn't killed anyone yet. But when it's time to step up and take action, we're truly crippled, even when it comes to something very, very small and insignificant, something that might turn us away from our constant routine of habit, ease, and laziness. That's when we show our true colors. That's when our evil nature shows its claws and bares its teeth. So now that we know who we are, why don't we just have our drinks, live our lives, and not think about it too much. Yes, it's better this way."

Mr. Teacher grew silent and lit a cigarette. The others were silent too. The marshal had not said anything for a while and had not dared interrupt with one of his jokes amidst the keen participation of the others in the conversation, but as the silence continued, he found an opportunity and said, "Well done, dear sir, we've learned a lot. Only the next time you want to give a speech, please don't speak at such a lofty level. Poor me, I don't understand concepts like 'bourgeois' and I don't have a particular liking for places like hamlets."

Nobody laughed. Everybody was silent. Everybody was thinking about the quickest way to escape this tormenting dead end. They were thinking of how their evening, an evening which had started out so well, was now ruined, and there was not a thing to be done about it. Everybody was thinking of forgetting. Too bad—they were saturated with liquor, and liquor was no longer the elixir of forgetfulness.

From the top of the roof, the multicolored city lights could be seen. The streets could be distinguished by the rows of white lights. They were all thinking about how they had to get up early again the next day, go to work, and get stuck in traffic and wait. They all had one wish: if only they could drive around the uncrowded, quiet streets now instead of tomorrow, so they could avoid the traffic jams.

Goli Taraqqi

1939–

The daughter of an editor, publisher, and member of the Iranian Parliament, Zohreh (Goli) Taraqqi-Moghadam was born and raised in Tehran. She attended college in the United States, returning to Iran with a degree in philosophy in 1961. She obtained a master's degree from Tehran University in 1967. During the 1960s Taraqqi served as an international relations specialist for the Plan Organization in Tehran and began publishing short stories, first in *Andisheh va honar* in 1965.

Her collection of short stories called *Man ham Che Gevārā hastam* (I too am Che Guevara) appeared in 1969. In 1973, she published a novelistic collection of related narratives called *Khāb-e zemestāni* (Hibernation). This was translated and published in France as *Sommeil d'hiver* in 1986, and in America as *Winter Sleep* in 1994.

In the 1970s Taraqqi was a lecturer in philosophy at Tehran University. Upon the temporary closing of Iranian universities in 1980, and her divorce from film director Hazhir Daryush, she emigrated to Paris with her two children. She returned to Iran for brief visits during the 1980s. A translation of Taraqqi's 1979 story called "Bozorg-bānu-ye ruh-e man" (The great lady of my soul), first published in the short-lived weekly *Ketāb-e jom'eh* (1979–1980), appears in *Iranian Studies* 15 (1982). Her mid-1980s short story which appears here, "Dandān-e talā'i-ye 'Aziz Āqā" (Aziz Aqa's gold filling), was published in an expatriate journal published in California called *Omid* 3 (1988). Since her emigration, two works have appeared in Iran: *Khātereh'hā-ye parākandeh: majmu'ah-e qesseh* (1992), and *Jāye digar* (2001), and one bilingual work in France, *Le bus de Shemiran = Utubus-e Shamirān.* (1990).

In 1991 Taraqqi was preparing to publish a new novel called *Ādathā-ye gharib-e Āqā-ye Alef dar ghorbat*(The strange behavior of Mr. A. in exile).

Aziz Aqa's Gold Filling

Translated by Farzin Yazdanfar and Frank Lewis

We try to catch bus no. 70, but it sets off before we get there. My little girl runs after it for a few steps, but gives up the chase before reaching the intersection. We will wait for the next bus.

Suddenly it begins to snow. The snowflakes, like translucent dust, swirl through the air. A pleasant calm has descended over the usual bustle of the city; everything is still and white. This is the first time in the eight years we have lived in Paris that such a heavy snow has fallen.

I still hear my grandmother's voice echoing in my ears: "The angels are busy cleaning house, dusting the clouds and sweeping the carpets of the sky."

I am thinking about the sunny winters when I was still in Tehran. I think of the Alborz mountains standing tall under the clear, bright sky, of the banter of the snow sweepers pushing the snow off the flat rooftops of the houses, and of the tall poplar trees, white like tall old ladies, standing at the far end of the garden.

As a child, when it started snowing it seemed it would never end. Saturday, Sunday, Monday, I would count the days and the centimeters, ten, twenty, half a meter. The snow would pile up and the schools would be closed for a week.

What happiness! What unbelievable joy! For a week I could stay under the covers in the morning, I could play with all my cousins in the streets. A whole week and no fear of seeing the headmistress or my bad-tempered math teacher. A whole week without opening our textbook on religious law or doing homework! No memorizing long, meaningless poems or practicing penmanship with reed pens and black ink. Seven days of play and freedom, released from school!

How wonderful it was to have company at home when the snow blocked the roads; our guests would stay for two or three nights until they could go back home.

One of those guests was my kind, thin grandmother. Night and day she would pray, wishing us all a long life full of health and happiness. Her older sister, Bibi Jan, would also be there. She was practically deaf and almost senile. She used to mistake me for my brother and my brother for one of my cousins and my cousin for our neighbor's son and our neighbor's son for me.

Dear, sweet, aunt Azar was another of those guests. Her crazy kids were always playing leapfrog in the hallways. They were worse than wild monkeys, always howling as they climbed up the walls and trees or slid down the handrails.

My uncle, Ahmad Khan, was the kindest dentist in the world, and couldn't bring himself to pull a single tooth. Every time one of us cried, tears would well up in his eyes.

Then there was my older uncle, who had been an artillery officer in the army. He was so scared of horses, rifles and cannons that right from the start he hung up his uniform and left the army. He decided to stay at home. He wore an apron, made delicious jams, and knitted colorful woolen pullovers.

Finally, there was Tuba Khanom. She was a fat, lazy lady, who knew weird stories and messed around with jinn and ghosts. She also knew sorcery and juggled for us. All these guests would stay in our house until the snow melted. I loved our guest-filled house and its crowded rooms with quilts spread side by side on the rugs and the tables on which one could see all kinds of dainty foods—pitchers of sherbet, bowls filled with pomegranate seeds, *sho'leh-zard*, pistachios, *sowhan*, Isfahani *gaz*, and the delicious baklava that my mother used to make.

How I loved the thousand intoxicating smells that would fill the nooks and crannies of our house and waft through the corridors—the smell of tobacco from grandma's hookah, the pleasant vapor steaming up from Bibi Jan's boiling concoctions, the fragrance of saffron on the warm rice, mixed with the smell of cinnamon, cumin, rose water, roasted onions, and half-charred kebabs over the hot charcoals.

I loved to fall asleep listening to the whispers and muffled laughter of the grown-ups in the adjoining rooms, to be lulled to sleep by the soothing sounds of my younger uncle playing the *tar* and the sweet humming of Aunt Azar and the clicking of my mother's slippers going up and down the stairs. I would wake up in the middle of the night and see that the lights were still on, the grown-ups were still awake and the kitchen was still full of people cooking and rattling the pots and pans. Then I would drift off to sleep again, a sleep as light as a feather.

Tonight, watching the snowflakes, I am happy and excited again, as in the days of my childhood. My daughter, too, is excited. She spins around, dances, and makes snowballs with her little hands, tossing them here and there. She is constantly running into the street and looking impatiently for bus no. 70 to arrive. Her impatience reminds me how my own little heart would beat anxiously every afternoon after school as I stood in the street waiting, counting the long minutes, to see my friend, Aziz Aqa.

I tilt my head back and open my mouth until the snowflakes fall on my tongue. How good they taste and smell! It's as if thousands upon thousands of jasmine petals are falling from the sky. I feel that my feet are no longer on the ground and I am floating in space as though I were in a glass bubble being blown backwards by a hidden breath to the days when I was a child.

I see myself as a ten-year-old kid standing at the intersection near the school waiting for the bus to Shemiran to come. Our new house is at the other end of the world. We live in the middle of nowhere behind the hills, where there are no other houses. Sometimes at night, we hear jackals howling. My mother is frightened. Our cook, Hasan Aqa, is scared too. He makes his bed in the hallway behind the door of my father's room. I love living in the middle of nowhere. I am not afraid of the huge water reservoirs or the pond which is full of frogs. I am not even afraid of the black shadows of the trees that look like wicked people. I use old sheets to make a small house for myself behind the boxwood trees in the back of the garden. Nobody can find me there. I hide my snacks under the bricks, and if my grades are too low I bury my homework in the ground so my mother will not find out.

The poplar trees are my playmates. Every tree has its own name. The taller ones are boys. As soon as school lets out and I get home, I toss my satchel aside and run to tell my playmates everything I have done. I show them my paintings and read them passages from my books. Some of them are stupid and yawn. Some of them are naughty and jealous. They don't listen. I kiss the ones who are my friends and stick my chewing gum on their leaves. I punish the ones who talk behind my back and tie their branches up with rope.

It takes half an hour to get to Firuzkuhi School if my father gives me a ride. It takes more than an hour to get there if we take the bus. My brother is older than I am and he is allowed to come and go by himself, but I can't even take one step without holding onto Hasan Aqa's hand. This is my mother's rule, but I do whatever I want to and I will skin Hasan Aqa alive if he tells my mother because I know that the key to the storage house, which is supposed to be lost, is in the lining of his jacket, and when my mother isn't home, he takes lentils, rice, and beans by the handful from their gunnysacks, puts them in a box, hides the box behind the outhouse in the back of the garden and takes it with him on his days off. For this reason we don't interfere with each other. We are even.

At four o'clock school gets out and Hasan Aqa comes to pick me up. We stand at the bus stop close to the intersection, waiting for the bus to Shemiran. It is snowing today. The snowflakes are so big that each one seems to be the size of a saucer. Everything is white with snow. Hasan Aqa, like a ghost, is standing by the wall. His face is like a wisp of transparent cloud, like the clouds I see in the sky every night and I know that these clouds look like the people who lived a thousand years ago. Some of these men are crowned and have long beards and ride their horses very fast. If you look carefully at the moon, you will see that there is a kid sitting there with his head on his knees, crying. I keep pointing him out to my stupid brother, but he can't see him. My mother is afraid of the full moon and tells me that I shouldn't stare at the stars. Sometimes the big dragon who lives up there appears in the dark blue of the sky and then disappears into the Milky Way. When I tell Hasan Aqa about the dragon, he gets scared and screams. He hides himself under the quilt and begins praying at the top of his lungs.

The bus that is supposed to take us to Shemiran hasn't come yet. I am excited about the snow and keep sliding on it in the middle of the street. I kick the trees and knock a little sprinkle of snow from the branches onto my head. Hasan Aqa, who has my backpack and lunch pail under his arm, is shivering. He opens his mouth and a white vapor comes out. He has my father's old shoes on. They are too big for him; so big that there is an empty space like a hole behind his ankle, filled with snow. His hands are small, too. He has my mother's gloves on, which don't match. One is made of leather red as jujube, and the other is black lace. My father always buys a new jacket, a new shirt, new underwear, and a new pair of shoes and socks for everybody at Nowruz, but Hasan Aqa doesn't wear his new clothes. He either puts them in his suitcase and waits until the end of the summer, when he takes them back to his village or sells them. If he sells them, he hides the money in the chimney. I am the only person who knows where he hides his money, but I don't touch it. I swear.

The sound of a bus engine can be heard in the distance. Hasan Aqa jumps up. I am happy and anxiously watch the small white structure clattering towards us. I say to myself, "If the driver gives me a signal by blinking the bus's lights, I will get on. Otherwise, I'll wait until the next bus comes, even if Hasan Aqa freezes and it gets very late and mother goes mad with worry or even if I die of starvation and exhaustion." This is a secret that nobody knows about. I mean nobody! It's a secret between Aziz Aqa and me. Even Hasan Aqa doesn't know about it. He doesn't understand why some days I refuse to get on the bus. It's because if the bus doesn't signal me by blinking its lights, the driver is not Aziz Aqa. I run from Hasan Aqa and ignore all his protestations and complaints. He has threatened me several times, and wants to tell my mother about it. Every time he threatens me, I bring up the key to the storage house which is in the lining of his jacket, and then he doesn't bother me any more. If the bus flashes its lights three times, it's Aziz Aqa. Every night before going to bed, I say to myself, "I won't get on any bus unless the driver is Aziz Aqa." I say this instead of the prayer that my mother has taught me to say. This is the silent promise that Aziz Aqa and I have made and we are supposed to keep this promise until doomsday. Of course, I have never spoken to my big friend, who is even taller than my father. I don't dare. Even the cops are afraid of his scary face.

The bus flashes its lights on and off in the distance. My heart spins like a top. The bus stops, and I get on, with Hasan Aqa in front of me. Aziz Aqa looks at me, greeting me with his puffy red eyes. His hair is greasy and curly. Hasan Aqa says that Aziz Aqa's hair has a six-month perm. His eyebrows are black and his thick bushy mustache covers his mouth. I sit on the seat behind him. Hasan Aqa sits in the back of the bus where it is warmer. As soon as he sits down, he falls asleep.

There are only a few people on the bus, all of them dozing. It's quite a journey from school to my house, especially in the winter time when it snows and all the cars that have no chains on their tires slip and slide, blocking the road. Some days Aziz Aqa is tired. He yawns. His breath is stronger than the smell of iodine that my mother puts on my scraped knees. I feel dizzy and my stomach has started making noises. He looks at me in the mirror and makes faces. He puffs out his cheeks, wiggles his nose, and pretends to be cross-eyed. I put my hands over my mouth so the rest of the people on the bus won't hear me laughing. I laugh hysterically to myself. My friend Aziz Aqa is like a demon. All the little kids are afraid of him. He has tattoos on his hand and his upper chest. A thick purple line stretches from ear to ear across his neck, as if someone had tried to cut his throat. My mother never rides the bus. She has her own car and driver, but she knows that there are demons like Aziz Aqa out there and that is why she worries about me. She doesn't like me to go to school by bus, but this is my father's order and it cannot be disobeyed.

Hasan Aqa has fallen asleep all curled up in the back of the bus. A cold breeze is blowing through the bus from a broken window. The passengers are freezing. Aziz Aqa takes off his jacket and covers my legs. His jacket stinks. I want the others to see me as I proudly touch the collar of his greasy jacket. My fingers become smelly; a strange smell which is neither in our house nor in my aunts', my uncles' or my cousins' houses. It is not even the smell of cats, dogs, cows, and sheep. It is a smell from an unknown world; the smell of the bad things that kids shouldn't do and the things they shouldn't know about just yet.

My mother's smell is different from any other. It is the smell of European perfume and powder, the smell of movie stars, fashion magazines, Lalehzar Avenue, and the ballroom of the Shahrdari Café. My mother's smell is the smell of the days yet to come, the smell of tomorrow and all the good things that I expect to have in the future.

With Aziz Aqa's jacket on my legs, I have become another person, a kid who doesn't have to be neat, or studious, or the best student in the class. A kid who doesn't have to wear huge bows in her hair, greet everyone and bow, or recite poems at all the parties she attends, poems that she has learned in school, but hasn't yet memorized very well. A kid who doesn't have to play her first piano lesson, which is nothing but a repetition of do—re—mi—fa—so—la—ti, for her talkative and impatient relatives. A kid who doesn't have to compete in the "Most Beautiful Child" pageant and lose.

With Aziz Aqa's jacket on my legs, I begin to look just like him. I imagine that I have tattoos all over my body and half of my teeth have gold fillings. I see myself walking around in the streets just like the daughters of Fatemeh, the laundress. I see myself giggling, riding a motorcycle with the most handsome boy in the neighborhood, and going with him to see a Tarzan movie.

As soon as we reach the Abshar Station, Aziz Aqa stops the bus. Most of the passengers get off to drink a cup of tea in the nearby teahouse. Hasan Aqa and I don't move. Before getting off the bus, Aziz Aqa takes a small bag out of the glove compartment and puts it on my lap. He looks at me in the mirror, and winks. His face is full of kindness and soft wrinkles. He looks like a rag doll. My friend Aziz Aqa is the best demon in the world. Something like a transparent vapor comes off his hands and his feet, his breath, his red eyes, and his old greasy jacket. A magical vapor which surrounds me; like a snowflake, I melt in it. This makes me so happy that I want to stay like this, here on the bus, for a thousand years without ever growing up or changing, like a statue made of stone.

Today, Aziz Aqa has brought me dried cherries. Hasan Aqa, who is sitting in the back of the bus, calls out my name and asks me what I am up to. I ignore him and keep counting my dried cherries. The passengers are standing outside drinking their tea. Aziz Aqa sips his booze and goes behind the trees to piss. I try not to look. I hold my face down and keep chewing my dried cherries, but I can see him in my imagination and my ears turn red as I blush.

The bus starts off again, moving like an ant very slowly toward Vanak Square. Sometimes the bus slides back. Other cars are sliding too. They come to rest in the middle of the road, blocking our way. It is getting dark now, and the whole world is white. Hasan Aqa, in the back of the bus, is scared and keeps calling out my name. I know that he is going to cry soon. He's always on the verge of tears. Every day he cries two or three times for no reason at all. My mother believes that Hasan Aqa's sorrow is like the clucking of hens—there is no special reason for it. My father says that Hasan Aqa is a stupid ass, which makes Hasan Aqa laugh, because he likes being an ass. As he takes the dishes and plates away, he looks at my father chewing the pieces of kebab that he has made. He is satisfied that my father likes his cooking.

Cold air is coming through the broken window next to me and blowing on one side of my face. My neck is stiff and my back is frozen. Aziz Aqa is anxiously watching me in the mirror. He stops the bus, and tries to close the crack in the window with old newspapers and a piece of an old rag. After he's done, he sits in the driver's seat again. I know his silent language. I know that he is worried about me and wants me to change my seat. I know that he is talking to me with his eyes and telling me: "Get up! Get up, you stubborn little girl! You will catch a cold. Sit in the back of the bus. It's warmer there. I'm worried about you. You may get sick." I answer him with my eyes and tell him: "No! I am not going to move. This is my seat and I am not going to give it up."

I like Aziz Aqa's concern. His motherly affection shows how deeply he cares for me. I close my eyes and travel through time to the glorious past, to the age of the great kings when loyal, brave men used to walk on red-hot coals in their bare feet, and fight with seven-headed dragons just to prove their honesty and allegiance to the king.

The bus has stopped. There is a traffic jam. It is cold everywhere. The right side of my body and my toes have grown numb and I can't feel my feet. My head is heavy and feels as though it has been filled with air. It grows larger and then smaller. I am freezing. Through my half-closed eyelids, I see shadows dancing and whirling in the snow. My nose is running and my eyes are burning. Suddenly, I feel a hot flash. I am burning and trembling now and my teeth are chattering. Tears are pouring from my eyes. I can't help it. Aziz Aqa is touching my cheeks with his rough fingers trying to wipe the tears from my cheeks and dry them. He smiles at me with a closed mouth. His assistants, who know him well, say that all of Aziz Aqa's teeth have gold fillings. I don't believe them. I ask my mother about it. She doesn't know either. She doesn't even know who Aziz Aqa is. She doesn't like my question and threatens to punish me severely if I look at bus drivers or if I talk to them. My mother believes that only no-good lower-class people have gold fillings and they are all thieves and murderers who do bad things to little girls. I don't believe it and I am sad that my mother is sometimes mean and tells lies. She makes fun of Aunt Azar and calls her fat and ugly. I get sad when I see that there are many things my mother doesn't know. For instance, she doesn't know the names of the capital cities in most countries and she isn't familiar with the basic rules of mathematics. In spite of this, I think she is the best and prettiest mother in the whole world. At night, I pretend to have a stomachache so that she will sit by my bed all night. I want to tell her about all the bad thoughts I have about her, but my mother is always busy. She is always in a hurry and doesn't listen to me. If she finds out that I eavesdropped on her while she was talking to my father, she will punish me severely.

Aziz Aqa is frustrated with the snow and the traffic jam. He tries to make his way through the snare, but he can't. It is almost as if we were lost in a big white desert. I hear Hasan Aqa's voice from afar. He is moaning. He is so scared that he can't stop hiccupping. I have a strange feeling. I feel I am getting sick. My stomach is filled with dried cherries and I feel like throwing up. With both hands I am holding Aziz Aqa's coat tightly around myself. I'm getting dizzy; I try to stand up but there is no strength in my legs. I open my mouth, but I can't talk. There is snow everywhere. The whole bus, the whole town and the whole world are covered with snow, and I am frozen under this arch of white. It seems I have been frozen for years. The only parts of my body that are not frozen are my eyes, burning like two furnaces, and my tears, pouring down. My mouth, dry and bitter, is gasping for water. Water, water, water…

A cool, perfumed hand, scented with powder and lotion, is caressing my forehead. Someone is praying in my ears and blowing on my face. Familiar faces are standing around my bed. Aunt Azar's big, sweet eyes are sparkling under the light and I can smell Bibi Jan's concoction. I recognize the feel of my own soft blanket and clean sheets. Now I know that I am in my own bed, with mother sitting by my side. My heart is filled with relief. I close my eyes and fall asleep. I see in my dreams that I am being carried piggyback by Aziz Aqa and he, like a flying carpet, is flying above the clouds and taking me to visit distant exotic cities. I wish he would open his mouth so that I could see his gold fillings. But what a pity that his lips are sealed and his mouth is closed like a jewel box.

I am terribly sick. Dr. Kawsari comes to visit me every Thursday. I have a rasping cough and at night am very feverish. Every time he comes to visit me, he changes my medicine, and I get sicker. I am thin and pale, and my hair is falling out. I look deathly ill. My parents have started consulting another doctor. He coughs more than I do and his medicine is not available in any pharmacy.

Days and weeks fly by. I have forgotten about school. I sleep during the day and cough even while asleep. My grandmother sits by my bed holding her prayer beads and softly reciting her prayers. When I am awake, she tells me stories and spoon-feeds me. Every day I look at the persimmon tree out in the garden. I see its bare, leafless branches, and I count the days until spring comes. Every day, around four o'clock, Aziz Aqa's bus passes by the intersection in front of the school. I see him in my imagination looking at my vacant seat as he passes by. Perhaps he has forgotten me by now and gives the snacks that he hides in the glove compartment to some other girl. This makes me jealous. My coughing gets worse. My mother gets worried and quickly calls Dr. Kawsari to come and see me. I hear my father giving orders to the servants to make preparations to take me to Europe.

I know that I will flunk school this year. This makes me sad and I cry. Aunt Azar says that there is nothing as important as one's health. I wish it was summer and the cherry tree would blossom. Our house is more crowded in the summertime. Our family is like a big tribe. I have dozens of aunts, uncles, and cousins. My father is the head of this tribe and everybody holds him in high regard. Every Friday these people eat in our house and my mother asks half of the guests to stay overnight. All of us sleep on the terrace in the garden, the kids lined up in a row and the grown-ups a little farther away under the poplar trees. They sleep on wooden beds under mosquito nets. My father sleeps in the arbor where you can hear the murmur of purling streams on either side all night long.

My grandmother sleeps next to the kids and watches them. For each child she leaves a glass of ice water beside the bed and a handful of jasmine under the pillow. She counts the kids and calls their names to make sure that everybody is there.

I love the sounds of nighttime; the faraway frogs, the nearby crickets, the persistent buzz of winged insects in my ears. Before falling asleep, I count the stars and gaze at the clouds, which are shaped like people. One of them resembles Aziz Aqa. Way up there, he calls my name and makes a face. My cousins whisper and my grandmother lashes their feet with a long twig, without moving from her bed. My youngest uncle snores, which makes the stray dogs in the vacant lot howl. Bibi Jan talks in her sleep and Tuba Khanom scratches herself all night. One of the kids keeps cutting the cheese. My grandmother jumps up angrily and wants to know who is doing it. Everybody pretends to be asleep. Nobody utters a word.

Sleep overtakes all eyes as a sweet-scented breeze wafts by and the stars glitter in the sky. Some nights it rains and my grandmother covers our beds with a long, wide piece of plastic which she keeps close at hand. My cousins and I cling to each other beneath that huge tarp like ants under the earth and listen to the raindrops falling one by one.

I have been a prisoner in my room since I got sick. Everything frightens me. Fear, like an invisible man, is everywhere. Sometimes in the afternoon, when all the grown-ups are taking a nap, he comes into my room to visit me. Sometimes he stands at the window or he hides himself under my mother's skirt. This morning I saw him in the mirror and it seemed he was making fun of me. I know it is fear that makes me cough. My mother doesn't believe in Dr. Kawsari anymore. She throws away his prescriptions. My uncle, who is a doctor, comes to stay at our place every night. He has made an arrangement with my mother to administer my daily injection. Today it is his turn and the next day it will be my mother's turn. My father believes that European doctors are brilliant. They can cure a patient with the first prescription even if he is seriously ill. Aunt Azar looks at me with her sad eyes. She kisses me as though she will never see me again. Hasan Aqa has an old post card with a picture of a fat blond woman dressed in velvet and lace. He believes that this woman is the Queen of Paris. She is wicked and does not believe in the Koran and the Prophet Mohammad. Hasan Aqa is worried about my mother and me. He begs my grandmother to pray for us every day and night so that we won't be harmed by the impious Queen. My mother is happy and busily packs our suitcases. I am sure that there is fear in Paris, too, and it will follow us around wherever we go. My grandmother is constantly saying her prayers and blowing on my face. Every day, when the sun goes down, Tuba Khanom feeds me a glass of cooked liver extract. All kinds of amulets and charms are tied to my neck and feet and, under my pillow, there are small pieces of folded papers with prayers and spells written on them.

I still think about school. I think about the afternoons around four o'clock when school gets out and the bus comes out of the distance to take me home, and like a half-forgotten dream, before it reaches me, it sinks in a cloud of white. Before going to bed, I still say to myself: "I won't get on the bus unless it is Aziz Aqa's bus." We have made this promise and we will keep it until doomsday. I swear and when I swear, I close my eyes and I hold my breath, and my heart beats like a drum. I am sure that Aziz Aqa will hear the pounding of my heart and respond to it.

We are supposed to leave for Paris in three days. My grandmother, who is sitting by the window, is making necklaces and bracelets for me out of jasmine blossoms. Everyone is so sad. Even Tuba Khanom, who is always dancing about and snapping her fingers, is very sad. Her eyes are tearful and she wipes her nose with her sleeve.

Someone is knocking. I say to myself: "This must be a new doctor or one of my aunts coming to visit me." These days everyone is knocking at our door, wanting to come visit with us.

Hasan Aqa comes in and stands by the door. He is stupefied and stares at my mother. He wants to say something, but doesn't have the courage. He is scared and has started hiccupping as he always does when he gets scared. He points at someone or something outside, but is unable to speak. My mother is irritated and impatient. She gets up and follows Hasan Aqa into the hallway. I hear my mother's voice asking, "Who?"

I can't hear Hasan Aqa's answer. I can only hear my mother's voice getting louder and louder. Siren-like, it makes everyone nervous. My grandmother gets up and closes the window. She pulls the blanket up to my chin. I hear my mother's voice again, saying, "The bus driver?"

My heart convulsing, I try to rise up and sit in bed. Hasan Aqa is bleating, just like a sheep about to be slaughtered.

My mother's voice rings in my ears: "Who? What? Which bus?"

Poor Hasan Aqa is scared half to death and stammering. I hear my mother shouting. She wants to know how a worthless bus driver dares to come to her house to visit her daughter. She orders Hasan Aqa to tell him that if he shows up here again, they'll break his legs.

I throw the blanket aside. In my bare feet, I jump out of bed and run toward the hallway. I am in my thin nightgown. Tuba Khanom tries to stop me, but I push her and bite her hand. My mother is astonished by my strange behavior. She orders me to go back to bed. I pay no attention to her threats and run down the hallway to my father's office. I go inside the room and lock the door. There is a window facing the street. I draw the curtain, and jump on the chair. Now I can see the poor, meek Aziz Aqa standing in the middle of the street like a shy, defenseless child. He doesn't know what to do. He is holding a small bag in his hand. His disheveled hair is neatly combed and his shirt is buttoned up to the collar. He doesn't want anyone to see the tattoo on his chest. I open the window and call his name. He looks around, but he doesn't see me. He decides to go. I call out again more loudly and wave my hand. He turns around and looks up to see me. His face is still kind. Tears are pouring from my eyes and I am saying words that are incomprehensible even to me. Aziz Aqa greets me by nodding his head. God knows how happy he is. He comes closer to me and stops. He looks around to make sure that nobody is there; he looks at the front door. He is holding the bag in his hand tightly. He comes closer again. Now he is standing by the window and I can smell that same odor again. I bend over to grab the bag, but I can't reach it. I would like to touch his tattoo. I'd like

to frighten my mother and Tuba Khanom, and Aunt Azar by showing Aziz Aqa and his tattoo to them. Aziz Aqa is happier than I am.
He holds his face up and laughs at me. With this laughter, something strange happens: he opens his lips so wide that I can't see his
nose and eyes. His mouth is like a dark cave. I am scared and my
heart is beating faster. I am hot and the sweat is flowing profusely
from my body. I'd like to throw myself into this dark cave which is
full of unbelievable sounds and odors. I stretch my body as far as I
can. I bend forward. Now Aziz Aqa's mouth is under my face and,
between his dark blue lips, I can see his gold filling, shining like
Aladdin's lamp. I know that this magic lamp will give me everything
I wish. I close my eyes and make a wish. I wish I could get well again,
I wish my coughing would stop and I wish my fear would go away.

We arrived in Paris and stayed at the Hotel Wagram. Three days
after our arrival, a French doctor came to visit me. He wrote a
detailed prescription. I was feeling much better and my coughing
had stopped. Nobody knew about my secret and the magic lamp. My
mother thought it was because of the French doctor that I was
recovering so quickly. But I knew who and what had cured me.
Every night, in the darkness of the room under the bedsheet, I
touched the imaginary Aladdin's lamp and said my old prayer.

We stayed in Paris for more than six months. We stayed there
until I got completely well and my mother did all her shopping and
my father visited all the museums and got to know all the animals in
the Paris zoo intimately. After we returned to Tehran, my parents
changed my school. The new school was very close to our house; I
could walk there. But every time I walked to school, my eyes
searched for Aziz Aqa's bus.

Years went by. I had become a respectable young woman. The old
buses were replaced by new cabs with young drivers. The vacant lots
around our house filled up with houses, small and large. The neighborhood kids had all moved away. My cousins went to the United
States, and I was supposed to go to Europe to pursue my studies. My
mother's chauffeur used to take me everywhere I wanted to go and I
hardly ever took a bus. I was bewitched and bewildered by my youth
and the bright future spread out before me. Every moment of my
life something new was happening and I, too, changed, along with
these events. But the passage of time, my mother's wrinkles, Hasan
Aqa's grey hair, my father's death, my marriage, my divorce, the Revolution, leaving my country and living abroad—none of them made
me forget about my old friend. I was still loyal to him. Every time I

was sad or faced a problem in my life, I could see his miraculous mouth in the back of my mind among my childhood memories, suddenly appearing with its gold filling shining like the morning star in the darkness of night.

I can see bus no. 70 turning at the intersection and slowly approaching us. I hear a childish voice saying: "I won't get on the bus unless it is Aziz Aqa's bus." My daughter wants to get on the bus before me. She waves her hand to the bus driver. Her eyes are full of playful thoughts and secrets. Perhaps she, too, has a secret, a secret that she doesn't want to tell me, just as I didn't want to tell my secret to Mother, Hasan Aqa, or even the poplar trees in the back of the garden.

Mahshid Amir-Shahi

1940–

Born into a well-to-do family from Qazvin, Mahshid Amir-Shahi attended secondary school and college in England, and received an M.A. in physics from Oxford. But once back in Iran, she embarked on a career of writing children's and other stories and producing translations, among them E.B. White's *Charlotte's Web*, James Thurber's *Legends from Our Times*, and P.L. Travers' *Mary Poppins*.

Kucheh-ye bonbast (The blind alley, 1966) was Amir-Shahi's first collection of short stories. Then came *Sār-e Bibi Khānom* (Bibi Khanom's starling, 1968) and *Ba'd az ruz-e ākher* (After the last day, 1969), from which the translated story "The End of the Passion Play" in *Modern Persian Short Stories* (1980) is taken. A translation of a story of hers called "String of Beads" was published in *Edebiyat* 3 (1978). The collection *Be-sigheh-ye avval shakhs-e mofrad* (In the first person singular) appeared in 1971.

A divorcée in self-exile since the early days of the Islamic Republic, Amir-Shahi published an autobiographical narrative called *Dar hazar* (At home) in 1987 in London and Encino, California. It relates the author's experiences and reflections during her 1978–79 visit to Tehran, with a premise of disapproving consternation at the Iranian Revolution and a tone of unmitigated contempt for the Shi'i Muslim clerics involved in politics.

Amir-Shahi spent the 1990–91 academic year as a Rockefeller Fellow in Middle Eastern Studies at the University of Michigan. In 1995, a collection of her short stories was published in the U.S. as *Suri & Co.: Tales of a Persian Teenager*. The same year saw the Los Angeles publication of a novel, *Dar safar* (In A Journey). A novel in three volumes was published in Los Angeles from 1998-2001 under the title *Mādaran va dukhtarān*. Two subsequent works, *Dāstānhā-ye kutah* (1998) and *Hazār bisheh: majmu'ah'i az maqālāt, sokhanrāni'hā, naqd'hā va mosāhabeh'hā-ye Mahshid Amirshāhi* (2000), were published in Sweden.

Brother's Future Family

Translated by Michael Beard

What I really wanted was just orange juice, but I was worried if I said orange juice they'd all think I was a dodo. So I said whiskey.

Brother's eyebrow rose slightly. I thought he was on the verge of knocking my block off while the waiter was still standing there. You can never figure out what this brother of mine is going to do. A few weeks before we had been out with Homa, Homayun and Auntie. Auntie and Homa asked for coffee, Brother and Homayun asked for beer and I asked for cookies and a glass of milk. Brother said, "Bring it to her in a baby bottle." Worst of all, Mehri and some of her friends were sitting at the next table.

At school Mehri won't drink a glass of water without my permission. If I say such and such is a good book, next day she's carrying it under her arm, telling everyone what a lovely story it is. If I say Hafez and Sa'di are dopey she'll start saying it too. All she does is copy me. But after that day when Brother treated me like a bad penny, Mehri didn't pay any attention to me until it was time for the next geometry exam. So I can't ask for milk, that's what will happen.

I can't ask for whiskey, this is what will happen. There's really no way
to figure out what Brother is going to do.

I looked over to Simin for moral support, but Simin was turning
away and biting her lip. Thank God her husband hadn't come. To
him I'm a half-pint infant. Whenever he introduces me he says,
"And here's the little crumb of bread that comes with the kebab."
Bread with the kebab means sister-in-law. The little crumb part is
his invention. Every time I say something worthwhile—and I'm
always saying something worthwhile, except that no one's ever listening—he'll say, "Eh, *barak-Allah!*" meaning "nice try." He seems
to have forgotten that when he married Simin she was only two
years older than I am now.

If he'd been there it would have been even worse. I didn't look up,
but I could see out of the corner of my eye that Mansur Khan had
quite an amused expression on his face, like someone who has just
heard a good joke. And he didn't have any right to look at me like
that! Every time he shakes my hand he squeezes it until his eyes
bulge out and turn red, and he holds it so long it gets all sweaty—
ick!—he doesn't have the right to look at me that way. But I'll pay
him back so he appreciates it. See if I ever bat an eye at him again.

The only person taking me seriously was the waiter. He asked,
"With ice and soda?"

I said yes. Uncle Ardeshir, who thinks he knows everything—and
why? Because back in the dark ages he spent six or seven months in
some dopey English school—said, "Isn't whiskey more of an evening
drink?" But I didn't even answer.

Maliheh said, "Now how long have you been drinking whiskey?"

"For a long time," I said, and to give a sense of time waved my
hand over my shoulder. I wish I hadn't waved my hand, though. I
made it look as if I'd started out drinking whiskey instead of mother's
milk. Everybody burst out laughing—except Brother, who looked at
me angrily, and Maliheh's father, who didn't look at me at all. He had
his eyes riveted to the hors d'oeuvres, studying them as if they were a
mystery story and he was about to find out who the murderer was.
Worst of all was Maliheh's mother, whose look was enough to turn
me into a cockroach crawling up the wall of the restaurant.

I should have ordered orange juice. They thought I was a dodo
anyway and the whiskey didn't improve the image. Actually it made
things worse, but it was too late now and I decided no matter what,
I'd follow it through to the end.

The waiter brought the whiskey and stuck it in front of me. Brother was shifting back and forth in his chair so much I thought he was about to grab my glass right out from under me, so I picked it up and—gulp, gulp, gulp—polished it off as if it were quince and lemon juice.

Since I knew everyone was looking, I managed to hold back the cough and, from sheer necessity, I even produced a smile. My eye fell on the mirror behind Simin's head, and gazing into it I saw something that looked like the double masks you see hanging over theater arches—not just one mask but both of them superimposed on each other.

Brother muttered under his breath, "You've really gone too far this time. If you've got to drink whiskey, you'd at least better drink it right!" Did I say muttered? Everyone in the restaurant must have heard him.

Brother really believes that I'm still five years old and he has to teach me everything. To hear him talk you'd think he was the world champion whiskey drinker. Fine, so I don't know how to drink whiskey. But it's not just whiskey; Brother thinks I'm a total nitwit. For example, he thinks I didn't realize what was happening when he and Maliheh were kissing under the trees in the corner of the garden. When they saw me coming, Maliheh pulled herself away and Brother began to whistle. I could easily have gone to Mama and told her everything and she would have really let him have it, but I didn't. I didn't even tell Brother that I know. I should have. If I had told him I'd seen everything he wouldn't have made such a fuss in front of everyone over one dumb glass of whiskey. Especially in front of that nasty Mansur Khan with that lovely smile on his muzzle. And those bulging eyes. Yuck.

My eyes fell on the mirror behind Simin again. The end of my nose was shining as red as a raspberry—as my mother would say. It looked just like a traffic accident. Until that moment, I had not realized what a traffic accident looked like, but suddenly I realized that a traffic accident was me in the mirror behind Simin's head. My head was swimming. I said, "Friends..."

Brother said, "Friends! You spoiled brat! And just who do you think you're talking to? Look at this half-pint infant..."

As if I hadn't heard what he said I began, "Friends, do you know what a traffic accident looks like?"

I don't know why, but my eyes were glued to Maliheh's father. He was sulking with a tragic look on his face, and I could see that he looked a little like one, too. I was scared he could read my thoughts, so I said, "No, no, I don't mean you."

Simin was straining at the leash to say something, but just then the waiter showed up with the food and saved us, momentarily.

A piece of meat was staring up from the middle of the plate, and Mansur Khan's fish was even worse than the meat. I was sure I could see it writhing, and when the sound of knives and forks started up it was as if they were cutting my flesh. It sent shivers down my spine like the sound of a fingernail running down the surface of a blackboard. I was scared that if I looked down at my plate, I would throw up. I put my napkin over it, but it was paper, so that water, gravy and the greasy green beans and peas soaked through. The outline of the food reappeared, only this time covered with a glaze that looked like a thin coat of spit. I was on the verge of heaving, but I managed somehow to restrain myself.

There was Simin, across the table, saying, "Aren't you going to eat anything?"

If that nosy sister hadn't said anything, Brother wouldn't have noticed, but the moment she asked about my food Brother stopped short whatever he was whispering into Maliheh's ear and in a sudden rage shouted, "And why aren't you eating?"

"I can't," I said, frightened he would force me and I would burst into tears.

Maliheh realized I was telling the truth about not being able to eat and said, "Why pick on her? Maybe she really can't eat." Maliheh really is a nice girl. Just to show her I knew she was nice I said, "Maliheh, I know what you were doing under the trees the other day was all Brother's fault."

I knew Brother wouldn't like it, but I didn't know it would be so bad. All at once he was half-standing in his place, saying, "If you don't shut up right now you'll be presented with a proper beating," and his eyes were staring so hard out of their sockets that I thought they were going to plop onto his plate and if I didn't take off fast he might slug me right there at the table.

I said, "Don't worry, I still haven't told Mama, but if you keep making such an uproar I'll tell her what you and Maliheh were doing."

Maliheh's mother raised one eyebrow and said, "What's this? I beg your pardon, dear?"

Maliheh's mother calls everyone dear and is always begging their pardon. And she always has one eyebrow raised. That's why Mama calls her Madame Orgueilleuse.

I said, "I wasn't talking to you, Madame Orgueilleuse. Do you know why...?"

Brother exploded again, shouting so loud that Maliheh's father looked up in shock and his fork flew out of his hand. Brother leaned across the table and hurriedly wiped off his shirt front and collar. He called for the waiter and said, "Bring the gentleman a fork. Immediately."

I said, "Maybe you'd better bring a dry pair of pants too."

Maliheh's mother said, "Well! Thank you very much! And what else do you have to say, dear?"

I said, "I beg your pardon, but that's all, dear." And my voice sounded so much like Maliheh's mother that I just about died laughing. But no one else laughed and it wasn't possible to laugh long.

All this happened very quickly, including the words people said—like a Charlie Chaplin film, or like a 33-rpm record played at seventy-eight.

I saw that Maliheh was on the verge of tears and I really began to feel sorry for her. I was about to cry myself. I said, "Maliheh, dear..."

But without the slightest warning Maliheh burst out, "Don't 'Maliheh, dear' me!"

I said, "Look, Maliheh, that day under there, it was all..."

But did Maliheh let me finish what I was saying? Her father snorted from his side of the table, and from the other side her mother let loose with so many *Allaho-akbars* that I thought she was going to pass out. Simin immediately broke in with "Oh, oh, this is awful; oh, what a disgrace!"

I said, "But Simin, what are you saying? You never liked them..."

Simin said, "That will be enough!"

"All I was going to say was—have you forgotten the day Mama was saying Brother will end up going so far with that Maliheh girl he's going to have to marry her? Don't you remember what you said?"

Total silence.

"You said all that Maliheh girl really wanted was for Brother to..."

Maliheh said, "Mother, let's go."

Maliheh's mother pulled on her gloves and picked up her handbag and said to Brother, "Now look, my dear, Maliheh is not your kind of girl. And we are not your kind of people. Since I seem to be Madame—whatever it was—and my husband some kind of a freak (no one called her husband a freak, but if someone had said one thing about her they must have said a hundred things about her husband; that way she'd still be on top) and a thousand and one other things… so I beg your pardon but we had better go before they say something else."

Brother said, "Ma'am, don't listen…"

"No explanations, please. First it's your mother and now this sister of yours (she waved her gloves up and down in my direction so we wouldn't think she meant Simin), dear."

And all three got up and began to walk out without a word of good-bye. Simin ran after them. Brother turned threateningly in my direction, but Uncle Ardeshir grabbed his hand and said, "Sit down, take it easy. Don't make the scandal any worse; not in the middle of a restaurant."

Every once in a while Uncle Ardeshir says something intelligent. Brother sat down again, but continued to watch me as closely as a four-eyed dog. When we got up from the table I didn't know if I was totally weightless or heavy as lead. Anyway, I couldn't walk straight, and to keep from falling down I grabbed hold of Uncle Ardeshir's arm. He said, "Let's go get this little lady a cup of coffee."

But Mansur Khan said, "Coffee?" in a tone that suggested coffee was some jewel you would never be able to find, and even if you could, it wouldn't be possible to drink it, and even if you could drink it, it wouldn't help anyway.

"Aw," I said under my breath, "go away. Leave me alone, you squashed toad."

Mansur Khan said, "Pardon me?"

But the sight of him was beginning to bother me. I scrunched my head down into my shoulders and bugged my eyes out to look like a Mansur Khan and said, "Pardon, pardon, you Casanuva—Casanova—whichever it is!"

Mansur Khan's eyes bulged out even farther and he began to shake. "You brat! You brat! You impudent little brat!" And each word rose one note higher in the scale. It sounded exactly like the washed-out insults you hear on dumb radio programs. I was dying of laughter, but I pulled myself together. I put my hand on my heart and recited, "Oh, my darling" in the same tone of voice, but Mansur Khan didn't wait to hear me laugh or to witness the continuation of my performance, but turned around and waddled like a crab out of the restaurant.

Brother grabbed my arm and squeezed so tight I had to yell. "Hey watch it, you're breaking my arm, you creep!"

"Stop yelling, you little idiot," he said, "I'd have broken your neck by now if I could."

"So who's yelling?"

Brother said, "One more word out of you and I knock your teeth down your throat."

I saw that people at the other tables were looking at us. I turned to the man sitting closest, who seemed to be wearing two ties and two pairs of glasses, and asked him, "And they call this a brother? Can you imagine it?" Then I noticed that both of his ties were crooked, and I went over to straighten them, but Uncle Ardeshir grabbed me and led me out of the restaurant.

Brother was saying, "Ooh, I'm going to serve you up what you've been asking for until even you'll be satisfied."

I said, "You and whose army?" By then I wasn't scared of Brother any more, not even scared of what would happen next.

Later I began to realize what I had done. Brother, naturally, kept his promise. He let me have it until I was truly satisfied, and for an entire month he wouldn't let me so much as drink a glass of water in peace. He laid down the law day in and day out and kept threatening he would tell Mama the whole story. He had done the same thing to me once before when I was seven or eight, all because I had been in the bathroom innocently trying on a fancy hairclip full of rhinestones. Brother can never wait when he has to go to the bathroom. He pushed his way in while I was still inside and saw what I was doing. The hairclip, completely by accident, had fallen out of my hair and I immediately flushed the toilet but it wouldn't go down. My mistake was flushing the toilet. By the time Brother banged his way in I had already flushed it three times but it was still stuck in the hole. I didn't get out of his clutches for a long time afterward.

For two or three weeks after that I had to be his slave to keep him from telling Mama. He'd call me away from my homework to get him a glass of water. I'd tie his shoes. He'd tell me to straighten out his clothes closet. Don't even ask me about the days when the plumber and masons were here to fix the sewer pipes.

One day he was pushing me around so much that Mama got irritated. She called him in and said, "Why are you making such a little girl wait on you all the time like that?"

Brother said, "She knows why she has to do everything I say. If she doesn't..."

I shot up like a bolt of lightning to do whatever he said next, but Mama said, "Stay where you are while I see why this big oaf doesn't do anything for himself."

Brother looked at me out of the corner of his eye and said, "I'm going to te-ell!"

My heart was boiling like vinegar. Mama said, "Tell what?"

Brother told her everything, and Mother said, "That's all? Fine, she dropped it. A cheap hairclip is an awfully small thing for a little girl's heart to melt over." Then she said to me, "Listen, Baby, if you'd only told me when it happened, I would have just fished it out so the men wouldn't have had to come and replace the pipes." I felt as if a mountain had been lifted off my shoulders, and Brother was just a speck on the snowy peaks.

So this time I made up my mind over and over again to go to Mama and tell her the whole story myself.

But this tragedy was more tragic than that one, so I didn't, and for an entire month—right up to the day of the engagement—Brother wouldn't let me alone for a moment.

The evening of the party Maliheh's mother begged my pardon so many times it was as if I had never said a word to her before. She grabbed my arm and personally introduced me to everyone who came by. It was as if I were the new bride in her family. I was even tempted to order whiskey again, but do you think Maliheh's mother let me out of her claws long enough? I just kept drinking orange juice, and to be completely frank, I must say I find it superior to whiskey, but I made up for it the next day by telling Mehri, "Brother's engagement party was last night, and I just wish you had been there. All I did was drink whiskey."

And that's how it came about that Mehri decided to try it herself.

The Smell of Lemon Peel, the Smell of Fresh Milk

Translated by Heshmat Moayyad

I am sure that it was the silence that woke me up. My eyes opened. Two faces floated before me in the air and my eyelids closed again. Then, even with my eyes shut, I felt their presence in the room. I wanted to look at them again, but my eyelids were as heavy as two pieces of stone. A biting thirst scratched my throat. I wanted to ask for water, but instead of words, a mute moaning came out of my mouth. I was terrified. All my energy was lost in big beads of sweat that poured from my body. Weakness overcame me.

I felt someone's heavy movement in the room and a head bent over my face. The smell of sterile muslin and toothpaste filled my nose. Two people were speaking to each other. All I heard them saying was "ch-ch-ch-ch."

Somebody said, "Did you ask for something?" I tried to nod, but I realized that my head had not moved. Once more, everything turned mute and pale, and after that I remember nothing.

I woke up again. The room around me was filled with sounds like "s-sh, sh-s, ch, ch, ch, ch…" and the noise of soft footsteps. The scent of some bitter medicine filled my nose. I opened my eyes but it was not the ceiling of my own room. My head remained motionless. I rolled my eyes in their sockets and they fell upon the china cabinet. "So, I am in the living room." Daddy, the doctor and the same two faces—one old and one young—were in the room. Mommy was not there. Where was Mommy? Why was she not there? …Then I remembered.

I remembered, Mommy, that you were no longer in our house. Since that summer afternoon you have not been in the house. How long ago was that? Was it a thousand years ago or was it yesterday? When was it, Mommy? Tell me, when was it that you, Ashi, Nini, Daddy, and I were all together in the basement rec room? You were piling our plates with cherries, strawberries, and gherkins. The day when the quarrel occurred. When was it, Mommy?

The doctor rushed to my bedside, took my pulse and asked, "Do you hear my voice?"

The word "yes" formed on my lips, but no sound came out. The "s-sh, ch-ch-ch" sounds grew louder, and then there was a droning silence, like a long-drawn "Sssss." I thought I had fainted. Yet I opened my eyes and looked. The doctor, Daddy, and two women were standing around my bed. Daddy was looking at me persistently. I returned his gaze. There were tears in his eyes and a slant smile on his lips.

He asked, "Do you want anything, darling?"

I nodded. His wet eyes flashed.

"What do you want, darling," he asked. "I will bring you whatever you want."

"I want my mommy," my voice came forth.

The word "mommy" dried both his tears and his smile. His lips quivered as on that day when he was arguing with Mommy, that day in the basement.

You certainly have not forgotten it, Mommy. Daddy was leaning back on the mattress with his elbows sinking into two soft pillows. His white and blue striped pajamas had rolled up to his knees. The upper part of his body was bare. You were filling the fruit plates and all three of us waited to snatch the heaviest one. Daddy was talking. His mouth foamed and his voice was very loud. A few times you said gently, "Not in front of the kids. Leave it for later." But Daddy would not give up. He sat upright in his bed, waving his hands in the air. His eyes were bloodshot.

Ashi's eyes were fixed on one spot of the wall. He clenched his fists. Nini and I looked at you and Daddy with terror. You were fighting off tears, talking chokingly, Mommy, begging.

You said a few more times, "The kids are here, please, let it be for now."

Ashi said, "Why don't you say or do anything? How long will you sit quietly and endure this?"

Daddy shouted, "Get lost, all of you! Get out of my sight."

Glasses, gherkins, and strawberries fell and rolled over the floor. Daddy's lips trembled. He looked swollen and ugly. I was afraid of him. I hated him. I was afraid that he would kill you, and hated him even more. Why didn't you say anything, Mommy? Why were you sobbing? I know the reason. Perhaps Ashi did not know it. I know, it was for our sake, Mommy. But, after all, why?

Daddy said, "This lady has come to look after the household, that is, to look after your needs. That there is her daughter." He smiled at the girl. She was fat and white, and had no neck. "If you kids need anything else…"

It was always like that. The things I was meant to desire were only those things that Daddy wanted me to desire. The day you left he held our hands and took us out. I have not told you this before, Mommy. First he took us to a toy store. The only thing I wanted was a small rubber mouse with a sad look on his face and a tiny tooth, who would wail when squeezed. I wanted that mouse. I wanted it to cry with me. Instead, Daddy bought me an entire menagerie of other animals and a whole series of cars, trucks and airplanes. He did not buy the mouse. Because it was worthless and dirty. It did not matter to Daddy that I wanted it. What mattered to him was rather his wanting me to want those other toys.

I closed my eyes. Something was pounding inside my head. The thirst was still scraping my throat badly. I licked my lips. They were so coarse and dry that I felt as if they bruised my tongue. Someone smelling of salty cabbage and acrid soap poured some drops of water in my mouth. I wanted to spit them out, but I did not have enough energy. They simply flowed down my throat. They had no taste but they felt cool. Like running tears that leave a trace on a dirty face, the water drew a line inside my throat and ran down. Then I fell asleep.

When I woke up—what time was it? Was it the next day?—that woman, the old one, was in my room. Daddy called her Madame, as did everyone else. Her daughter was thus titled "Madame's Daughter." I thought that they must have never had names.

Madame always smelled of salty cabbage and acrid soap. Her daughter smelled of starched white cloth and toothpaste. With eyes closed, I knew by their smells who was in the room. People were identifiable only by their smells. Daddy was the cigarette smell, my nurse was the smell of bath steam and henna, and grandmother that of urine.

You have the smell of lemon peels, Mommy, sometimes the smell of fresh milk. You smell clean, you smell of human skin. And every time I think of you, my nose remembers your smell.

Madame told me that Nini is ill; she got it from me. The thought of Nini being sick is awful. Even barring sickness, she has always been weak and frail. I wished to know more about Nini. But all I managed to ask was "What about Ashi?"

"Ashi is all right. He is staying with your uncle."

Mommy, I don't want anyone, except those whom I like, to mention names that are dear to me. You should have been at my bed, telling me that Ashi is staying with my uncle, and that Nini is sick. I am crying for you, Mommy, both for you being away from me and for Nini being ill. The left side of my pillow is wet. Perhaps if the right side gets wet as well, the moisture from both ends will join in the middle and then everything will be all right. When the moisture seeps through the pillow, the door will open—I imagine—and you will come in with Nini following behind you. And so I trail my fingertips on the pillow, drawing the moisture down. It absorbs my tears in the middle. Look now, the wet from both ends has seeped through the entire length of the pillow. But why, then, haven't you come? Perhaps because I have cheated. I should have let the tears penetrate the pillow on their own.

When Daddy came I told him that I wanted to see Nini. He said I should wait a few days. I became obstinate and refused my medicine. Next day they transferred Nini's bed to my room.

Nini had the smell of chicken feathers. She was two-dimensional, flat. Her face consisted of just two large, black eyes. We both burst out crying. Her condition was better than mine. She was able to sit up in bed. Looking me up and down, her eyes registered terror. It was as if she was looking at something that was about to leave and never return. Just as she had looked at Mommy the day she went away.

I could not see my own face and was not in the mood to worry about myself. The only thing that frightened me was that my breasts, which had started to bud before I got sick, had now shrunk. The cartilage circle around the nipples had disappeared. I was afraid I would turn into a boy. I could speak about it with no one. I would have told Mommy about it had she been there. Maybe I could talk to Ashi about it, but he was not there either. They only let us see him once every two to three days from behind a glass window.

Ashi would smile at us from behind this glass. The image of his teeth and eyes remained on the windowpane long after he had left. Nini and I would cry after he left. But as long as he was there, we just kept looking at him. He was the only link between ourselves and the world of the healthy people.

I could not speak with Nini about my breasts. She was only a child and did not understand such things. I did not speak with her about Mommy either because I knew that she could not bear it. Each time she huddled in her bed and did not speak, I knew that she was thinking of Mommy. But I did not have the courage to say anything. Closing my eyes in order to avoid looking at her, the expression of her face on the day Mommy left appeared before me.

You got in a *droshky*, Mommy, and as it started, its wheels clicked on the street's stone pavement. The driver whipped the horses to speed them on. Nini ran barefoot into the middle of the road and screamed. Her face was fiery red and her eyes… you did not see her eyes, Mommy, but I did. They were filled with fear, fear of losing you. She had stretched her little arms out toward the *droshky*. Her feet could not keep up with her torso, which strained ahead so as to reach you. When they took her back to the house, she was kicking. Her screams pierced the air. Ashi carried her into the room in his arms. I hugged myself, put my face against the wall and scratched it, drying my tears on the plaster. I wished that Daddy would hold me. Forgive me, Mommy, for wishing to be held by Daddy. Forgive me for not having disliked Daddy except that day in the basement, and for always having loved him. You yourself, Mommy, taught me to love him.

Nini asked, "But who is this girl?"

"She is Madame's daughter."

Enraged, Nini went on, "To begin with, who is Madame herself? What is she doing here?"

I shrugged my shoulders.

"I hate them," said Nini. "I hate them so much."

"Me too," I said, and swallowed my tears.

"Do you believe that God exists?" asked Nini.

"No," I answered, and I was afraid that he might exist and hear what I said and be angry with me. I was afraid and repented.

"I believe that he exists. I say my prayers every night."

I knew what prayers Nini said. She prayed for Mommy to return to us. She prayed that Grandma, Madame, and her daughter would all leave our home. She prayed that we would both recover and eat ice cream, chocolate and dried fruit rolls again. I hoped that God did exist and that he heard Nini's prayers. But I laughed at Nini, with repentance still in my throat and on the tip of my tongue. Nini rounded her lips and said, "Go make fun of yourself."

The smell of powder, eau de cologne and cigarettes. I opened my eyes. Azar Khanom and Daddy were there.

That day Daddy took us from the toy store to Azar Khanom's house. I have not yet told you this, Mommy. There are many things I have not told you, only because I do not want to make you sad. There was a party there, at Azar's place. Everyone there was friends with Daddy. They spoke of you as if you were dead. I wished the ground would swallow them up or that the sky would fall down on them. I had no desire to play with other children there. I did not want to forget my grief. I believed that if I stopped feeling sad for you, I would betray you, cheat you. I was afraid that something bad might happen to you if I did not cry. In my thoughts I kept begging you, "Mommy, do something to make me cry, something to stave off my hunger, something to make them take the cream cake out of my sight." Could you hear my voice on that day, Mommy?"

Now Azar Khanom asked, "Do you feel all right, my dear?" I just looked at her.

Nini said, "Why have you come here? I don't like you."

I was both embarrassed and delighted.

Daddy said, "Stop it, Nini! How impolite and spoiled you have become! What kind of way is that to talk?"

Azar Khanom said, "Let her go. She is not feeling well. None of them like me. I can see it in their eyes. It doesn't matter. They're only kids."

Both of them left the room. Nini was grinding her teeth.

"I am glad you said it."

Nini grinned. But she was pale as white plaster.

I said again, "I am glad you said it." I wanted to kiss her.

"Has she come to stay here too?" asked Nini.

"Oh no," said I.

Mommy, you occupy only as much room as a sparrow. Why should so many people fill your place? Grandma, Madame, her daughter, and occasionally also Azar Khanom. They are all corpulent, each one of them takes up enough space for three people. You smell of lemon peels and fresh milk, Mommy. Drive the other odors out of the house!

Nini said, "Do you remember that? On that Friday, when we returned home, this Azar Khanom was here?"

"Yes, the first Friday."

The first Friday that we went to visit you, Mommy. The nurse took us to you, do you still remember? You had rented the second floor of a two-story building. Your place was small and depressing. You yourself are so small, Mommy, but you can't be boxed in. I mean, you have a certain aura which requires open space around you, like a bird. But in your small, second-floor flat, you were exactly like a caged bird. You looked thinner and pale. You could not embrace all three of us at once. Nor, however, could any one of us wait for a turn. Your delicate neck was bent under the pressure of our weight, and your hands caressed whomever's head they could reach.

The nurse unwound us from around your neck, all three of us weeping. Your eyes usually grow larger when you are about to cry. Do you know that? And like a bird when drinking, you tilt your head up. Why do you do that, Mommy? Are you struggling to prevent your tears from running down?

Overjoyed at the sight of you, Nini's tears dried quickly. Ashi sought to hide his. I kept wiping my eyes in order to see you well.

You said, "It is nice here, isn't it?" and you looked at us with concern.

No, Mommy, it was not nice there. It was depressing: gloomy and small. You knew it very well yourself.

You said—and how hard you tried to make your voice sound steady and cheerful—"I have cooked meatloaf and *albalu polow* for you."

But the nurse had instructions to bring us back by noon.

This second separation was more painful for me than the first. I don't know whether this was the case for you too, Mommy. Nini, poor little Nini, my little sister. She was writhing like a wounded animal. She scratched her own face and the nurse's hands. You had bitten your fingers and no longer struggled to stop your tears.

First we postponed our trip home by ten minutes, then by five minutes more and again by another two minutes. But in the end we did leave you.

When we got home, Azar Khanom was there.

Days, weeks, months—they had no meaning. They belonged to healthy people. We lived by the hours: 7:00, tea with milk and a piece of rusk. 9:00, an injection. 10:00, medicine drops and syrup. My tablets, just before noon. 12:00, chicken soup and yogurt. After 12:00, tablets. 4:00 p.m., an injection… Invisible hands did all the work. Just like in fairy tales and witches' houses. The active people were invisible. Beyond the four walls of our room was the fairy world, as well as the thought of our favorite dishes. These thoughts were but dreams and imaginings. During the day Nini would sit at my bed and we would speak of different foods.

"Meat loaf, *albalu polow*!"

"Dried cherries!"

"Yum!"

"Cream cake, ice cream, *faludeh*!"

"No, no *faludeh*, please! Tell me about cream cake and ice cream!"

"*Khoresh-e bademjan*!"

"Eggplant kuku!"

"No, don't even talk about it!"

"*Polow! Lubiya polow!*"

"With its golden crust! Will it ever be possible, Nini?"

"Who knows?" said Nini. There was sadness and disbelief in her eyes.

"They say that we will get boiled rice next week."

"Hmmph! Boiled rice? What is boiled rice?" She did not wait for an answer, but continued, "Oh well, let it be what it may. After all, it is rice of a sort, isn't it?"

"Yes, of course."

Our mouths watered and our stomachs ached.

Nini dreamt overnight of tables laden with colorful dishes and would report to me in the morning.

I sat in my bed and listened to her with bittersweet pleasure. And I watched the winter through the windowpanes. That year I saw nothing of autumn. I did see the first snow, though. It was untouched and pure as it settled lightly on the branches of the pomegranate tree and on those parts of the flowerbed and courtyard I was able to see. As Nini spoke, I watched the snowflakes settling softly and weightlessly upon each other. The snow looked to me like *polow*, cotton candy, and cream cake.

Again, forgive me, Mommy. When I thought of food you were still at the back of my mind. It was you who set Nini's dream tables. It was the memory of your dishes that whet my appetite. Nevertheless, food came to mind first, and you only second. You will forgive me, won't you?

When I woke up in the morning after the first snow, everything I saw through the windowpane was white. There was only one bush of ice plant outside which disrupted the continuous stretch of white snow. I could feel the cold in the warm room even from underneath my blanket. Everything I looked at was cold except the ice plant. Sunlight and warmth had nested between its yellow, crystal-shaped petals. I was afraid the sun might melt the tender crystal of its flowers; it worried me the whole day. However, the flowers clung to their naked stalks and did not melt away; they warmed my heart.

My bed was warm and had the smell of my body and its bitter medicines. I wished that they would put the bed outside in the snow. Nini could tell me about her dream dishes and I would be able to feel the clean and virgin coolness of the snow against my skin.

It snowed for several days. Branches bowed down under the weight of the snow. Muddy footsteps soiled the snow and dirtied it. It balled up and smudged like the cotton lining of a worn-out mattress. At night, however, it appeared clean; its white shone through the window in my room making it so bright I was unable to sleep.

The night before we were promised boiled rice for lunch, I couldn't fall asleep until very late. It was bright in the room and I watched the blue sky with its lead-colored clouds. The moon sat behind the clouds. It looked like a woman dressed in delicate silks. I felt like a peeping tom. My heart beat fast with excitement at this stealthy action and the anticipation of boiled rice the next day.

Nini started mumbling. At first I thought she was talking in her sleep.

I asked, "Are you awake, Nini?"

"Yes," she said after a moment of silence.

"Were you saying something?"

"No, I was praying."

She turned on the light near her bed to see whether I was making fun of her again.

I wasn't making fun of her, Mommy, I was praying too. I prayed that Nini and I would stay alive long enough to eat the boiled rice the next day. I prayed that you also would be awake and perhaps look at the moon at the same moment as I. I prayed you might not find out I had thought more of boiled rice than of you.

I said, "Turn off the light, Nini, and look at the moon. The clouds look like the waves of the sea, and the moon is about to drown."

Nini turned off her light and looked at the moon.

"No, the clouds look like two fat cats and the moon is like a ball between them," said Nini.

With eyes fixed on the sky, and thinking of boiled rice, I finally fell asleep.

How long were you sleepless, Mommy?

From early morning on we spoke only about lunch. Hours stretched longer. Time was not passing. The day was to be a celebration for us and we were to lunch with Daddy in the dining room. We felt much better. We could both walk. I walked from my bed to Nini's, and Nini from hers to the door, to my bed and on to the window. On condition I did not move from my bed at all, we were to be permitted to lunch in the dining room. Accordingly, I stayed in bed. My hip was pierced like a sieve and it ached from all the injections. Sitting up was difficult. It even ached lying down. However, on that day all these pains were bearable.

At 11:30 they fetched us to the dining room. The house was quite warm. As we passed through the hallway, I peered eagerly at the stairs leading to my own room, the handrail and the small telephone stand from which the telephone was now missing. We passed by Grandma's room. The scent of urine assaulted my nose. Grandma sat sunk in her armchair. Her legs were dangling off the floor. Her round, fat body moved like a pendulum from right and to left. She held her index finger to her temple and hummed.

Fati—who had the odor of dung—was hopping up and down near the doorway.

"Are you all right, Fati? Did Grandma beat you again?"

Fati nodded yes and laughed.

Grandmother called, "Fati, you vicious child-of-a-genie, where the hell are you?"

The world of the healthy people was definitely not the fairy world. It was nice, nevertheless. Nothing had changed. Oh yes, the dining room looked different. The picture of Mommy and Daddy was no longer on the wall. Nor was the picture of Aqajan, Mommy's father. There were no flowers on the table.

Where are you, Mommy? There are no flowers on the table today. You see, Mommy, the napkins you used to fold into the shape of a flower aren't there either. Where are the tulip-shaped lamps on the mantelpiece? Where is the turquoise box, with a gold pear and two broad leaves on the lid?

The table was set for four people. The bread basket was on the table as well as rusks and glasses of milk for Nini and me. We two sat next to each other.

"Beware not to eat bread," we were told while Daddy was called to the table. Two pieces of fresh baked bread quickly disappeared into my lap. They were warm and crusty.

Daddy entered the room with Madame's daughter following behind him. They sat at the opposite side of the table, facing us. The two ends of the table remained empty.

Daddy rubbed his hands. "Well, children, you're waiting for boiled rice, aren't you? Are you hungry enough? Are your mouths watering?"

Nini and I nodded to every question like mechanical dolls.

First the boiled rice dish was brought in together with yogurt jars. The pomegranate stew, *fesenjan*, *polow* and cutlets followed.

If you were here, Mommy, the pomegranate stew and *fesenjan* and cutlets would not have appeared together with our boiled rice on the table. And your picture would be hanging on the wall. You would take your seat and Madame's daughter wouldn't be at the table at all. Where are you now, Mommy? On the second floor of that same depressing house? Mommy, take me there, please! That place is much better than here.

Nini's eyes gazed at the stew pots, her nostrils flaring.

My hands moved between the folds of my nightgown and placed a piece of bread on Nini's lap. The second piece fell noiselessly on the floor. Gently I bent down to pick it up. Under the table Daddy's and Madame's daughter's hands and legs were entwined.

I was carried back to my bed in someone's arms. The plate of boiled rice remained untouched on the table.

Mahmud Dowlatabadi

1940–

Born in the Khurasan village of Dowlatabad (near Sabzavar), short-story writer and novelist Mahmud Dowlatabadi was the most prominent Iranian novelist of the 1980s. Self-educated and forced to work from childhood, Dowlatabadi spent part of his younger adult years as a stage actor in Tehran.

His first collection of stories was called *Lāyeh'hā-ye biyābāni* (Desert strata) and appeared in 1969. A second collection called *Do dāstān* (Two stories) appeared in 1970. Then came a series of novels: *Safar* (The trip, 1969, revised 1974), *Owsaneh-ye Bābā Sobhān* (The legend of Baba Sobhan, 1970), *Gāvāreh-bān* (Cowherd, 1972), *Bā Shobayru* (With Shobayru, 1973), *Hejrat-e Solaymān* (Solomon's emigration, 1974), *'Aqil, 'Aqil* (Aqil, Aqil, 1974), *Mard* (Man, 1974), *Didār-e Baluch* (Visit to the Baluch, 1978), and *Az kham-e chanbar* (Through the hoop, 1978) are his chief writings before the Revolution.

Dowlatabadi's 1979 novel *Jā-ye khāli-ye Soluch* (Soluch's empty place) treated the decline of Iranian village life in the 1960s. His magnum opus is the monumental 3,000-page saga called *Klidar* (1978–83), which narrates the lives of Kurdish tribespeople and peasants in a poverty-stricken village in Khurasan in the mid-1940s. A second saga, *Ruzgār-e separi shodeh-ye mardom-e sālkhordeh* (The bygone days of old folks) was published in three volumes from 1993–2001. Other works include *Ahu-ye bakht-e man, Guzal* (1989), *Radd, goft va gozar-e sepanj: maqāleh'hā, naqdhā, goft va shonudhā, sokhan-rānihā* (1992), and *Otobus: filmnāmeh* (1993).

A volume recording a series of interviews Dowlatabadi gave to a group of writers and editors, *Mā niz mardomi hastim* (We are also a people, 1990), gives a clear picture of his views on writing, as one of the first Iranian writers of interpretive fiction to support himself exclusively or primarily by writing. Dowlatabadi lives with his family in Tehran. He traveled to Europe and the United States in the early 1990s, lecturing on literature and politics.

Hard Luck

Translated by Cyrus Amir-Mokri and Paul Losensky

The stable was quiet and a cluster of stars appeared through a circular tear in the roof. At the base of a wall, Rahmat was sitting silently in a pack saddle and the whites of his eyes glowed. A pale, round platter of light had fallen on the stable floor. Standing against a wall, a white animal was shivering, its body erect and its hair on end.

The door of the adjoining room creaked. The gypsies' conversation broke off, the platter of their light disappeared from the stable floor, and the sound of a man's footsteps in the snow faded into the distance ...

The night was yet young.

Rahmat shifted in the pack saddle. He pulled a sheet over his ears and fixed his hat snugly on his head. He pressed his knees against his chest, placed his hands between his thighs, and huddled his head as far down as he could between his shoulders. He closed his eyes... no matter what, he wanted to catch a little nap.

The cold had kept him from resting in any one place since morning. His bones ached—it was a deep, dull pain—and he felt pins and needles in his leg wound. When he had gotten to the stable early that night, he had scraped together what was left in his tin, made a pill the size of two lentils, and eaten it. It seemed as if the pill was beginning to take effect as Rahmat started to feel hot. His back was becoming warmer, his head grew heavy, and his eyelids drooped. But his thoughts would not leave him in peace and buzzed in his head like a bumblebee.

2

From birth he was frail and epileptic. As far back as he could remember, his mother had been an invalid: she was so bedridden that she'd give up the ghost if you so much as blew your nose. He was just beginning to know his left hand from his right when his father left for the city one day, promising to bring him back a hoop and a new pair of espadrilles with leather heels. For two days, Rahmat was so excited he couldn't sit still... The third day went by, then the fourth... and the umpteenth, but there was no news of him. All the fathers who had gone to the city came back. Rahmat asked every one of them about his father. They replied that they had not seen him. Worried and choked with tears, he went to his mother and said, "Every day you say, 'He'll come. Today he'll come. He'll come.' So, where is he? Everyone has come except him."

"He'll come, tomorrow... tomorrow he'll come. I'm sure. Go meet him on the road tomorrow." She moaned and pulled the blanket over her head.

Next day, before the sun cast any shadows, Rahmat hurried to the city gate, climbed to the top of the tower, and fixed his eyes on the road gleaming in the desert. Every black dot that appeared on the road excited him. But when it drew near and he got a better look, his hopes were dashed, and he leaned on the crumbling battlement of the tower to wait for another dot.

The call to prayer was sounding and the road was disappearing in the sunset when Rahmat felt himself trembling—a symptom of a seizure. As he was about to descend, the fit stopped him cold; he passed out, twisted about, and was thrown from the top of the tower, a distance two-and-a-half times the height of a man... The people of the village would talk behind the back of the prayer leader. Everyone had something to say, and said it—some even said, "He escaped his fate." Rahmat's mother was not long for this world and soon died. The villagers said, "She died of grief," but God only knows. Whatever the case, the result was that Rahmat remained alone, broken down and sickly, like a cracked goblet. He had a spindly neck like the stem of an apple, a huge head, sunken eyes, a flat nose, and a chin as pointed as the edge of a piece of crockery. When he reached manhood, only a few strands of soft gray hair appeared on his chin. People said that opium had burned the roots of his hair, but hair grew all over his head, from the top of his protruding forehead to the edge of his neck and ears. He never shaved his head, always keeping his hair so long that it stuck out from under his squalid skullcap and rubbed against his collar.

The villagers performed the burial services for Rahmat's mother. The sun had not risen on her grave a second day before Rahmat was given, along with a handful of alms, to Kawkab, who was alone and had no one to look after her, so that she could be rewarded in the hereafter—and so that Rahmat could support her in her old age.

People said that Kawkab was an adult orphan. Her parents were among some Baluchis from Sistan who had run into famine and sickness on the way back from a summer migration. Kawkab was the only one of them to survive. She was a tall, middle-aged woman. Her bony shoulders protruded through her garment, and her face was as sallow as amber.

Her narrow, lean face was dominated by black eyes and eyebrows. She covered her graying hair with a faded headscarf. People said that in her youth she had been the village beauty: she had long, braided hair that hung down to her waist and eyes which were unmatched in all of Khurasan.

Now she owned an opium den. It served both as her residence and as her place of business, and as the village playground. It was also a hangout for the unemployed and the shiftless, for men who had no one waiting for them at home by the *korsi*, or had no home at all.

All in all, it was the top opium den in the whole village.

So it was that they brought Rahmat to Kawkab's house. Kawkab did not embarrass the villagers and took Rahmat under her wing. First she had his dislocated shoulder put back into place, but it did not heal well, making it seem as if Rahmat were hiding a goat's head underneath his jacket. They also set his ankle, and it healed by itself, though crookedly.

Every night Kawkab applied an ointment of dates or eggs or some other poultice to his fractures and laid him down by the *korsi* and covered him up, but Rahmat's wailing did not cease, nor did his pain subside. She needed a drug to quiet him. Kawkab was desperate and had no choice.

This was something she had brought upon herself... so, what remedy better than opium? It could send Rostam himself reeling, let alone Rahmat. Moreover, it was ready at hand and convenient... She would take four long drags and blow the smoke in Rahmat's face. Rahmat enjoyed it. He would inhale the smoke with pleasure until he got dizzy. His body would go numb and start to itch. The pain in his body would diminish, eventually subside, and then he would fall asleep. Kawkab was happy for Rahmat's tranquility and proud of her charity. Her name was on everyone's lips, and they would say, "Manliness has nothing to do with a beard and moustache."

3

A little over a year went by. Rahmat grew stronger and began moving about, but his right leg was a little bent at the ankle and shorter than his left. His left shoulder too had been pushed upward and was nearly behind his head. With every step he took, his body bent forward and his head shook... In the course of little over a year, though he was never free of pain, he was able to learn the things that he needed to know and some that he didn't, the things that he would put to use in the future and some that he wouldn't, and he came to accept, like any other child, every condition laid down by his elders. He listened to anything they might tell him, eagerly going wherever they might send him, and zealously carried out any chore they might set for him, so as to be a good and obedient child.

Kawkab's house had fixed rules and regulations that were as incumbent on Rahmat to learn and carry out as religious commandments. He must greet the customers pleasantly. From time to time, he must go fill the jug with pure water from the top of the creek and bring it back. He must sweep the basement and dust the windowsills and ledges. He must wash his clothes and Kawkab's, rinse them out, spread them on the wall, and gather and fold them when they were dry. He must make the tea perfectly and pour it in the cups in such a way that there were no bubbles on the surface. He must lie down on his side at the foot of the kerosene burner and prepare the opium for smoking, and he must smoke a little opium himself once in a while to clear the inside of the pipe.

He must tidily scrape the inside of the pipe and neatly place the burnt remains of opium in their box. He must also take care not to irritate Kawkab, who, after all, had taken his mother's place… and a lot of various other chores that sent him running about under Kawkab's smoke-stained roof like a chicken with its head cut off. Of all the chores, Kawkab took responsibility only for preparing the stew, and this only because she believed that no one could make stew with her expertise. She claimed that in her youth she had been the housekeeper to Haj Molla Mir, God rest his soul… Some days after lunch, Kawkab would sit on her roof in the sun and stretch out her legs, crossing one over the other; she would place her head on Rahmat's lap and tell him, "Pick through it." She would let her head of withered hair flow over Rahmat's legs. Rahmat would run his delicate fingernails through her hair and inspect it carefully. If he found any lice, he would pull them out with his fingertips and crush them between his finger and thumbnail until they burst open and dark blood spread out over his nails.

Crushing each bug brought a smile to his lips, and he was as happy as if he had prevented some disaster from befalling Kawkab. Sometimes he became so enthralled with searching out and killing lice that mucus from his nose would whistle down and plop onto Kawkab's face, but he wouldn't notice and would keep on searching just the same.

4

The months of Scorpio and Sagittarius were approaching, and everyone returning from the fields was bringing firewood home with them and stocking up for winter. One morning before breakfast, Kawkab sent Rahmat to gather and bring back four piles of dry firewood so they would have fuel at the ready and not be caught unawares by winter. By now Rahmat had experienced much and gained some expertise in daily affairs; besides, he was as sharp as a tack, and before noon he returned with four men, each carrying a load of firewood. They unloaded the firewood and Rahmat paid them with Kawkab herself looking on. Then he carried the wood to a storage room and stacked it right by the wheat urn. After he was done, with fatigue evident in his every word and movement, he picked up the cast-iron pitcher, went to the edge of the ditch, and washed up. He returned to the house, tired but proud, and sat next to the kerosene burner, across from Kawkab.

He had the air of a wrestler who had pinned his opponent with his mother looking on. Kawkab cleaned the stem of the pipe with a poker, and Rahmat put the pipe to his mouth... then another round... His knees gained some strength and he straightened up. He picked up a cigarette from next to the plate and lit it. He then placed his elbow on the pillow, crossed his legs, and leaned back like the most indolent of her customers. Kawkab shifted about and got up. She boiled six eggs and a cup of grape syrup in half a ladle of mutton fat, poured it in a copper tureen, and put it by the large serving tray. She placed three pieces of soft bread left over from the previous day beside the tray too, and gave it all to Rahmat. She draped a small piece of sackcloth over his shoulders and sent him out onto the roof. She then picked up her small kerosene burner, a pillow, and a felt carpet, followed him up the stairs, and went out onto the roof. Rahmat put the tray and the sackcloth by the wall and came back down at Kawkab's request to carry up the yellow Nasrabadi melon that Kawkab had hidden under the bread container. They had each noticed that melons and opium complement one another very well, each contributing to the inebriation caused by the other, and that the sun capped them both. So it was that they frequently settled themselves on the sunny roof.

Kawkab had spread out the felt carpet and the sackcloth and placed the tray in the middle. She was dividing the bread into small pieces when Rahmat arrived. He rolled the melon over next to the pillow and sat flush against the wall facing Kawkab. After lunch they had the melon, then two bowls of opium and a cigarette... and they leaned against the wall to soak up the sun and to get their strength back.

The sun was warm and the air tranquil. Kawkab slid back her headscarf and ran her fingers like five baby snakes through her hair. She opened her eyes and moaned to Rahmat, "Pick through it." She then crawled over by Rahmat's knees, turned her back to him, and leaned up against him.

As Rahmat's slim, smoky fingers were running through her hair, Kawkab fell asleep. Her body slackened and fell into Rahmat's embrace. Rahmat stretched out his leg, which had fallen asleep. Kawkab's back pressed tightly against Rahmat's abdomen, and her head with its mane of hair lay against his chest just under his chin. Rahmat's legs were extended alongside hers.

Looking at them straight on, you would have thought they had merged into one: a large body with outstretched legs, propped up against the sunny wall.

Rahmat's fingers had grown damp in Kawkab's hair, and with every breath Kawkab moved up and down in his embrace. The odor of Kawkab's hair wafted into his nose, and his whole chest, abdomen, and thighs were burning and drenched with sweat. A fever ran through his body, and he felt as if he were being held in front of an oven. His cheeks were inflamed, and it felt as though fire were pouring out of his small, sunken eyes. His heart was beating faster and something seemed to be dripping from it. Such a languor came over him that he felt himself becoming as insubstantial as a cloud.

A novel sensation had taken hold of him. His face was flushed, and it seemed as if blood were trickling from his ears. His mouth and lips were as dry as sandpaper. His throat was parched and his tongue felt like a sun-dried brick. Head to toe he was consumed by a delightful fire—wine seemed to run through his veins. He did not himself know how old he was. Thirteen? Fourteen? Or, as some people had it, fifteen or more and an adult? Whatever it was, it was the season of passionate ecstasy. He closed his eyes and cast aside all reserve. He passed his hands under Kawkab's arms and knit them together beneath her breasts. He nestled his head against Kawkab's neck and buried his head under her hair. He embraced Kawkab, as if he wanted to absorb her, with a strength that he had never known he had. Kawkab shifted her weight a little, then a little more. Rahmat trembled and tried not to lose touch. He shot a lightning quick glance about him—not a shadow stirred.

Walls surrounded three sides. In front of him there was an alley, and beyond that a few ruins. Beyond the ruins, there were the sandy plains and hills, deserted and still.

"What if someone comes through the alley?"

He heard her, but pretended not to. He pulled away from Kawkab and laid her down next to the wall. He pulled the sackcloth from under them and covered them with it.

When they were about to come down, Kawkab smiled at Rahmat from the top of the stairs. Rahmat blushed and lowered his head, and at night they spread their bedding next to each other.

5

Rahmat was squatting in his place and looking at a spot in the darkness. His eye sockets were dried out and his lips locked tight. He had been motionless in this position for over an hour, as though he were made of wood.

At this time the night before, he was an uncrowned king. He had the run of things under Kawkab's warm and lively roof. He was openhanded and a generous host. The opium pipe was at hand next to the brazier. Whenever his mouth got dry and he felt the urge, he poured himself some tea without a second thought. The box of opium in the tray at the base of the kerosene burner was at his disposal. He could put as much opium in the pipe as he wanted, give it to the customer, and smoke what was left over to "clear the pipe." Their small, two-person pot was simmering and steaming. Bread was on the table and salt, pepper, pickles and everything else was prepared and laid out.

The *korsi* was warm and surrounded by people of every sort you could desire. Everyone had something to say. There was talk of everything—the harvest for the year or the month, dry farming, the drought and cold, the brides who'd been brought to bed and the potential grooms who were engaged for the following year, how last year's snow had flattened several flimsy houses and put one person out of commission—may God have mercy on us this year—and how the snow that had fallen twenty years before had imprisoned people in their own homes, forcing them to dig tunnels and move about under the snow. And the good old days, when wheat, ghee, raisins and walnuts were stacked high in the storage rooms and when purified syrup cost the same as barley, and barley cost one *qeran* for every five *man*. And there were stories of legendary heroes such as Amir Arslan, Fayez and Rostam, the battles of Ohod and Khaybar and 'Omar ebn Abdud, mayhem and massacre, and other such things... these conversations were designed to while the night away and attracted many listeners.

Asadollah Charyari, who claimed to have trekked through every corner of Zabolistan and Baluchistan and to know the streets and alleys of Tehran and the area of Rayy like the back of his hand, would spin yarns about his youth and the trip he had made to Ashkhabad in Russia. Sayyid Musa, a tall man who tied a blue scarf around his waist, sat in one corner leaning against the wall. If he got the chance, he would murmur a few lines of poetry by Najma.

Halimeh was there too. She was mature, corpulent, affable and cute as cute could be. She had rosy cheeks, and a smile never left her lips. She was the life of the party. She never worried about some meddler going to her husband to stir up trouble. She had wrapped up some wheat in the corner of her veil and brought it to obtain a chickpea's weight of opium, the equivalent of two bowlfuls, which she smoked to ease the pain that flared up occasionally in one of her molars. In Rahmat's eyes, her eyes were like those of a mountain gazelle, her thighs like those of a mare. Beneath her veil her fair and plump body was like the tail of a fat-tailed sheep. Her lips were like fire, and she moved about with the elegance of a peacock.

Rahmat had had a crush on Halimeh for a long time, but he was afraid to show it. If anyone caught wind of Rahmat's fantasy, they would make him the town's laughing stock, sitting him back-to-front on a black mule and parading him through the streets.

Rahmat and Halimeh, the wife of the financial officer for the pious foundations, were a world apart. If he set a foot out of bounds, he'd get it chopped off. He knew as much and made do with just looking at her. With all his heart, he wished Halimeh were in his sight every moment, like most of the other customers you couldn't get rid of and who kept coming back for more. They never helped out and just puffed on their cigarettes and pipes, drank their tea, smoked opium, bitched and moaned, brought down curses on heaven and earth and went on their way.

These people only added to one's grief. But Halimeh was not like that. He never tired of seeing her and wanted to smell her. The only time he could see her face and hair up close and feel her breath was when she lay on her side next to the kerosene cooker, rested her head on the pillow, and put her lips to the opium pipe. Sometimes, if her veil fell off, her large, full breasts could be seen through her blouse. But Kawkab denied him even this. She gave Rahmat no opportunity to get up next to Halimeh. She immediately found something for Rahmat to do and took care of Halimeh herself.

Only the night before Kawkab had seen Halimeh pick up a pair of scissors, twine the hair above Rahmat's ear around her finger and say, "I'm going to trim the fur of Kawkab's baboon," just to irritate her and get a laugh. Rahmat laughed then. Kawkab sent Rahmat to a corner of the room and made him sit next to the primus and keep an eye on the cauldron on the kerosene burner to make sure that the opium boiled evenly. She also had Halimeh sit next to her so that she could give her her opium before it was her turn and get her to leave.

It was obvious that she did not want Halimeh's shadow darkening her door, and if she could, she would have kicked her out. She had even lost all her appetite for the half *man* of wheat that Halimeh brought in from time to time. But Halimeh paid her no mind. She had put her hands by the tray and was leaning forward. Her veil had slipped back onto her shoulders, her headscarf was pushed back and her dark hair fell down along both sides of her face. She was telling a story about her husband's night blindness: one night during the holidays last year, his foot had gotten caught in the opening of the well. He hollered so loudly that she was almost scared to death as she sat in the alcove. The neighbors poured into the house from every direction. She complained that she had given him all the liver she could find in the village, but it had done him no good—it only made him fatter and his breath fouler. She described how he counted sugar cubes and put them in the sugar bowl…

She told these stories and laughed along with those sitting with her, all around the *korsi*. Kawkab continued grumbling and fretting. Rahmat was sitting on one knee next to the primus, pricking up his ears and keeping an eye on those waiting their turn with sidelong glances.

Flames from the fire were rising and forming a halo around the cauldron, but it seemed as if he were trying to melt down a kettle of rocks. Rahmat watched a customer move around by the kerosene burner and his spirits sank. Halimeh had taken her hands off the *korsi* and was pulling her headscarf forward, tucking her hair up under it and getting ready to leave. Rahmat was furious and started pumping air into the primus. He felt that the primus and the cauldron were at fault here: were it not for them, Kawkab would go prepare dinner and he would be able to serve Halimeh when it was her turn.

Rahmat worked the pump, and with every stroke the pressure in the primus built up and the basement rumbled more loudly. He did not know what he was doing. When he felt that the flames were dying and saw that Halimeh had gotten up and gone toward Kawkab, veil in hand, he reached the boiling point. He gritted his teeth and pumped more air into the primus. Just then… Kawkab's voice, as though from the bottom of a well, "What's going on? The damn thing is going to explode. May you end up in hell!"

Rahmat jumped up in surprise, as though branded in his sleep. The pump was pulled toward him. The primus shook and the boiling cauldron fell on his leg. He screamed, jumped up and landed on the floor. His leg hit the primus, hurling it toward the dinner pot on the stove, and he rolled about on the floor. He ripped open his pants and freed his leg. A hand's width of his calf was covered with blisters and looked like a camel's tongue. He grabbed it with both hands. The blisters burst under the pressure of his hands, and a colorless liquid seeped through his fingers. He screamed to high heaven and writhed and twisted about like a snake that had just been hit with a shovel.

He howled and flung himself on the floor. He hit the wall, pulled himself up, sat back down, rubbed himself against the floor, got up, fell down, and on and on… until the customers snapped out of their daze. Asadollah Charyari jumped on Rahmat and held him tightly, and the others circled around him.

Rahmat hammered his heels on the floor a few more times and nestled his head against Asadollah's chest until, bit by bit, foam came to his lips and he calmed down. He was seized by a fit of fainting and, as always, his head tilted over onto his shoulder and rested there. They bandaged the blisters. They laid Rahmat down by the *korsi* and everyone sat sourly around it and sobered up.

Half erect, leaning stiffly on her elbows, Kawkab began to speak, "By God, this is the first and last fit he'll have here. By Fatemeh…" Her face raised to the blackened ceiling, she made a fist and struck herself on the chest. Then, in front of everyone present there, she vowed to expel Rahmat the very next day, and may God care for him. She swore that what she had put up with so far was more than seven men could have dealt with.

She made good on her promise.

But to Rahmat, it was as clear as day that Kawkab's heart would not be able to stand firm and that she would send someone to fetch him. But the day passed and there was no sign of anyone. Nightfall was accompanied by a brisk wind. Rahmat was left alone in the alleys of a village where people went to bed at the same time as their chickens. So it was that he came to a public poorhouse, slipped into the pack-saddle belonging to the gypsies' animal, and waited for morning.

6

The moon had risen and the wind carried with it from the desert the sound of a pack of jackals howling. The animal was in the manger and its jaws were moving. The stable was quiet and a cluster of stars appeared through a circular tear in the roof. Rahmat had crawled under his cover like a porcupine, and the whites of his eyes glowed. A man's footsteps approached through the snow. The door of the adjoining room creaked. A pale, round platter of light had fallen on the stable floor. It seemed as though the night had almost passed.

Rahmat went toward the hole and brought his face up to it, so that he saw all of the adjoining room. On the wall across from him, a lantern hung on a nail. A man stood next to it, his eyes fixed on a single spot. He had a bony, dark face like unleavened barley bread. He had a work-hardened body, as coarse as an unfinished piece of lumber. He wore a black cloak that hung down below his knees and had tied a yellow shawl around his waist. His nose was long and rough. He had dark eyes and eyelashes like daggers. His ink-black eyebrows extended almost to his temples, and he wore a camel-colored scarf around his neck and part of his chin. The man looked like a pillar of steel. His was a figure that Rahmat always dreamed about and hoped for; he could do a lot of things with such a body.

The man bent over, undid his boots, took off his cloak and went toward the woman. He sat next to her, leaning on his elbow, and caressed her cheek with his rough hand. Then he lowered his head and kissed her knuckles.

The woman closed her eyes. When she saw her man, a warm smile came to rest on her dark, thick lips. She took his fingers in her hand and pressed them against her chest. They looked at each other for a little while and then the man put the dark brown sackcloth aside and held the woman in his arms. He laid his head by her neck and ear, hooked his hands firmly behind her shoulders, and pressed himself against her for a long moment until the woman's dark hands settled on the back of his neck.

Rahmat, desirous and lustful, watched the gypsy man and woman and could not tear himself away, as though his face were glued to the edges of the hole. The gypsy, still holding the woman in his arms, picked her up and carried her toward the lantern. He turned down the flame and went back under the sackcloth. Three rays of moonlight came through the door, falling on the blanket like three delicate feathers.

Rahmat's throat was dry and his temples were hot. His ears were blazing, as red as pomegranates. His body was burning, as though wine were coursing through his veins. He had never been so seized by passion and, had he been able, he would have torn the earth open and pulled Halimeh out of its depths. The animal snorted and twitched its ears.

Rahmat turned away and sat on the manger. He heard intermittent moans. From the tear in the roof, moonlight shone down on the animal's back, covering the extent of a small felt carpet, and revealed its form more brightly and elegantly. It was lean and fit with firm legs, short, pointed ears and a long, straight neck. It was an animal that one could trust to carry the baggage of two families going from country to country. Its loins were smooth, its thighs corpulent, and its rump round and white, like two dishes of rice.

He was struck by a thought. Desire swept over him from head to foot like a wave and lifted him from the manger... he had forgotten the pain in his leg.

7

Clip-clop... The gypsy recognized the sound and jumped out from under the blanket. In a panic, he turned up the lantern and put on his cloak. He thought a wolf had attacked his donkey... it was snowy and cold and there were no sheep in the fields. The stable door was as flimsy as a breeze and would cave in under a wolf's weight. He picked up his sledgehammer and went to the stable. The donkey had reared on its front legs when the gypsy whistled, and he pushed it aside.

Bent over holding his stomach, Rahmat straightened up. Full of anger, he struck his head against the wall and splayed out at the foot of the manger. The man went toward him and held the lantern near his face. Rahmat's mouth was open and foaming. His eyes were yellow, like two cooked chickpeas lying at the bottom of a bowl. His temple was fractured, and rivulets of blood flowed over his face and mingled with the foam.

The man felt a pain run down his spine and was moved to pity. He looked bitterly at his restive donkey. The donkey stood in a corner of the wall and stared at them. What could he have done to it? Fear overwhelmed him, but to the man who was always on the road such things often happened.

He took the blanket off Rahmat and laid it over him securely. He tied the packsaddle on the donkey and led it out. He latched the stable door and went to the adjoining room. He gathered in the blanket, picked up the anvil, and began packing his belongings.

His wife asked, "What was it?"

The desert was barren. The moon was setting. The woman was catnapping on the donkey. The lantern swung from the saddlebag frame. And the man was still silent.

Nasim Khaksar

1944–

Expatriate short-story writer and political activist, Nasim Khaksar was born and raised in Abadan. He graduated from the Institute of Higher Education in Tehran with a degree in teacher education and began literary activity with the publication of short stories from the late 1960s.

His collection called *Man midānam bacheh'hā dust dārand bahār biyāyad* (I know children want spring to come) appeared in 1974. But because Khaksar was imprisoned from the early 1970s until early 1978, his writing from this period did not get published until the end of the 1970s; examples of such works are *Agar ādamhā hamdigar rā dust bedārand* (If people would love one another, 1978), *Giyāhak* (The embryo, 1979), and *Rowshanfekr-e kuchek* (The little intellectual, 1981). Four of Khaksar's stories appeared in *Ketāb-e jom'eh* (1979–80) and two in *Nāmeh-ye kānun-e nevisandegān-e Irān* (1979–80), while his collection of three connected stories called *Gāmhā-ye paymudan* (Measured steps) appeared in 1982.

Khaksar fled Iran for Europe in the early 1980s after being imprisoned by the Islamic Republic. Consequently, from the mid-1980s on, Khaksar's stories have been published outside of Iran: *Qesseh-ye kucheh-ye biqavāreh va chahār pir-e zan* (The tale of the crooked alley and the four old women, 1988), *Baqqāl-e Kharzavil: majmu'eh-ye dāstānhā-ye tab'id* (The grocer: a collection of stories of exile, 1989), and *Morā'i kafer ast* (Mora'i is an infidel, 1989). *Akherin nāmeh; va, Bāyad haqiqat rā be-mardum guft: dunamāyeshnāmeh* (1990), *Qafas-e tuti-e Jahān Khānum* (1991), *Badnomāhā va shallāqhā* (1996), *Ahuvān dar barf: dāstānhā-ye tab'id* (1996), *Mā va jah_n-e tab'id: majmu'eh-i maqāleh, mos_hebah, naqd va goftogu* (1999), *Māhi'hā-ye sardin: va, namāyesh'nāmeh'hā-ye digar* (2000), *Rāsteh-e Arizunā: majmu'ah-e dāstān'hā-ye tab'id* (2001). In addition to fiction, Khaksar also wrote a book about his travels in Tajikistan, *Safar-e Tājekestān* (1994).

In the late 1980s Khaksar served on the board of directors of the European-based Association of Iranian Writers in Exile. He also contributed articles to the London-based journal *Fasl-e ketāb* in the late 1980s and early 1990s.

Night Journey

Translated by Fariba Zarinebaf-Shahr

The driver turned the wheel when the light hit the fellow's chest, but
was unable to drive on. He would have if he could. The man was
standing in the middle of the road, making it impossible for the driver to pass. When he put his foot on the brake, the man lowered his
hands. He was crippled from the waist down, like someone who had
been shot in the leg.

The driver said, "Lame son of a bitch."

The cold rushed in when he opened the door.

The driver said again, "Lame son of a bitch."

He had wrapped his face in a kaffiyeh, leaving only his eyes visible. He placed the sack he was carrying on his back by the door and
closed it.

The driver was still angry. He said irritably, "What do you have
on you?"

"Nothing. Don't be afraid." His voice came out muffled by the
kaffiyeh.

The driver said, "I'm not going to give you a ride. You've got to
tell me what you have with you."

"Henna."

"Yeah, right! Sure you do! Do you want to ruin my reputation?"

His eyes were small and deep-set; he was small himself. The way he had bent under the sack made him look smaller. The shoulder of his worn-out jacket was torn. It was torn on both sides.

He said, "That's not my style, brother."

The driver said, "What a way to stop a bus! Weren't you afraid of being run down?"

He pulled himself together. "Why should I? I've been waiting for a bus in the cold for two hours. If you hadn't run me down, I would've frozen stiff."

The driver calmed down. "I'd throw you out if you weren't lame. Why should I make trouble for myself?" And he slowly stepped on the gas. "I haven't been able to drive on this goddamned road one single night without saying prayers for protection. I swear I'm not going to drive at night anymore."

He turned his head. "I got stuck in the police station for two days on account of one of these bums, only last week." And he pointed to the man. "Pardon me, mister, maybe you don't do these kinds of things."

The man did not even blink. The bus was moving slowly. It had rained all day long. The reflection of the headlights on the road shone brightly. The night was dark and hazy. No stars were visible in the sky. A thick layer of condensation had fogged the windshield. The road was so wet that the bus could not move any faster. The man was sitting on his sack, his back against the door, not moving at all. He was still feeling the cold. He had put his hands in his pockets, and his shoulders shivered from time to time.

It started drizzling again. The droplets of rain speckled the windshield. The driver turned the wiper on. The bus had only one wiper, which cleaned a space in front of him. The road was wet; headlights were reflected brightly. As soon as the driver stepped on the brake, the man understood. He knew before anyone else.

The driver said, "Hell! Now we're in for it!"

The man stood up, looking through the window at the road. They were oil-company guards. Their guns glinted when the light fell on their wet, brown uniforms. Two of them were armed.

The man was half-standing on the sack. With one hand he was holding the sack, and with the other, the door. As the first guard opened the door, the man sprang like a tiger, pushing him off, and jumped down as fast as lightning. The second guard, who was standing by the door, fell down. By the time he had gotten up, the man had run away through the mud. They both chased him. In the midst of splashes in the darkness and the constant noise of the falling rain, the voice of someone shouting "Stop!" rang out. It was repeated twice. The third call was drawn-out and frightening, causing the listeners to hold their breath. When the sound of two shots rang through the air, the road was blocked to traffic.

The driver thought, I would get the hell out of here if my lights were working.

The driver was so scared he was shaking. The road was lost in the darkness. The guards returned alone. The man had gotten away. There was a lot of mud, so much that it had blocked their way.

Climbing into the bus, the guard said: "Did you warn him? We'll fix you! Obstructing an officer, eh?"

The driver said, "I swear I didn't know," and rose from his seat. "Ask the passengers. Ask any one of them."

Everybody was silent. They were numbed by the cold air that had rushed in.

The second guard was wiping the mud off his boot. The guard who had been knocked down asked, "Are you claiming you didn't know him?"

The driver said, "I swear by the life of my children that I didn't know anything. Nobody knew anything. He tricked us all by saying he was carrying henna."

The guard looked around, then looked at his colleague. The second guard came up; he was an acquaintance of the driver. He said to the driver: "Bravo, Jabur!"

The driver said, "I swear by our friendship that I didn't know anything. The passengers can testify to it."

One of the passengers volunteered, "He is telling the truth — we're all shocked, the driver is paying for his kindness. You know, officer, he felt guilty leaving someone waiting in the cold night. Besides, we urged him to do it."

The guard who had been struck was even more irritated. They ordered the driver to move, after they completed their investigation. They decided to get off at the police station. It was still raining.

The first guard said, "I'll catch him even if it takes me till morning."

The second one was putting on his gun.

"The rain will take care of him. He can't stay in the mud forever. The cold will finish him off."

It began to warm up again. The bus was moving slowly. The tires were sticking to the wet road, sounding as if they were rolling over melted asphalt on a mid-summer afternoon. The dim lights of the police station looked even dimmer in the rain. The guards got off after the bus stopped. The first one warned the driver, "Mind who you pick up!"

The driver said, "You bet!" He was relieved.

"What a strange fellow he was... whew!"

One of them added, "Strange all right, acting so innocent!"

The driver said, "I'm glad he pulled it off, but I'm afraid he'll get caught."

Someone said, "If he is caught, they'll make mincemeat out of him."

"Those animals are mad as wet hens," the driver agreed as he stepped on the gas. "We were lucky."

It was pouring. The sound of the tires squeaking over the wet road could be heard. The light hitting the road signs made them look like someone crouching by the road. From a distance they appeared ready to leap up. It was dark, with lightning occasionally illuminating the plain, bringing the rocks and hills into view for a moment. The driver stopped the bus before a teahouse.

"I'm going to check the engine and smoke a *qalyan*, if you don't mind."

Four loaded trucks were standing in front of the teahouse. The drivers were relaxing in the corner, drinking tea. The bus driver checked the engine. In addition to the drivers, a few rough-looking men were sitting on a bench in their raincoats, smoking *qalyans*. When the driver entered the room, the boy prepared a *qalyan* for him. A bus stopped in front, its passengers trooping into the teahouse. The driver stood up after finishing his tea. Everybody else followed him out.

It had stopped raining. The man appeared before everybody had sat down. He came out through the trailers. He was wet through and muddy up to his knees. The sack was still on his back. When he opened the door, the driver said gently: "Where the hell did you go?" and made room for him. "Come on, get in and get warmed up."

The man was relieved. He was wet all over. When he took off his kaffiyeh, his face appeared. It was wrinkled and brown. His unshaven beard made him look older. A thin furrow reached under his chin. His eyes, which had no lashes, appeared deep-set and small. As he squeezed the water out of his kaffiyeh, he said, "I knew they were not brave enough when I ran into the mud."

The driver asked, "Didn't they catch you at the station?"

Still squeezing the kaffiyeh, he said: "I walked through the mud until I came up behind the station."

He was leaning his head on the seat and his thin shoulders were shaking.

"I was lucky enough to catch a ride after that point."

The driver said, "Weren't you afraid of being run down?"

He laughed weakly. "Someone who sets out on the road at night shouldn't be afraid of being hit."

He was still cold. His voice was trembling when he spoke.

He said: "The tea sack was wrapped in plastic, but all the cigarettes still got wet." And he turned his head toward the back.

"Is anyone interested in buying cheap Winstons?"

The driver said, "Yes."

"They're wet."

"It doesn't matter."

The bus was moving faster, the sound of its wet tires getting louder.

The man said, "I'm selling them real cheap, the same price I bought them for."

The driver turned his head and looked at him from time to time. The man was sitting peacefully, arranging the cigarettes he had taken out of his shirt. It was dark outside and occasional flashes of lightning lit up the plain and the hills, so that they looked like figures lying in ambush in the dark.

Amin Faqiri

1944–

Born and raised in Shiraz, Amin Faqiri began writing when was nineteen, concentrating on poetry. He served in the Iranian Literacy Corps in the mid-1960s as a teacher and community developer in various rural communities in Kerman and Fars provinces. That experience inspired Faqiri's focus in his writing on specific rural Iranian settings and issues.

His first book, a collection of seventeen stories called *Dehkadeh-ye por-malāl* (Depressed village, 1969), received immediate critical attention and approval, especially for its realistic depiction of village life. It was reprinted in 1970 and printed a third time in 1974. Faqiri followed that book with five other collections of stories in the 1970s: *Kucheh bāgh'hā-ye ezterāb* (Garden paths of anxiety, 1970), *Kufiyān* (The Kufans, 1971), *Ghamhā-ye kuchek* (Small sorrows, 1973), and *Sayri dar jāzbeh va dard* (A journey into rapture and pain, 1974). Two novels were announced as published in the 1970s: *Saqqezi* (The person from Saqqez) and *Daf barā-ye 'arusi-ye hamsāyeh* (Tambourine for the neighbor's wedding).

From 1979 to the end of the 1980s, Faqiri published *Sokhan az jangal-e sabz ast-o tabardār-o tabar* (I talk of green woods and axmen and axes, 1979), *Do cheshm-e kuchek-e khandān* (Two small, smiling eyes, 1986), *Tamām-e bārānhā-ye donyā* (All the rain in the world, 1988), and *Muyeh'hā-ye montasher* (Spreading lamentation, 1989). His output decreased in the 1990s, being limited to *Gozideh-e dāstānhā-ye Amin Faqiri: 1347-1368* and a 1996 novel, *Raqsāndagān*.

The Sad Brothers

Translated by Sholeh Quinn

We were always afraid of the basement. If you stood in it for ten minutes, your eyes still would not get used to that strange and hideous darkness. Grown-ups would say, "That place is as dark as the grave." When we took a lamp with us, it would not light up more than one meter around us. I was never brave enough to go there alone. Perhaps my brothers were the same way. When they went down the five stairs and reached the basement, they would be terrified even by my soft, small footsteps. My eldest brother would say, "Is it you again?"

I would laugh and fix my eyes on the darkness. My next-older brother would say, "He must have lost someone down here. The darkness seems to have cast a spell on him." There was still enough light next to the basement steps that the dense darkness would try to ward off even that tiny bit of light. My father would advise us, "At least don't go there barefoot. There are many snakes and scorpions. Who knows what creatures are stirring there?"

My father would often drag someone over and show him the basement, in order to get rid of all the junk in it. But each time when the man came up the basement stairs, he would be white-faced and stutter, "This place is as dark as the grave."

My father would say, "I'll set up a light for you. If something catches your eye, keep it."

The man would not be taken in by this fanciful offer. At evening time my brother and I would go and close the basement door, which was full of cracks. As soon as the sun went down, the high walls of the house and the pamelo tree, which reached above the walls, made the house appear sad and weary, and the stained-glass windows would take on a turbid and lifeless appearance. We were afraid and would say to ourselves, "Let's close the basement door to postpone, perhaps, the coming of night to our house."

Father would just read the paper. Even if he was not home we would still feel his presence sitting next to the stone lion's head near the pond and watching our imaginary world. During one of these evenings, when the sky was full of clouds and the leaves of the pamelo seemed darker, and the water of the pond was dirty and gloomy, and the clouds' black shadows made the water seem as if it was far from being water, the basement door shook violently. All at once the color left our faces. Terrified, all three of us looked at each other. Father was not at home. The noise grew louder and louder. Should we open it?

We were frightened and uncertain. My next older brother said, "Let's go tell the neighbors."

After thinking a while my eldest brother said, "Do you want them to say there's a jinni in the teacher's house? Everyone will say our house is haunted and that would be very bad."

His logic was sound, but there was no limit to our fear. The shaking of the basement door went on and on. It was as if all the small doors and the windows, with their faded window panes, were shaking. Something must be done. This thought passed through all our minds. We must do something, because if we did not, all these earthquake-like shocks might destroy all the supports of the house. Frightened and trembling, all three of us advanced. A soft light broke through cracks in the basement door, which mightily astonished us. A hundred years seemed to pass from the time my brother put out his hand to open the door until he undid the latch. There, on the top step behind the door, a small creature somewhat resembling a chicken regarded us with brown eyes, and light was emanating from its body. We were enthralled.

I do not know how long we looked at it. Our hands involuntarily reached out toward it. It did not startle or draw back. It only acted a bit coy. A moment later, the shining creature was in my brother's hands. My brother looked at it lovingly. We were all enamored of it. At that very moment, we wished to possess it. Despite its being so magnificent, it seemed very, very helpless.

My brother said, "We will raise it."

My next oldest brother asked, "Should we tell father or not?"

I said, "What about Grandmother?"

Our eldest brother angrily shouted, "No one! Only us!"

We said, "Where will we keep it?"

"Right here in the basement."

We said, "Let's hope it will eat what we eat."

My eldest brother said, "Bring a piece of bread."

We tore up the bread. The bird seemed to have been hungry for years. In the twinkling of an eye, the pieces of bread disappeared.

Then we brought water. It drank and was satisfied. The rays of its light totally illuminated our bodies.

It did not have feathers yet. It had no wings. But its size had increased. It had the fragrance of a naked baby, and its flesh was just like soft cotton. The basement was very bright. We looked all around. There wasn't anything there except for some junk, which smelled old and damp.

Father said to grandmother, "What are they doing in that basement, which is full of scorpions and snakes?" Then he looked at us and said, "You mean you aren't afraid of the dark? At least take a lamp with you."

We looked at each other in astonishment. Doesn't our father know anything? Has he not even seen the light when it shines through the cracks of the door at night? He definitely had not seen it, otherwise he would have looked in the basement out of curiosity.

Grandmother said, "We must pray for the children. God forbid that they have had any dealings with jinn! Certainly harm has befallen them. Poor kids, they are always busy with themselves. Heaven knows what they are doing."

And immediately, without father's consent, she went to the amulet writer, obtained prayers in leather bindings for each of us, and pinned them to our lapels. This brought us closer to each other and to the strange creature.

We would sit there for hours and stare at it. The basement had become our playroom. Sometimes we brought our food there, concealed from Grandmother's eyes, and we ate next to the shining creature. That wingless bird shared the food with us. It took each morsel straight from our hands.

How? We were puzzled. Anything in our hands simply disappeared straight into its mouth.

Brother said, "Everything about it is like a bird except it doesn't have feathers or wings. It must learn how to fly."

My heart trembled. If it flies, our basement will be dark forever. On the other hand, this damp basement is not worthy of such a creature.

From the next day on, we set about collecting feathers. We stood in the bazaar and kept an eye on everyone who came to Sayyid Ahmad the butcher with a chicken to be slaughtered. The next day, we took the feathers from his rubbish pail. We washed them clean and stuck them into the body of our featherless bird. This was a torment for it, but it bore the pain. Soon most parts of it were covered with feathers, and the amazing thing was that the feathers grew. Whatever color the feathers had been, they grew out in a fiery red color. A color just like the flames of a fire—a purple red—perhaps a shade of red without a name. Our bird had everything except wings. How could it fly without wings? But then it happened that we got a chicken in our house because of the holiday. All three of us took the chicken to Sayyid Ahmad the butcher's shop. We saw our eldest brother quietly saying something to Sayyid Ahmad the butcher, but we could not understand it. Only when father stared into my brother's face, saying, "Where are its wings?" did we understand that Sayyid Ahmad had cut the wings from the body.

My brother said, "To make up for the missing wings, I will not eat anything."

Father's anger soon subsided. At the table, no one was thinking about the wings except for us. We knew that the strange creature now had the shape of a bird. When it flew everyone would envy us and say to themselves: The teacher's house has a bird the color of fire!

The wings grew. The years passed. Despite the fact that we kept the basement door open, the bird did not attempt to fly away. We thought: What better place than the pomelo tree, which has abundant branches and leaves? We stood across from it and flapped our arms, to teach it that it must fly, otherwise it would rot in that basement with the dense color of night. And as a sign of agreement, it flapped its wings; but it did not fly. We were heartbroken. All birds fly. Even those that are in cages break open the doors and tear off into the sky. Why didn't our bird, which was more beautiful than all

other birds, fly? We must be proud of it. It should not stay in the basement, not even able to walk around the stone pond.

In the depths of despair, when we were sadder than the bird, suddenly we saw the fiery bird standing in the yard, flapping its wings. Together we flapped our arms with it. The brick patio and the dampness of our house had come alive. The trees once again had turned to spring. We, in a mystical rapture, continued to dance passionately around the bird. Time seemed to stand still. We did not understand anything. Our existence had become one with the bird's. We circled around each other. The bird smiled at us as if it was thanking us. With each round of dancing it grew. Now its body was the size of a stork's. All at once we all became silent. We were waiting for something to happen. Our anxiety communicated itself to the bird. Painfully trying, it rose from the ground and got itself to the edge of the pond. We waited for hours and our hearts bled, until it moved. It alighted on the shortest branch of the pomelo tree. We hoped that after perching there a few moments it would again alight at the edge of the pond. But suddenly it flew higher—three meters—to the edge of the roof. We quickly went to the rooftop. We were happy. It flapped its wings a few more times and flew to the top of the small roof.

The neighbor's wall was higher. My brother yelled, "If it flies over there, they will steal a bird of this beauty. Who has a bird this color? Like a ball of fire! It has turned everything purple. Wherever it lands it turns that place to fire. Oh, my God. It's flown."

The bird flew up and alighted on the neighbors' rooftop. The yard of the house turned red. The green leaves were no longer green. The windows were all red.

The neighbors asked, "What are you doing on our rooftop?"

We said, "We want our bird."

They looked. Their yard had turned red. It seemed as if they had not noticed it until now.

They looked for a while together. A strange glow filled their eyes.

"Your bird? This is ours. If it was yours it would be in your house. No one here knew that you had such a bird."

My brother yelled, "You're lying! You didn't have the slightest inkling of its existence. You were surprised to see it."

The neighbors said, "We'll not listen to anymore of this. Whoever catches it keeps it."

We felt confident. We had kept the bird for years. It was impossible for it to give its heart to someone else. I could still feel its beating heart in my hands. I was certain my brothers felt the same way.

The bird took off again. It tried to choose a higher place. The city had turned red. People had poured onto the rooftops. We were lost in the mass of people. The sky was red. The sun could not be seen. You could not tell whether it was day or night. No one paid attention to our shouts and cries. Our bird flew higher each moment, but it didn't look much like flying: it was more like struggling. It flew like a dead weight.

My brother said, "It's afraid. It can't fly into the sky. People will catch it. There'll be a tremendous row."

Our bird flew, ten meters, five meters, two meters at a time, soaring even higher. We did not have anywhere higher than the tall city tower. Somehow, it managed to fly up there. It stood in such a way as if it wanted to speak to the people. My brother started to climb up the base of the tower. All the people stood anxiously under the red umbrella which was spread over the city. We were anxious for our brother; we told the people that this was our brother, and we described how we had raised the bird.

The people treated us like fools. They mocked us.

"How did you get hold of such a bird?"

No one believed our story. They thought it was childlike imagination. My brother got closer to the bird. It was strange that no one else had found the courage to climb the tower. Everyone stared at my brother. Even though we were scared, we also felt proud.

The wind blew and constricted the red expanse. My brother reached out his hand to grab the bird.

The bird made as if to throw itself into my brother's arms. But it dropped like a stone into the air, and no sound arose upon its impact with the ground. It flapped its wings two or three times and fell silent.

A strong wind blew from the far side of the world. It whirled everything into confusion. It pounded everything together. The tower broke from its center and collapsed. The bird was no longer a bird. It wasn't anything. The crowd burst like a bubble and melted away.

Shahrnush Parsipur

1946-

The daughter of an attorney in the Justice Ministry originally from
Shiraz, Shahrnush Parsipur was born and raised in Tehran, studied
Chinese culture in France from 1976-79, and graduated from the
Faculty of Letters at Tehran University. Her first book was *Tupak-e
qermez* (The little red ball, 1969), a story for young people. Her first
short stories were published in the late 1960s. Her novella
Tajrobeh'hā-ye āzād(Trial offers, 1970) was followed by the novel *Sag
va zemestān-e boland* (The dog and the long winter), published in
1976. Then came a volume of short stories called *Āvizeh'hā-ye bolur*
(Crystal pendant earrings, 1977).

By the late 1980s, Parsipur was receiving considerable attention
in Tehran literary circles, with the publication of several of her stories and several notices and a lengthy interview with her in *Donyā-ye
sokhan*. Parsipur's second novel was *Tubā va ma'nā-ye shab*(Tuba and
the meaning of night, 1989), which Parsipur wrote after spending
four years in prison. Right before her incarceration, she had published a translation called *Zanān-e romān'nevis* (Woman novelists,
1984) of a book by Michelle Mercier.

In 1990 appeared a short novel, again consisting of connected stories, called *Zanān-e bedun-e mardān* (Women without men), which
Parsipur had finished in 1976. The Iranian government banned the
novel in mid-1990 and put pressure on the Parsipur to desist from
such writing. Thus, from 1992 on, all her fiction has been published
overseas, primarily in California and Sweden. These works include:
Tajrobeh'hā-ye āzād: majmu'ah-i dāstānhā-ye be-ham payvastek(1992),
Adāb-e sarf-e chay dar hozur-e gorg: majmu'ah-e dāstān va maq_lah
(1993), *Aql-e ābi* (1994), *Khāterat-e zendān*(1996), *Mājarā'hā-ye sādeh
va kuchak-e ruh-e derakht* (1999), *Shivā: yak dāstān-dānes* (2000).
Despite being published in exile, Parsipur's influence on other writers has been huge. In 1999, a collection of short stories by Iranian
women dedicated to her appeared: *Az rāh residan va bāzgasht:
majmu'ah'i az dāstānhā-ye kārgāh-e dāstān'nevisi-e Shahrnush Par-
si'pur*. An English translation of *Women Without Men* was published
in the U.S. in 1998. The only work of Parsipur's to appear in Iran
since 1990 is her translation of Chinese stories, *Tārikh-e Chin*.

Trial Offers

Translated by Paul Sprachman

The man was dancing—or doing something like it—in the rain which jumped steamily from the street. I was depressed and had left the house in search of relief, going all the way down the road in the rain that continued to fall and clung to the skin like the dampness of a cold dawn by the sea.

The man was on a street—green from end to end—and his outline, which thanks to the rain was barely visible, broke the continuous line of trees. The man raised his right leg, did a half-pirouette and spread his arms. It was as though he wanted to embrace some form that embodied the rain. Now he put his right leg and his arms down. He waited a moment and then raised his left leg. It was clear that he wanted to reverse his previous move and that he was not as deft with the left foot as he was with the right. Clumsily he made the half-turn and all of a sudden fell flat on the ground.

"What are you looking at?" he asked. "Doesn't anybody have rights around here? God almighty, isn't it a free country? I'll file a complaint against you."

Then he got up from the ground in anger. His raincoat was completely soiled. "I swear to God, that's what I'm going to do. Where does a person have to go to get away from these busybodies, tell me, huh?"

Having removed his raincoat and given it a few futile shakes in the air, he muttered something and turned on me. Intruding was the last thing on my mind.

He said, "It seems like you people have nothing to do but butt in on folks when they want to be left alone. Who gave you permission to be such a snoop? Where the hell can I hide to be rid of your prying? Damn bodywasher take the lot of you!"

"Sir, you'd better be civil," I said. "I didn't intend to watch you. You were dancing in the street when…"

He said, "So I was dancing, what's it to you? Are you some kind of self-appointed representative of the people? Doesn't a man have the right to dance? Is that so unusual? Isn't dancing one of man's God-given gifts? Did you think that you're the only one who has the right to dance? Quite to the contrary, may it please you to learn… bastards!"

"Mister… but… b…" I said.

"That's right, I'm Mr. B, what's your point?" he answered. "You want to turn me in? Go ahead, the hell with you. Who's afraid of you?"

"Mr. B," I said, "your dance was quite beautiful. I was just passing by when I saw you and was taken by it."

"Why, what was so special about it?"

" 'Cause you were dancing in the rain and I hadn't seen anyone dance in the rain till now."

Mr. B put his raincoat back on and became quite involved in buttoning it. It appeared that I no longer interested him. But, when I started to go, he said, "Wait!" I returned and looked at him. "You said something that…" he continued, "I sort of liked. Could you say why you find dancing in the rain so interesting?"

I told him that I hadn't thought about dancing in the rain till then, and so on. Sometimes things just happen that way.

"Yes, yes," he said, "it's like that when the spark of genius ignites— for example, if you and I were in America, we would put our heads together and make dancing in the rain the latest craze, and in a few years we'd be millionaires." He laughed suddenly and said, "After we'd become millionaires, the tax notices would follow and, if we had earned two million, we'd have to give half to the tax collector… There'd be nothing left for us but to flee to Switzerland immediately."

He then watched me in the rain and carefully tried to read the reaction in my eyes. "But we live here now and have no such commercial opportunities; we won't become millionaires and naturally won't flee to Switzerland. See how simple it all is?"

Mr. B had now worked himself into a frenzy and was cackling. "Do you see? If we were anywhere but here, it would be different... I mean that even if we were right here but different people, the possibilities are endless... it's fascinating."

Mr. B's eyes were a little red and his pupils quivered imperceptibly. I couldn't tell whether he was making fun of me or had something else in mind. He even seemed to be an affectionate person. There was a light in his eyes that you might say was a spark of affection.

Smiling, I asked, "Mr. B, are you drunk?"

"Oh no, I just wet two centimeters of my whistle, that's all. You see? Now you are accusing me of being drunk—is it any of your business, really? I don't think there's any refuge from you people... what did you say your name was, by the way?"

I told him my name. Mr. B explained that a strange feeling always came over him when it rained, "Like sometimes when I hear the beat of a drum, tada tada, tadadum... I must dance. How can you keep from dancing when the drum beats?" Suddenly he looked at me and said, "You seem to me like a well-fed girl." I looked at him in astonishment. He added, "I mean that you haven't wanted for food."

"That's right."

"Me too, I've almost never been hungry."

"It's good for a person never to feel hunger."

"Yes, very good."

He thought for a while and then quickly added, "As long as you don't go hungry just for the hell of it. I'm often hungry. You know, sometimes I eat like a cow but then I'm hungry again. It hurts... I just lied to you: I'm hungry most of the time." Then he asked, "How about you?"

"What about me?"

"You're not hungry, you don't feel hungry?"

"No, sir," I said and smiled at the thought that just occurred to me.

"Why are you smiling?" he asked.

"Look, I'm not hungry exactly, but I do crave something."

"What's that?"

"A good, upstanding, and noble husband."

B said, "Odd. Poor child, and how are you going about finding that husband?"

"I go out walking the streets hoping to get lucky."

B looked at me very seriously and asked, "Excuse my asking, but you're making fun of me, aren't you?"

I was taken aback. I said, "No, Mr. B, not at all. I just thought I would joke a little."

"Fine, fine, no problem, go ahead and joke."

He then returned to his previous mood. This was the first man I had ever encountered who would get himself worked up so quickly and then just as quickly become quite calm. Later, during our long walk in the rain among the trees, he said that an avenue was the most beautiful of God's inventions. "The best of man's inventions," he corrected himself. And then he said that of course the avenue issue is rooted in economics and urbanization and, in short, in other kinds of chicanery, but an avenue itself is genuinely good. An avenue is the continuation of a thought that reaches a square, turns round and goes back for one hundred and twenty million years with one hundred and twenty million years of decomposition and growth again behind it. Then he said, "Despite all this, when I'm out on the avenue, I'm afraid of people... you're not afraid?"

"I'm not sure," I said, "sometimes I have weird thoughts, but I don't know whether it's fear of dying or whether I'm just imagining things."

He asked, "For example?"

"For example, I thought that my yesterday was on Mars."

"So why should it be on Mars?"

"I don't know... see, it was yesterday and I remember that it was, but now I don't know where it is... maybe each of my days goes to one of the planets... couldn't it be like this, what with all the planets in the universe?"

"Sure," he said, "but why? Must it be that way?"

I said, "It's got to be somewhere, after all."

"Certainly, certainly," he replied, "it's got to be somewhere." He thought for a while and asked, "Where's tomorrow? Do you know?"

I said, "I have a theory of my own. Some of the planets are negative and others are positive. Our tomorrows are on the positive planets and our yesterdays are on the negative ones. Then the days just change places until they reach today, here."

"O.K.," he said, "so it's like that. What does that have to do with dying?"

"This," I replied. "Today I died on one of the positive planets. Maybe during the next four years, but it may take four years for the days to change places for the day to reach here and for me to actually die. It will take four years and a day for my death day to reach the first negative planet and on and on until the end... until on one of the remote negative planets I'm conceived once again, while at the same time I have already died on some of the other planets."

B said, "Even so, you still have to die, there's no escape in the end. One day you will die here." He nodded his head impatiently. "We've become regular philosophers."

We walked on in silence for a while. When we stopped in front of a little hole-in-the-wall liquor store, B asked, "Is it okay if you continue walking like this while I stop in for a quick one? I'll gulp it down and be right back, you know."

"Fine," I said.

B almost ran into the store. I went on slowly. I had been strolling with this newfound friend for a couple of hours and the time had passed quickly. For a moment I was terrified of being alone. I thought that I would go as far as the trees and if he did not return I would go home quickly. The trees were five or six steps away. Before I reached the trees, B took me by the arm and asked, "You didn't wait long, did you?"

"No," I said, "you returned quickly."

He said, "I didn't have anything... would you mind if I nursed this as we walked?" The front of his raincoat was puffed up.

"No," I said, "go ahead."

"So let's talk," he said.

"About what?"

"What we've been talking about until now."

We had arrived at the first avenue; until that moment it felt as though we had returned to the avenue several times. We sat in the archway of a house. B drank a little from the bottle and lit a cigarette we both smoked. Whenever a stranger approached we would hide in the archway and cover the smoke with our hands. There was a terrible silence.

I said, "Mr. B, I think that it's really good for a person to make friends on the street like this. It has one advantage at least: you don't have to explain the obvious."

B's mind seemed elsewhere, "Explain what, my dear?"

"Explain the obvious." I didn't know what that meant myself, I was just making conversation.

He said, "Look, don't call me 'Mr. B,' okay? Just B. It's better that way."

"Have you ever made friends with somebody like this before?" I asked.

"I have made nearly all my friends that way."

"Women too?" I asked.

"Them even more. Mostly late at night, just like this."

"B," I said, "I hope our friendship lasts. I like people who are direct and sincere."

"How do you know I'm one of those people? Tell me," he said as he took my hand and kissed it.

"I don't know," I said, "I just think so."

"Don't think that I can become a friend to you like other men. You are, after all, a woman. Understand?"

"Yes, I understand," I said.

"In any case, don't think that I can be like one of your girl friends. I don't know girls very well. I taught in a girls' school once a long time ago, until they threw me out."

"Why did they throw you out?"

"I slapped one of them. By the way, why are girls so coy?"

"I don't know," I said.

"It doesn't matter. We will just become friends. It'll happen somehow." Then he placed the palm of my hand on his rough cheek and we remained that way for a long time.

We talked a lot as we were going back. His father and mother had died a long time ago. He worked in an office, but always dreamed of a business of his own. He once had the idea of escaping to Canada, but they didn't give him a visa. When he finally got a visa, he had already given up the idea of Canada. "I don't think about positive and negative planets. I learned long ago to live for the moment. If it snows and my room is warm, I can stay in bed a million years and listen to the kettle boil. You don't know how good it feels."

We were in front of my house. I said, "B, this is my house."

He said, "Fine. Can we see each other again?"

I said, "Of course." We made a date. Then he kissed my hand like an English gentleman and said good-bye. His looks and clothes made such a spectacle that you would think he was acting. But it seemed that he was serious.

2

One day my father returned from work accompanied by a prospective suitor. My suitor was perfect. He was as tall as a cypress. Of course he wasn't that muscular, and now that I think about it, he wasn't all that tall, either. What recommended him was his good position as a deputy head—he had prospects. There was this also: my suitor was not actually there to woo me. Apparently he was a friend whom my father had designated "company." In our courtyard there was a large wading pool full of blue waterlilies which my father liked. The suitor was also the kind of person who could extol water lilies. In addition to all this, his first name was Fereydun and his surname was Yaganeh.

In the beginning, when Mr. Yaganeh was not a suitor, we were friends, and the first time we had a serious conversation was toward the end of some gathering. He was quite frank when he told me that I was the type of girl whom he had always praised, "...affable and talkative. The man who gets you will be lucky indeed." Later I realized that this was the moment that he was to make his choice. Afterwards he was found in our home more frequently, bearing little gifts for me which he would present to me in front of the family so I couldn't refuse them.

Mr. Yaganeh was twenty-seven years old, but he had the gravity of a forty-year-old. His suitorship little by little became unquestioned.

One day I saw B in front of the university. He had come looking for me. Without a hello, I said, "B, I'm almost engaged."

I wasn't sure whether B's reaction was one of surprise or chagrin. He said, "Congratulations."

We went to B's house. On the way we bought something for dinner. I said, "I think that my fiancé is waiting for me at home right now."

B said that if I preferred I could leave. I didn't want to. When we were eating, I said, "B, he is a man of substance, a deputy head."

"Oh!" B said, laying his fork, with which he had speared a tomato, on his plate. "No, no. Not a deputy head, for the love of God."

"What's the problem?" I asked.

"Look, my dear, what good is a deputy head to you? A deputy is neither here nor there. He's not a director, nor is he directed."

"B," I said, "my fiancé aspires to chief directorship, while his head inclines toward bald and his physique toward fat."

B said, "No. No. Look, either wait till he becomes a chief director or don't marry him at all. Don't make trouble for yourself."

"Why?"

"Well, there's always the possibility that he will remain a deputy forever. Then what'll you do?"

"My task will be to consider myself the wife of a deputy director."

"No," said B, "it's not right at all." He was completely lost in thought. Then he remembered that my fiancé had notions of becoming chief director and burst out laughing. We both laughed for a time. B began to make fun of me: "Do you really want to become Mrs. Deputy? Of course, you will become active in women's organizations, too. Right?"

He was really happy now. It occurred to him that the source of all this happiness was probably the finding of a fiancé for me. I said, "B, if you want me to get rid of this fiancé,"—he was not listening—"If you want, I can marry you."

I felt my ears getting red. B said that he had never given the matter any thought. We lay together on the bed. Outside it was cold and B's stove was quite warm. B kissed my fingers and spoke with them. How much I would have loved to become his wife. Until that moment I had never considered this to be a good idea. I asked him, "B, what's wrong with our getting married?"

"And having children."

"Yes, and having children, at least one child."

"Who will be a beautiful roly-poly girl."

"Nope, a boy. I like boys better. I want to have a boy."

"You're so old-fashioned. What's wrong with girls? Think of it: she'll babble for you, put your shoes on. Then grow up and fall in love and all the rest of it."

"I don't think I like the idea of continuing myself."

"You wouldn't be continuing, the girl would."

"No, B, a boy is better."

"I say a girl."

"No, a boy."

B said, "Did it ever occur to you that there's a twenty-year age difference between us?"

"Doesn't make the least bit of difference."

"It's very important, I feel. You ever get a good look at me? The difference is that every day you'll have to wake up to this wrinkled, baggy face."

"I'll probably get used to it."

"Then I won't be able to stand it. I'll watch you blossom and shine with your smooth skin... do you really want to cause a quarrel between me and my mirror?"

"What nonsense, B," I said. "You know that these things are really not important. It's not your wrinkles that I want to marry."

"You will marry all of me. My complexes and my scars. The wife of a wise man who has yet to become a deputy director." He sat up and laughed, "Phew, and when we fight you'll probably say that you once had a deputy director fiancé who wanted to become a chief director and was much younger than I..."

He laughed again. I said, "B, why can't you take anything seriously?"

"There are many things that I take seriously; this you definitely know."

He was right. There were many serious things: clouds driven by the wind, fine drops of rain, and a leaf that falls from a tree—in the fall—and a man walking quickly down the road as if he didn't want people to hear him crying. All were serious matters, and B was always serious. A man cannot always explain why he says stupid things. B said, "You probably think I'm some kind of hero, right? It makes you feel superior to become a hero's wife, rather than a deputy's. Just let you wear old clothes, let your hands get calloused, and let you learn the theory behind handling weapons, and you'll be able to look down on a lot of people... You probably think I'm going to give you all of that. That's what you're thinking, isn't it?"

I said, "B, I don't know what you can give me, I just know that I feel better when I'm with you. I... I think, actually I feel, that I could feel relaxed with you in a grave."

"O God! ...I wish I could understand why all women must eventually find themselves a husband."

I think he was about to cry. "Dear girl, I have known many women, you know? But you haven't been with any men, have you?"

I said, "B, it's not like that. I have seen some men. I have seen you. This alone means a lot."

"Well," said B, "it certainly means a lot. No doubt."

I said nothing after that. It was as though a dark valley suddenly appeared before us. It was like this for me: there was only the latticed reflection of the stove on the ceiling and outside was the wind. I didn't dare lay my head on his arm. If I had, all of these things would lose their reality. If I had dared to do it, something could definitely have happened; we could have melted together—at the very least we could have shivered together. I just fell asleep.

It was B who woke me. He said, "They might be worried about you."

I was very thirsty and there was water on the table. B brought me some. Later we left together, because it was so late that I couldn't go home alone.

B described some Italian film that he had enjoyed very much. When we reached my house he said, "I wasn't joking before, but, my darling, please don't become the deputy's wife."

"Of course I won't, B," I said.

"Look, don't marry me even if I ask you."

Knowing myself well enough to realize that I would break my promise, I said, "Very well."

3

B very much wanted to become a poet. Of course, many people have the same ambition, but B was different. B had a world of things to say, but was not able to. When he got drunk, he would pull his hair out, as if to say that it was all his hair's fault. Once, when he was drunk, he recited this line to Harand and me: "I shall say to the whole of the heavens: woe unto us, woe unto us."

I laughed like an idiot and temporarily ruined the moment in such a way that repairing it was nearly impossible, and if it had not been for Harand it would have been ruined forever. Harand said, "Fine, B, don't worry about it, listen to this."

He recited a translation of a short Armenian poem. B said, "It's strange. Why must I be the one who can't write poetry?"

We were gathered around a table at B's house talking this way. B's house was not at all a fine house. It was one of those houses that sprouts from the ground like a weed. It was a ridiculous house. Harand could not stand cigarette smoke, and would go over to the window from time to time to breathe and later on would just sit by the window. B would say, "Haru, we won't smoke if it bothers you." Harand would answer, "No, B, it doesn't matter."

And we would go on smoking. Harand, instead, drank a lot and had this bad habit of ruining his drinking by not getting drunk.

Harand once told me about the time when, after many years, he saw B on the street and his heart almost stopped. Then he thought: Should I go up to him or not? What should I say, not say? He was still debating when B approached him and without any fuss just took his hand and asked him how he was. Then they stood still staring at one another and finally went to a tavern where they drank their fill. Late that night they got a little wild on the street and found themselves crying on a bench. In the end they decided to see one another. B said, "We've been housemates for two years."

They were living on the second floor of the house of a man who had a young wife. For Harand's sake, the wife would put on her chador in the evening and sell newspapers in the deserted streets. When the man went to the village with his friends, Harand and his wife would sleep together—they had an excellent relationship. B would say that theirs was the best relationship he had ever seen.

Later on the husband said to Harand, "Armenian dog, you're a no-good bastard," and pulled a gun on him. The woman got between them and, not having the nerve to kill her, her husband threw the gun into a corner in disgust and began to weep and weep. He must have been drunk. B explained, "This woman was not your everyday type of woman; a woman like this doesn't come but once in a thousand years."

They left the man's house with the woman, and the three of them lived happily together.

Then B and Harand did not see each other until that one day on the street several years later.

Apparently the man hurt Harand so much that his left arm became nearly useless and finally, after several months, went limp. One day when they were alone in their room, the man said, "What must you have to make a whore happy?" and stroked Harand's twisted arm, as though he were a woman. Harand thought that if he wanted to, he could now get himself out from under all of this. Harand's thoughts had now become quite perverted as he wracked his brain for a solution. He could very easily have treated the man to what he had given the woman. But memories of the woman would always enter his thoughts, and the woman tasted like honey which, in his difficulties, was exactly the thing that made him sick. He admitted, "I thought that other people were doing this thing and that, here and everywhere, and I started thinking of using my filthy, hairy body as a way out. That's the way it was."

But things did not go that far. The woman agreed just for Harand's sake to return to her husband and the husband immediately agreed to take her back on the condition that Harand be banned from their lives forever. And it was this act that convinced Harand that the woman was a direct descendant of a great romantic heroine like Leyla: "Any person who could enslave scum like that with her body must be quite a person."

They see each other occasionally in the street and nod. Harand said, "It's as if all of that was just a dream."

B said, "Haru, I can't sleep at night. It's like there's an ant walking around inside my head. I track it down, and I see, by God, it's a poem. But as soon as I try to catch it, it escapes. What can I do?"

It was not clear whether he was serious. Harand said, "You can die."

B rented the second floor of a taxi driver's house. His landlord did very well for himself. When I visited the house, the driver's wife's head would pop out of the kitchen window, and she would stare at me in a curious and condescending manner. The television was always on in their house. You couldn't figure out what they had on during the day when there wasn't anything on TV. B said they had the radio on and listened to all of its programs.

"How could anyone listen to that?" I asked B.

He said, "You'll learn, don't worry about it." He kissed my hand. It was as though I had brought tidings of spring for him. I was happy and several meters beneath our feet there was the street and life seemed good to me.

One night Harand brought a man I had not seen before to B's house. The man was slightly built. He and B embraced for a long time. Then they looked at one another and embraced once more. "How old you've gotten. God, how old you look!"

"Speak for yourself, buster!"

B was quite excited, and a bottle of newly bought spirits fell victim to the slender man. I learned that the man was a poet. He spent the entire night reciting poetry as though he had written his entire opus for this one night. B said, "It's good, we are together again; so what if there are one or two more wrinkles on our faces, what difference does it make?"

He took the poet's hand, which was nervously drumming the table, and patted it. Then he rose, poured another round of drinks for everyone, and sat down. Nothing else to do, he just stared at the table. It was quiet. I was afraid that he was holding back tears, so I said to the poet that B himself had made a poem and, with a gleam in my eyes, recited it to the poet. He said, "So, B, if you can't write poetry, is it the end of the world? For God's sake, man, give it up." Then he bent over and kissed B's face. B's spirits fell a little further. Then the man continued reciting and we all must have been so tired that we fell asleep right where we were.

The sun had long since risen when B woke us. He had fixed a feast, having arranged butter, cheese and quince, carrot, orange and I don't remember what other kinds of marmalades on the table. All of these were for the poet, who seemed content with performing his ablutions with *araq* and appeared to have no stomach at all for food. Several days later, when we read of the details of his suicide printed alongside his photograph in the newspaper, B was so depressed that for a moment I thought he was mourning all the marmalade that he had left, having set it aside in expectation of another night of poetry. B never for a moment thought of visiting the poet's grave, but I think he was spending his nights walking the streets. When we were together his indifference was maddening and felt like a slap in the face to me.

The weather was truly stifling and B's house on the second floor was quite hot. I asked B several times if I could live with him. I was always at his house and sometimes spent the night there, until the time the driver's wife came up and, not overly concerned with being polite, said we had created an intolerable situation and that our behavior was ruining their reputation. B moved and I visited him less frequently. He left for the village and I was afraid that I would cause them to throw him out of the village too.

4

In an effort to convince Mr. Yaganeh that I did not want to marry him, for a time I would invite him out to dinner on Wednesday evenings; up till now I had asked him four times.

This Wednesday evening, Mr. Yaganeh told me that another four dinners must be endured. When I asked why, he said, "I've asked you to dinner eight times so far, and naturally you want to match my invitations to the number until I agree that we are even."

What a mistake. Though, in a way, he was right. I did want to reciprocate his invitations lest he think that I had accepted them as prenuptials. As it turned out, however, he thought that the women's movement against millennia of coercion and oppression, which had come to fruition of late, had put me on my mettle. I asked, "Mr. Yaganeh, what makes you feel this way?"

He was very put off that I used the formal pronoun. "Because you are a very outspoken and hot-tempered girl. I'm afraid that you'll go so far as to make me do the dishes."

"And where do you suppose you'll be doing them?" I asked.

"In our home."

"Oh!"

Mr. Yaganeh quickly looked me in the eye. Though he was very careful not to show emotion, I could see that his ears had reddened. He asked, "Why? Is there something wrong with my washing the dishes?"

"No," I said, "but you always have the wherewithal to hire a servant to do them for you."

"Of course, if you want we can hire someone."

"Why should I want?"

Mr. Yaganeh laughed and winked (his right eye opened and closed mischievously). He said, "Why are you always being so coy—let's be frank, shall we?"

I was overjoyed. I felt that this was the time we could be open. I said, "What a really good idea, why shouldn't we speak frankly."

"That's very good."

"Do you want to marry me?"

"I want with all my heart to marry you, if you desire to be my wife."

"Fine, I don't desire to be your wife."

Mr. Yaganeh's eyelids fluttered. Scarcely noticeably. He quickly regained his composure. Despite his efforts to hide it, it was obvious that he had been shaken. I was enjoying myself now. "Look," he asked, "why are you using the respectful 'you' with me?"

"Because you're a respectable gentleman."

We ate in silence, and no matter what I did, Mr. Yaganeh would not let me pay for dinner. We left together in silence and got in Mr. Yaganeh's car. It was the first time that I saw Mr. Yaganeh speed, and when he had to brake suddenly, it was startling. "Why won't you marry me?"

"Because you are a respectable man—your life is all neatly planned out... we are quite different and couldn't possibly live compatibly."

Mr. Yaganeh showed his irritation with a nervous laugh and told me that I had fallen prey to the delirium of adolescence and was being guided by youth and that I didn't know what was best for me. I told him that this was possible, but whatever the case, such was the situation and there was nothing that could be done about it. He braked suddenly and said, "Someone else has put you up to this. I sense that you are not behaving normally. You probably think that you are something special?"

"The thought never occurred to me."

"Of course you do. Look, there are a lot of other girls like you—and you aren't even that good-looking, you know?"

"Yes, I have a full-length mirror."

"I am certainly not trying to insult you. Your face is fine as far as its form, but your looks are entirely ordinary. For another thing, you don't dress very well."

"My apologies."

"Of course, none of this matters very much. I don't want a woman for the way she dresses. Moreover such things can be corrected . . . It's only that I really don't understand why you can be so perfectly satisfied with the way you are."

I said, "Why don't you come out and say it. You think I'm just trying to have it my way."

He let his breath out. It was clear that this is what he had wanted to say. He said, "It's not important now, I have always felt that we could reach an understanding, but you are proving the opposite. Why?"

I said, "Mr. Yaganeh, I could never explain exactly why... This notion was your own invention. It's not my fault."

"Nevertheless, when I asked you out to dinner you accepted; in your own home I was showered with so much attention that... My God, your mother... that mother of yours treated me as though I was already her future son-in-law... Why shouldn't I have taken it for granted?"

"I am genuinely, genuinely sorry—really sorry. But what can be done? The woman is a mother and dearly wants her daughter to marry. It had nothing to do with me."

Mr. Yaganeh started the car and said, "Why are you acting as though you have no shame? Can't you speak more ladylike?"

I didn't exactly know what speaking ladylike meant. But Mr. Yaganeh was upset and this worried me greatly. I said, "Look, my friend, I am genuinely sorry, really sorry. You should marry someone who's right for you. A girl who appreciates your worth. I am not such a person, so why don't we nip this domestic tragedy in the bud?"

The young man curtly told me not to waste my pity on him. He was right. We arrived in front of my house in absolute silence. I was at a loss trying to find the most natural way of exiting the car. Finally I tentatively reached for the door handle and mumbled, "Good-bye."

Mr. Yaganeh nearly screamed, "Wait!" I will admit I was a little frightened. I sat immobile. He leaned toward me, his eyes flashing, and said, "You are the filthiest girl I have ever known." I didn't exactly catch everything, as he continued, "You're like these women who go with everyone. What a fool I was to want to marry the likes of you and spoil my life forever!"

Without saying a word I tried to leave again. Mr. Yaganeh gripped my arm tightly and, had he had the nerve, would have killed me. He said, "You women are all mentally inferior, your minds are flawed, you can't tell the difference between what's good and what's bad for you. I swear, they ought to hitch your hair to a horse's tail and let it drag you through the desert!"

"Try to be civil, Mr. Yaganeh," I said.

"What a shame—all the time I wasted on you."

"Two or three months, that's all."

"I'm out at least ten thousand."

I was beside myself. I said, "Sir, let go of me." I came close to wrestling with him, but Mr. Yaganeh knew better than to start wrestling with a woman that late at night in his car, and he quickly released my arm. He muttered, "The whole lot of you is worth a single, putrid strand from a European woman's hair." Then he started his car to leave. I was upset. I walked toward the house feeling defeated, and was on the verge of fainting when a hand grasped my arm firmly. Terrified, I turned to see Mr. Yaganeh. I couldn't see his face clearly in the dark alleyway, but I was sure he wanted to get even. He was like one of those angry Greek gods who were always taking revenge on humanity. "Let go of me, little man."

I watched in utter amazement as he let go of my arm. I now walked unsurely toward the house. Almost inaudibly, Mr. Yaganeh said, "Slut." This was too much. I was livid now. I turned around and said, "Yaganeh, sir, you're a true son-of-a..."

In the dimly lit alley I could see shock on Mr. Yaganeh's face. He was so shocked that if I had been able to wrestle him to the ground, I could easily have pinned his shoulders. He said, "Unbelievable." Then he quickly got into his car and left, and I never saw him again.

B became quite angry when I described what had happened. He said, "You just stood there and listened while this miserable deputy director spoke to you like that?"

"B," I explained, "I was very insulting to him," and repeated the insult for B. "Oh! Oh!" exclaimed B, "Really foul. Not becoming a fine young lady. Oh, no!"

He burst out laughing. He laughed so hard that I started laughing too. Tears came to our eyes. In mid-laugh, he said, "You know that it's not right for a young lady to use such curses. But confidentially I'll tell you that you did a good thing."

We laughed a great deal as we walked the length of the avenue. I held his hand so tightly that I felt we were locked together.

5

The coop was on a hill. From the bottom of the hill, a place which hung like the hem of a poorly cut cloche-shaped skirt, a dirt road led to the village. At sunset, the donkey riders would use this road to travel there.

On a slope of loose earth behind the coop, B had dug a number of graves for burials. At dawn, after he had watered and fed the birds and washed his face and hands, he would sit before the loose earth. On the other side you could see the road going halfway around the hill toward the village, and the white line of the horizon, becoming slightly more and more vermilion, receded farther into the distance. And there was the sound of crested larks chattering together with thrushes and a few swallows that had lost their way. All of this was a feeling, and if it were possible for a person to sacrifice himself for the sight of such a sunrise, he would have this feeling and this is what B would do.

From afar the hill looked poorly shaped. We had come a long way. Three days before Haru had said, "We'll take a car as far as the paved road goes, the rest we'll go on foot—it's no more than six kilometers." Then the trip stretched on and on, and we had quite a hike with the dust and sand choking us. We had gotten an early start to see the sunrise from the hill. Haru walked in silence. He had not spoken since the asphalt road and was in a good mood.

Auntie was smoking her waterpipe. Summer afternoons she would spread her prayer rug in a place where it was always shady in the compound, which she had watered down before. As the water evaporated, the scent of mint and roses would rise from the rectangular, baked bricks of the compound. With the sun gone, she would water the small garden. The dark, sunburnt boy Mortaza watered with the watering can. The geranium pots gasped for breath and several oleander petals fell into the wading pool. Auntie sat on the rug. First she broke off chunks from a sugar cone, then brewed tea, and finally lit her waterpipe and several red rose petals fluttered up and down with each puff.

I said, "No, Haru, no absolutely no one can say who's right, all of these are absurd claims. So why should a person create a situation where he thinks that he's responsible for the whole world and, in the end, is forced to squat down in the corner of some room and cry? Can you answer me this? No, you can't, and why, incidentally, should you answer? You know, after you sit in that corner and have a

good cry, so much that your sockets bleed, you'll look in the mirror
and see that you're fifty years old—then you'll be forced to rent a
compound with a small garden and you'll plant some roses, sweet-
briar, two myrtle bushes—say—one boxwood, and one fir, and you'll
spend your afternoons watching them."

Mandi was like a piece of gold cloud. When she walked, she
didn't just move, she rippled along. Her smile was like honey, like
the honey of the wild hives of Mount Sabalan. The curl of her smile
was like a trail of honeybees moving toward flowers. This Mandi was
a piece of gold.

I said, "What now, when you can be a scorching hot wave and
your entire body can exude femininity—Oh, Haru, the best thing to
do when the ruler proves very much the tyrant, is to go under his
throne and sleep with your mate."

B said, "You're late, you must have dawdled; the sun's already up.
So, how are you? Everything in the right place?"

We sat on the wooden flat. He had made a good house. Though
the occasional smell of chickens seeped in through the windows, he
had set up two really decent rooms.

B said that he was serving grilled chicken for lunch, had bought
five bottles of wine and had twelve bottles of beer cooling in the
stream, and had one or two bottles of *araq*, some melon seeds and
pistachios, even some fruit and a blanket. After lunch we were going
to spread the blanket on the ground and each of us would stretch out
in a corner, drink the wine slowly—before lunch we would drink the
beer, the beer was ice cold and would taste like polar snow. B said that
when, toward sunset, the dew settled on the grass, we would go and
have a look. Then they would sound the call to prayer in the village
where they had bought a loudspeaker which brought the call all the
way to us. We were going to listen to it because it was beautiful. We
could also read. He said that he had a lot of books. He said that there
was also tea and that tea at sunset when there was a little nip in the
air, before the *araq*, would hit the spot. We could also read poetry,
because he had books of poetry, and quite a few. Indicating with his
hands there was no more, he said that he thought we were going to
have a good time—these were all of the things that we could do.

"How does a man come to commit suicide?"
"I don't know. I've never wanted to."

"It must occur in some way; like one day the history and geography teacher clears his snout and proclaims that civilization is the product of humanity's suffering. Then you go and sit down and think to yourself: So, am I ready to suffer or not? And thinking this way causes you to suffer. Naturally, after that the thought of suicide crosses your mind."

B said, "Ideas that people learn from books are likely to have such consequences. A person can experience things easily; it's better for a person to commit suicide out of experience than from a book. Believe me, it's much better, and some even have better methods; they commit suicide as part of their experience. They prefer to play the role of laboratory rat, not just an ordinary rat. Their names go down in history and you use them as role models."

I said, "No, they're not rats, B, they embody all the values that people have, in history. How could you say such a thing?"

"I said that I hope that people would commit suicide this way, was it a bad example? Okay, fine, but it was eloquent, dear."

Haru had gone to sleep and was dreaming. I was sure he was dreaming for he had put his hands over his eyes to shield them from the sun.

"I knew a girl who was quite beautiful, like a goddess, you wouldn't believe how beautiful, nothing like it. One spring day she comes home and her mother sees that she is very sick. The girl had a fever and was shaking, really badly. She had been golden and was going pale, pure white like plaster. The girl goes to bed, pulls the covers over her head, and sleeps. The next morning they go to see her and she's dead; she had written a note saying that she was very sorry, but her heart had been utterly broken."

B said, "Well, her heartbreak was no doubt the bookish variety— what a stupid way to go."

I said, "No, after they examined her, they found she had been pregnant."

"Oh!"

B said, "Let's stop this silliness; it's simply a sign of degeneracy. How could such a golden girl get rid of her baby? Fool."

"What about my Auntie, did you know her?"

"No."

"You know, one day they found her stiff on her prayer rug still smoking the waterpipe. Died just like that. You know she was deaf. She had been deaf from the age of five. Never heard anything her entire life—no, I forgot. Just recently she'd started to wear a hearing aid. One day I saw that she had put the hearing aid on the pipe. I think that the red petals moving in the pipe bowl gave her the idea that she could somehow hear the sound of them moving."

"Haru, lad, get up. Let's go pick some viper grass in the field."

Haru rolled over onto his arm. He eyes were red. He said, "I had a good sleep, didn't I?"

Then he got up and stretched.

A black cloud covered the sky and rain was in the air. The three of us went to the porch and looked out at the wasteland. Nothing could be seen. It was dark and quiet and in an instant one part of the sky flashed and there was sound, fierce and monstrous. The downpour began immediately. We returned to the room.

"You're very alone here, aren't you?"

"It's not that bad. It's not a hardship. Only at night it's a little depressing when the quiet is everywhere; you can hear the silence—the sound is so bad, it's like rubbing two pieces of honey-brittle together."

I said, "B, you can go back. Why don't you? The winter will be suffocating. You aren't used to it, then the snow will come and all the mountain roads will be closed—you'll freeze to death all alone, it's really awful."

B said, "You don't understand. You don't understand a lot of things."

"B, I understand," I said, "Why is it necessary for a person to die at a specific moment in his life? The world has become one of expertise, you know; you can acquire a certain expertise, then another, and another, and while you go on getting new ones, your previous ones will get old; then you'll be forced to keep on updating your various specialties . . . Don't you know that medicine is advancing so fast that even if you work at keeping abreast of new developments twenty-four hours a day, you still won't get anywhere?"

He said, "I've thought about it; last night I thought I would go and learn something, dear—how to make a statue out of wood. I will carve a woman, from wood, all of her body will be root; I'll leave her belly empty and put a wooden fetus in it. I'll carve her hands as though they were tree roots. I'll open her breasts and show the veins and sinews. An old man will hang from one of her breasts and a thousand babies from the other. Male babies. You see, dear, I am thinking of a specialty, except I envision the end right at the start; it will take a thousand years of my time. It could be, say… say the manifestation of fertility… besides these things, I have a more important task, dear. You know that one day this may happen."

It was raining heavily. B lit his portable heater and the light filled the room. Outside was the sound of the downpour and the raindrops striking the metal roof. Haru had closed his eyes. I slept on my back next to B.

"One day an evil man decides to take a walk. He goes beyond the asphalt road and reaches a stretch of grass. This man is fifty years old and upon seeing the grass, his breath stops. His heart tells him, 'God, how beautiful!' and without knowing it he goes walking in the grass. He has been to the doctor and the doctor told him that the condition of his heart was not reassuring. Then, when he's walking in the grass, his heart tightens up. For a moment he looks back and examines his entire life, and, since he is on the verge of death, he looks at history also and says to himself, 'Oh, history, see how they've killed this figure and that?' He thinks for a while and then remembers the rest of mankind in history, and his body breaks out in a cold sweat. He gets the idea to set up a personal foundation that will aid poor children, offer a helping hand to widows, lift the spirits of the downtrodden, in short, to become a martyr. The grass ends and he reaches a barren desert in the late afternoon. He rounds a hill and sees a light on it and is drawn to it. Slowly he climbs the hill. In the beginning the going is very easy. The slope is slight. But halfway up, the slope suddenly becomes steep. The man gasps for air and the light is near. Gasping, the man sits on the ground and clutches his beating heart; his distress is immeasurable.

"I go to him and he, seeing me, says, 'Sir, help, I want to reach the milk and honey, but I'm afraid that the hill has become too steep.' I say, 'It's not far, believe me, it's also not that difficult.' The man looks me in the eye and pleads, 'Then I beg you, finish me off with one blow.'

"Then it's all over in one moment. The man was at least lucky enough to travel the course of history once."

"Haru, you awake?"

"I'm awake."

"You bored?"

"No."

"Should we read poetry?"

"No."

"Should we read, talk, commiserate?"

"No."

"Then what should we do?"

"Just let's be quiet, listen to the rain."

"Okay."

6

B had been spinning himself in silk for the last fifteen years. By the time I made his acquaintance, he claimed that the cocoon had reached almost to his waist. Naturally, such a problem would have had an adverse affect on his drive, and I guess that this was the very reason why he would be late for the office most of the time. B made every effort to arrive early, but at the last moment something would happen; since he was unable to walk properly with all those strands, he was forced to ride and this was the reason that the taxi became the principal agent of all his tardiness. At times going to bed late at night would push his mornings beyond their usual times, thus delaying his arrival at the office. B would say, "Now I'm ready to go to the office, but just as I am about to stick my foot out the door, a bird starts chirping outside. Or it's one of those cloudy mornings when the only thing you want to do is spend the whole day listening to the kettle boiling on the stove... Is the fault really mine?"

I believe that until that moment they were very considerate of his condition. But it appears that B had made fun of the director and he found out about it. B said, "It wasn't like that at all, I merely said that this gentleman reminded one of a funhouse mirror; couldn't he smile, at least?"

The director said to B, "Mr. B, you are late every day—this is an absolute breach of office decorum."

B said, "Mr. Hosayni, I'm surprised to learn that you would know about this."

Perplexed, the director asked him why, and B simply replied, "Because you come late every day yourself."

B was actually unaware of the fact that the office menials and doormen were the director's eyes and ears. The director merely scowled and B left the room. He went to his desk to remove his briefcase from the drawer and left the office. "It was only natural that they would fire me."

We agreed that there was really nothing else that could be done.

B decided to go into independent work. The first partner he chose was me. I said, "B, I don't have a penny to contribute."

He chose Harand. After Harand heard B's proposal, he scratched his scalp, parting tufts of hair, and thought for a time. Finally, he said that in general it was a good idea and that he was ready to become B's partner. They had all the requisites for investment except capital. This was the reason why they decided to plan the business first. B was married to the idea of an *araq* store, but Harand was completely opposed, "Friends will make us go broke. After all, wouldn't you yourself volunteer to drink *araq* for free?"

B said that he would do so religiously. So they shelved the plans for the *araq* store. Harand proposed: "A country-wide chewing-gum distribution center."

In B's view this plan was so laughable that it was beyond ridicule. No grocer would be ready to take a penny less than ten cents' profit on a twenty-cent pack of gum.

I suggested that they start a center for wooden handicrafts. They mulled this over for a while. It was good, but would be difficult. You would have to find some one to go and collect wooden handicrafts from the countryside to sell. B was not made for this work and Harand had a regular job that paid him a salary every month.

In the end they agreed upon a modern coffeehouse, and had even chosen the place where they would set it up. Now they just needed capital. Two months passed, and the nightly brainstorming which revolved around the issue of money cost them two bottles of *araq* and a lot of pickles and bologna.

In the meantime B had found another job. He contracted with a laundry to find it well-heeled clients and in return receive a percentage of their trade. This new job caused the coffeehouse plan to be shelved for a short time, and B for his part had to sell his radio, transistorized stereo, old records, and his rug to prove to the owner of the laundry that in today's investment world the right advertising and hiring men who take a percentage as payment for honest work was a very shrewd step. The only problem was that the owner was content with a small income, and B's wages for services rendered, I guess, covered only half of his expenses in the discharge of his duties. In return he found detailed information about the operations of the hospitals and the hotels. (These places were B's main hunting grounds.) He found out, for example, that the hands of the old washerman at Alavi Hospital were utterly useless. As it turned out the washerman used the same hands to nearly tear B's throat out. B said, "Believe me, I had absolutely no intention of taking the bread out of his mouth; I don't know what gave him that idea. Really, do I look like the kind of man who would do such a thing?"

Of course he didn't look like such a man. B wasn't the kind of person who would take the bread out of another man's mouth, he only knew how to do this to himself and was not willing to admit it.

After the laundry work, B once again succumbed to the coffeehouse temptation. He made interesting innovations. He placed an old gramophone in the coffeehouse and played seventy-eights. There was also the possibility that the coffeehouse would be used from time to time as an art gallery. Young artists would display their paintings, and B would find customers for their work from those who frequented the coffeehouse. In exchange for every ten thousand tomans in coffeehouse sales each artist would present B with a painting. In this way young artists could earn an easy annual income of twenty thousand tomans without having to do business tricks and B would gradually amass a collection of the works of young artists.

Occasionally the coffeehouse would show the works of amateurs, helping to introduce deserving, unknown artists to the public. Likewise young singers who had not made names for themselves could also be debuted.

Then B found a job with a pharmaceutical company. He had to introduce drugs made by this company to doctors. B lasted only a month. Some doctors were very surly: "Though you were only giving away free drugs, these guys thought that you owed them their paternal inheritances."

B said to the head of the pharmaceutical company, "Sir, I can do other things—office work and the like."

The boss rejected B's offer. The company had its fill of office employees. On the other hand B's three years of medical studies made him a more suitable candidate for the sales job.

At this juncture B bought a small shop adjacent to the coffeehouse from its owner and removed the wall between the two shops. The coffeehouse was much wider now. B built a small library in one corner. After eating, customers could sit on dark leather couches and read books. B proposed to young writers that for every hundred books they gave to him to sell, they would contribute a complimentary copy to the coffeehouse library. The young writers agreed to this to a man. B was becoming the proprietor of a large library.

Around sunset on a late summer day, Harand visited B's house. This was the house that Harand had scrounged for B. It belonged to an old Armenian lady who was always drunk, so we could make as much noise as we wanted on the second floor without the woman saying anything. Harand said that the place where he was working was an empty spot which was entirely appropriate for B. Because of this world-shattering event, Harand decided to get drunk as he customarily did every night.

When they were drunk, I said to Harand, "Harand, I wish B would let me live with him." B laughed. I felt that he didn't know what he was saying. He said, "Haru, the poor child's begging for it— thinks I'm a real man, ugh!"

Then his laughter grew so raucous that I was able to forget the flush in my ears.

Harand said, "B, I think it'd be a good idea if you shut your trap."

B said, "God help us! Now look who's become chief, the stink bug!"

Then he got up and started to pace the middle of the room, "Poor little stink bug, all of his efforts to prove the proposition that he is a sniveling worm have gone to waste; the girl with the dark brown eyes just had to gaze admiringly at him and say: 'Precious stink bug of mine, you are my idol.'"

B was annoyed. I couldn't tell whether he was laughing or raving. The situation was very bad and I couldn't stand it anymore, so when Harand went out to get some water, I left the house.

Some time later I saw Harand in the street. B's new job had lasted just fifteen days. B told Harand, "You see, brother, I can't, I really can't."

Harand said, "He's just bought two rooms over the coffeehouse, because there are too many books. He also needs a respectable art gallery. He says that he doesn't want the coffeehouse atmosphere to depreciate the value of the paintings."

B devoted one of the upstairs rooms to the paintings and divided the other into two entirely separate sections. The front part was a library which the coffeehouse customers used and the rear section, which had a secret door, was B's private library, full of books that would make your hair stand on end. According to Harand, B now had ten thousand volumes.

7

B sent me a note. He wrote: "Please, if you think it wouldn't be too tedious, come and visit me, on hill N, under the tree, 4 o'clock."

He had written everything wrong. It should have been: 4 o'clock, under the tree, on hill N—or actually Avenue N. B was in no way ready to accept that all of these hills had become avenues. He would say it was shameless that some people would retreat into the hills to make love and for this reason lurid names, which drove him crazy, came to be associated with some of them. There was also this, that these hills at some time could be good hiding places. It was this second aspect of the hills that excited him the most.

I thought about going for quite some time. My instincts kept telling me: Don't be a fool, don't be a fool.

The fall was charming and so cold that a pullover was necessary. Just in case I also took along an overcoat. Hill N is relatively high, so I had become quite warm by the time I reached the top. I saw B sitting under the tree. From far away he looked like a roach. I thought that there was still time to return—let him sit and be suffocated by the loneliness.

B sat under the tree with his arms wrapped around his knees. He smiled when he saw me. He seemed on edge and drunk to me. He said, "Can I apologize and all that?"

I forced a smile and said, "No problem."

B was wearing a thin shirt under his summer jacket. Standing close to him, I saw that he was really chilled. I said, "B, I don't think it's a good idea to go out dressed like that anymore. You'll catch your death."

B stared at me in surprise, "Darling, I've got a fever."

"Don't joke about it, B, you're shaking."

Astonished and helpless, B looked at me. His eyes bulged and were red. I couldn't tell whether it was from drinking or weeping. He said, "Believe me I have a fever, I'm so feverish that I'm burning up."

I put my hand on his forehead. It wasn't hot. I said, "B, why must you lie?"

"God! Why must I be so tired?"

He got up and paced a bit. "My dear, listen, an unpublished book by Dale Carnegie has come my way, you know it's really amazing. I don't know how it made its way to me... the book begins: 'To people, to those human beings who pain without gain, to those gains that they gain, to those pains that they pain or those pains that they gain or gains that they pain.'" Then he resumed his seat under the tree and shook with the cold that wracked his body.

"Dale Carnegie writes: 'one cold winter's night on which it had snowed heavily and the air was getting somewhat frigid, I was at home when all of a sudden I lost hope. My despair was so great that it seemed limitless. Yes, hopelessness is a misery without remedy... but despite this feeling, I continued to struggle with myself. This struggle reached its peak during the late hours of the night. So I went to the mirror and looked at the man in it and said, mister, if you think that Dale Carnegie is the kind of person who would succumb to the power of painful temptation, you are mistaken. Then I spat hard into the face of my reflection. And the strange thing was that my reflection spat back in my face.' Dale writes, 'My astonishment was boundless and I quickly wiped the spit clean with a handkerchief that Mrs. Carnegie had washed and ironed that day. I wanted very much to beg my reflection's pardon, but I knew that this would cause him promptly to reply in kind, and I was in no mood to be shamed, and I needed to remain irritated to bolster my resolve..."'

I said, "B, for God's sake, don't kid around."

"God knows that I'm serious... 'After this incident,' Dale writes 'I told Mrs. Carnegie that I had to leave the house on an errand... On that night of the terrible storm, I wandered the streets alone and miserable, and thought about life, hope and despair, success and failure, and I wished with all my heart that I had a brother who would act as my Cain and put me out of my misery.'"

"Then Dale goes to a bar and decides to have a drink, but, after struggling with his evil side, emerges victorious with his head held high... 'When, dejected but nevertheless proud of my power to resist temptation, I passed the river, I met a man who was drunk. He was so drunk that he had difficulty walking..."

I said, "B, If you want we can go sit in a café and warm up. Right near here there's a café."

B asked, "You don't want me to go on with the story?"

I noticed that he had tears in his eyes. It might have been the cold that made his eyes run. I shut up.

"Dale asked the man, 'Are you drunk, friend?' The drunk said something unintelligible. Dale helped him walk and the man finally did what he ordinarily should have done from the beginning: namely, he sat down and vomited. Dale began to massage his back and the man's spasms caused drops of vomit, which looked like a suspicious, coffee-colored goo, to fall onto Dale's clothes. Dale never showed his annoyance, rather he led the man down the jetty steps and lowered him headfirst to the neck into the cold river water. This sobered the man a bit and his nervous spasms turned to cold shivers... Then Dale asked the man, 'Dear friend, in your opinion what is the source of despair? Doesn't a god exist for despair... Isn't life beautiful? Don't birds chirp? Isn't snow beautiful? Isn't... Isn't... Isn't...'

"The man listened to Dale carefully and Dale's own nervous stimulation caused him to chatter like a broken record: 'Shouldn't we mark our friends' birthdays on our calendars and send them cards in time so they can respond in kind, make us happy, and purge the despair from our beings? Shouldn't we begin each morning with a bright smile on our faces and say hello to one and all? In fact, each day shouldn't we tell ourselves: Try and try and try? Shouldn't we eat nourishing foods and make milk one of our staples? Have I written all of this advice in my books for nothing?'

"Dale writes that the man nodded like an idiot, pretending to understand him. At times he stared at him in amazement, and to the end Dale did not know what his voice was like, for he did not utter a word, but Dale's despair receded.

"Dale got the man to his house around morning and returned home elated. He writes, 'When I got home I washed the handkerchief I had used to clean the spit and gave my clothes to the cleaners. Mrs. Carnegie was sleeping. I woke her and made love to her; I repeated this for seven nights. The glow on her face increased day by day…'"

I was quiet as I leaned on my left leg and watched B. He was sitting under the tree, and when he finished the story he looked at my face.

"Was it such a bad story?"

"B, are you pulling my leg?"

B said, "I swear to God, I never would do such a thing. It just seemed to me that it was an eye-opening story… I told it to you because for a while now I have been searching for my own Cain…"

"You got me to come all this way just to tell me this?"

"You probably think I'm crazy, right?"

"Crazy? God almighty, you're just banal, you're just acting to prove that all of this wasn't for nothing."

"What wasn't for nothing?"

"All of the things that have driven you crazy and made you spin this absurd yarn and pull whatever other garbage you've pulled."

B said in surprise, "It's odd, how can it be for nothing?"

I said, "Your kind act like martyrs… To hell with the lot of you— why blame me?"

B rose suddenly. His eyes were sober. He said, "Don't be silly, don't be silly."

"Oho," I said, "look at the poor martyr! Spineless little martyr!"

B slapped my face. He slapped me hard, making my head spin for a moment. I wanted to hit him back, but I couldn't. I can't hit anyone. I said, "B, you've been stricken by God. I'm not going to hit you."

B screamed, "You bitch, slut, you're scum, spit-up, you're all puke… O God, who are we fighting over? Who?"

Then he hid his face in his hands. A woman who looked like some maid had emerged from a villa-type house on the right side and was looking at us curiously. The right side of my face stung. I realized that the woman had seen me stupidly getting slapped. Even if I had a thousand years and the guts for a thousand slaps, I could never have slapped him back. Something snapped in my mind and this was what was pitiful. The slap itself I could endure. But I was certain that it wasn't my fault. I was certainly blameless and all the facts were in my favor. But the woman, a local villager, kept looking at me. I ran down the hill and B ran after me. He said, "You're not getting away that easily. You have to pay, tramp, you're the tramp of tramps."

He got to me, breathing heavily, and violently grabbed my arm.

I said, "B, I swear I'll hit you. I've got no patience for this bullshit. It's not my fault that I wasn't born earlier... I haven't done anything... I just hope that all you troubled souls drop dead and get a decent burial."

B said something and we started to shout at one another. Then it was as though a strange feeling came over both of us and quieted us. We came down arm in arm. The policeman who came forward was skinny, but a policeman nevertheless. I said, "Good afternoon, officer, excuse me, could you tell me if the home of Mr. Javan is on this avenue?"

The officer said that he honestly didn't know, and scratched his head in perplexity. I said, "Thanks, officer." We went down a little farther, our arms now unlocked.

B said, "I must have been quite an asshole, thinking all this time that I could talk to you." I didn't answer him. He continued. "I'll be damned if I ever trust one of your kind again. Bitches, bitches!"

I wanted to tell him to shut up, but couldn't. He said, "What am I going to do?" and slammed his hands together. I thought: Why won't he just go and get lost, and no sooner had I thought this than B was gone.

I walked for a while. The sun was setting and it had become biting cold. I went down the incline and on my left were the hills made avenues and the thick stands of trees which were a comfort in themselves. I said, "B, goddamn you, your greatness is like a stream, and I'm looking for an ocean."

I realized that I was consoling myself. I said, "I'll be a bitch in heat if I don't shame you for what you did, just wait!" I said, "I'll be damned if you don't come around and ask me to forgive you." I screamed, "B, even if I have to stage it, I'll have my martyrdom, my martyrdom, my martyrdom..."

Now I was crying. The evening was getting quite dark, and it was not a good idea to walk in the street.

8

A narrow alley, with twenty-eight thousand ash-gray doors and windows, the width of two men shoulder to shoulder, went a thousand feet, then turned, and at the turn there was a yellow door, and behind the yellow door there was an old Armenian woman, and above her there was B, who lived inside himself while the old woman was always drunk.

I knocked on the door, the old woman poked her balding head out of the window and said, "Who is it?" It took a long time for the door to open, and the first thing to emerge was the smell of her breath, followed by the woman herself with her bloodshot eyes; the hallway smelled of mixed pickled vegetables and mold.

"Is B here?" I asked.

She said he was, and stepped aside. In her woolen housedress she was like an old parrot in winter after a spat with a mate or like a young female parrot who had taken a splash bath.

As I went up the stairs, she said, "B has not been out of his room for three days, he's barricaded himself in there. I think he's reading or playing the martyr or something; he's an ass—my poor house, and what's wrong with having some manners, anyway? These Muslims are absolutely uncivilized, they haven't an ounce of good sense—what a shame that a woman is forced to rent her home to them! They're absolutely incorrigible, and one day some bomb, some swarm or other, something will let them have it from above and, I hope to God, a prophet will be sent down to this folk."

I said, "Madam, he's probably sick or something."

"Uh-huh," she said, "that may be, but he's still an ass and very rude."

"Madam," I answered, "his *araq* is still good, isn't it?"

She said "Uh-huh, with the rent he pays, I would have dumped him into the garbage, if it weren't for this one good thing," and had a good laugh. It was difficult to tease a good drunk who was both aged and spent every night in bed crying for a man who had died years before.

B must have huddled himself in a corner of his room. When I knocked he did not answer. I knocked again. He said, "Madam, may your father burn in hell, goddammit, leave me alone, whore!"

I knocked again and went in. I asked, "What have you done with your furniture, B?"

He said, "Sold it. What's it to you?"

"Nothing. Has Haru been around to see you?"

"That son of a slut!"

"Why are you cursing?"

"He's the lowest person I've ever known."

I said, "B, to you everybody is the '-est' something. How is that possible?"

"These Armenians," he said, "they're all '-ests' of one kind or another; take this Madam, she's the drunk-est."

"Will you come with me to get something to eat? Let's go somewhere and have coffee or something?"

"Fuck all the somewheres and coffee there is!"

"B, you look like a man who hasn't eaten for a week."

"That's about it."

"Well, why?"

He said that he was at odds with himself, the world, me, Haru, Madam, and any other son of a bitch who wanted to harass him, and that he wished that they'd all get their heads chopped off, and he told me this so that I would leave him the hell alone as soon as possible.

"You see that all I do is smoke cigarettes, now run along to that Armenian dog, that Haru, tell him to get over here and do his own preaching."

I said, "You certainly are drinking *araq.*"

He said, "I'm drinking my *araq* all right—you tell him also to screw himself!"

"Why should he?" I said. "You can talk to a sensible person once or twice, but then you say to yourself: okay, screw him, let him do whatever the hell he wants."

He said, "Now what, I wonder who put you up to coming around and start preaching here? I'm drinking *araq*? Why not? A person in the process of metamorphosis has some rights, doesn't he?"

"Of course he does."

"Do you know whether they want to build a natural history museum here?"

"What's your point?"

"Do you mean they don't want to build a natural history museum here, after all? They do need one, don't they?"

I said, "B, I haven't heard anything; but they may be. With all the different kinds of universities around here, they'll need something like it."

"You're sure?"

"I'm not sure. I guess that they'll build one eventually."

"Very well then, listen you so-and-so, they can put the most amazing thing in their natural history museum. The entire world will be dumbstruck, and they'll probably take in considerable amounts of cash from curious tourists; then 'tourist hotels' will start to have some meaning, really mean something. Mosques and historical landmarks will also mean something. The tourist will say: Look, how extraordinary. On their ancient ruins look how far their knowledge has come. In brief, the strange and incredible things that so many tourists say will cause millions to rush in eagerly, the hotels will always be full, full of guests, filled to overflowing with people."

I said, "Well, well! You haven't so much as stepped out of this room and what a big talker you've become! There are so many great and tremendous museums in the world..."

"Where have you been all this time?" he asked.

I said, "Nowhere. Where was I going to go?"

We remained silent for a time, smoking a cigarette. Then he said, "By the way, by the way, how's it been going? Everything okay?"

"I walked, I walked a long way," I said. "You know the condition of the roads. There isn't much security, so I went through the alleys. What alleys—dizzy with the fragrance of acacia—full of honeysuckle and lilacs which—large and dark—brought perfume to the sorrow of passersby. And if you knew the fragrance of the gillyflowers on summer nights, at the end of the alleys, what a riot they make! The summer was good, very good, full of loafing, and wandering about.

"Then winter came and I went somewhere to drink. The wine was good and homemade. When I was a little drunk I returned to the alley and turned up my raincoat collar, because the fine rain that was turning to snow soaked my neck. You know, before that I had danced, really danced, and then in the alley and the biting cold I saw the light. I saw that everything was just as it should be. Nothing was wrong in the world, only one thing was missing, and that was love. This was why all at once I fell in love. Then love began in earnest, and continued in a bad, bad way; and so it was that I hit my head against a brick wall.

"One day I woke up in the morning and I had a bad taste in my mouth and my head hurt. I looked at myself in the mirror. I said, 'Are you me? Is this actually me?' You don't know the half of it, B, somehow you're really in bad shape, dead almost, as though you've lost your wits in an accident. I said, 'I'll go and visit B, go and tell him what happened,' but it was a long time before I actually did it; something always got in the way to postpone it, and besides, I said, 'go and say what? B has his own problems, what can he give me? What can he do for me?' ...What have you been doing?"

He said, "Well, how can I put it? In summer when you open the window, you see that your neighbor's window across the way is closed, rarely opening. I looked at the spots of rain on the plaster walls of my neighbor's house, and followed the motion of the sun through a crevice between the two houses. Late afternoons Madam would make tea and we'd sit out on the platform bed in the garden, drink tea, and shoot the bull.

"After winter came, you could have popped in anytime and had some tea. The kettle was always boiling on the stove and there was always that good, fragrant tea that Haru had brought from Ahwaz. I thought of getting in touch and inviting you for tea several times. Haru would come around occasionally and we'd fight.

"Then my money ran out and I sold my furniture, and one day I looked around and found that I was always selling. Always. I have even been selling myself and got nothing in return. I realized that I was no good for you, I was no match for your youth and couldn't let your body become my property; with a face full of wrinkles and a creaky voice, I saw that I was all pus and scars and good only for a museum. I would serve as an obvious example of an age that elegizes the obvious. So, Madam and I drank away the money from my furniture sale. Nights we'd sit in Madam's room, Madam would listen to Tchaikovsky and cry and I would grieve for Tchaikovsky. You see, Madam's record player is in bad shape and her records are old. It was pitiful, and the misfortune continued until I realized that I was undergoing a metamorphosis, see."

I moved the blanket aside and saw that the cocoon reached to his waist.

He said, "I'm becoming a butterfly, it's happening. It's a shame that you can't see, my legs are starting to change shape, it won't be long before I'm a true butterfly."

I said, "B, this was to be expected."

"Now what?" he said. "I'm the first man to change into a butterfly, a fifty-kilo butterfly."

"Maybe even sixty kilos," I added.

"No, I've gotten really thin, it's fifty, no more, but that's something anyway."

I said, "The people of this age are trying hard to turn into light."

B said that a butterfly was his limit, he couldn't go higher, but I too, if I tried hard, could change into a gillyflower, and he would fly in my fragrance.

"Should I come to see you again, B?" I asked.

He said, "Stop by if you feel like it—no, wait a month. All this while I have been thinking how I could be of some benefit to you. When you come then you'll be able to sell my butterflyhood to them to put it in their museum. You'll get a hell of a price."

"B, they haven't started the museum, and they may not even buy you," I said.

"To hell with 'em. Dry me out and mount me on a wall… it's the old story, isn't it? You can say to your guests that I was one of your lovers. All the girls will die of envy."

I said, "Do you want me to stay a bit longer so we can talk?"

He said, "No, there's no need, why should we? Go back to the alley, where there are a lot of things to do, lots and lots of things; you'll get some real experience there."

"So I should go, B?" I asked.

He said, "Go, but before you do, just open the window, it's very stuffy."

"Okay," I said.

9

Finally, one beautiful spring day when the sky was so blue and the sun was bright yellow, our doorbell rang. When I looked down I first saw a round head covered with shiny, curly black hair, but then I made out Haru's familiar eyes. "Ready?"

I nodded yes and quickly ran to the stairs, and we held hands on the shiny mosaic tiles in front of the house. We were both fresh from the bath. We were clean and both smelled of cheap cologne. Haru's shirt radiated spotlessness, which made me think that he had discovered a new kind of soap powder. My blue dress was also immaculate.

He said, "Whatever it takes, we must get him out of the house."

And we started off.

The alleys, the streets, and the people were all so clean and radiant that you'd think they were waxed. The whole way we talked and laughed, and apparently everyone felt as we did. But we both got cold feet in front of Madam's house. If he threw us out it would be difficult to continue our friendship with him.

Haru said, "Leave it to me. We'll force him to sit in the wheelchair, and even if he screams bloody murder, we'll pay no attention, right?"

"Fine," I said.

Some moments after the bell rang, Madam turned up behind the door. She was wearing one of those Armenian-type embroidered flower dresses, which was clean and bright, and had lipstick on. When she opened the door, she laughed and said, "You've come just in time."

The three of us went up the stairs. The wheelchair that Haru had ordered was on the landing. Haru with the utmost daring opened the door and was naturally met with a dried orange peel on the forehead.

"Ouch!"

"Son of a slut, who said you could open the door?"

Haru's eyes flashed with anger as he rubbed the spot where the orange peel hit him. But it was not a day for anger. He said, "Okay, fine," and laughed.

B said, "It looks like you've been reading Dale Carnegie lately."

"That's what you want to think, fine. Guys."

He nodded to me and Madam. The three of us advanced and surrounded B. He seemed very frail under his blanket, but apparently had taken advantage of his perpetual confinement to learn all the ways to escape. So he violently waved his frail arms in the air, and the three of us patiently endured his struggles until we finally subdued him. Haru grabbed hold of both his hands. Madam locked her arms around his chest under the shoulders, while I tackled his legs in their cocoon, and we walked to the wheelchair this way. B yelled, "Scoundrels, scum, heathens, murderers!"

But there isn't a human on earth who can allow himself to become angry on a spring day which also happens to coincide with a great national festival.

B said, "I'll swear out a complaint against you, I'll throw the three of you in jail. I'll fix you!"

Perspiring, we sat him on the chair and roped his hands to its arms; as he cursed, we gagged him with a piece of cloth and tied a blue handkerchief over the gag.

B's hunger-stricken, feverish eyes were a sight then. It was as though he wanted to stare a thousand daggers at us. Then Haru bent over him and said, "Now you shut up and sit still like a good little boy."

Poor B. It was so warm out you didn't need any kind of a coat, and he was covered in blanket to the tip of his nose. He had to appear normal. Then, panting, the three of us hefted the chair down the stairs and entered the avenue. B squirmed in the chair. He turned red sometimes and sometimes white. Madam said, "Good heavens, look how he fusses!" B looked at her furiously. Madam said, "I'm not afraid of you anymore, don't waste your stares on me." Poor B.

Haru asked, "Do you hear that sound, B? From the square just down there."

In the square, the Navy band was playing marches. Children had gathered around the band and were sucking on candies. The square was wall-to-wall sandwich-seller stalls. Haru said, "If the sandwich had not been invented, how would people be able to fathom the concept of recreation?"

No one had an answer for him. Then we reached the second square. Here the Air Force band was playing marches. It was obvious that people were more interested in sandwiches than marches. The bandsmen blew into their instruments with an admirable flair. We then reached the third square, where the police band was performing, and the fourth with the children's orchestra, and the fifth with the workers' band, and the whole time B perspired under the blanket. He gave off a bad smell. Haru asked, "How long has he been without a bath?"

"I think it's been about a year."

As Madam said this, she distanced herself from the wheelchair.

Then we entered the city park. A band from the Gendarmerie was playing marches in one corner of the garden. They were mostly playing the tune from *The Bridge On the River Kwai*, as people walked and ate sandwiches. But they didn't throw the sandwich wrappers on the ground; the wastebaskets were filled with paper. The central section of the park was festooned with lights and banners, and every child had a balloon. They had lined the area with folding chairs and the chairs were gradually filling up. Haru chose one corner and the three of us sat down, and placed the wheelchair before us. The Army band entered the park and began to play a march. Our discussion centered on the leader of the band. Haru believed that he definitely didn't need to twirl his baton in the air and that this was more showmanship than leadership. I disagreed and it seemed that B wanted to join in the debate. His eyes moved furiously, and he listened to us intently. When Haru saw this he laughed and winked at me. B did not react anymore. He was essentially no longer angry, he only seemed listless.

After half an hour the band departed and the panel of judges came. All were chosen from among the respected members of the community, a departure from precedent. Haru recognized a green-grocer among them. The respected members of the community all wore the dignity of judicial robes, which had gone to their heads and even rubbed off on the people. Even the children had fallen silent, and when Haru began to speak, everyone glared at him. Then they led in the accused. He was a bald-headed man wrapped in a shroud. Here and there, on his face and body, his flesh had peeled away and his bones were visible. Half the skin on his skull was also gone. We knew that he was bald from the other half. Even his shroud was decayed. It was a mixture of colors—grey, yellow, and black. His body gave off a very foul odor; it made many ill. B, his eyes bulging in their sockets, stared at the accused. Haru asked, "You know him, don't you?"

B shook his head violently. Haru whispered, "If you promise not to yell, I'll ungag you." B nodded in agreement and Haru took the gag out of his mouth. He removed the handkerchief from his mouth and untied the ropes from his arms. No one paid any attention to us. Everyone was staring at the accused.

The chief judge asked, "Do you admit, sir, that times have changed?"

The accused said, "Yes, your Honor, it appears that the world is full of bands."

The accused's right cheek melted away and we saw his jawbone and teeth, and when he spoke his mouth made a whistling sound.

The chief judge said, "Yes, exactly, you see the change."

"Yes, sir," said the accused.

The chief judge asked, "Well, you know that we are an ancient people and have always been able to escape catastrophe because we have acted rationally? Isn't this so?"

"Perhaps. I was always bad at history."

The chief judge disagreed. "You're lying, you have written many tracts in the field of history."

The accused bowed his head. The chief judge became milder. "Never mind. This is not a real trial. It is merely a warning. Do you remember your old friends?"

"Some of them."

"Very well. Do you know how they are?"

"No, your Honor."

The chief judge whistled and a number of men, B's contemporaries, emerged from behind the tribunal. Their clothes were fresh and firsthand, and though this was the Day of Purity, it seemed that these men had been pure for all time. The chief judge asked, "Are the gentlemen satisfied with their state?"

To a man they nodded in agreement, and one of them claimed that he had been inspired in a dream by one of the Imams, another said that we were a small nation and it would be foolish for us to sacrifice ourselves to the flow of world events, and a third said that it wasn't worth the trouble.

The chief judge faced the accused and said, "My dear sir, note that our intention is to restore your dignity, although no one knows you now."

To the crowd he called out, "Does anyone know this man?"

No one uttered a sound, except B, who shouted, "Me."

"What?" said the chief judge.

At this Haru, horrified, jumped from his seat and shouted, "Your Honors, excuse him, this man is sick. He's only worth a silkworm's cocoon."

The chief judge did not investigate further and again turned to the accused. "Your existence is a matter of indifference to us; however, we prefer that, when we live in happiness, not even the slightest cloud darken the skies of our lives. It is for this reason that we would like to restore your dignity. You only have to admit that you are sorry you committed suicide and that you died in vain, for nothing."

The accused was silent and the crowd began to mutter. I saw some of them had become pale and the friends of the accused begin to fidget.

The chief said, "Say you're sorry."

The accused answered, "I'm sorry that I'm not sorry. In any case, dying was better."

Then all hell broke loose. I noticed that B was crying silently. The friends of the accused shook their heads sadly. The chief judge motioned with his head and they led the accused away. When they were leading him away, he turned and looked at B. He may have even smiled; his features had changed so much that it was impossible to remember how he looked originally.

The chief then delivered a speech to the effect that there has never been a shortage of fools in the world, to which the people paid no attention. They were restless until the honorable panel of judges left the tribunal and were replaced by the Army band. Haru said, "So, let's go."

We left.

That night we sat together in Madam's room, drinking tea. Outside were the sounds of fireworks.

Haru said, "Well, B, you were the only one to recognize him, and that's why I brought you. It's a shame that you are also going to die in a cocoon, isn't it?"

He didn't answer. Haru said, "I don't have the nerve to do something, and it's not even certain that something could be done. But you can take a trip, move about, look, listen—anything would be better than becoming a butterfly, doing something at least."

B said, "My becoming a butterfly is something."

"That'll just cause a stir and bring publicity; you don't need that, do you?"

"No."

"Well, go then, at least you'll have a change of scenery."

"What about you three?"

"Oh, we can take care of ourselves, all right."

Then the three of us got to work removing the cocoon from B's legs and waist. A thick sheath of silk piled up in the room, and B's deformed and scrawny legs emerged from the mesh.

"I'm really in bad shape, aren't I?"

"No, not that bad, in six months you'll be as good as new. B, I'm sure that something can be worked out, I can't tell you how certain I am of this."

B smiled bitterly. Then Haru gave Madam some instructions. The next day they took B to the public baths and cleaned him up. Then several new suits of clothes, a valise, and a bus ticket were in order. The rest was left to fate.

I never saw B again.

Moniru Ravanipur

1954–

Short-story writer and novelist Moniru Ravanipur was born in the village of Jofreh and raised in the provincial capital Shiraz. She completed an undergraduate degree in psychology at Shiraz University.

Ravanipur's first book was a collection of nine short stories called *Kanizu* (1989, reprinted in 2001). In the winter of 1989, Ravanipur published her first novel, *Ahl-e Gharq* (The people of Gharq). A year later, she published a second novel, *Del-e fulād* (The steel heart). In 1991 her second collection of short stories, *Sang-e shaytān* was published. This was translated into English and published in the United States in 1996 as *Satan's Stones*. Ravanipur's novel *Kowli kenār-e ātesh* (The gypsy by the fire) was scheduled to go to press in 1991. In 1991–92 she published a pair of children's books, *Sefid-e barfi* and *Golpar, māh va rangin'kamān*. These were followed in 1993 by her third short story collection, *Siriyā, Siriyā*. Her next work didn't appear until 1999, a novel called *Kawli kenār-e ātas*. Her fourth collection of short stories, *Zan-e forudgāh-e Ferānkfort*, was published in 2001.

Ravanipur's productivity during the first twelve years of the Islamic Republic makes her a leading figure in the generation of fiction writers who began publishing after the Iranian Revolution. Her productivity likewise signals the mainstream presence, begun in the 1960s, of female narrators and voices in Iranian fiction. Simin Daneshvar, Mahshid Amir-Shahi, Goli Taraqqi, Shahrnush Parsipur, M. Shahrzad, Ghazaleh Alizadeh, Mihan Bahrami, and Farideh Lasha'i were the chief women story writers from the 1960s, all of them active in Iran or abroad in the 1980s, when Ravanipur began adding her distinctive narrative voice to theirs.

Ravanipur's success further signals mainstream acceptance of regionalism in Iranian fiction. Sadeq Chubak, Ahmad Mahmud, Mahmud Dowlatabadi, and Amin Faqiri offered regional focus and local color in fiction from the 1960s onward, while Ravanipur gives her distinctive texture of Shiraz and Persian Gulf littoral life in her narratives.

The Long Night

Translated by John R. Perry

The village of Jofreh was dying under the effects of Golpar's cries. A keen autumn wind blew in from the sea, snaked round the palms, and carried off with it bits and pieces of rubbish and crumpled paper. The night was half over. Maryam rolled over where she lay. "Mother, close the shutter."

"All the shutters are closed. Go to sleep."

"Is he hitting her, Mother? Is Uncle Ebrahim hitting her?"

"No, Maryam, he's caressing her. Now go to sleep."

"Will she come and play tomorrow? Will she come to the beach?"

"Yes, I'll go and fetch her myself. If you go to sleep, I'll fetch her."

A piercing scream rent the darkness and crashed into Maryam's head. Maryam sat up in fear.

"She's dying, Mother, she's really dying…"

She heard her mother's soft laugh, and her father's calm tone as he whispered to her mother: "The child's scared…"

"I've closed all the shutters, and still that noise won't let her sleep."

"Now that a pigeon's fallen into his clutches, d'you think he's about to let it go?"

481

The shutters of the room's five windows were closed. A half-extinguished lantern guttered above the water jug. Maryam slept some distance from her parents, next to the wall. Noises tumbled about alarmingly inside her head. The howling of the wind, the banging of the shutters, the muffled cries of pain from Golpar's palm-log shack that were growing less and less recognizable with each moment: "Please... please, don't... you're killing me... killing me..."

For a week now, Golpar's call had not been heard through- out Jofreh after cockcrow. That clear, loud call that brought the children rushing outdoors and the gulls flocking to the fishing fleet's moorings.

The sun was not yet up when the children, stark naked, would squat in a row on the beach to do their business before the sea embraced them in its cool and welcoming waters. Golpar's arms would cleave the air, cut through the water and race on. Fishermen riding at anchor far offshore would haul in their nets at Golpar's shout and get under way for Jofreh.

Hey, hey, anchors aweigh...! Hey, for the waves...! Hey, hey, hey!

The seagulls did not peck at them, but would fly round about them, lighting on their bare shoulders or snatching playfully with their short red beaks at Golpar's golden hair as it spread out on top of the water and bobbed up and down with the waves. For a week, Golpar had not called out to anyone, and now her heart-rending screams had driven sleep from everyone in the village.

Maryam trembled, her mouth was dry, and she looked at the water jug and the half-extinguished lantern in fear. "Why are you sitting up? Go to sleep..."

"Water..." The word broke in her throat. She heard her father's sleepy voice: "Get up and give her some water. They're really piling it on!"

Her mother got up grumbling, filled the bowl with water and came over to Maryam. "Damn him and this wedding of his!"

"Mother... it's dark..."

"Here... drink your water and sleep."

"Turn up the wick, it's very dark."

The howling wind battered at the door. The faint light of the lantern wavered. Maryam clutched at her mother with both hands: "Did you hear that? She's crying, I can hear her crying."

"It's the wind, dear, just the wind."

"No, she's run away—go and open the door."

"Maryam, dear, it's the wind; Golpar's inside her house."

Once again the wind launched an assault. It sounded as if someone with disheveled hair and bloody hands were begging to be let in.

"Take the lantern to the far corner, it's going to go out." It was her father, who was sitting up and lighting his cigarette.

"Daddy, tell Mother to open the door, she's outside, Daddy…"

"There's nobody there, it's the wind, the wind."

"No, no, she's screaming, she's screaming!"

"It's just the sea roaring, and the gulls screaming because they're afraid of the storm. Go to sleep, it's nearly morning."

"Open the door, please, Mother!"

"A fine fix we're in! Are you going to get to sleep or not? Others get the pleasure, we get the aggravation."

Maryam's mother took hold of her arms and forced her to lie down. She threw the bedcover over her. Her father leaned back on one elbow, smoking.

"Mother, bring the lantern closer, I'm scared, I'm scared of the dragon."

"God save us, what dragon?"

"Uncle Ebrahim's dragon." She heard her father laugh; her mother brought the lantern over and set it at her head. "Go to sleep now, there's nobody at the door."

"Nobody?"

"No, it's the wind and the waves; and the bogeyman is prowling the streets, sniffing out little children who are still awake. If he finds out, he'll come and carry you off, and he's so strong no one can stop him…"

"How come the bogeyman doesn't hear Golpar? The boogeyman is so tall that his head touches the stars, and his fingers are like fishhooks, and he prowls round Jofreh at night, stops outside the windows and reaches inside with his hands just like fishhooks and carries off children who are still awake—God send the bogeyman, make him hear Golpar's crying, let him know that it's Golpar, Golpar the child who hasn't grown up yet, who doesn't have bracelets on her arm, who doesn't have a painted face…"

Tears moistened Maryam's face. No, the bogeyman certainly wouldn't recognize Golpar, all his sniffing wouldn't do any good… this wasn't Golpar's voice, this was the grating cry of a woman whose arms and legs were being sawn off, the screams of a woman assaulted by a dragon; Golpar's voice was lost, had gone far, far away, was sitting weeping somewhere among the stars; Golpar had lost her voice for a week now…

On the first day that Golpar failed to call out to them, the village children gathered behind the shack. The row of dry, frowning doors and shutters blocked their view.

"It's no use thumping with your fist, let's use a stone!"

"Let's call to her—Maryam, you call to her!"

"Suppose she isn't in?"

"Maybe she's sick."

"Knock with a stone, so her ma won't know it's us."

They battered at the door with stones, until they heard the shuffling of Golpar's feet approaching and her chubby little hands opened the door.

"Come on, Golpar, the sea… the gulls are flocking at the moorings." Golpar stood there as if putting on a bold front. She wore bracelets and a white, flowered headscarf.

"The thing is, I'm a grown-up now, I can't play with you."

"A grown-up? How do you mean?"

"Ma says I have to keep house and stuff."

"Is she sick or something?"

"Not for her, for myself."

"Keep house for yourself?"

"Uh-huh. Uncle Ebrahim wants me to set up house for me and him."

"Uncle Ebrahim?"

"Uh-huh. He bought me these bracelets, and the headscarf, and soon he's going to buy me a pair of shoes, and a pair for ma too, so's her feet don't get blisters."

The children's mouths opened in astonishment like those of fish. One by one they fingered the bracelets. Their yellow sheen dazzled them.

"They're so beautiful; and your headscarf has flowers, too!"

"Golpar, just let me try on the bracelets."

"They don't come off; you have to rub them and rub them with soap, but they don't come off anymore."

"When did he buy them for you?"

"Last night. My old nurse was there too. And soon he has to pay three hundred tomans on top."

"On top of what?"

"On top of… I don't know. Ma knows."

"What about a doll, Golpar? Did he get you a doll?"

"No, he says he's going to make me a doll."

"What sort of doll?"

"I don't know. He says if I wait he'll make me a talking doll."

"Oh, wow—lucky you!"

"Don't worry, I'll ask him to make one for you as well--only ma mustn't know, 'cause when a person gets to be a grown-up, she has to look after her own household. She can't play any more... Now ma's coming—come again this afternoon, when she goes to bake bread... late this afternoon."

Someone was pounding on the door, groveling on the ground, trailing her unkempt hair over the earth, and strewing handfuls of dust through the shutter into the room; the lan- tern's pale flame writhed and twisted; Maryam cradled the lantern in her hands, the small, pale lantern.

"How hard it is to be grown up! Dear God, let nobody grow up, make Uncle Ebrahim die, let him die so Golpar can come to the beach again."

Until late afternoon they sat on the beach without Golpar. The gulls gathered morosely at the moorings, bobbing up and down waiting for the silver fish scales, as if without Golpar the sea were alien to them.

"Maryam, let's go swimming."

"No, it isn't good."

"They're here, the gulls have come too!"

"No, there's nobody at home." That afternoon, they saw Golpar. Her emerald eyes glistened, and seven long, golden braids lay over her shoulders. "Wow... When did you go to the beach?"

"I didn't, ma washed my hair at home; at noon when Uncle Ebra- him came home, he brought me a comb." And she showed them the crescent-shaped, gold-colored comb she had stuck in her hair. "Any- thing Uncle Ebrahim brings home now, he gives one to me."

"Lucky you, Golpar..."

"I've asked him to bring one for you."

"When will he bring it?"

"When we get married."

"Married? You want to get married?"

"Uh-huh."

"Will he buy candies?"

"Oh, yes. And he'll get musicians."

Maryam sat up again at the howling of the wind and of Golpar, which had become one. Her mother was snoring loudly; Uncle Ebrahim's bushy mustache and the dragon on his chest stayed before her eyes and would not go away.

"Golpar, aren't you afraid?"

"What of?"

"Of his dragon."

"Nah, it's not a real dragon, it's a picture; I even touched it once, and he told me himself, he said, 'Come on, don't be scared,' and when I touched it I found it wasn't anything."

"What about his mustache? Aren't you afraid of that, either?"

"No, that isn't scary. He's a very good man. Next year he's going to build us a house, a stone house like yours, and after we're married he won't let ma bake bread for other people, only for us. Uncle Ebrahim's a very good man."

Everyone in the village knew Uncle Ebrahim. Once a week the sound of his motorbike would draw people around the square. He would bring out wares from inside the small cabin that he had constructed on the back of his motorbike and display them. His collar was always wide open, and a tattooed dragon with a long tongue and a sharp beak would send the children fleeing from the motorbike.

The wind howled and assailed Maryam through the cracks in the shutters, the roaring of the sea frightened her, the water jug in the darkness made her thirsty. She got up, made her way toward the water jug, found the bowl in the darkness; on top of the jug there was a plateful of sweets. Alarmed, she withdrew her hand, put down the bowl, and went back. The sweets seemed to smell of blood.

From noon on, the children had been hanging about the shack; the village houses had emptied and the women, one by one, had appeared in all their finery. It was a wedding; the piper's playing was heard far and wide, and the women sang: "Long live the bridegroom! The groom is king!"

That afternoon, Golpar took her seat in the ceremonial bridal chamber. She wore a green cloth over the back of her braids. Her eyebrows were drawn long and fine, and her cheeks glistened with thick red paint. Her lips were bright red, as if smeared with Mercurochrome. Golpar's eyes wandered in astonishment over the crowd of people and the plates of sweets. Candles gleamed in bowls of henna. There wasn't room to turn round. Maryam pushed her way through to Golpar. As soon as she saw her, Golpar stood up. The nurse hissed at her from behind her hand, "You're a bride now, sit down!"

"But it's Maryam...!"

"Woman, sit back down!"

The colors on Golpar's face had run together. Perhaps she had smiled, the smile of a mask, the mask of a child who suddenly grows up and realizes she has no say in her life. She cannot even speak to

Maryam, cannot get up and leave the bridal chamber and go with
Maryam to take some sweets, crumble the sweet cakes and feed the
fish, the tiny, silver-tailed fish that forever swam hungrily among the
pebbles on the seabed...

The wind whirled around itself and howled. The endless roaring
of the sea carried for miles. The banging of the door terrified
Maryam. Someone with hennaed hands was scratching at the door.
"Do you want to have your hands hennaed, Maryam?"

"No."

"Why not?"

"You don't come to the beach anymore."

"No, but when the wedding's over, I'll come, first thing tomorrow
morning. I'll wake you all up at the crack of dawn, I told Uncle
Ebrahim I would."

What a wicked man Uncle Ebrahim was! Golpar barely came up
to his knees, and as the nurse placed Golpar's hand in his, he was
smiling with his yellow, golden teeth. The wedding had no purpose
except to spoil the children's fun and keep the gulls waiting at the
moorings and make Golpar's face all painted and oily, and at night,
after they had all left, to make Golpar scream. Maryam's eyelids felt
heavy, darkness swirled about her head; tired and fuddled, she lay
down. She heard the pad of footsteps approaching, someone running; maybe the bogeyman had found Golpar, reached out with his
fishhook hands and snatched her from the dragon's mouth and was
even now carrying her off; the bogeyman was running, running on
his long, thin legs, heading for the sea, with Golpar under his arm;
Golpar's cry was stifled; Maryam called out to her and Golpar leapt
free of the bogeyman's grasp. Like a seagull on outstretched wings
she flew once round Maryam; Golpar's wings were broken, bloody.
Maryam wanted to take hold of her wings, to take her and bathe her
in the sea, but Golpar looked at her. The same way a seagull looks,
the way the little silver fish look at you. She looked at her and
soared... flapped her wings and was gone. Maryam ran after her as
fast as she could, but couldn't catch her. She cried, "Golpar! Golpar!" Golpar's wings were broken, and drops of blood fell onto
Maryam's face.

She woke up with a start. Her arm struck the lantern and knocked it
over. The lantern sputtered and went out. Her mother and father,
alarmed, ran to the door. A shrieking could be heard that was not Golpar's voice. Maryam rushed outside. It was a yellow, misty morning.

Everyone was running toward Golpar's shack. When Maryam reached the shack, Golpar's ma was holding a bloodstained shift to her face and screaming. Two men were carrying out something wrapped in a sheet. Golpar's golden hair hung out from the sheet; the underside of the sheet was bloodstained. The women wept and rocked from side to side, and the nurse waved the ends of her headdress in the air and keened: "Woe, woe, the child bride is no more!"

Hushang Ashurzadeh

Hushang Ashurzadeh published two stories in *Dāstānhā-ye now* (New stories, 1987), a collection compiled by established author Jamal Mir-Sadeqi, who points out in his preface that the stories are mostly by writers not yet forty years of age. Ashurzadeh thus signals the continued and increasing popularity of short stories in Iran today and the opportunities open to younger writers to publish their work. Hushang Golshiri edited a similar volume of short stories mostly by new writers called *Hasht dāstān az nevisandegān-e jadid* (Eight stories from new writers, 1984).

In 1991 Ashurzadeh republished one of the two stories in "New Stories" in *Qamar dar 'aqrab* (The moon in Scorpio). His earlier works were *In sālhā* (These years, 1980), a short tale for young people called *Dar jangal* (In the forest, 1980), and *Gol-e sorkh va bād-e muzi* (The rose and the pernicious wind). His latest book is a collection of stories titled *Khāneh'i por az gol-e sorkh*, published in 1999.

Narcissus, Get Your Nice Narcissus

Translated by Yaseen Noorani

The cars took off, and the man took himself out of their way to the side of the road, and stood there. He coughed from the smoke of the exhaust pipes. He rubbed his face with his hand and fixed his gaze on the traffic light. As soon as the light turned green, he quickly went back out into the road. He moved the flowers from one hand to the other and wound his way between the cars: "Narcissus, get your nice narcissus!"

He held the flowers up high, so that everyone could see them. The flowers were white and fresh. Beside a large black car he raised his voice:

"They're narcissus, sir, fresh narcissus!"

He stared at the man sitting behind the steering wheel.

"Buy some flowers, sir!"

The man raised his window. He turned his head and continued his conversation with the person sitting beside him.

He continued past the black car and went to a small car behind it in which a young woman was sitting behind the wheel.

"Wouldn't you like some narcissus flowers, ma'am?"

The woman looked at the flowers.

"They're really fresh, ma'am!"

He took out a small bunch from among the flowers and gave it to the woman. She took the flowers from him and smelled them.

"They smell really nice, ma'am!"

The woman laughed and put the flowers on the empty seat beside her.

"Nargesu, what are you laughing at?"

Nargesu was kneeling on the hay in the stable milking the cow. "Is it you, Abbas?"

"Yeah."

Nargesu picked up the milk pail and walked over to where Abbas was standing. "Our cow's pregnant."

"Really?"

"Ah, yes."

The woman opened her purse and gave him a twenty-toman note.

The cars took off again. They sped by, he was stuck between them. The blast of a horn made him jump. Startled, he ran to the sidewalk. He leaned against a wall. A light breeze blew. The smell of rain struck him. He looked toward the mountains, and said to himself, "It must be raining in the mountains."

"Abbas!"

"What?"

"Something on your mind?"

The sun had settled in the center of the village square. Men were squatting by the coffee house.

"It's the middle of spring and no trace of rain, Haydar. It seems to me our crops are going to burn this year too."

Haydar struck his pipe on the ground, and the burning tobacco fell out into the dirt. He looked at the sky and said, "But it might still rain…"

A small girl was standing in front of him and staring at the flowers. The little girl's hair was jet black.

"Could you give me one of these flowers?"

She was carrying a doll under her arm. The doll's eyes were closed, as if it were sleeping.

"Get lost!"

She stood as before, staring at the flowers.

"Papa, could you buy me a doll?"
Rababu was sitting on the porch with her arms around her knees.
"Sure I'll buy you one. Just wait until the harvest comes in."

The man pulled out a stem from among the flowers and said, "Here!"
The girl took the flower and smiled. The cars stopped.
"Narcissus, get your nice narcissus!"
He went to and fro among the cars.
"Fresh narcissus!"
A man wearing sunglasses yelled to him from a station wagon: "Hey, flower man!"
"Yes."
"How much are the flowers?"
"No fixed price. You give however much you want."
The man rummaged in his pockets.
"They smell really nice, sir."
The light turned green. The cars took off. The man hastily spilled a handful of change into his palm. He took the flowers and drove away. A woman with loaves of flat bread passed by. He caught the scent of the freshly baked bread. He felt a hollow pit in his stomach. The little boy who sold balloons walked up beside him. The little boy was thin and black as a cinder. He looked up at the boy's balloons, which rode high in the sky and looked like a bunch of multicolored grapes as they swayed back and forth with the wind. The balloons were tied to one end of a thick cord and at the other end was the little boy's hand.
The man laughed.
The boy asked, "How's business, pop?"
"God provides."
The boy said, "Give the flowers some water. They're wilting."
The man looked at the flowers, which had lost their former freshness in the sun.
"You can't let them wilt."
The sky was clear and bright. In the distance a few clouds cast their shadows on the mountains. He thought, "If it keeps getting hotter like this, our crops are going to burn again this year."
He said to himself, "Please let it rain."

"Nargesu, look how its raining! The Lord's blessing us. I think we'll have a good harvest this year."

The rain had soaked him from head to foot. He remained standing in it anyway.

"Why do you keep standing out there? You'll catch a cold."

The rain fell hard and fast. He stuck the shovel in the ground. Spreading out his arms he said, "If our harvest turns out good this year, I'll stay here with you and the kids over the winter. I don't like the city. The city wears a man down."

The boy said, "What is it you're saying to yourself?"

"I'm saying I hope it rains enough this year."

"For what?"

"Rain is God's blessing."

"I can't stand it when it rains."

"You don't like God's blessing?"

"What blessing? When it rains, the water washes us all out."

"You mean you never want it to rain?"

"Father, rain's a killer. When the awful stuff comes, everyone runs home, fast as they can. It kills business. I wish that God would make it sunny every day."

"Don't speak such blasphemy, child! How could it not rain? God does everything for a reason. If it didn't rain, we'd all starve to death."

"I hope we get a hundred black years with no rain."

The man shifted on his feet.

"If only it would be sunny on Fridays. Then everyone goes to the park. I could sell every single one of my balloons. God just save me from when it rains…"

He gave the balloons some rope. They rose higher into the sky.

"Get your balloons!"

A girl and a young man crossed over to their side of the street. As soon as she saw the flowers, the girl said, "Won't you buy me some flowers?"

The young man walked up to him.

"Let me see the freshest bunch out of those."

The girl was standing and looking at the flowers with her dark eyes. Over her head was a scarf with pretty flower patterns. He gave the flowers to the girl.

"What is it, Nargesu, why are you staring at me like that?"

Nargesu took her dark eyes off of him. She bent over, picked up the basket of plums from the garden and put it over her shoulder.

"Hey, Nargesu, are you listening?"

Nargesu lowered her gaze and laughed. "I'd really like to have a pretty shirt with flowers…"

He thought, "If I have good luck and it rains enough this year, I'll buy her a satin shirt with flowers on it."

He lit a cigarette and sat beside a stream. The water was filthy and carried along its course orange rinds and rotten fruit.

He thought, "If this same water flowed on the parched earth of our farmland, it would bring the wheat back to life…"

He looked at the flowers in his hands. The flowers were wilting in the sun. A blast of wind kicked up some dust. He looked at the mountains.

"I think it's raining."

He took a drag on his cigarette. Slowly, he walked out into the road.

"Narcissus. Get your nice narcissus."

Farahnaz Abbasi

Farahnaz Abbasi began her writing career with the publication of a short story called "Ayeneh" (Mirror) in an early 1988 issue of the Tehran literary journal *Ādineh*. Her first collection of stories was published in 2000 as *Rāz-e sar be-moh*.

The Mirror

Translated by Farzin Yazdanfar

She used to wear it every year and sit in front of the mirror. She would pick up the Koran too and read verses from the Surah "Women." Then she would close the book and put it in the middle of the tablecloth and wait for Rahman to come. As she was waiting, she would stare at the flickering flames of the candles melting away. With the sound of the key turning in the keyhole, her heart would beat faster. The door would open. Rahman would take four steps into the room. Mahbanu would rise, making sure that her dress was tidy and her hair, which she had patiently set for hours, was hanging on her shoulders neatly. She waited for Rahman until he had come in. Seeing Mahbanu in that dress would make Rahman laugh. Mahbanu would hug him and lay her head on his shoulder. She would stay in that position for a few minutes, and, out of habit, she would close her eyes while drawing away from him. Rahman would reach into his pocket for the present that he had bought and scrupulously wrapped for her. He would put it in Mahbanu's warm, soft hands. Mahbanu would laugh and rejoice like a child. She would open her big black eyes and drag Rahman toward the tablecloth. They would

sit in front of the mirror for an hour and Mahbanu would recite
from the Surah "Women." Rahman, bored, would ask, "Haven't you
read enough?" And Banu would always frown, knitting her eyebrows. And Rahman would keep silent...

Banu has been sitting alone in front of the mirror for hours. She has
been alone for years, although Rahman comes every year to see her.
Always on time! Rahman stands behind the door and calls her with his
warm friendly voice. Banu looks through the keyhole. He is dressed in
white from head to toe. She says to him, "No, Rahman, go change
your clothes." Rahman goes away. He has gone, but Banu is still staring at the mirror and the dancing flames of the candles. She hears the
sound of the key turning in the keyhole and the footsteps getting closer: one, two, three, four. Banu's heart beats faster. The footsteps stop
at the door. It is him, Rahman. Banu wants to get up, but she has no
energy. She has rouged her cheeks and the make-up has sunk into the
wrinkles of her rouged cheeks, but her face still looks pale. She has
braided her completely gray hair, which is hanging over her breast.
She sees herself getting up and walking toward the door. She looks
through the keyhole. Rahman is once again dressed in white. Banu
says, "No, Rahman, change your clothes."Rahman answers, "Banu
aren't you going to open the door?" Banu's hands, which are normally
shaky, start trembling even more than usual. She turns the key in the
keyhole. She can no longer ask Rahman to change his clothes. She can
no longer stay separate from Rahman. The door opens and Rahman
comes in. He comes closer. How frightening he has become in this
white garb! Banu pulls herself back. She doesn't want to hug him the
way she used to. Rahman says, "Banu, how many times have you worn
this dress in your loneliness? Now I have really come to you." Banu
looks at Rahman's weak, slender body. Rahman takes her hand and
asks, "Don't you want your present?" Banu laughs, but not the way
she used to laugh thirty years ago. She laughs calmly and noiselessly.
She closes her weak-sighted eyes. Rahman says, "No, Banu, not with
your eyes closed. Will you come with me?" Banu, terrified, answers,
"Yes Rahman, it is time to go." Rahman pulls her to himself. Banu
turns her head toward the room and sees herself dressed in white sitting in front of the mirror. She says, "Rahman, look at Banu...!"
Rahman pulls her harder. As she is being dragged out of the room, she
sees herself dressed in her white wedding gown gradually falling on
the tablecloth and knocking down all the candles, and Rahman taking
her away.

Glossary

Aban, 24th of: Aban is the eighth month of the Persian year; 24th Aban corresponds to 15th November.

aftabeh: A metal ewer with a long spout, typically used for ablutions in the lavatory.

albalu polow: A dish of rice cooked with sour cherries.

Alborz College: A prestigious private preparatory school for boys in Tehran, founded by American Presbyterian missionaries in the nineteenth century. It grew into a college in the 1930s, was nationalized in 1940 and continued as a state high school.

akhund: A scholar, teacher or student of the religious law; one of the Muslim clergy *(ulama)*, a mullah.

Ali: see Imam.

Allaho akbar: Arabic, "God is great," an exclamation of triumph, surprise, consternation, etc.

Amir Arslan: A *dastan*, or popular romance, written in the nineteenth century as a bedtime story for the Qajar monarch Naser oddin Shah by a courtier, Naqib ol-mamalek. Amir Arslan ("Prince Lion") has a variety of martial and romantic adventures, notably after he falls in love with a portrait of the daughter of a European king, Malekeh Farrokh-Laqa ("Princess Fairface"), and journeys westward in quest of her.

Aqa: Sir, Mr., etc.; form of address for a man, placed after the forename or before the surname or other title (cf. Khanom).

araq: (also *arak*, *arrack*), a spiritous liquor distilled from grapes; vodka or similar liquor.

Aryamehr [Technical University]: A polytechnic college founded by (and named for one of the titles of) Mohammad Reza Shah Pahlavi.

ashrafi: A gold coin minted in Iran from the fifteenth to the nineteenth century, formerly worth one toman (q.v.). The term came to refer generally to gold coins.

Baha'is: Members of a religion that derives from a nineteenth-century millennarian movement (Babism) within Iranian Shi'ism. Regarded as heretics by the Shi'a, they are now banned in Iran.

Behesht-e Zahra: "The Paradise of [Fatemeh] the Resplendent," name of the chief cemetery of Tehran, occupying an extensive area southwest of the city. Since the eve of the Islamic Revolution it has been a shrine of great symbolic importance and a site for mass religious commemorations and political demonstrations.

besmellah: "In the name of God [the Compassionate, the Merciful]." An Arabic invocation pronounced before any solemn or ceremonious undertaking, such as a sacrifice, or before embarking on any new or potentially hazardous action.

bile dig, bile choqondar: "As the pot, so the beetroot." An Azerbaijani Turkish proverb, meaning that complementary parts of a system should be, or tend to be, of an appropriate size, shape or kind. A tale associated with the saying goes as follows:
A man said, "In our village they grow beetroots as large as houses." Someone else present said, "In my native town they make cooking pots as large as mosques." "Whatever for?" asked the first man. "To cook your beetroot," was the reply.

It corresponds to sentiments expressed in English as "They deserve each other," or "Suit the tool to the job," or "What's sauce for the goose is sauce for the gander."

bowl hotter than the soup, a: A Persian proverb equivalent to "More Catholic than the Pope," said of one who is more enthusiastic about something than those more intimately involved in it.

chador: A sewn sheet of cloth, generally black, worn by Iranian women in public as a head-to-foot covering to comply with Islamic prescriptions of modesty.

Cockaigne, Rosebud of: Cockaigne, in medieval Anglo-French tradition, was a fabled land of indolence and luxury. The actual Persian word (in the story "Mirza") is *Quppeyna*, an imaginary place-name coined from the colloquial term *quppey* or *qupi*, "boasting, putting on airs."

Dar Khevin: A village on the Karun river, south of the city of Ahvaz, about 75 miles from Abadan.

depilation ceremony: Persian *band-andazan*, one of the rites of preparation of a bride-to-be. Her facial hair is removed by means of a taut string manipulated by older women experienced in the art.

Divan: A council of state; the central government. Jamalzadeh's derivation from *div*, "demon, ogre," is of course humorously intended and has no etymological basis.

do-hezari: A coin worth two riyals, i.e. one-fifth of a toman (q.v.).

faludeh: A dessert consisting of starch jelly squeezed through a strainer to form thin fibers, served with lemon juice and rosewater syrup.

Farhad: See Shirin.

Farrokh-Laqa, Princess: see Amir Arslan.

Fatemeh (Persian), **Fatima** (Arabic): A popular Muslim woman's name, originally that of the daughter of the Prophet Mohammad. She married a paternal cousin, Ali ebn Abi Taleb, the first Imam (q.v.) of the Shi'a; eleven of their male descendants, starting with their sons Hasan and Hosayn (q.v.), complete the line of the twelve Imams.

fesenjan: A stew of pomegranate juice, ground walnuts, saffron and other spices, generally served with duck or chicken.

Five sheltered under the Prophet's mantle, the: Refers to the Prophet Mohammad, his daughter Fatemeh, her husband Ali, and their children Hasan and Hosayn—the "holy family" of the Shi'a. These five are said once to have slept all together under Mohammad's mantle.

Fourteen Innocents, the: Collectively, the twelve Imams, the Prophet Mohammad and his daughter Fatemeh.

gaz: A white, nougat-like candy, a specialty of Isfahan.

Haj, Haji: One who has made the pilgrimage to Mecca; term of address for a respectable member of the traditional bourgeoisie.

Hajji Baba of Ispahan, The Adventures of: A satirical novel by diplomat and traveler James Morier, recounting the picaresque adventures of the son of an Isfahan barber who rises through luck and guile to high rank in the service of Fath 'Ali Shah Qajar (1797–1834). Published in 1824, it was issued in a Persian translation in 1905, and was thought by some to be an original Persian work.

hammam: The traditional "Turkish bath."

Hasan (Imam): Eldest son of Ali and Fatemeh (q.v.), the second Imam of the Shi'a.

Hejri: Pertaining to the years of the Islamic calendar, beginning in 622 C.E., the year of the Prophet Mohammad's emigration (*hijra, hejreh*) from Mecca to Medina. When reckoned by the Arabic months, the year is lunar, and is thus some ten days shorter than the solar year (and currently 42 years ahead of the latter). In Iran it is nowadays reckoned as a solar year of 365 days, beginning on the vernal equinox, i.e. March 21 or 22, the festival of Nowruz (q.v.).

Homa cigarettes: A coarse brand of cigarettes, popular with working men.

Hosayn (Imam): Grandson of the Prophet, younger son of Ali and Fatemeh and the third Imam of the Shi'a. Hosayn and his family and followers were massacred in 680 C.E. at Karbala, in Iraq, by an army of the Umayyad caliph. This tragedy is commemorated annually in Iran during the month of Moharram.

Imam: According to the Shi'a, one of the twelve rightful leaders of the Muslim community by virtue of descent from the Prophet through his cousin and son-in-law Ali (the first Imam). In several of the stories, the reference is to the eighth Imam, Ali Reza ("Imam Reza;" d. 813 C.E.), whose tomb at Mashhad is the most important Shi'i shrine in Iran.

kaffiyeh: Diagonally folded piece of checkered cloth, used as a man's headdress.

Karbala: see Hosayn.

Karbala'i: Term of address or nickname for a lower-class male; originally, one who has made the pilgrimage to the shrine of Hosayn at Karbala in Iraq (cf. Mashdi, Haji).

kebab-e shami: Fried meatballs made from a paste of ground beef and roasted chick-pea flour.

Khanom: Lady, Madame, etc.; form of address for a woman, placed after the forename or before the surname or other title (cf. Aqa).

Khaybar: A fortified Jewish town north of Medina, which the early Muslim community besieged and captured in 628 C.E. According to Shi'i legend, Mohammad's cousin Ali played a heroic role in this action, wrenching open the city gate with one hand.

Khizr (the prophet): A legendary immortal saint widely venerated in the Middle East under various forms of this name. He is traditionally identified by Muslims with the anonymous guide of Moses in Surah 18 of the Koran ("The Cave"). He is sometimes said to possess a supply of the Water of Life and to be able to revive the dead.

khoresh, khoresht: A stew or sauce of meat or poultry with vegetables and/or fruit or nuts, served over steamed rice; e.g., *khoresh-e bademjan*, made with eggplant.

Khosrow: See Shirin.

korsi: An arrangement of quilts spread around a wooden framework over a central brazier, under which people sleep at night and relax during the day in winter.

Lalehzar Avenue: "Tulip field," originally a garden walk inside the palace grounds, later a popular shopping and entertainment thoroughfare in central Tehran.

Lata'ef ot-Tava'ef: "Jokes about [various] folks," a collection of humorous anecdotes about prominent figures of Islamic history, compiled by Ali Safi in sixteenth-century Herat.

Leyla, or Leyli: Heroine of an old Arabian legend, the beloved of a shepherd called Qays. She was betrothed to another, and Qays roamed the desert distraught, being henceforth known as *Majnun* ("crazy, possessed"). The story was widely used by Persian poets, often with mystical and other symbolic overtones; "Leyla and Majnun" have become the Eastern archetype of star-crossed lovers, the equivalent of Romeo and Juliet.

Liqvan: A village near Tabriz in Azerbaijan, known for its butter and cheese.

Majlis: The Iranian national assembly, or parliament. The Fourteenth Majlis was elected during World War II while the Allies were occupying Iran, after they had deposed Reza Shah in 1941. It inaugurated a period of vigorous political activity involving a variety of parties, including the Justice (*'Adalat*) party founded by the writer Ali Dashti, and culminated in the nationalization of the Anglo-Iranian Oil Company and confrontation with the Shah under the ministry of Mosaddeq (see Mordad).

Mashdi, Mashti: Term of address or nickname for a man of the lower classes. (From *Mashhadi*, title of respect for one who has made the pilgrimage to Mashhad; cf. Haji).

man: The maund, a unit of weight nowadays equivalent to 3 kg. or 6.6 lb.

Mesgarabad: A village near Rayy, south of Tehran, where there is a large cemetery.

Moharram, Safar: The first two months of the Muslim lunar year. Since they contain many days of mourning for martyrs, they are generally avoided when scheduling happy occasions such as weddings.

Mordad, 28th of: Mordad is the fifth month of the Persian year. In Mordad of the year 1332, corresponding to August 1953, Mohammad Reza Shah failed in an attempt to arrest his powerful and popular Prime Minister, Mohammad Mosaddeq, who had nationalized the Anglo-Iranian Oil Company and alienated many of the pro-Western elite; the Shah fled the country, but on 28th Mordad/19th August, Mosaddeq's government was overthrown by the army under General Zahedi and other loyalists, aided by the CIA, and the Shah was restored to power.

National University: Persian *Daneshgah-e Melli*, a private university in Tehran.

Nezami: See Shirin.

Nowruz: Lit., "new day," the Persian new year, celebrated at the spring equinox on approximately March 21 and for twelve days thereafter with feasting, visits, the exchange of presents, and spring cleaning. The thirteenth day is traditionally spent out of doors at a favorite picnic spot.

pashmak: A sweet resembling cotton candy.

Paykan: "Arrow," an Iranian-assembled passenger car.

polow: Rice cooked in combination with other ingredients (as distinct from *chelow*, plain boiled rice).

Plan Organization: The body founded in 1949 to channel Iran's oil revenues into implementing a seven-year plan, and subsequently a series of five-year plans, for economic development.

Purusis: A fictitious tribe of predatory nomads.

Qajar period: Effectively, the ninetheenth century in Iran. The Turkoman dynasty of the Qajars ruled from 1796 to 1925, when the war minister Reza Khan, who had seized power in a coup d'état four years earlier, crowned himself shah and inaugurated the Pahlavi dynasty.

qalyan: A tobacco pipe in which the smoke is passed through a jar of water and drawn through a long, flexible tube; hookah, narghile.

qebleh: The direction of Mecca (from points in Iran, approximately southwest), to which Muslims face when praying; the dead and dying are also laid with the head toward the *qebleh*.

qeran: The smallest monetary unit, one-tenth of a toman (q.v.).

qormeh-sabzi: A dish of meat chunks, beans and other vegetables, sauteed in oil with various seasonings, served over rice.

rowzeh-khan: A professional reciter—generally a cleric—of the lives and deaths of the early Shi'i martyrs, especially those of Karbala (see Hasan and Hosayn). These emotional commemorations, known as *rowzeh-khani* (from the title of the best-known martyrology, the early sixteenth-century *Rowzat osh-shohada* or "Garden of the Martyrs") take place before large audiences during the months of Moharram and Safar (cf. *ta'ziyeh*).

reshveh: Bribery, bribe, kickback.

Rostam: The mythical hero of a series of Herculean adventures in the Persian national legend, the *Shahnameh* ("Book of Kings"), composed ca. 1000 C.E. by the poet Ferdowsi. Rostam is the archetype of martial prowess, able single-handed to kill elephants and rout armies.

Safar: see Moharram.

Sahib: In India and Iran during the early twentieth century, a respectful term of address for Europeans and, by extension, their native clerks and associates.

sangak: A long, flat, unleavened bread baked on a bed of gravel, some of which adheres to the bread when it is taken out of the oven.

santur: A musical instrument of the dulcimer family, the strings being struck with light wooden mallets.

sayyid: One descended from the Prophet Mohammad, and thereby entitled to special respect and privileges; often wears a distinctive green turban.

Shah Abdolazim: A town just south of Tehran, on the site of the ancient city of Rayy, named for the tomb of a ninth-century Shi'i ascetic around which the town grew.

Shemiran: A northern suburb of Tehran, on the southern slopes of the Alborz mountains, where well-to-do residents of the capital have summer villas.

Shirin: Heroine of a verse romance, *Khosrow and Shirin*, by the Persian poet Nezami of Ganjeh (ca. 1141–1203). Shirin (the name means "sweet"), a princess of Armenia, falls in love with a portrait of Khosrow, prince of Iran, and sets off to find him. On the fourteenth day of her journey she stops to bathe in a wayside spring, and Khosrow, who has fortuitously arrived at the same spot, covertly spies her and is enamored—an episode popular with miniature painters.

Farhad, a sculptor, also falls in love with Shirin. Khosrow challenges him to cut a channel through Mount Bisutun (Behistun) in order to win Shirin; and when Farhad has all but finished this superhuman task, Khosrow deceitfully sends a messenger with false news of Shirin's death. Farhad leaps from the rocks to his death.

Khosrow's life is ended by an assassin's dagger as he sleeps beside Shirin; after preparing the body for burial, Shirin takes out the dagger and kills herself.

sholeh-zard: A rice pudding flavored with saffron and rosewater, sprinkled with cinnamon and almond slivers.

snake stone: Persian *mohreh-ye mar.* A legendary jewel said to be found in the head of a snake and endowed with aphrodisiac powers. It is sometimes identified with the bezoar stone (from Persian *pad-zahr*, "antidote"), a concretion found in the intestines of animals and anciently believed to be an antidote to snakebite. For the motif of a snake's gift to a human, cf. Antti Aarne and Stith Thompson, *Motif Index of Folk Literature*, No. B 103.0.4.1.

sowhan: A hard honey-and-almond confection for which the city of Qom is famous.

tar: A plucked string instrument, having five or six strings and a wooden soundbox faced with stretched sheepskin.

Taqi's pocket to Naqi's purse: A Persian proverb, equivalent to "robbing Peter to pay Paul."

ta'ziyeh: A dramatic re-enactment of the martyrdom of Hosayn (q.v.) and his companions in 680 C.E. at Karbala; one of the Shi'i rituals of mourning during Moharram (cf. *rowzeh-khan*).

toman: The principal unit of Iranian currency, comprising ten riyals. approximately 7.5 tomans = \$1 during most of the Pahlavi period, and between 100–150 tomans = \$1 since the Revolution.

tonbak: a goblet-shaped drum of wood or pottery, played with the fingers (also called *donbak* or *zarb*).

Uhud: One of the battles of the nascent Muslim community of Medina against the Meccans, fought in 625 C.E., in which the Prophet was wounded and the Muslims were put to flight.

Usta: As in Usta Ja'far, a term of address for a craftsman or bazaar shopkeeper (a variant of *ostad*, "master, maestro").

Zamzam: A well within the precinct of the Great Mosque at Mecca, supposed to have miraculous healing powers.

Bibliography of Sources

Jamalzadeh, M. A. (What's sauce for the goose) *Bileh dig bileh choqondar* from *Yeki bud yeki nabud*. Tehran: Kanun Ma'refat, 1339/1960. *Yeki bud yeki nabud* was translated into English by Heshmat Moayyad and Paul Sprachman as *Once Upon a Time* and published by Bibliotheca Persica, New York, 1985.

Hedayat, Sadeq. (Abji Khanom) *Abji Khanom* from *Zendeh be gur*. 5th ed. Tehran: Amir-e kabir, 1342/1963.

Alavi, Bozorg. (Mirza) Title story from *Mirza*. 1st ed. Tehran: Amir-e kabir, 1357/1978.

Beh'azin, [Mahmud E'temadzadeh]. (The snake stone) Title story from *Mohreh-ye mar*. Tehran: Nil, 1344/1965.

Chubak, Sadeq. (The wooden horse) *Asb-e chubi* from *Cheragh-e akher*. 1st ed. Tehran: 'Elmi, 1344/1965.
——. (The gravediggers) *Gurkanha* from *Ruz-e avval-e qabr*. 1st ed. Tehran: 'Elmi, 1344/1965.

Daneshvar, Simin. (The half-closed eye) *Chashm-e khofteh* from *Be ki salam konam*. 3rd ed. Tehran: Kharazmi, 1362/1973.

Golestan, Ebrahim. (Esmat's journey) *Safar-e 'Esmat* from *Juy va divar va teshneh*. Tehran, 1346/1967. This translation first appeared in *Major Voices of Contemporary Persian Literature, Literature East and West*, Vol. 20 (1980): 191–95.

Al-e Ahmad, Jalal. (The American husband) *Showhar-e Amrika'i* from *Panj dastan*. 2nd ed. Tehran: Ravaq, 2536/1977.

Mahmud, Ahmad, (The little native boy) Title story from *Pesarak-e bumi*. 2nd ed. Tehran: Amir-e kabir, 1354/1975.

Mir-Sadeqi, Jamal. (Through the veil of fog) *Az posht-e pardeh-ye meh* from *Shabha-ye tamasha va gol-e zard*. 2nd ed. Tehran: Nil, 2535/1976.

——. (Glorious day) *Aftab-e 'alamtab* from *Mosaferha-ye shab*. 2nd ed. Tehran: Raz, 1350/1971.

Nazari, Gholam Hosayn. (Moths in the night) *Parvaneh'ha dar shab*. *Sokhan* 15 (1344/1965): 670.

——. (The cast) *Qaleb*. *Sokhan* 24 (1353/1974): 106-107.

——. (Adolescence and the hill) *Bolugh va tapeh*. *Sokhan* 24 (2535/1976): 1200.

——. (Mr. Hemayat) *Aqa-ye Hemayat*. *Sokhan* 24 (1354/1975): 586-589.

——. (Shadowy) *Sayeh'vash*. *Sokhan* 25 (2536/1977): 1094–1095.

Fasih, Esma'il. (Love) *'Eshq* from *'Aqd va dastanha-ye digar*. Tehran: Amir-e kabir, 2537/1978.

Sa'edi, Gholam Hosayn. (The two brothers) *Do baradar* from *Vahemeh'ha-ye bi nam o neshan*. Tehran: Nil, 1346/1967.

——. (Mourners of Bayal, 1st story) from *'Azadaran-e Bayal*. 3rd ed. Tehran: Nil, 1349/1970.

Ebrahimi, Nader. (Sacred keepsake) *Yadegar-e moqaddas* from *Makanha-ye 'omumi*. 2nd ed. Tehran: Amir-e kabir, 1350/1971.

Sadeqi, Bahram. (The trench and the empty canteens) *Sangar va qomqomeh'ha-ye khali*. 1st ed. Tehran: Zaman, 1349/1970.

Golshiri, Hushang. (The wolf) *Gorg* from *Namazkhaneh-ye kuchek-e man*. 1st ed. Tehran: Zaman, 1354/1975.

——. (Portrait of an innocent) *Ma'sum-e sevvom* from *Namazkhaneh-ye kuchek-e man*. 1st ed. Tehran: Zaman, 1354/1975.

Tonokaboni, Fereydun. (The discreet and obvious charms of the petite bourgeoisie) *Malahat'ha-ye panhan va ashkar-e khordeh borzhua'ha* from *Rah raftan ru-ye rayl.* 1st ed. Tehran: Amir-e kabir, 2536/1977.

Taraqqi, Goli. (Aziz Aqa's gold filling) *Dandan-e tala'i-ye 'Aziz Aqa. Omid* 3 (1988): 68–79.

Amir-Shahi, Mahshid. (The smell of lemon peel, the smell of fresh milk) *Bu-ye pust-e limu, bu-ye shir-e tazeh* from *Sar-e Bibi Khanom.* 1st ed. Tehran: Taban, 1347/1968.
———. (Brother's future family) *Khanevadeh-ye ayande-ye dadash* from *Sar-e Bibi Khanom.* 1st ed. Tehran: Taban, 1347/1968. This translation first appeared as Brother's new family, in *Short Story International* 11 (1978): 75-83.

Dowlatabadi, Mahmud. (Hard luck) *Edbar* from *Layeh'ha-ye biabani.* Tehran: Golsha'i, 1352/1973.

Faqiri, Amin. (The sad brothers) *Baradaran-e ghamgin* from *Muyeh'ha-ye montasher.* Shiraz: Navid, 1368/1989.

Parsipur, Shahrnush. (Trial offers) *Tajrobeh'ha-ye azad.* Tehran: Amir-e kabir, 1357/1978.

Khaksar, Nasim. (Night journey) *Shab-e jaddeh* from *Giahak.* Tehran: Sazman-e ketabha-ye jibi, 1357/1978.

Ravanipur, Moniru. (The long night) *Shab-e boland* from *Kanizu,* 2nd ed. Tehran: Nilufar, 1369/1990.

Ashurzadeh, Hushang. (Narcissus, get your nice narcissus) *Narges, ay gol-e narges* from *Dastanha-ye now.* Tehran: Shabahang, 1366/1987.

Abbasi, Farahnaz. (The Mirror) *Ayeneh. Adineh* 49 (1366/1987): 63.

C O L O P H O N

This print-on-demand and e-book edition is a Mohammad and Najmieh Batmanglij book published by Mage. It was designed and set by Tony Ross in a digitized version of Janson using Framemaker 5. The photographs of the authors were all taken by Maryam Zandi. The bazaar photographs are all by Mehdi Khonsari and were taken in bazaars throughout Iran. The jacket photograph was taken by Laurence Lockhart (1890-1975) in Iran in the 1920s and is reproduced courtesy of The Lockhart Collection at the Faculty of Oriental Studies, Cambridge University.

CPSIA information can be obtained at www.ICGtesting.com
Printed in the USA
LVOW090213260312

274743LV00001B/13/A